November

1

2

3

Andrew McDonnell

This book is a work of parody. This book is purely fiction. Names, characters, places, and events either are products of the author's imagination or are used fictitiously and satirically. Any resemblance to actual events, locales or people, living or dead, is wholly coincidental. The public figures portrayed in this book would never behave, think, or speak in the manner depicted herein.

Copyright © 2020 Andrew McDonnell
All rights reserved, including the right of reproduction in whole or in part in any form.

The cover design includes an image of a pipe gleaned from the British Library's magnificent public domain collection of over 1 million images. You should visit and appreciate their fantastic work:
www.flickr.com/photos/britishlibrary

ISBN: 9798607936426

This book is for my parents.
It is also definitely *not* for my parents.
With love and all apologies.

Forewarning:

This is a work of satire. The events foretold in this novel are set in the future and are therefore inherently a work of fiction. None of the words, thoughts, or actions attributed to the public figures or corporations in this book represent their actual character, words, thoughts, history or actions, past or present. Unless they choose to say or enact them. In which case, the author is a soothsayer or the wronged victim of plagiarism. Only time will tell.

November I
Sunday Funday

Sunday, November 1
8:18 a.m. E.T.

Three men and three women in their late 20s are seated around an oblong table in the Old Hickory Suite of the Manzanita Hyatt on L Street. Their clothes are expensive but rumpled, as they've been working in this room for 51 hours straight. Six blue jackets are draped on the backs of chairs. The air is thick with the smell of coffee sweat, medicinal energy drinks, pepperoni grease and the general funk of human miasma. They've stopped leaving the room to fart. Politeness died somewhere around the 19th hour, common decency had rapidly followed, and now any-sense-of-humanity is making apologies, brushing imaginary dust from his top hat, and avoiding eye contact as he heads for the door.

The white board on wheels has been wiped clean of every word but two, plus a comma and an exclamation point: "Think, Goddammit!"

Six laptops are open on the table, but no one is typing. Conference call equipment is laid out as well, but no one's called anyone in 26 hours. In fact, no one has said a word in over an hour. Not a syllable.

The sound of a woman clearing her throat cracks the silence.

"Skywriting?" croaks Michelle, the blond woman with the furious black unibrow.

Team Leader for Cell 20-L is a slender man named Atticus from Utica, New York. Pinched features, black hair, and thick-framed black glasses, Atticus hasn't uncrossed his arms in 14 hours. He is a hardened wonk at 29. "Bernie's got all the sky time reserved in every major metropolitan area through next week," said Atticus. "Plus midterms pre-booked, as a sweetener. Skywriting and banner draggers. There's nothing left to buy in the sky."

"He's gobbled up all that old shit," says a man with white-blond hair. "All of it. We've been over it. He's cornered the market on Barbershop Quartets and One-Man-Bands. Polka Combo naming rights in Milwaukee. Square dance callers in Bernie Bibs. Fucking unreal."

"Blimps?" says Michelle.

"President's got the dirigibles. Goodyear and Snoopy."

"MetLife."

"I think GEICO bought that one?"

"I fucking care."

"Do you have to swear so much?"

"Yes."

"How much does a blimp cost?" says the short intern from Chicago whom they call Limey because she always wears lime green Chucks in the (surprisingly correct) belief they make her memorable. "Like, to buy? Not borrow?"

The room was silent.

Atticus ran both hands through his hair and sighed. "Let's find out," he says. "We've got more money than things to spend it on, so let's find out."

He wrote "Blimp$?" on the white board.

Clacking of laptops fills the air. But there's no levity. "Blimp purchase" is surely just another cul-de-sac waiting to be u-turned, and all of them know it.

The six young people are members of a MIC, a Mobile Idea Cell, one of 20 independent cells arrayed across the city (over

100 across the country) scrambling to sway public opinion in some new, previously unfathomed fashion. All in favor of the independent candidate who pays them handsomely in the cryptocurrency they had founded.

Traditional media outlets sold out of ad time two months ago. AdWords and Facebook ads, InstaAds and (despite their "ban" on political ads) Twitter and Snapchat have been bid beyond all reason by entities, both foreign (especially foreign) and domestic. Plus, more importantly, the social channels are so saturated, so overwhelming and ugly, that people are logging off, leaving their phones at home, making more eye contact. Social broke politics, and now politics is breaking social. Seems only fair.

Even newspapers are turning advertisers away, saying their insurers are done; they've maxed out on inserts and extra pages and fear repetitive stress injury lawsuits among their delivery people. Newspapers saying no to revenue. What evil actuarial genius calculated that shit?

The only way left to sway the populace is... as yet unknown. That's why they're here. One of 120 cells assembled by mysterious Bitcoin inventor and multi-billionaire Satoshi Nakamoto in support of an independent run for office.

Each cell is tasked with the same charge: Change my mind.

Nobody's sure what it means or who exactly Nakamoto is. But the name appears on the ballot in all 50 states and the District of Columbia.

Polls will open in less than 47 hours.

Sunday, November 1
8:23 a.m. E.T.

There exists a sub-basement beneath the wine cellars of a well-known seaside resort in Palm Beach, Florida. The employees of that golf club are not permitted to enter. Most of them don't even know it's there. Entry to the sub-basement is guarded by a rotating crew of ex-military dressed in black track pants, black turtlenecks, and black facemasks, contracted through a company called Stern Microsystems. The guards themselves do not enter the sub-basement door. Ever. They are gatekeepers, tasked with one unambiguous chore: permitting the entry of authorized personnel, of whom there are merely four, and denying all others at any cost.

They are contracted via the Queen's Guard Package, which means they don't say a word when they're on the clock. Even less in their free time. Stern Microsystems' headhunter scours the world for introverted mercenaries. The pay is good. Extraordinary, in fact. More than enough to tamp down any curiosity they might otherwise feel.

The four people permitted to pass between the guards' cocked and loaded short-burst submachine guns are well-known to the former marines at this point, four being a modest number to memorize. Three of the personnel are citizens of the Philippines, resident in the United States: two doctors and a maid. The doctors visit once a day, alternating every day. The maid arrives four times a day and stays in the sub-basement for longer stretches. Sometimes she's carrying food. Sometimes she's hauling a box with a new television or an armful of books. Sometimes pushing a small shopping basket full of cleaning supplies and toiletries.

The sub-basement is accessed by a small forgotten freight elevator that shuttles the guards, the doctors and the maid between the sub-basement landing and, aboveground, what appears to be a maintenance shed on the southeast lawn, but which is in fact a steel-reinforced concrete bunker surrounded by a modest white shed.

The maid has visited the sub-basement every day for the last 19 years. Without exception.

The doctors have alternated their daily visits for 19 years. Never missed a day. Never skipped a beat.

Only one other person is authorized to enter the sub-basement. He first visited 19 years ago, on September 12, 2001. He's been back 18 times since. And unless something curious happens, he'll be back again on September 12, 2021.

He has yet to miss the milestone, but it hasn't been easy to make it every year.

Especially since he was elected President of the United States of America.

This morning, the maid arrives as she always has. She carries a discrete backpack picnic hamper over her shoulder and a single red hibiscus flower in her right hand, which she moves to her left hand as she leans her face towards the retinal scan and places her right hand on the door handle. The guards aren't watching her. They never do. The scan beeps twice, the electric latch disengages, and she sweeps through the door. It swings shut behind her.

Five minutes pass.

The guards hear the double beep of the retinal scan from the other side of the door and the door opening again.

The maid emerges but something's different. She stops as

the door closes behind her, two feet into the sub-basement landing. She looks around wildly. The guards glance at her, taken aback for a millisecond before regaining their Queen's Guard discipline and returning their eyes level in front of them.

The maid's eyes are a different story. She looks crazed. Wild. Lost. And most of all, frightened.

Sunday, November 1
10 a.m. E.T.

Father Hildebrandt says grace. He drops the big "Amen," and one hundred bowed heads look up as they parrot the valediction. Then slip the napkin from beneath their cutlery and lay it across their respective laps.

Places are laid across white linen tablecloths and every seat is filled. Ten tables of ten guests each. Waiters appear from the wings, bearing meticulously chosen red plates loaded with beef bacon, eggs, beef sausage, potatoes O'Brien, corned beef, beef brisket, filet mignon hash, fried cinnamon apples, and white toast topped with pats of perfect, soft, salted, melting but not melted, white butter.

A satisfied guttural hum rings across the oak-paneled room, and a man wearing a headset stands in the shadows next to the coffee tureen in the shadows and whispers, "Joyeuse. Joyeuse." The waiters evaporate from the room. Doors swing silently on oiled hinges in their wake.

Aaron Burr VI sits third table from the dais and eats far more with his eyes than he does with his mouth. The society is only three years old, but manifests the trappings and gravity of one much older. Centuries older. Many of its members possess membership in societies and organizations more ancient than this, but undeniably, for each of the 100 present today, this is the society they hold most closely to their heart and their vest. For it is theirs and not their fathers'.

Here is power.
Here are secrets.
Here is danger.

Burr has been looking forward to this event more than any on the BUR calendar. The Sunday election breakfast. But he knows that his anticipation is akin to that of the masochist, pulling on their chicken mask and lubricating their velvet socks, unsure of what may follow. Dread and titillation laced with safety, but still, ever at the jagged edge of control. He feels history pressing in on him from all sides, pulsing through the room. He has borne the weight of history his entire life, so the feeling is a familiar one, but now, this morning, the sensation is amplified beyond anything he has ever known.

Here he sits, Charter Member of the Brotherhood of Uncomfortable Republicans. Bowtie Republicans. United in ambivalence. Moved by the force of collective unease to decide what to do about this, once and for all. For this was more than a simple re-election. Four years ago, the network wonks had deemed the primaries a "battle for the soul of the Republican Party", but that conflict hadn't truly arrived until the daily shocks of the years that followed. Now it is time to decide whether the party, the Real party, had perished in the horrors of a fiery orange cataclysm. And if so, what remains? What fresh form should rise from its ashes?

Four years earlier, the men gathered in this room had been scattered across the country in their various constituencies, having written off the president in the days leading to Tuesday. They felt no love for Hillary, but at least she was sane. She could be managed. At the time, the men had considered the pending election in 2016 a lost cause. A necessary loss. A cleansing loss. They would pretend to lick their wounds while whispering to one another, "We told them so." They would regroup and galvanize. The senate and the house were still safe, they reasoned. In 2020 they would rise again, lifting a man they could believe in, one of their own, over the stanchions and onto the third throne.

Then that imbecile had somehow won the electoral college. And they'd had to appear to fall in line. Zip it. Swallow their pride. But it had become too embarrassing. Too transparently unprincipled. A prosperous embarrassment, but there it is. The man himself in three words.

Standing by for another four years would kill what was left of the party they revered and leave in its stead an unlovable husk. The whole party nothing but a soulless Golem crushing all in its path, the scroll in its clay mouth a handwritten speculative script for an untitled Johnny Knoxville project written in magic marker by a 13-year-old in Wildwood, New Jersey with impulse control issues and a mouth like a Tarantino pirate.

It is time to take action. The price will be steep initially. If things are as bad as they appear, there will undoubtedly be harassment. Lawsuits. Alienation. Sacrifices will be necessary by every member of B.U.R. in the days and weeks ahead. Today is the final all-members meeting to define the necessary actions for the week ahead. Secrecy is of the highest priority. If their plans are discovered too early, they might still be foiled. Depending on how the vote goes on Tuesday, there might be no need for action.

If the Democrat is elected on Tuesday, they can stand down. Breathe easy. Shake their fists with conviction and get down to the business of reclaiming the Grand Old Party.

But if the President wins, or appears to, they will have to stand tall, the 100.

For each of the 100 members in the room was a member

of the electoral college. Selected by their state parties for their loyalty. Their financial contributions. Their faithful party history. And each of them hails from a state without laws binding them as faithful electors. That is to say, no matter the popular vote in their state, they are free to vote their conscience when the final tally arrives.

They come from Georgia. Tennessee. Texas. Kentucky. Indiana. West Virginia. New Mexico. Utah. Louisiana. The Dakotas.

Burr and his men scouted them carefully and thoroughly. Multiple discrete meetings with each member before they could even be made aware of the organization's existence. Deep background checks. Late night visits. Burr had spent a significant sum. He had shared gallons of very old whiskey and smoked a crate of embargoed cigars. Traveled far and frequently. He'd become skilled in the clandestine meeting.

The Electoral College had been the incumbent's end-around past the popular vote four years ago.

The B.U.R. was the end-around around the end-around.

These 100 men can elect whomever they choose if they need to. Acting on their plan would mean the end of the Electoral College in all likelihood. It would lay bare what some call the vulnerability of the system. But to others, it will lay bare its purpose.

That was surely for the best.

Sunday, November 1
10:14 a.m. E.T.

The Democratic nominee for President of the United States of America is standing on a pleather ottoman in the center of a hotel suite with her arms spread wide, a crumpled ball of polling information strangling in each hand. She releases a shriek. One of her pollsters, an avid bird watcher, reflexively identifies it as the hunting cry of the red kite. A high, plaintive cry with a menacing undertone, a darkness slinking through the wavelengths.

"How can I be losing? How can I possibly be losing to this cretin?" she shouts at her assembled highest ranking staff members. "Answer me. What haven't I done? What haven't we done? What must I do?"

The string of rhetorical questions is chased by a silence far too long to not require some sort of response. The assembled staff don't know where to look. Definitely not at their phones. She hates that. Not at each other. At her? Probably not, as she will interpret that as a desire to speak. Many resort to pensive lip-biting as they stare at her knees. Some tilt their heads and look towards a ceiling corner as if they nearly have the solution to that which has no answer. The wiser heads in the room are swiveling back and forth in sympathetic understanding, as if to say, "I know, I know. It's true. God dislikes you, and the world is peopled with dumb animals undeserving of your goodness."

"I am asking you," she says, descending to calm in that alarming way she has, from hysteria to icy tranquility, faster than a sneeze. "Is there anything left to do in two days that we

haven't already done?"
More silence.
She isn't letting it go this morning. She will stare them down until somebody speaks.
At last, a hand tentatively rises. An older woman in a gray suit. "Yes?" says the candidate.
The woman with the raised hand doesn't actually work for the campaign. She has been tasked with liability risk assessment (LRA) by the candidate's insurance company. An LRA specialist is present for every minute of every meeting; it's the only way the company would agree to cover the candidate in the face of the legendarily litigious President. "I know it isn't my place," says the woman.
"Go ahead," says the candidate. "The rest of these idiots won't even look at me."
"You need to be more pleasant."
The candidate inhales sharply.
The woman continues, "We've seen you tough. We've seen you smart. But people ought to like you by now. People don't like you. You need to spend the next three days smiling. Wherever you go. Really smiling. No grimaces. No sarcasm. No chagrin. A real smile. Real joy."
The candidate glares at her. She isn't smiling. "So you're telling a woman that she needs to smile more?"
"Yes."
"You're telling the woman who would be the first female President of the United States of America that she would be prettier if she'd just smile more?"
"That's right. But not prettier. Well, maybe prettier. But more likeable. That's the important part."
"I can't just walk around smiling all day."

"Why not?"
"Well, for one, I don't want to. I shouldn't have to. And two, I just can't physically do that."
"Why not?"
"Because it's a strain. My jaw will lock."
"It isn't a strain if you're actually happy."
"How am I supposed to be happy?"
"Now there's a question."
"Can anybody tell me how to be happy?" The candidate pivots on her ottoman. She drops her disappointing poll numbers to the carpet. "Can any one of you idiots help me find happiness?"
"Puppies?" says a man in a striped tie.
"Ice cream," says another.
"Se–"
"Shut the fuck up, Karl."
"Love?"
"But what's love, really?"
"Well, I for one–"
"Karl, don't say it."
"I was just going to say–"
"No, Karl. Sit on it."
"Well that's exactly what–"
"Release illusion."
"What are you talking about?"
"The Buddhist concept of maya. Of releasing all illusion. The source of all suffering–"
"No," says the candidate. "That won't make me smile for two days."
"Food?"
"I can barely wear my clothes as it is. All those buckeyes

and ribs and cheese curds and, fucking, local fried everything around the 50 states. So no."

"I still think it's love."

"Well that's just not going to happen," says the candidate.

"Maybe some of these?" says a voice with something of a Tennessee hill-country lilt. A young man in a smart gray shirt holds a rolled-up plastic bag aloft, and allows it to unfurl to reveal five black tablets, each the size and shape of a licorice Good 'n Plenty.

"Doubtful," says the candidate. "What are they?"

"Oh hell no," says the campaign manager, a tall permed woman in a checked pantsuit. "You can forget about that." She charges the young man, seizes the back of his collar and frog marches him towards the door.

"Wait!" says the candidate. "Wait."

The campaign manager closes her eyes and pauses mid-ejection. Without releasing her grip on the young man she says, "What?"

"What are they?"

The young man looks back at the candidate over his shoulder with a charming grin. "I'm only trying to help. If you're fixing to smile for two days, there's your golden ticket."

"What are they, though?"

"Can't show you from this position," he says, still smiling, his arms clamped behind his back by the campaign manager's merciless pinch.

"Let him go," says the candidate.

The campaign manager relaxes her grip. She scowls at the young man. "This is not smart," she says.

"What are they?" says the candidate.

The young man straightens his shirt, tucks it back in, ignoring the campaign manager's scowl and the fact that she's still standing between him and the candidate. He takes a wide step to the right, then walks past the tall woman and approaches the candidate with the bag still unfurled. "Nothing harmful. Nothing illegal. Just a little seasoning for the spirit. Just a little boost."

"What kind of boost?"

"Some folks call them EFJs. Easy Facial Joy. Others call them Southern Smileys. Cheshire Specials. Grinney Smiths. I've been thinking of tossing one into your coffee when you weren't looking. Truth be told. Opportunity never presented itself."

"You're Max, right?"

"Yes, ma'am. Assistant liaison to the southeastern state offices."

"Okay, Max. What are these made of?"

Max's eyebrows rise and the corners of his mouth follow suit. "Well I'm no pharmacologist, ma'am. I've been told it's a special compound designed to relax the stiffest of smirks into a nice, soft, pillowy smile. Real likeable. Welcoming. But again. I'm no doctor."

"But if I were to ask one–"

"I imagine he'd say dive right in. Head first, if you will. Non-habit-forming. Non-drowsy. Non-motor skill impairing. Non-judgement-impeding. They just make you smile."

"Where'd you get them?"

"A buddy."

"You on those right now?"

"No, ma'am," says Max, smiling all the while. "This is my natural comportment."

"But not mine, eh?"

"I wouldn't speak to that, ma'am," he says.

"But you would dose me on the sly."

"Just enough to slap the lemon out your mouth."

"Is that a saying?"

Max shrugs. "Dunno. RBF is, though."

"Ruth Bader... Finsburg?"

"Resting bitch face," says the campaign manager.

"What?!" says the candidate.

"Some of the memes were getting kinda mean," says Max. "So I thought–"

"What memes?" says the candidate.

A deluge of sidelong glances floods the floral wallpapered room.

"What memes?" she repeats. Again, no one speaks. The candidate pulls out her phone and does a quick search. "I'm the... first result when you search for 'resting bitch face,'" she mutters. "It's all..." she swipes quietly as the room watches. "What's all this... stepmother stuff." After two minutes she looks up. "What's a Pink Yeti?"

"I don't know," says the campaign manager.

"Why?" asks a man.

"It says my husband must love the Pink Yeti," says the candidate.

"Oh," says the man. "That's where you put your dick in a freezer."

"What?"

"Karl!" someone shouts.

"What?" says Karl.

"Why would anyone do that?" a voice whispers.

"Why didn't anyone tell me!" the candidate demands. "It's

too late to fix this now. Way too late," she says.
"No," says Max. "Not too late at all. Wednesday is too late. If there's ever a time for a charm offensive, it's now. And these little beauties..." he shakes the bag. "These'll give you that boost."
The candidate takes the baggie and studies the pills. "It's not black cocaine or something, is it?"
"No, ma'am. Like I said. Nothing illegal."
"Will I feel high?"
"No. Maybe a little happier. It's your face that will feel the effect. Stuff just makes you smile."
"I can't have a big, stupid grin."
"You won't. It gives you a nice, relaxed smile. Specially formulated. Nicest smile you'll ever have. There's enough there for five days. Each one's about twenty-four hours."
The candidate looks around the room to gauge the reaction of the assembled. Mostly, she sees a flash of hope in their eyes that she hasn't seen in a while. Not in weeks. It's been a festival of sad bastards and bad news for as long as she can remember. Now, even the insurance lady is nodding a little bit of encouragement. The candidate sighs. Opens the baggie. Pops two of the black pills in her mouth and chases them with a swig from a diet cola someone's left on a table.
Max gasps. "Not two! Never two! Spit it out!"
The candidate clutches at her throat. "I already swallowed them!" she says.
"But you've got–" Max begins, but then trails off, takes a step back from the candidate.
"What?" she says.
The insurance lady screams.

Sunday, November 1
10:45 a.m. E.T.

Things had been going so well. And then, as so often happens, they weren't.

Although there is no written agenda, of course, the meeting of the B.U.R. is planned down to the second by Burr and his lieutenants. Tightly scripted. The National Anthem into the welcome address. The acknowledgements of each attendee. There needs to be no anonymity in this room, and each member needs to feel seen and heard. They need to feel like an equal among powerful men. Then the main presentation. Here are the possibilities. Here is the plan for each possible outcome. Here is what you do and how you do it. Here is what you say afterwards, word for word. Here is how you say it. Recommended tone. Demonstrations of recommended facial expressions and hand gestures. But that's just for interpersonal response. Do not speak on camera. Ever. Give no interviews. You will be supplied with press releases, customized to your region's preferences and linguistic tendencies. Here are some things you must not say and never admit to.

An emergency fund has been established for members facing threats, legal challenges, serious financial loss, or other problems that may arise. All of this information is presented in the same even tone. But when the time arrives for questions and answers, every question is pointed at the need for this emergency fund. Specifically, what kind of threats might they face?

Burr watches the proceedings from his seat. Even though he is the founder of the society, he prefers to play the role of member, equal to all, neither superior nor inferior to any. His spokesperson on stage, Willoughby Sandtide, is capable, a state legislator from South Dakota with enviable political bedside manner and a crisp side part. He's done a good job, thus far, thinks Burr. But the questions coming from the gathering are becoming barbed.

"What if I can't sell any properties for the next three years?" one man from West Virginia says. "Will the fund underwrite my losses?"

"The fund will help any member in serious need, yes."

"I'm not necessarily looking at poverty," says the real estate agent. "But I would like to be made whole, if that's possible. For my sacrifice."

"The fund's focus is on serious need first. So depending on how much you lose–"

"Well who's getting to decide who gets what, exactly? Serious to me, might look like chicken feed to some of the people in this room."

"The B.U.R. Funding Committee members will make those decisions."

"And who's on that committee?"

"Well, there's–"

Another member stands, a very tall, thin man in checked blazer, and interrupts. "We're all making sacrifices, Reilly! We knew it walking in the door."

Reilly of West Virginia holds his hands up. "Now I know all that. I'm just trying to get a little clarification on this fund."

"Let the man ask his questions!" shouts a discount liquor chain mogul from North Dakota. "Just cause he's from West Virginia don't make him less of a man."

"Thank you, Mister Schneider. Wait. Was that a crack?"

Schneider cackles from his seat.

"You son of a bitch."

The room erupts.

"But wait! Can the fund pay for bodyguards?" shouts a drycleaner from Tennessee. "I've got neighbors that'll come with guns if we end up doing this thing."

Sandtide nods into the microphone. "Viable threats will be answered appropriately and the fund will help members in need and good standing if things escalate to that level. But I'd like to repeat that we don't believe they will."

"And why not?" shouts a man nervously twiddling a dollar bill bowtie from the back of the room. "We don't know how this will go! It's never been done!"

Sandtide nods again. "Gentlemen, we've been over this. This is well-trod ground. We've had this conversation in smaller groups. And on our own, with our own conscience. Each of us. The risks to ourselves are miniscule compared to those of our party and our country."

"Easy to say in South Dakota!" someone shouts. "You only got to worry about 62 people coming after you!"

Sandtide blushes at the microphone. More shouting follows, not all of it intelligible.

There is more cowardice in the 100 men than Burr had anticipated. That much is becoming clear. And the questions are beginning to unspool into conversations and arguments between members of the crowd.

Burr stands. Checks with a practiced motion of the hand to ensure that his subdued, maroon bowtie is straight. Brushes his lapels with the palms of his hands. Walks onto the stage. The shouts from the crowd die down.

"Gentlemen," he says into the microphone with a soothing

cadence that lacks none of the firm command that marks him a leader. "You have abused the question and answer format. It is concluded."

The room is nearly silent. Someone coughs. They are abashed.

Burr continues, "Ours is a sacred calling. We are the Republican Party's one, final, true hope. I have spoken with each and every one of you, and I know you feel the same. If you had not, I would never have made you aware of this august society in the first place. You were vetted. You were challenged. You were chosen. For your integrity, your spirit, your values. Now. Mister Sandtide has done an exceptional job of laying forth the operations of the next two days. Let us acknowledge him."

Applause fills the room. Universally, the room applauds and not a single pair of hands abstains. Burr watches, vigilant, to make sure that is the case, and it is.

He continues: "This President. Is a crass, hedonistic, atheistic donkey lacking all moral compass. None whatsoever. You know and I know, that so many of our supposed brethren in the party will counter that by saying, '"Yes, but he's our crass, hedonistic, atheistic donkey devoid of moral compass.' And I tell you there is no such thing. Not in our party. And he may not continue to pretend to represent this party as he chases his own interests. He will not. Because we will stop him. And we will do it. Together."

The room is on its feet and the cheering is thunderous. Burr raises his hands and walks off the stage, but the noise continues and the eyes in the room follow him to his table. And even then, the noise grows and crescendos until Burr swears he can hear it, that vaunted Angel of History herself,

eyes forever staring backwards as she flies, watching the carnage gather in her horrible wake, Burr can hear her wings beating the air, and picture the look in her eyes, puzzled, curious, maybe a little fearful? Turning her head to steal a glimpse, just this once, at what's ahead. What is that noise?
    What's to come?
    What will these men achieve?

Sunday, November 1
11:30 a.m. E.T.

Codename "Moshi Yakamoto"'s shoulders barely fit through the metal doorframe of the Western Union. She's used to it. Nearly has callouses on her shoulders. The clerk behind the counter does that thing people do to Moshi. They're looking down at their hands, typing or reading a screen, and their eyes turn up to her chest, the height where most other people's faces are, then slowly tilt up, past her neck, pause at the size of her strong jaw, continue up to the mouth, nose, then finally eyes.

The man behind the Western Union's counter gives Moshi a gratifying wide-eyed response before tilting his head back to look her in the eyes. The clerk wears a green turtleneck and is heavily pierced: lower lip, ears, nose. "Good morning," he says.

"I'm here to pick up a transfer," says Moshi.

"Transfer number and ID," says the man. The snag in his voice makes Moshi suspect she may be the first person this man has spoken with today. She passes the clerk a slip of paper with the number handwritten on it and her Coast Guard ID, which identifies Moshi as "retired".

"Oh," he says, studying the ID. Moshi's punky shag haircut had belied her expectations. "Thank you for your..." he pauses. Coast Guard? Is that...? She can hear him think it.

"You're welcome," she abridges the interaction. People don't know what to make of it, especially in the Midwest, and she doesn't care to delve into it with every Western Union clerk she meets. But Moshi did serve her country in an elite D.O.G. unit (since disbanded) the Coast Guard equivalent of the

SEALS.

The clerk punches in the transfer number, furrows his brow. He looks up at Moshi, "46 cents?" he says.

"I won a bet," she says.

The clerk shrugs. Fishes four dimes, a nickel, and a penny from her cash drawer and hands it to him. "Your friend spent $11 to send you 46 cents," he says.

"Bet's a bet," replies Moshi.

"Fair enough," he says.

"I need the receipt," says Moshi.

"Oh," he says, "sorry." The man had mindlessly crumpled it and dropped it in the wastebasket. He fishes it out and smooths it against the countertop with the palm of his hand. "Most people don't. I figured for 46 cents..."

"Thanks," says Moshi. She takes the receipt, turns, and leaves.

Standing outside the business, the cold wind rakes her face. The sidewalk is empty and three doors down an orange "Open" sign buzzes in the window of a coffee shop in need of a paint job. Perfect.

She slides into an empty booth and flips over the empty coffee mug. A woman with a tightly curled gray perm appears and fills the mug without a word. "I'll be back for your order," she says.

Moshi pulls the Western Union receipt from her pocket and studies the numbers and symbols in the "Notes" section of the receipt. She has the code memorized so well at this point that she can decipher as she reads. It isn't much of a code, a simple 1:1 character replacement, just enough to keep WU clerks from reading her notes. If anyone were tracking her, they'd crack it by hand in a few minutes.

No one's tracking her, though. She'd know.

After committing the details of the message to memory, Moshi balls up the receipt and pops it in her mouth, washes it down with her first sip of coffee. Her real name was on there. No point in leaving that lying around.

The food in the diner is greasy enough it slides around on her plate as she chases it with her fork. Fried eggs and potatoes. The coffee is good, though, and her mug never dips below the halfway point before the waitress appears to top her off without a word. She couldn't wish a better waitress into existence. No prying questions, no idle weather chat, just keep the coffee coming.

Moshi doesn't ask for a check, leaves 46 cents stacked on the paper placemat, slides a twenty under the saucer (twice what she owes) and leaves.

As she walks through the empty downtown, she pats her pockets to inventory. Dental floss in her left pocket. Thick wad of 20s and 100s in a money clip, a debit card, and Coast Guard ID in her back pocket. The clothes on her back. Her worldly possessions are accounted for. Time to get to the airport.

Sunday, November 1
12:13 p.m. E.T.

After six hours of scrounging, scrapping, scouring, and searching, the six members of MIC20 in the Old Hickory Suite have come to an agreement.

"Blimp's not gonna happen," says Atticus.

The other five shake their heads. They've exhausted all leads. And even with billions at their disposal, there isn't an operational or salvageable blimp for sale in the entire world. To have one built is possible, but not in 24 hours. Not if workers are bumped to $1,000 an hour and labor around the clock; it just isn't possible. One manufacturer in Manitoba calculated that he could get it done if the whole company went balls-out for 48 hours. Said it would cost $50 million. Atticus told him the price wasn't a problem, it was the time. Said he'd probably be able to pay him $75 million for a blimp in 24 hours. Needed to be over New York City in 30 hours. The Canadian man actually wept over the phone. It was so much money. Just out of reach.

It just can't be done.

The room is silent. Atticus swipes "Blimp$?" from the whiteboard with the side of his fist.

The tall kid from White Plains starts biting the sides of his hands. White blond's left eye is twitching every fourth blink.

"What if?" says Limey. She sucks on the button end of a blue retractable pen. A pad of paper beneath her elbow is filled with lines of penciled text, each one struck through with vicious blue ink. Pencil to create. Pen to rule out. "What if we flip it?"

"We're going to sell a blimp?" says a bleary-eyed lobbyist, formerly of the marine life lobby (AKA tuna fisheries).

"No?" says Limey. "We advertise from the ground, looking up?"

"Sidewalk art?" says white-blond.

"No? Or," Limey corrects herself. "Yes, and? Foliage carving? Design tree-clearing? Corn maze?"

"Holy shit," says Atticus.

"Crop circles gone wild," says White Plains, cheering up.

"Rent land next to every airport in America?"

"Shit," says Atticus. "Fucking buy it if we need to. Remember who we work for."

"How many people get in a plane on any given day in America?"

The sable haired woman with the white streak down her center-parted hair who hasn't spoken since Friday night looks it up. "1.73 million people."

"That's cable news ratings," says white-blond. "Prime time."

"And how many people are sharing that on social? Pictures out the window?" says Limey.

"Fucking organic reach," mutters Atticus. "Out the fucking moon's fucking ass."

"Fucking Mars."

"Fucking Neptune."

"Do we really need to swear this much?"

"And the news coverage. The spectacle. Every small market. Every large market."

"Can we clear that much land this fast?"

"Trees fall faster than they grow."

"I had a roommate from Brazil whose family does this on

a planet-killing scale."

"Call him," says Atticus.

"The environmentalists will pitch a hissy."

"We pledge the land to reforestation afterwards." Atticus waves the complaint away. "We pledge to build orphanages. Forest orphanages. Sustainable treehouse orphanages. Organic vegan sustainable farm-to-table, tree-fort orphan communities for the blind. Who gives a fuck? I gotta call Yoshi and pitch it. You guys start making calls. Keep it vague. Don't use the name or give the reason. Kate, make a folder called "Below from Above". Everything goes in there. Start with airport lists by traffic, columns for polling percentiles, electoral point values, and anything else you can think of. We'll build from there."

There are smiles for the first time in a long time. Intern Limey especially.

"Okay," says Atticus. He writes "Ground Game" on the whiteboard and walks into the bathroom to make the call to Yoshi Nakamoto, primary dogsbody, wallet caddy, and campaign manager to the candidate.

Sunday, November 1
12:21 p.m. E.T.

The Stern Microsystems Rapid Action Team (RAT Squad, in the vernacular) has been on the scene for two hours at the Palm Beach resort when the CEO, Johann Microsystem himself, pulls up to the scene in his black armored Land Rover. The RAT Team leader meets him at the elevator and they descend together to the sub-basement bunker. They don't say a word until they are well underground.

"How the hell did he get out?" says Johann.

"Tunnel, sir."

"Unbelievable. I mean, I actually don't believe you."

"I wouldn't believe it if I hadn't seen it myself. 20 yards long, through mostly limestone. Straight into the primary wine cellar. And once there, no problems maneuvering up and out."

"What's our cordon? How far could he have gotten?"

"If on foot, our most ambitious estimate is 80 miles. If he jogged for 12 hours."

"That's ridiculous. We can certainly tighten that down."

"Sir..."

"What?"

"It looks like 80 miles is realistic. He's had a treadmill for a few years down here, and even though he wiped the memory, judging by the use it's had, our forensics guy says someone's been doing some ultramarathon-level training down here."

"Who the fuck gave him a treadmill?"

"To help with general fitness. The... principle... said his cheeks were looking doughy a few years ago, didn't want him to get fat, even under the circumstances."

"Even though no one would ever see him."

"Well, the principle sees him. He's sensitive to weight. Apparently."

"I told the principle... I told him they needed to restrain the client as he got older. Or consider... alternate arrangements. I fucking told him."

RAT Leader nods sympathetically. The customer isn't always right. Normally, when the customer wouldn't take their advice, Stern protocol dictates you refuse the job. A strict our-way-or-highway policy. But this isn't the sort of client you turned down, especially now.

But no more did you want to fail the client. Especially now. Especially now.

"Show me," says Johann.

RAT Leader walks the CEO through the sub-basement dwelling. It never fails to surprise him just how nice the whole arrangement is. For a prison. The walls are immaculate white with gold wall fixtures, and there are false windows embedded in the walls with photo-perfect LEDs designed to mimic natural light. The lights rise and dim according to the position of the sun in relation to the above-ground world, in an attempt to create an above-ground sense in a lair that is anything but. Unusually high ceilings, lofted ceilings almost, help enhance the sense that one is in a normal, extravagant even, Manhattan penthouse apartment. The client has everything they'd needed. Queen-sized bed, still made. Living room set-up, gaming systems, couches, gaming chair. The posters all over the walls are the only thing that throw the décor off its upscale stride. Anime action figures in power postures, wild explosions in their background. And a few pin-up girls in bikinis. It produces the air of a privileged teen's rec-room bedroom set-up.

Or maybe a rich kid at a city university set up in his own apartment for the first time.

The place appears immaculate, as it should. Spotless. That's the other thing that distances itself from normal teenspace. There should be socks in strange places. Food wrappers. But then the maid's been in every day. Four times a day. So what do you expect?

"The maid helped," says the CEO. "Had to."

"We've been interrogating her since we got here. Her and both doctors."

"And?"

"Nothing. They're all pleading ignorance. Confusion. They have a lot at stake here. Everything. They know what happens to their village if this goes down."

The CEO shakes his head. "They have to have played a role."

"Inadvertently," says RAT leader.

"You believe her?"

"I doped her up. She's telling me things about herself she wouldn't tell her priest, her sister. Things she probably doesn't tell herself in a quiet moment. But she has no idea how the kid did this."

"Where is it?" says the CEO turning slowly in place. "Bathroom?"

"No, sir. It's right there." RAT leader points to a poster of a blond woman with breasts the size of wall clocks dangling, tenuously sheathed by an unlucky bikini top as she bends forward. Her hands are buried in sand, and cool blue waves roll in towards the slope of her buttocks. Rat leader pulls the corner of the poster back and reveals a neatly carved circular hole in the drywall at the mouth of a tunnel that curls back into darkness. "Straight out of Shawshank," says RAT leader.

"Has he seen it?" says Johann.

"He has cable, sir," says RAT leader. "Premium cable. He's seen everything."

"Jesus," says Johann. "So he knows. He knows who he is. Who the fuck gave him... never mind. The principle."

"Said television was an important part of his education," says RAT leader.

"Who the fuck cares about his education if he never goes anywhere? And if nobody ever sees him. Or knows he exists? The whole point of this– Never mind. This whole thing was always so... I never should have signed onto this. Even if..."

RAT leader remains silent. Awaits instructions. The CEO is not the sort to think aloud, normally. He regains himself.

"The resort's been searched?"

"Yes, sir. Thoroughly. Tact was exercised, but in light of circumstances we were as intrusive as we needed to be. Thorough. Complete. And nothing. Closets, ducts, cabinets, luggage, car trunks, everything. The whole place is locked down and I can state with certainty that he is no longer on the property."

"The golf course?"

"Swept. Nothing."

"What's the staff say?"

"Nada."

"Nobody saw him?"

"Nunca."

"The cameras?"

"There aren't any in the wine cellar. Tech is going over the tapes everywhere else. Nothing yet."

"We need to find him fast. Everything about this is fucked."

"Yes, sir," says RAT leader. "Yes it is."

The door to the sub-basement apartment opens and a jumpsuited tech hustles in. "He's not on foot," says the tech. "He jimmied the valet box and grabbed a Tesla fob."

"Do we know what time?" says RAT leader.

"Midnight," says the tech. "He's been in the wind for 12 hours."

"It's a Tesla. Talk to the owner and have him find out where it is on the App."

"Already did. The kid disabled tracking."

"Impossible. This kid's been down here without the internet his whole freaking life. How could he possibly work that out?"

"Well actually, it's a very intuitive interface, sir," says the tech. "Elon has personally put a lot of time and thought into the UX and bringing electric vehicles to the lay pers–"

"Shut the fuck up," says Johann. "How far can he have gotten on the charge in the vehicle?"

"He unplugged it from a charger on the lot here, and it had been parked for a day and a half," says the tech, "so it was definitely fully charged."

"How far?"

"370 miles," says the tech. He seems strangely proud, as if he'd built the car himself. "Until he'd need to charge again."

"How long does it take to charge?"

"All the way? Around 9 hours. They're working on bringing that down to 6 in the next model year–"

Without even looking at him, the RAT leader punches the tech in the throat. The tech crumples to the ground with his hands wrapped around his neck, gagging and sputtering.

"Sorry, sir," says RAT leader to the CEO. "I can't stand that shit."

"No. That's fine," says the CEO. "So if the kid drove five hours, found another charging station, charged for five hours, then drove another couple hours, he could be..."

"Anywhere within 500 miles, sir," says RAT leader.

"He's not even necessarily in Florida anymore," mutters the CEO.

The silence that ensues is long and layered, interrupted only by the tech's whistling gasps as he crawls towards the elevator. Johann and RAT leader watch him crawl in and tap the button that will send him back to the surface. The silence resumes.

The CEO finally speaks. He has decided. "Use your contacts in the Highway Patrol to track him through their cameras. No point in chasing him if we have no idea where he is in a 500-mile radius. If we're lucky, he's still on the move."

"And if we're unlucky?"

"He's already talking. And we'll see him up there any minute," says the CEO pointing to the television, where an anchor, looking odd and awkward in his everyman sweatshirt, is interviewing patrons at a Michigan Steak 'n Shake about their feelings regarding the upcoming election.

On the screen, a woman wearing a Spartans sweatshirt wipes ketchup from her upper lip with her pinky finger and says, "I think he'll bring a breath of fresh air. Plus I trust him. He's not like the others!"

"Shit," says the CEO.

Sunday, November 1
1:05 p.m. E.T.

Late brunch in Lincoln Park and it's still crowded as hell at Trixie's Mimosa Brunchaterium. Lauren and her five friends wait 45 minutes before they finally get a prime booth, next to the cinnamon-butter bar.

Five of them are wearing pink "pussy hats" with petite cat ears popping from either side. Lauren wears a modified version with intricate pink knitted labia in place of cat ears.

After their drinks are ordered (three donut-capped bloodies, two lemonade mimosas, and one Triple-B (Basic Bitch Bellini)) Lauren taps her knife against the side of her water glass.

"Girls," she says. "Real talk. After the march, what's next?"

"Get stitched up at the Urgent Care, likely," says Brigid.

"And after that?"

"Kombucha brinner at Lackey's," says Jess.

"Friends, Fries and Fingers at Friday's on Sundays," says Dakota B.

"Empowerment night at Uno's," says Dakota S. "Half off well drinks."

"I'm not talking food and drinks," says Lauren. "I'm talking about what's next, next. I'm talking about the system."

"Well, it needs to be overthrown."

"Toppled. Clearly."

"Redistricting is key?"

"So key?"

"Question is. How do you bring the country to Chicago?" says Jess. "Like rural, country."

"How do you get people to vote in their own interests?" says Dakota S.

"It's all fucking Facebook's fault, you know?" says Brigid. "Like it's the newspaper for old people now? And that is fucked up."

"Right?"

"Everyone should just move to Insta."

"You know Facebook owns Insta, right?"

"Wha?"

"Shet."

"That's fucked."

"Did you see those BB-FoBs when we came in?"

"How could I miss those lemon-head bitches. Like eight of them."

"Fucking traitors."

"They're gonna fucking Nader this whole thing."

"What the fuck are they thinking?"

"Like the only thing they care about is Medicare for All. Which is great. But you're gonna end up with Medicare for My Ass if he gets reelected. Right?"

"Preaching to the choir."

"Right?"

"One of them's coming."

"So?"

A thin woman wearing a yellow pussy hat walks past the table, giving the six women the side-eye as she passes.

"What are you looking at?" says Lauren.

"Hard to say," says the woman. "Gender is a spectrum so, you know... hard to say."

"Most things are with an old, white, Vermont cheddar dick in your mouth."

"What you say?" says the woman in the yellow hat. She stops, stares at Lauren. Lauren returns the stare, but in the periphery sees the woman's hand move towards the pocket of her jeans where a bulge resembling the outline of a switchblade is unmistakably visible.

The women in pink hats tense. Dakota S. tightens her grip on a fork. Brigid's hand slides slowly towards her ankle holster. Lauren stands. Harder to defend yourself from a seated position. She applies her warmest smile and holds up her hands, palms out. "Hey," she says to the woman identifiable as a Bad Bitch for Bernie by the yellow bonnet. "We should all be friends here. We may not be voting the same. But at least we're voting the same. If you know what I mean. The enemy of my enemy is my friend. You know."

"The lesser of two evils is still evil," says the yellow cap. "And we ain't friends."

"Fair enough," says Lauren. "We don't have to be friends. But we haven't even ordered our entrees yet. And we'll have time to talk at the march. Plenty of time."

Yellow cap nods slowly. "Yeah," she says. She studies the six pink hats. They look pretty hard core. Like maybe they've been juicing. The little one with the crazy eyes sipping on a Bellini's got forehead veins like a UFC bantam weight. "Yeah, we'll talk there. I.R.L."

"Couldn't be realer," says Lauren.

"K," says the woman.

"KK," says Lauren.

The woman walks towards the restroom.

"I have to tinkle," says Dakota S., still gripping her fork.

"Leave it," says Lauren. She sits. "We'll see her at the Tower."

"I can't wait," says Dakota S.
"I know," says Lauren.
"Right?" says Dakota B.

Sunday, November 1
2:24 p.m. E.T.

There are more private clubs in Washington D.C. than there are members of the U.S. House of Representatives. Something for everyone. Everything if you're someone.

You want to meet your mistress for an old fashioned and an "old fashioned" (less commonly known as the Charles Kuralt Undulating Kazoo Ride) you go to the Red Rose on F Street. It's not on Google Maps. It's not on Apple Maps. It's not on MapQuest. It's not on OpenMaps or ArcGIS. Good luck asking Siri. You have to know about it to know about it.

If you want to meet your mister for a "How's your father?" and a Yankee Doodle Sandy, you creep to the Blue Violet on G Street.

If your assignation is with your lawfully wedded spouse but you're looking to preserve your bad boy or naughty girl image, throw the press off your trail at the Jolly Molly Private Club for Couples. Abraham Lincoln was a member. So was Polk, not that anyone cares who Polk poked. Again, for the sake of discretion, no sign above the door. It's on L Street this year. The plan is to up stakes and make for a shoreside manse near Foggy Bottom next year. The year after that: who knows? Subscribe to our newsletter for updates. Just kidding. You might as well ride a Segway to the Watergate if you have to ask.

Those seeking the company of strangers in the strangest of company find an alley off of N Street, knock three times on the triangular window at the back, then proceed at a clip to the side door and introduce themselves to the maître d'hôtel as Monsieur de la Pout, then open their jacket to reveal a red kerchief in the left breast pocket. Pass through the feather tunnel, remove their socks, but keep their shoes on, and bow three times before proceeding past Michael Dukakis (or is it a wax likeness?) without making eye contact.

All that to say, if you need a discrete place to meet, Washington D.C will provide.

Mid-afternoon on a Sunday is the ideal time to convene if you most sincerely want to be ignored (there are abundant clubs to visit, of course, if you're looking for attention.) So it makes sense that mid-afternoon on Sunday of election week, three executives from three cable television networks climb the unadorned concrete steps of a nondescript building on M Street, not a half mile from the Farragut North Metro stop. They don't climb the steps at the same time, of course. Ranya, the Aussie from the Right Wing News agency makes the steps at 2:20. Loretta of the Leftist News Organization wanders up five minutes later. Cindy, of the Centrist News Television Network pretends to be waiting for an Uber at the stoop for a minute, checking her phone, scouting the windows, before following suit at 2:30.

They each speak the prearranged message (provided via encrypted text on Signal) "I need a word with Walter," and are shown to a wood-paneled study on the third floor containing three folding chairs arranged around a card table with a plastic Wander Suero Day collector's cup from Nationals Park in front of each seat and a wooden pitcher of Tang in the center of the table.

"Tang?" asks Ranya with the Australian accent, as she pours herself a glass.

"God, you people are weird," says Loretta.

"Bit early to hit the Tang?" says Cindy the Centrist.

"There's not even any fucking ice," says Loretta. She pulls a silver handled hairbrush from her bag and starts brushing her hair with wild vigor. "Fuck your Tang."

"If I wanted Tang in my mouth, I'd suck off Ted Cruz," says Cincy. She sneers and pulls a copper flask from her vest pocket, takes a pull.

Ranya giggles. Loretta knocks her empty glass over. Cindy throws her empty plastic cup into the fireplace where it bounces with an unsatisfying plock. Ranya drains her Tang with relish and fills it again from the pitcher.

"What are we doing?" says Loretta. "I've got a deadline in two hours and I have to pump before dinner or the whole batch will taste like ham and we're keeping baby kosher."

"Why?"

"I don't fucking know. I read it online. Mind your business."

"What the fuck are we doing?" echoes Cindy. "What's your boy got planned?"

"He's not my boy," says Ranya. "He's America's boy."

"Shut the fuck up and speak up. What's up?" says Loretta.

"A Block features the American President giving a speech to a group of supporters in a recently reopened airplane hangar in Paducah."

"Big whoop. What's the angle?"

"He's going to start calling her the Witch of the West."

"Why not wicked?" says Cindy.

"Didn't poll great," says Ranya.

"He couldn't say it," says Loretta.

"Not true," says Ranya.

"My girl on the inside says he couldn't handle three "W"s in succession. Kept saying 'Wicked Witch of the Rest.' Had to trim the wicked in rehears-os."

"Fake news," says Ranya.

"If you say so."

"Fuck off. B Block is a feature on illegals on the contracting crews building shoddy sections of The Wall for later use. C Block is a wrap-up of the polls."

"Conclusions?" says Cindy.

"Inconclusive," says Ranya.

"Anyone's game," says Cindy.

"That's what we've got," says Ranya. "You?" she gestures to Loretta.

"A Block: Nakamoto polls. B Block: Nakamoto identity. C Block: Nakamoto supporters. Who are they?"

"You seeing something we're not?"

"Usually."

"Hallucinations don't count."

"Nakamoto's making a dent in the disaffected," says Loretta. Cindy and Ranya grunt.

"It's hitting both sides equally," says Ranya.

"That's our take," says Cindy.

"I don't disagree," says Loretta. Coy.

"A Block, though?" says Ranya.

"The disaffected is a large voting bloc," says Loretta.

"Not large enough," says Cindy.

"Ten percent in one poll," says Ranya. "Less than five in the rest."

"Polls have been asking the wrong questions."

"What should they be asking?"

"Tune in and find out," says Loretta. "You?" she says, gesturing to Cindy.

"A Block: Russian hacker threat to voting machines," says

Cindy. Ranya yawns. "B Block: Polls roundtable." Ranya refills her glass of Tang. "C Block: Dem on the stump."

"What's her closer?" says Ranya.

"She's still calling him a fat cat," says Cindy.

"People like cats that are fat. People like Garfield. And Heathcliff. She should have ditched that months ago."

"Racist didn't work," says Cindy.

"Everyone's racist."

"Out of touch billionaire didn't work," says Cindy.

"Becoming an out of touch billionaire is the new American Dream," says Ranya.

"Nothing sticks long enough," says Loretta.

"I heard she tested 'Bald Billionaire,'" says Cindy.

"Can't alienate the balds," says Ranya. "Lotta balds vote."

"People like Daddy Warbucks more than they like Annie," says Loretta.

"I heard they floated 'Anchor Husband,'" says Ranya.

"Self-defeating," says Cindy. "I heard they gave 'Pussy Grabber' a go."

"Didn't work four years ago," says Loretta.

"Nobody wants to hear it," says Ranya.

"Nobody wants to say it," says Cindy.

"I heard," says Loretta. She pauses. Pauses are rare in this trio. "I heard she floated 'Child Rapist of New York.'"

The pause echoes.

"Ew," says Ranya.

"Nasty nasty," says Cindy.

"Didn't stick?" says Ranya.

"Oh it stuck. But insurance lawyers said no-no-no," says Loretta.

"Missed opportunity," says Ranya.

"Surely we're in a post-slander world," says Cindy.
"He is. She isn't. Lawyers make the man."
"It's a man's world."
"It's a lawyer's world."
"It's a man's lawyer's world."
"For the moment."
"Nakamoto?" Ranya says to Loretta, still puzzling.
"Tune in." Loretta smiles.
Ranya hums in a speculative fashion.

Cindy leaves the room. Five minutes later, Ranya follows. Five minutes after that Loretta puts on her Bulgari shades and makes for the stairs.

Sunday, November 1
3 p.m. C.T. / 4 p.m. E.T.

Corner of Washington and Liberty, at the light in downtown Peoria, and Gary Crest is back in his lawn chair. Same as every day since the 4th of July when the idea first struck him. 9 to 5. The red trucker hat with white text across the front is perched neatly atop his head and the American flag anchored to the back of his chair flaps in the stiff wind. Despite the cloudy cold, he's got his aviators on. He likes to look where he wants to look and it's no one's business where he's looking. There's a GoPro screwed onto the top of the flagpole above his head, just in case anyone tries anything. No one has, but you never know. There's just the minor irritation, now and again. Some hippy in a Prius leans on the horn here and there, the occasional middle finger, and sometimes someone shouts an obscenity out their window as they drive by. Of course, that's their God-given right and Gary will go to the mat to preserve their right to verbally abuse him. That's freedom of speech. Theirs is his.

His lawn chair is a good one with two cup holders and a little flip-out ottoman to prop his legs on. Like a little recliner. He keeps an American-made green, 30-ounce, Polar brand bottle filled with iced tea in his right holder. In the left holder, he maintains a small clutch of American flags. When there's a honk or a shout, he'll pluck one of the flags up and wave it with the biggest grin he can muster. Hostile or friendly, it doesn't matter. Most of it's friendly. There's a lot of like-minded folks around.

If a kid wanders by with their parents he hands them a flag.

One time, a woman pushing a jogging stroller walked past, trailed by a toddler decked out in full Osh Kosh B'Gosh suspenders and denim cap. Gary waved a little flag and the toddler took it gleefully and put the golden end in his mouth without hesitation. The mother clocked it and snatched the flag out of the little kid's mouth and hand with a scowl, tossed the flag on Gary's lap.

"No thanks," she said.

"God bless you," he'd replied.

She started to storm off, dragging the toddler behind her, looking like he might start crying any minute. She paused. Turned back towards Gary. She had her hands on her hips. "I have to know," she said. "It's one thing to vote for him. But what are you doing out here?"

"You got an open mind?" he'd asked her.

She paused. "Not about him I don't," she said.

Gary nodded. "Might as well enjoy your walk then."

"Seriously, what's the appeal?"

"My wife asks the same question. Know what I tell her?"

"What?"

"Simple enough. Three things. We gotta get out the Middle East. We gotta stop killing babies. We gotta bring jobs back. Too many people free-riding."

"It's been three years," she'd said. "And he hasn't done any of those things. Even if I agreed with them."

"Wife says the same thing. I say: Can't do it alone," Gary had told her. "Gotta vote in some friends. The swamp is deep and full of monsters."

The toddler had started to squirm out of her grip. "Okay," she said. "But at least admit he's a dirtbag."

Gary had nodded. "They're all dirtbags. Good people don't

run for president. He's just honest about it. Gotta respect that. I'll take the honest dirtbag over the lying dirtbag. We need three things, and he's trying to get 'em done. That's all I care about. I hope you'll think about that."

The woman had shrugged and rejected his repeated offer of a small flag for the kid. Which hurt a little bit. The flag wasn't wearing a hat.

The flag was the flag.

Two days until the big day. His phone buzzes against his hip and he pulls it from the belt holster and looks at the number. 309 area code, but he doesn't know the number. He flips it open and holds it to his ear. "Yup?" he says.

He hears a click, nothing for two seconds, and then a semi-familiar voice. "Hi, this is Alan Alda." Gary flinches. "Election day is around the corner, and it's time to make a change. If you want a return to traditional American values, if you care about American workers, you'll vote the fat cat billionaires out of office by saying Yes to–" Gary flicks his phone shut and clips it back in his holster. Fifth call in two days. Martin Sheen, Elliott Gould, that guy from Law and Order, Robert Redford, and now Alan Alda. It's like they're begging him to vote against her. How on earth has Gary ended up on their list anyways? He wonders. He suspects his granddaughter, Trinity. The things she posts to his Facebook... She's relentless. He'd almost be proud of her if she weren't so danged wrong about everything that matters.

A green car pulls up to the light. Big engine, not enough clearance to roll a tennis ball under the axle. Two black kids with the windows rolled down. The kid driving wears a White Sox hat and the kid in the passenger seat has a black bandanna tied around his forehead and a logo-less white baseball cap pulled down over the bandanna. Neither of them seems much interested in Gary. Music is blasting out of the car. Thrumming bass shudders the metal frame of Gary's chair beneath him, and from the radio, a woman's voice is saying... something. He can't make out most of it over the bass. The bass drowns the words out, but it's definitely a woman.

The light changes and the car rolls forward, and for a moment the words crystallize in Gary's ears: "I'm far from cheap, I smoke skunk with my peeps..." and then the Doppler effect twists the whole thing flat, and the car is gone.

Not exactly the Beach Boys, thinks Gary. But that's their God-given right. Gary will go to the mat to preserve their right to sing about smoking skunks if needs be. Though they might think of turning it down a skosh for the common peace.

People think he's a racist when they see the red hat, but he's not that. Before he retired, he worked with a lot of good black guys and he liked them fine. Never quite crossed the bridge to socializing with them after hours, not because he didn't want to, it just never... happened, but a good working relationship, absolutely. Got along with nearly everyone. He disliked more of the white guys than he did the black guys. And the Mexicans were the best workers he ever hired. Those guys hustle. Most of them couldn't speak a lick, but dear God, could they work. President was wrong there, in a lot of ways, right in others. There ought to be a way for people to get over here and work. Get paid. Pay taxes. They shouldn't be breaking the law. But we shouldn't be locking kids in cages. That was stupid. Gave the liberals exactly what they wanted. Not smart.

Gary gave Kanye a fair shake after he saw some that footage from the White House and came away liking some of it. He likes that gold-digger song. And can't fault the man's taste in women, my goodness. My goodness.

Not so sure about Kanye's father-in-law anymore, but you know what? Not his monkeys, not his circus. People have a right to privacy. Not that it appears to be that particular family's primary concern. But people think he's going to be a racist gay-hating codger as soon as they see the hat. That's part of why he wears it. Let them see a nice decent guy who agrees with the President and what he's trying to do. Mainstream media paints all the President's supporters with the same ignorant brush and it isn't right. It isn't fair.

Yeah, there's loonies out there, for sure, saying some pretty extreme stuff, dressed up in flag pajamas and Uncle Sam hats and sparklers stuck up their ass, playing up to the cameras at the rallies. There's a thousand Garys for each loon, though, and you never see them on camera. They don't get the air time. Plenty of loons on both sides. Snorfing up that oxygen.

That's why he's here. Just a normal guy, waving hey, handing out flags, saying: I love this country and I want it to get better. Like it used to be. Only better. It wasn't ever perfect, but it used to be nicer. Three squares and a car in every garage. A place where babies are loved and valued, where his taxes aren't pissed all over the desert. Where a man can provide for his family and isn't always looking for a handout.

A car horn beeps. Short and friendly. Gary waves a tiny flag.

Sunday, November 1
4:33 p.m. E.T.

"You tell him."

"You tell him."

"I'm above you in the Orgchart. So. You tell him."

"We're level on the Orgchart. I don't answer to you."

"My name's first."

"It's alphabetical."

"My name's first."

"I'm not getting fired two days before the election just because your mom fucked an Alsatian."

"Alston. And no. You're getting fired because your Mom fucked a Polack, Zabrocski."

"Someone's gotta tell him."

"Then maybe you should do the right thing."

"It's not our fault."

"Right. Tell him that too."

"If he hears it from outside, we both get shitcanned."

"So I guess you'd better tell him."

"Wrong conclusion."

"I'm not telling him."

"Yes you are."

"I heard the Demanetwork running it tonight. In a few hours. Then Rupes will roll with it right after, late night into the morning show. Everyone else will too."

"You want a morning show to tell him?"

"Maybe."

"No."

"No. I want you to tell him."

"You know what?"
"Yes."
"No. I mean it. You know what? I will tell him."
"Sure you will."
"No. I will. For a hundred grand."
"Fuck you."
"I'll tell him for $100,000. Severance pay."
"He's not giving you a nickel."
"No. I know. Draw it from one of the RNC accounts. We both know there's plenty of casino milkshake left."
"You serious?"
"I'll tell him."
"You're serious."
"I'll tell him."
"Why would you do that? I don't get it."
"$100,000."
"What's your angle?"
"I'm just tired of this shit."
"We're all tired of this shit. Fuck you. Tired. It's the end of the fucking marathon. Rubber legs all over. Everyone's drenched in their own piss. Our nipples fell off in September. You wouldn't just walk away now. You know something."
"What's your problem? I said I'll tell him. $100,000. Plus I finally get some sleep."
"You know something. What do you know?"
"I know that I'm tired."
"Bullshit. Nobody walks away two days before the day."
"You want me to tell him. I'm telling you, I'll tell him. My price is a modest severance package."
"Never mind. I'll tell him."
"What?"

"Yeah. You figured something out. I'll be the one to tell him."

"Don't be crazy. You think he's stopped shooting messengers?"

"No. I think you have an angle."

"What angle?"

"I don't know yet."

"I don't have an angle."

"So you're just stupid?"

"I'm tired."

"Bullshit."

"Fuck it. I don't even need the money. I'm just gonna go tell him."

"Oh no you don't. You're not telling him shit."

"You're gonna stop me?"

"Yes I am."

"I don't think you can."

"Oh I can."

"You gonna hit me? You gonna hit me?"

"Maybe. Is that what I have to do? You wanna sit down, bro?"

"Don't fucking bro me, bro."

"Better take your glasses off, bro."

"You gonna slap me with that legal-sized notepad, bro?"

"Take your glasses off, bro. Don't want to lose an eye over nothing."

"They're not prescription anyway."

"I fucking knew it. Poser."

"Yeah. Nice class ring."

"Nice chin dimple."

"Nice 'fiancé.'"

"We doing this?"
"---"
"We doing this?"
"---"
"That's what I thought."
The door closes behind him.
"Sucker."

Sunday, November 1
11:42 p.m. Moscow Standard Time/4:42 p.m. E.T.

[In Russian]

"What is this?"

"I'm sorry, sir. I know it's late."

Viktor Paralinka throw his gloves at the GRU technician, whose name is Igor Simonchev. They bounce off his shoulder, fall to the ground and land with a sound like raw, wet chicken meat.

"It couldn't wait for tomorrow?"

"I didn't think so, sir."

"What?"

"We're blocked, sir."

"From what?"

"Everything external, sir."

Paralinka slaps the technician at the next terminal in the side of the head and gestures for him to stand up. The tech scutters away, and Paralinka takes his chair, rolls it next to Simonchev. "Show me," he says.

"Internal network is fine," says Simonchev, running his finger down on a column on the screen. "Everything's up. Everything's good."

"I didn't come down for you to tell me what's working."

Simonchev points to a second window on the screen. "Everything else is not working. Nothing outside the country."

"Not possible."

"I tried everything. Every VPN. Couldn't connect."

"Switch to the pipeline auxiliary fiber."

"Tried. Nothing."

"Switch to satellite."

"Tried all of them. All of them. Wouldn't connect. Like they're gone."

"Even the ISS?"

"Silence."

"You called Moscow?"

"I did. Same for them."

"Provideniya?"

"Same."

"Go through Ukraine."

"Called Ukraine. They can't move traffic beyond Ukraine."

"Not even the Turkish line?"

"Pings aren't rebounding."

"Someone would have to physically cut... how many lines?"

"I don't know, sir."

"It's impossible."

"I don't know."

"This doesn't make sense."

"There's more."

"What?"

"Cell towers are down along the western border."

"How many?"

"All of them."

"It isn't possible."

Paralinka inhales a long, slow breath through his nose. "Call Paris?" he says.

"No answer," says Simonchev. "Or–"

"What?"

"Couldn't get through."

"What do you mean?"

"It rang. But it wasn't the right ring."

"What?"

"I called Paris. But it was the American ring. When I called. You know." Simonchev trills his lips. "Brrrrrrrr." Pause. "Brrrrrrrr." Pause. "It should have been: booop booop. Booop booop."

Paralinka stares at the tech. "You think Paris has been taken to America?"

"No. I don't think my call made it across the border. I think they've cut us off. Physically."

"So the ring tone?"

"They're... trolling us?"

"It isn't possible," says Paralinka. Simonchev shrugs. Paralinka runs his finger down the column of network ports on the screen. "All of these?" he says.

"Yes," says Simonchev.

"There's one more," says Paralinka. "Only for emergencies."

"Okay," says Simonchev. He is unsurprised. He's privy to many secrets. But even the secrets have secrets in the IRC. "Should I empty the room?"

"No, just move." Paralinka scoots towards the keyboard and Simonchev makes way. Paralinka pulls the gold wedding band from his finger, rotates it slowly between his index finger and thumb, squinting into its interior rim. He opens a window on the screen and types in 12 digits. Four groups of three numbers separated by periods. He taps enter.

The cursor blinks for thirty seconds and neither man says a word.

A message appears on the next line.

"Connection Timed Out"

Paralinka stares at the monitor in disbelief. "Nobody knows about this line," he says. Paralinka had overseen the laying of the fiber himself, five years ago. It runs from a repeater station inside the Russian border to a small lakeside town in Finland called Potoskavaara. The line terminates in a modest lakeside cottage. Spanish tile roof, but otherwise simple and inconspicuous. He'd purchased it in cash from an old woman who couldn't believe her good fortune. Paralinka had learned fucking Finnish for the operation. He'd cultivated a Hämeenlinna accent and backstory.

Finland has permissive laws about camping on unfarmed land. He and three others had trekked by day and camped and dug and buried endless fiber cable in the cold Finnish nights for weeks, carefully replanting disturbed foliage, upset tree limbs, everything restored to its former state as they moved.

On the last evening, the line buried through the cottage's backyard and run through a length of pipe into the cottage's basement, Paralinka and his companions cheered as the cable poked its head through the wall.

Then Paralinka pulled a muzzled Glock 9 from his pocket and plugged the two men standing beside him. Soon, the third man jogged down the basement stairs grinning like a golden retriever, until he saw the two dead men laid out side-by-side on a tarp in the basement. Paralinka gave him an "Ours-is-not-to-reason-why" shrug, raised the Glock once more, and plugged the third technician in the forehead.

Then he started unpacking the rest of his equipment and finished setting up in silence.

Five years later, that line is down for the first time since he plugged in the brand new Telia router in the basement of that humble cottage.

"Nobody could possibly know," says Paralinka.

"Someone does," says Simonchev.

Paralinka repays Simonchev's words with a look that could sublimate vodka back into a potato. Simonchev withers in his seat.

Paralinka stands, walks to his office and closes the door behind him.

[/In Russian]

Sunday, November 1
5:10 p.m. E.T.

"You tell him?"

"Yup. An abridged version."

"What he say?"

"Didn't go well."

"What he say?"

"A number of things."

"You don't say?"

"He was upset. Flipped his wig, as it were."

"I'll bet."

"Yup."

"I can't believe you told him."

"Yup."

"You get fired?"

"Not yet. Momentarily, I assume."

"Two days before E-Day? Bro."

"I hate you."

"Yeah, Bro?"

"God dammit."

"You did it to yourself, right?"

"God."

"And that's what really hurts?"

"You're an animal. A fucking animal."

"Universally true. I'll see what we can do about a little severance, though. A little sugar. Tide you over."

"Fuck you."

"Now. Clearly it's you what's fucked."

Sunday, November 1
4:29 p.m. C.T. / 5:29 p.m. E.T.

Codename "Yoshi Nakamoto" (Moshi's deskbound counterpart (no relation, however)) wears wireless headphones and sits before a $300 plastic Chromebook, nodding to a voice delivering instructions to him over the phone. Seated on a Starbucks stool in Austin, Texas (one of nearly 50 Starbucks locations in the city proper) Yoshi wears a white Adidas windbreaker, torn black jeans, and spotless, white Pearl Izumi running shoes. The day Izumi announced they were discontinuing their running line, Yoshi bought 50 identical pairs online. When you find a shoe so perfect, you marry it, surely as a spouse.

Computers are a different matter. The Chromebook will be incinerated at the end of the day. A new one purchased with cash in the morning at a new location.

Same with the phone.

If anyone bothers to look for him, that isn't how they'll find him. His genius is pedantry. Details.

The voice in his ears provides Yoshi five concrete directives and he commits them to memory as he hears them. He never transcribes directives from Satoshi Nakamoto, not on anything more tangible than his own mind.

Satoshi finishes dictating instructions and Yoshi says, "I have heard every word."

"Repeat them back to me," says Satoshi.

Yoshi says, "I'm in a Starbucks." The voice call is over Signal, encrypted, safe enough, but repeating it aloud in that environment is probably a bridge too far.

Satoshi sighs and says, "Step outside. Please."

Yoshi gathers his possessions and stumbles outside, messenger bag on his shoulder, and walks behind the dumpster. Starbucks dumpsters are a nice, quiet place to talk if you're feeling paranoid. "Okay," he says. He repeats Satoshi's instructions, verbatim, standing in the bright Texas light on a blacktop parking lot.

"Good," says Satoshi. "Tonight is an important night."

"Tomorrow is an important day," says Yoshi. "And let's not forget Tuesday."

"I fire you on Tuesday," says Satoshi.

"Then it can't come fast enough," says Yoshi.

"Have everything you need?"

"All that I need. More than I want. Everything's good here."

"Good."

"Ready to be president?"

"Ha!"

"Laughter."

"Yes."

Satoshi ends the call.

Yoshi hitches the messenger bag to a more comfortable angle and abandons the dumpster's shadow. Nobody is waiting for him. He's a husky man with a limp, wandering away from the back of a dumpster in Austin. Not much to interest the casual observer. Incognito.

Yoshi has calls to make. Starbucks is making his clothes smell like a French Roast tire fire anyways. He walks five blocks from the coffee shop into a residential neighborhood that reminds him of diagrams he recalls from his high school biology textbook, illustrations of kidney components. Street after street of blind nephrons, branching off of curving main channels. His ride today is an incongruously compact Honda Civic hatchback, parked in front of a house that has been for sale for nearly three years. He feels the automobile tilt towards him as he climbs into the driver's seat. Not cool, car. Not cool. He starts the ignition and tears out of the neighborhood with a tinge of anger evident in his driving.

The headset still on, Yoshi makes calls as he drives.

There are 20 cells in D.C. that need babysitting. Five in L.A. Five in New York. Five in Chicago. Solo cells all over the place. Ironic that the entity supposedly responsible for blockchain keeps his cells completely detached from each other. Their only connection is to Yoshi, the hub at the center of the wagon wheel. And that's it. That's the campaign staff. There aren't any public appearances to deal with. No baby kissing or hand shaking. There are speeches but they arrive as press releases or video ads or highly polished cinematic quality mini-features or underproduced low-fi cellphone veritas films delivered by real people on behalf of Satoshi Nakamoto. Who we promise: is a real and marvelous person.

There are also the usual volunteer centers across the country that want to hear the voice of someone named Nakamoto. If it can't be Satoshi, and it can't, then Yoshi will have to do.

Yoshi has the right voice for this work, and he knows it and Satoshi knows it. It's a pleasant deep voice, open and trustworthy. A radio voice with none of the corniness. Friendly but direct. Even when he tells you things you don't want to hear, you're willing to accept them coming from Yoshi's voice.

But money will only get you so far. People need sleep. They need rest. The handsomely paid cells have been working for days. Their condition has gone beyond strained. People are beginning to warp and crack. Some of the ideas coming out of cell 14 in Washington D.C. are just bizarre. Frightening, even.

Thus one of Nakomoto's directives, which Yoshi is now scattering across the country: Go to sleep. Immediately. They are working in hotels for a reason after all.

Nine hours from now, you will be expected to be awake again and rejoin your cell.

The directive is delivered to every cell except one. Cell 20 had a bright idea, and their reward is to make it happen.

Keep going.

Sunday, November 1
5:42 p.m. E.T.

Sunday sibling dinner had been their sister's idea, and the boys found themselves looking forward to it. It had been years since they'd done anything like it. Decades, actually. No spouses, no kids, no Mom. And especially no Dad. Just the three of them. Back in the city.

Since it was her idea she'd gone ahead and laid out a program and put a good bit of thought into arrangements. She didn't tell them what she'd planned. She just told them to dress as casually as they could and plan for a long evening.

These days, she could almost forget they were siblings. They were more like extras in each other's films. Adulthood had twisted them in different directions. They still saw each other, but it hadn't been just the three of them, brothers and sister, in so long that a part of their relationship had drifted away. And after stumbling across her childhood diary, she felt like she had unearthed a glimpse of some purer aspect of herself, something she'd lost along the way. When she was eight she'd had no pretensions. She was unadulterated. She hadn't thought about the implications of that word as much as she had over the last week.

And so her simple scheme was this: recreate the night of November 1, 1989. Not a date of note, not particularly. Which in some ways was of note. Their childhood had not been a normal place. A normal time. But she had kept a diary. Secret from everyone. And reading the entry from 31 years ago had flooded her with a nostalgia she could hardly believe possible. She doesn't think of herself as a sentimental woman. But it turns out, maybe she is. She just needed to find something worth being sentimental about. November 1, 1989 was it. The three of them together in the basement of her parents' old place. Sleeping bags. Movies. Sodas and snacks. "Best night ever," she'd written. They'd been nice to each other, she wrote. Did they only do that when left alone? Had they ever been left alone before that night?

The food was crucial, but it wasn't a question. Pizzas and garlic twists from their favorite childhood pizzeria, Marianaro's. Cans of New Coke in the fridge (she'd got lucky there, thanks to a recent promotion tied to Stranger Things). Plain Ruffles. E.L. Fudge cookies to follow. For entertainment, she'd found a VCR in a long-dormant closet and connected it to the projector in the living room. All on her own. Plus, bonus, she'd found a milk crate full of tapes. She couldn't believe what all was in there.

They'd start with "See No Evil, Hear No Evil" (Richard Pryor and Gene Wilder, oh yeah) and then into "Police Academy 6". If the boys fell asleep, they usually fell asleep in front of movies, she'd switch to "Dead Poet's Society" as she'd done so very long ago.

Back when she was eight years old. And Junejune was eleven. And Rico was five.

1989 had been a difficult year, the first of a few. But in the midst of it all, through all the fighting, the divorce, the moving, the parental timeshare, the embarrassment at school, the only constant had been each other. They didn't always get along, but just in the usual way that siblings don't always get along. Fights over the remote control. She'd borrowed their jackets or shirts or Oaklies without asking. Normal namecalling. They were the best part of her childhood.

Junejune arrives at her apartment first. He is wearing a red plaid flannel shirt tucked into white jeans and holding a large bottle of red wine in the crook of his arm.

"Hey Vonkers," he says. He looks down at her toes and then back up to her eyes. "The fuck?" he says.

"I'll explain," she says. "Come in. You can put that on the counter." He pauses, clearly reconsidering the decision to accept her invitation, which she'd done in crayon on a square piece of lined paper and folded into an origami fish. He should have seen that as a cry for help. Not an invitation.

She nearly has the door closed behind him when she hears Rico in the hallway.

"Hey," he says. She opens the door wide and waves to him.

"Hey," she says.

"The fuck?" he says, pointing his finger down to her toes and back up to her head.

"The fuck?" she replies, mimicking the gesture. He is wearing a tuxedo. She is wearing red adult-sized onesie pajamas. "I said casual as you can manage," she says.

"Tie's a clip-on," he says.

"Gross," she says.

"I just came straight from a thing. What do you want from me?"

"Forget it," she says. "Don't worry. I've got stuff you can change into."

"The fuck?" she hears Junejune say from behind her. He is holding up an extra large pair of adult green footed pajamas. His name is embroidered in white cursive letters over the left breast. An identical blue pair sits folded on the counter next to him with "Rico" stitched in the same tidy font.

"The fuck?" says Rico.

"So I was reading my diary..." she says.

Sunday, November 1
6:12 p.m. E.T.

The President is lying on a black kangaroo leather sofa with gold rivets in the Oval Office. His head is propped up on a throw pillow that the wife of a gasket plant's manager in Sandusky, Ohio had given the President last year at a rally. It features a somewhat cartoonish rendition of the presidential seal, and the text on the thin, ribbony banner clenched in the beak of the bald eagle that normally reads "E Pluribus Unum" reads "Make America Great Again." It is the most perfect size for a head prop against the sofa's beautiful arms.

He squints through his reading glasses as he scrolls through his Twitter feed at an impressive pace. He is the fastest reader in the world, perhaps. He has recently received some potentially bad news from one of the Stats Bros, he can't remember which. Stats Bro 1 or Stats Bro 2. He knows he fired one of them but he can't remember which. He'll have Jessica fire the other one tomorrow morning, just to be safe. Why did he even need stats guys in the first place? They were wrong more often than they were right. Statistically speaking. Or anecdotally.

He sighs. Nothing new in the feed to spark joy this evening. He retweets Hannity, as a courtesy. That's all he can muster. His heart just isn't in it. Maybe he's sick. Is he sick? He does a little inventory, clears his throat, experimentally. Sounds fine. He checks his pulse. Good. He considers his joints. His left knee's a little sore. What's new? Maybe he's just tired. The morning rally in Kentucky took a lot of juice. He holds the back of his hand against his forehead. It's a fine temperature. A great temperature. Is he hungry? Maybe his blood sugar's a little low is all.

He switches to his messaging app and types "KFC" into his ongoing text conversation with the kitchen steward. It's not a thread he cares to review. He'd only get more depressed.

Is that what he is? Is he depressed? Maybe he's just horny. Sometimes, when you think you want KFC, what you actually want is a blowjob. Sometimes when you think you might be sad, what you actually are in need of... is a blowjob. He hasn't had a blowjob in... he scrolls backwards through the years in his mind's phone... before the primaries, definitely... oh yeah. He remembers. Her. Bulgarian beer girl on that course in Tampa. That had definitely not been worth $15,000. That is what it had cost him, though. That, and some citizenship papers for her and her baba. Which had done the trick. She gets baba to a dialysis center in Loxahatchee Groves, he gets leverage. Everybody wins. The American way.

It really isn't fair. Things used to be so dignified. Classy. Presidents used to have a free pass to fool around a little bit. Everyone was on the same page. A gentleman's agreement. The presidency was too important for reporters to get hung up on a little sex, back then. If a reporter even wanted to write that story, there wasn't a publisher in America that would touch it. Now, if there's a typo in his tweet, there's an op-ed on the front page of the Times questioning his fitness for office.

He sighs and shifts his head on the pillow. Turns towards the Resolute desk. Jack Kennedy gave it to thirteen different broads on that desk. True story. Not a rumor, and not a myth. He read it in the man's own handwriting. There's a presidential journal locked in the lower cabinet of the desk. Obama handed him the key at the swearing in ceremony, passed it in a handshake. A significant nod. Said, "No one else." That's how it's done. No middleman.

First time he was alone in the office, he pulled the key from his jacket pocket and opened the cabinet. Big stack of notebooks. Big whoop. Each one has handwriting in the corner: "Presidential Eyes Only." Sure, sure. He's already been walked through the machinations of the Football. The Roswell Report.

Then he reads them. Holy shit.

Hot stuff.

Kennedy's entries are the first. So maybe Johnson started the passing of the key, thing. Probably got into the office, found this little locked cabinet door. Asks the steward. Steward tells him Kennedy had the only key. Had to call down to Dallas for someone to find that fucking suit and check the suit pockets for a key. Which they found, eventually, little secret pocket where pockets normally aren't. A courier brings it up directly. Johnson unlocks the cabinet, doesn't know what the hell he'll find. Just a notebook. Opens it up. Holy Moley.

Hot stuff.

Stuff so hot, you want to tell a buddy, but you can't tell a buddy about this particular stuff. But you have to tell someone. So then Johnson realizes, here's the torch you pass, right here. Add your own chapters. Get it out. Safe space. Lock it away. Hand the key to the next guy.

And maybe a year into your term, you meet up with the former presidents at such-and-such a thing, a funeral usually, and you get corralled together for a photo, and you're the president, so you can say things like: "We need the room." And everyone else clears out, and you can turn to the other guys and say things like, "The Dock at Hyannis?" and the whole room just about dies laughing.

Kennedy wrote these stories, unbelievable. Nearly made the President lubricate his pants, just reading them. The guy was a grade-A cocksman. And he could write. Boy. Oh boy. He had an ear for smut.

Staring at the Resolute he can hear Kennedy's words in his mind's ear.

"She was the daughter of a family friend from up North. French Canadian but red hair, so she had to have some Irish in her. She just had to.

Her family was in the lumber business. But I was the one in the room with all the wood.

"I want to talk to you about my family's mining interests on the border near Caribou," she said.

"That's funny," I replied. "I want to mine your interesting border."

"Oh Mister President," she smiled. "You're not a bad man. Are you?"

"You see this Bill?" I said. I walked her to the desk. "Put your hands on it."

"Is this real legislation?" she said, caressing the folder.

"It doesn't get realer than that, baby," I said.

"What's it do?"

"You wanna know?"

"I really do," she cooed.

"It appropriates $1.7 billion dollars for the National Aeronautical and Space Administration," I told her. My hands clutched her waist. A bead of her sweat dripped down the back of her neck, and I licked it thirstily.

"What's that?" she said.

"We're gonna shoot rockets into heaven, baby."

"Oh Mr. President," she said. She ground her hips into the edge of Resolute, my trusty desk. Its brown walnut accepted her gyrations with the stoicism of a cowboy's horse getting brushed down by strange hands in the stable after a long day on the dusty trail.

"We're gonna put a man on the moon, darling. That piece of paper under your hands? That's rocket fuel."

"Oh Mister President," she squeaked.

"You ever made love on the law?" I asked her. Her hair was pulled back into a flawless, tight bun. I placed my mouth over it, took the whole thing in my chops, stuffed the whole of its soft, beautiful ginger between my teeth and burrowed my tongue into her follicles like a snake lost in a haystack. My breath shot in hot plumes out my nose and ruffled her bangs.

"Oh Mister President," she whispered breathlessly.

I had her ears in my hands as I suckled on her hair a while longer. She was nearing climax. I could tell. I can always tell.

I opened wide, reared my head back, and released her hair from my trembling maw. The bun sagged, heavy with my glistening saliva.

"Are you ready?" I asked her.

"Ready?" she gasped. "I'm nearly done."

"Oh sweetheart," I said, sliding the rubber bands over my wrists. I took off my left shoe. "We're just getting started."

A knock sounds at the door. Shave and a haircut, the President's signature. He tucks his erection into the waistband of his gold, silk boxer shorts. "Come in," he shouts.

The steward appears with a broad, gold tray, bearing a red-and-white striped bucket of chicken, a golden plate, a gold trimmed silk napkin, solid gold fork and knife, and two gold finger bowls, an empty one for bones and one in which a single seedless lemon slice floats in a pool of Evian. Next to that lies a pair of white linen gloves.

The steward lays the tray silently on the coffee table level with the President's face.

"Original Recipe?" says the President.

The steward nods. "Of course, Mister President."

"Leave," says the President.

The steward bows his head and departs in the manner customary to every presidential steward of the last 240 years. Without lifting his head from the hand-stitched pillow, the President extends his arm and grabs the gloves. He pulls them on. First the left. Then the right. He reaches over and fumbles in the wax-lined paper bucket before wrapping his fingers around a breast. He snatches it out and brings it to his face, smells it, cautious yet eager. He buries his teeth in it and tears a swathe of meat out. Chicken juices cascade into his mouth, dribbling around the edges, and mingling with the salty tears streaming down his cheeks.

Sunday, November 1
6:34 p.m. E.T.

The fundraisers are over. There's nothing left to do but spend that cash.

Crystal May, the President's director of Swag Ops has already purchased everything they need (and more) for the congratulatory acceptance speech rally (or concession speech mourning, if you want to take a negative-nelly approach to the situation, and she doesn't). The fact is, all involved understand that even a loss will be painted as a win or a challenge. There's no such thing as a loss in her world. There are just wins waiting for the right Supreme Court to recognize them.

If anyone thinks this will all be over in two days, they are sadly mistaken. Unless the President wins. Then they are happily correct.

She has purchased more balloons for election night than the nation of Paraguay consumes in a decade. Public performances for the event are set. She's expecting a bouncy crowd for Jars of Clay, Scott Bayo's Bayou Band, the Posey O'Donnell's, the Real Spruce Bringsteen (better than the original, if you ask her, and considerably more on-message with the banter), Ted Nugent, Kid Rock, and if the stars align, fingers crossed, Kanye himself has offered to perform a preview of his forthcoming interpretation of Walt Whitman's "Song of Myself." She wasn't familiar with the poetry, but Crystal knows West is a White House mainstay and a Kardashi-man. Big deal all around.

Her budget for sparkling grape juice would make New Hampshire wealthy for two years. She is creating jobs with her peel and eat shrimp order, single handedly responsible for the building of new boats in gulf coast Mississippi. Between catering, design, venue, pyrotechnics, security, entertainment, and event logistics, Crystal is spending upward of $43 million. Hopefully, the president will be re-elected in a timely fashion. But if not, the money is spent either way and will be enjoyed.

Not just spent, but truly, in escrow, ready to be spent-spent. Vendors have grown a mite wary of the President's payment strategies over the years and they are demanding money be a tad more upfront, a little more concrete than in years past. Slightly less theoretical.

Her phone buzzes against her left breast in her jacket pocket.

Him again.

"Hi," she says.

"Crystal? J-Kiddy here. Just triple-checking. Will the microphone on the dais be wireless? You know dad likes to walk around?"

"Absolutely," she says.

"Is the water Evian? He's got this thing?"

"All Evian. Nothing but."

"You got my email with the guest list for security?" he says.

"I did. I wrote you back with a few questions," she replies.

"Oh right?" he says. "And then I wrote you back with answers?"

"Yes, and then I wrote you about whether it was okay that the smoked salmon was farmed and not wild-caught, and you wrote me back and said that would be fine as long as it was American-farmed. And I wrote you back and said that yes it was. And you wrote me back and said, that's good, because the last thing we need is for the media to find out that we were serving Chinese farmed sockeye salmon, and I wrote you back and assured you that this was a guaranteed 100% American-made and planned event and you need not worry. And you wrote back and said 'Good.' I think that's about where we left it."

"So the salmon is American-farmed?"

"That's correct."

"That's a relief? The last thing we need is for the media to discover we were serving Russian-farmed Chinook?"

She waits to see if she ought to laugh. She decides she ought not. "Absolutely not, sir," she says. "This event will be as All-American as the President himself."

"Hm?" says the man, as if to imply that might not be good enough. She knows most of the President's wives had been foreign-nationals and reconsiders her choice of words silently. "Sounds good, Crystal? We're looking forward to it?"

"Best of luck," she says.

"Why would we need luck?" asks the President's son-in-law.

"I just mean, generally."

"The general election?"

"No. No no no! I know that's in the bag."

"What are you suggesting, in the bag?"

"I just mean, broadly speaking, best of luck, in that sort of mindless way, that people... you know. Like, don't fall and break your arm, or anything?"

"Oh? Okay? Yeah? You don't break your arm either?" He hangs up. She shakes her head and replaces the phone back to her pocket. God knows what's wrong with that man. He's about as secure as an octopus at a Yakitori bar ever since they took him off the Middle East and immigration and left him with event planning. She couldn't wait to be done with these people. And with the percentage she is skimming, she won't have to wait long. Win or lose, she'll be retiring in three days.

This might as well be the best party she's ever thrown.

Sunday, November 1
6:41 p.m. E.T.

Moshi Nakamoto adjusts the five-foot ladder hooked over her right shoulder and walks past the security guard without a glance towards nor from the uniformed man at the front desk. The guard is otherwise focused on a tablet tucked beside the surveillance monitors beneath the black marble counter. Moshi knows the job, knows the man. His only real responsibility is to sit behind that desk for eight hours shifts, signing for packages and groceries and upscale cuisine. He is as much a luxury as the white marble countertop he sits behind, but he serves little necessary function. Moshi hears a nasal, tinny woman's voice from beneath the countertop say something about open floor plans. Moshi strides past and heads for the stairwell beyond the reflective golden doors of the elevators.

The stairwell, like all those in upscale apartment buildings, is pure utility in stark comparison to the subdued lighting and luxury of the brass and dark wood lobby. Moshi adjusts her grip on the ladder so it rests vertically on her left palm and climbs the steps two at a time at a steady jog. Her legs chop up and down as she ascends the flights, ten steps, turn left, ten steps, turn left. Her small backpack is cinched tight and the waist strap, with its useful utility pocket, keeps the bag from bouncing as she goes. The gray cinderblock walls are a blur in her periphery as she climbs and climbs, scanning for the odd surveillance camera or crossfit weekend warrior heading the opposite direction, neither of which appear. The building has an old style fussiness that invites an older tenant. The stairs are seldom used for anything, least of all exercise, and this evening is no different.

After ten flights of stairs she can hear her breathing. After twenty, her back begins to sweat beneath her backpack. Her pace never slows, but after thirty flights her thighs have reminded her of their presence. After forty, the sweat on her forehead loses surface tension and releases a trickle down the left side of her nose. At the 42nd floor she stops and rests the ladder beside the entrance to the hallway. Moshi pulls a small hand towel from the front of the pack and wipes down her face. Her greige coveralls have thick cotton patches sewn into the places she sweats most heavily: armpits, belly, between the breasts, back. People notice sweat. Something animal about it. People notice. She waits for her body temperature to cool and reins in her breathing. Five minutes, accounted for in the planning.

It is essential to appear unremarkable in Moshi's diverse line of work. Difficult when you're a tall woman, six-foot-three, so she has to make everything else nondescript. If she's done it right, the best anyone will be able to say tomorrow, should anyone come asking, is: tall person with a ladder.

Hair color? Hat? Clothes? Distinguishing marks?

They won't remember. They'll have nothing. If she's done it right.

Five minutes. She doesn't wear a watch. Carries no cell phone, for obvious reasons. She just knows: five minutes. Hooks the ladder over her arm, empties her eyes of any residual spark. She flips out her pin-kit, and leans over the lock on the door handle. Seven seconds of subtle manipulation, a satisfying click, and she opens the door, slides the pin-kit into her pocket as she walks through the doorframe.

Again, the contrast. Like stepping into Oz from the gray

fluorescent-lit stairwell. Golden light seeps from antique sconces along a dark-wood hallway. Original oil paintings on the hallway walls that Moshi halfway studies in her peripheral vision as she walks down the singular hallway of the 42nd floor. Tasteless works, she notes, though expensive. Women in unfastened robes sprawl across settees and bathtubs and grand staircases, women who died over 150 years ago, immortalized in thick, smeary daubs of oil paint to be hung in an empty hallway. Mortal women undressed playing the role of this or that goddess in the midst of vaguely recognizable myths. Persephone closing the lid on Hope (while her robe swings open). Diana, her bow strung, sighting a hind through one squinting eye (as her hunting gown slips open). Ariadne extending a length of thread from a red ball of silk (as her robe quivers with the movement required to pull a bit of thread from a ball of the same).

Moshi shakes her head but steps silently past them to the final door, the only door on the left side of the hallway. She knows the names and faces of every tenant in the building, prepared for unexpected encounters, but has yet to encounter a single resident of the Park Avenue structure. She is almost disappointed. Almost. As she pulls her pin-set from her pocket, she prepares for the possibility she might finally encounter one inside the enormous apartment, the only half-hall (as the residents term it) in the building. The click, a sharp turn of the handle, and she leans the ladder into the apartment first, followed by her head and shoulder.

She is alone.

Moshi pushes the door closed and locks it.

"Building maintenance!" she calls. Nothing. Scanning the room, as she expected, no cameras. No alarms. Cameras create evidence as much as they create security, and people such as these do not want their activities captured on hard drives. Nor do such people want the police summoned to their homes by an alarm under any circumstances. The occupants of Apartment 4242 are careful people.

The apartment is sleek and modern. The walls, the furniture, the marble floor are white, and everything else is seamless and gleaming metal (the lamps, the enormous window frames, the contents of the kitchen). It does not exude the feeling that people live here. It is an idea of an apartment. Moshi props the ladder against the closed front door so it straddles the hinges, a crude alarm set to clatter to the ground should someone enter the apartment before she's finished.

Moshi isn't expecting anyone to interrupt. Her surveillance says she'll be fine, but the world is a garden of chaos. If you have a ladder, prop a ladder.

Moshi isn't looking for anything clever. She expects to find a wall safe in either the office or a bedroom closet. Usually, an office if the subject is married, the bedroom closet if they aren't. Following this logic, Moshi checks the bedroom first. She circles it once and opens the two enormous windows parallel to the king sized bed, allowing a freezing whorl of air to chill the room. The streetlit view is extraordinary below. Central Park's pastoral landscape fenced in by pickets composed of brick, steel, and stone structures, speckled with light. Turning her back on the city, Moshi closes the bedroom door, pulls a wooden doorstop from her backpack, slides it under the edge of the closed door beneath the doorknob, and gives it a kick to lodge the wedge in place. She opens the bedroom closet's sliding, mirrored doors and shifts a row of tailored white shirts to one side of the closet, taps the back wall until she hears a change in pitch and feels wood shiver beneath her fist. She runs a finger along the edge of one wood panel and finds a small metal catch in the lower-left corner that she flicks with her index finger. The wooden panel pops forward to reveal the safe. It has both a fingerprint panel and a combination lock; either mechanism will open the door. Moshi has brought no fingerprints other than her own for this particular task.

It will have to be the combination.

Every safe cracker has their own means of registering the dropping of a pin on a correct digit. Some still arrive on the scene toting the stethoscope, some rely on the naked ear, and others boast of superior fingertips that sense the quivering resistance in the combination wheel itself. Moshi is a tongue cracker.

After giving the combination wheel its initial spin, she rests her left cheek against the safe's door so she can watch as the wheel turns beneath her fingers. She stretches her tongue as far out of her mouth as she can and curls it to the left, where its moistened pink tip rests against cold steel. As the numbers click by, Moshi relaxes her jaw and feels the metal strum beneath her preternaturally sensitive taste buds, attuned to the most minute vibration as the clicking combinations pass. Her fingers stop, and she allows her eyes to blink for a moment. "23," she thinks. She focuses her faculties and continues again, picking off the last two numbers in less than three minutes. Knowing the numbers but not their order means there are only six possible combinations, but Moshi gets lucky and the safe snaps open on the second attempt.

Inside she discovers more than she had hoped for. Three rugged-case hard drives. A manila envelope stuffed with glossy photos. A pile of passports. 15 bricks of rubber-banded $100 bills, probably $150,000 just sitting there. A snub-nosed handgun and a smooth, ebony box filled with bullets. A wooden case containing a bottle of Van Winkle that has just turned 30 years old. Moshi stuffs her backpack with the hard drives and manila folder, the passports, and leaves the rest behind. Limit the possibility of a police report. How would they describe the stolen items? "They stole my false passports and my blackmail materials!" Seems unlikely.

Moshi swings the safe's door shut and just finishes wiping it down when a metallic crash sounds from the living room.

"What the hell?" a man's voice shouts.

The ladder.

Moshi slides the closet door closed, pulls on thick gloves and pulls a device that looks like a thin, black metal flashlight from her backpack and hurries to the open windows. She depresses a switch on the side of the flashlight and two gleaming metal claws spring from the top of the device. Moshi swings onto the windowsill, crouches, and hooks the claws around the lip of the window sill. The sill's thick stone, embedded in the wall, is up to the task. Moshi twists the black rod once, and it separates into two half-units, connected by a thin black thread. Moshi clips the base to the waist strap of the backpack and gives the thread a sharp tug with her leather work gloves to pull it taut. The bedroom door shudders with a thump as someone throws a shoulder against it. Moshi hops backwards off the ledge of the building into the chilled November air.

The mechanism in the clever device feeds the thread out at a rate of 10 feet per second. Fast, but not so fast that her ankles will break at the landing. The thread is remarkable stuff, Kevlar carbon-fiber hybrid, and Moshi is able to hold herself vertical, parallel to the building, by keeping one gloved hand loosely wrapped around the thread as she descends the 42 flights. In the dusky darkness, no one sees her sliding down, a shadow among shadows.

Moshi lands on the sidewalk in front of the building and startles an elderly woman stooping forward with a plastic bag over her hand clutching a warm curl of shit from her King Charles Spaniel. Moshi ignores the woman's noises, unclips the black rappelling tool from her backpack. She peels a small rubber cover from one edge of the tool, revealing a red plastic button. Moshi presses the button, and an electrical charge shoots through 42 stories of thread, leaving behind only a thin wisp of black smoke. Back in the apartment, she knows, the charge is igniting a coil that will melt the anchor and leave two metal hooks in a black puddle beneath the windowsill.

Shame to leave a perfectly good ladder, Moshi thinks, as she crosses the street and passes through a gap in the black iron fence. She fishes a pair of black roller blades from the hedge where she'd stowed them two hours ago, swaps them with her shoes, pulls on a neon orange windbreaker and chucks her shoes in the backpack.

Witnesses to her transformed self would have little to say. A leggy woman rollerbladed past them on the path with speed and grace made all the more remarkable by her enormous frame. But they wouldn't recall her. Moshi remains invisible to the too-cool eyes of the city's denizens who will see fifty things stranger than she before the sun rises on Monday.

Sunday, November 1
6:00 p.m. C.T. / 7:00 p.m. E.T.

Peoria's evening rush hour has passed, and Gary begins packing up his patriot rig. The large flag comes down from the back of his chair first. He knows he ought to fold it every day in the correct manner he was taught by Scoutmaster Harry so long ago. However, there's no acceptable surface on which to do the folding out here. It can't touch the ground. So he twists the flagpole until the flag is wrapped around the pole. He puts the small flags in a black pouch, stuffs them in his backpack, closes his chair, and bungees it to the backpack, along with the flagpole. He wishes he could stash all of his supplies at one of the businesses on this corner, but he'd asked, and they'd all said no. Classic lib-cuck fear of the patriot, trying to act like you can separate your business from your politics. Everything is political now, everything, and they ought to take a stance and not hide away as if they're impartial. Gary throws the strap over his shoulder and makes for his Ford pickup.

He's back home by 6:30 p.m. and his wife, Jean, must be getting peckish, so he drops the bag in his office and heads to the kitchen to get supper underway. There's leftover beans and rice and half a smoked venison sausage in the fridge that should do good. He tosses the sausage in the casserole with the beans and rice and microwaves the whole pile for five minutes. He's never been much of a cook, but with Jean otherwise occupied for the last two weeks, he's getting to know his way around the kitchen a little.

He sticks a plastic fork in the steaming casserole and pours some milk in a plastic Peoria Chiefs souvenir cup. He's got a pot holder in the crook of his arm, under the casserole, because the casserole's borderline thermonuclear, and he struggles to open the doorknob while holding the milk, but eventually twists it open and heads down the wooden stairs.

Jean's waiting for him on her couch, looks up from the cable news. "Hey there," he says. It's a pretty good little set-up they've got down here since they finished half the basement into a sort of second family room slash guest bedroom. Got a little half-bath. Got the nice 50-inch TV. Little mini-fridge. He sets the food and the milk down on the coffee table in front of her. "How's today? How you feeling?"

Jean looks up at him and annoyed doesn't do it justice. She shakes the chains on her wrist in his face and shouts, "Change the fucking channel, Gary! I'm losing my mind!"

Monday, November 2 / Sunday, November 1
12:12 a.m. Moscow Standard Time / 7:12 p.m. E.T.

[In Russian]

Paralinka stands as tall as he can before the Russian president's desk, his hands at his side and his head held level. He understands that to survive the current dilemma, he has to proffer the appearance of a man who can fix this problem. Even though he isn't yet sure how to do so, precisely, he'll need to offer the beginnings of the solution. Or appear to for a few hours.

"I was watching Netflix," says the President. He is speaking softly. "Ozark. I am in the second season. It is an important moment. This man has a gun, he is heading towards the family's house, and then, the little blond girl, you know the one?"

"No sir," says Paralinka.

"She is so cunning! You don't watch this program? Ozark?"

"Not yet, sir. It is in my watchlist."

"It is very good. You should watch it. Jason Bateman is very good."

"He is Teen Wolf."

"Yes. He is the second Teen Wolf."

"Oh yes. After Michael J. Fox."

"Yes, so. I am watching this man approach... what is her name? The little blond one? I never remember her name. Anyways, I am watching, and then..." Putin holds up his palms and flicks his fingers backwards like a magician showing an audience that something has unexpectedly disappeared. "Gone."

"The entire nation is experiencing an outage, sir," says Paralinka. "To external connections."

"I am aware," says the President. "How long will it last?"

"We do not yet know."

"What has caused it?"

"We are yet unsure."

"The timing on this?" He raises an eyebrow.

"It cannot be a coincidence," says Paralinka.

The President nods. "What does it mean for Operation Double Eagle?"

Paralinka shakes his head. "Nothing. It will proceed as planned."

"How, if there is no connection?"

"If we cannot get a connection restored, I will take our men to a place where they can gain access."

"You will?"

"If you see fit to permit it, Brother President."

"Are you still necessary to this operation?"

"I will be useful."

"Where do you propose?"

"We need to find out more about the outage. If it's happening here, it may be the same for China. And Kazakhstan. And North Korea. But cut-off as we are, we can't yet determine."

"So if it is, where?"

"Finland, sir."

"You think they wouldn't turn the lights off in the EU?"

"That's right."

"Where in Finland?"

"Well," he considers his old off-books internet safehouse. He won't suggest it. But he also knows better than to deny its existence to Putin. "I have a place in a small town called Potoskavaara. I believe it would be unwise to use it."

Putin nods. "I may know a place," he says. "Send me updates as you learn more. If we need to export the manpower, I'll have Stormont assist you in the logistics." Stormont is Putin's head of security, a towering mass of muscle and lethal cunning. He is everything Putin believes himself to be, physically and mentally, which is quite a thing to be, even in one's own mind. Paralinka is also well aware that Stormont is one of the most lethal bipedal forces on the planet. Sending Stormont along means there will be assistance if heavy lifting or heavy dropping is required. But it might also mean that Paralinka might find this a one-way trip.

Hopefully they will just get the network running again from here and not have to interrupt Stormont's hectic schedule. Because if Stormont gets involved, there will be nowhere for Paralinka to hide.

"What does the American Embassy say?" asks Paralinka.

"Nothing. They say we are doing something to them. They can't communicate with their Department of State. They can't get to their satellites. Which figures, as their satellites are our satellites, so to speak. They have attempted contact via shortwave radio transmission without success."

"No?" says Paralinka.

"No. Our offices have also had difficulties with transmissions."

"Have we...?" Paralinka starts to puzzle out the problem, and realizes that he has not been summoned to speak.

Putin stares at him for a while, then continues: "We've been monitoring their internal communications, of course, and if the Embassy's confusion is a charade, it is convincing.

They are considering evacuations, but the ambassador has exhibited the decisiveness of a child in a sweet shop told he may have only one thing. My little Katerina was the same way when she five. It is cute in a child. But not for a man."

"No," says Paralinka.

"Fix this."

"I will."

[/In Russian]

Sunday, November 1
7:30 p.m. E.T.

Yoshi had called back five minutes after hanging up on Atticus, who had stayed in the Hyatt suite's bathroom to smoke a joint, to say that MIC-20 had the go-ahead.

"Wait. What? Which part?" Atticus said.

"What do you mean?" said Yoshi.

"Which part of the plan."

"Whole thing."

Atticus nearly swallowed his phone. He gathered himself sufficiently to sputter the age-old question: "What's our budget?"

"$100 million. I've transferred it to your cell's operating account for immediate access."

"I don't understand. The whole thing?" Atticus had felt the anxiety creep beneath his sternum, his breathing was becoming labored.

"Yes. Exactly as you described it to me. Yes. It's a good idea. Your cell was hired and handsomely remunerated for this exact moment, Atticus. Do it and be legends. Million dollar bonus for each of you if you do."

"Right," Atticus had said. Yoshi had hung up before the "-t" was enunciated.

Atticus took two minutes to gather himself in the bathroom. In the adjoining room, his group could hear him slamming his fist against the wall. Not usually a good sign.

When he emerged, his face had lost what little color it had ever possessed, but he wore a startling smile. "They said do it. Do it all. Just like we said." The other five members of the cell were numb with surprise. They hadn't had an idea greenlit. Ever. Atticus had continued, "And there's a million dollar bonus if we pull it off."

The surprise morphed into delirium in a moment.

"Wait, an extra $160,000 each, or?" said Limey.

"No, no, no," said Atticus. "A million dollars each."

Limey shrieked like she was being murdered. The man with white-blond hair had pounded the table and kept shouting, "Fucking yeah! Fucking yeah!" Michelle had grabbed the giggling former marine life lobbyist by the head and planted a loud squeaking kiss on the entirety of her ear.

But the tall kid from White Plains had started tapping away at his laptop immediately. Gradually, the rest of the room turned their attentions from celebrating to the gangly kid working away. He lifted his eyes to them but continued typing. "I have student loans," he'd said. "Let's go."

And go they had.

That was five hours ago. Their exuberance has transformed into focused labor. Truth is, they're relieved to finally be doing things, not just thinking about what things to do. Now they have a plan. A goal. The means to reach it. And an extra dash of incentive to say the least. These are driven, brilliant young people and a task in hand is meat in their mouths. Plus Atticus keeps handing out something he keeps calling "Mother Trucker Pills" and the little beauties do the trick.

Work is divided, assigned, and the documents are piling up in various shared folders. Organizing the tasks is perhaps as large a job as any of the tasks themselves, and Atticus was born for this moment. Even as he hammers away at the meta-problem, the micro-tasks he's assigned are underway. Project management is his genius. Not many bother to envy him.

But while some people can compose symphonies for twenty instruments in their head, Atticus can take a job, break it into 1,000 component jobs and arrange them into logical and chronological perfection. He can identify and align the skillset of a staff far larger than the six currently in the room, and assign tasks large and small to meet their abilities, tendencies and personality.

The whiteboard is his canvas and the one word invocation to "Think, Goddammit!" is erased and replaced with an ever-burgeoning web of connected rectangles containing words and phrases.

Limey and Michelle are researching and calling real estate brokers and landscape artists across the country. In an era where email has become the main means of business, the phone is still king when it comes to doing something now, and Limey and Michelle are both bouncing from phone to phone tracking down the only people who can do what needs doing. To get there, they are dropping sums of money on people from the clear blue sky on a Sunday afternoon, sums that pull people yelping from their recliners and away from the afternoon NFL game. Sums that will change the years to come for men, women, children, and limited liability corporations alike. Sums that cause hair to rise on arms. Sums of cash that make "No" impossible. Enough money to change the face of the earth overnight.

Or small chunks of that face, in any event.

As the money flies all over the place, Tuna is laying out messaging and designs that will match what she anticipates she'll need for each ground location, each design and message customized to match the region, the city, the landscape on which it will appear. Typing so hard she's sweating, White

Plains has meanwhile constructed a fifty-two tab spreadsheet, the sight of which would strike the majority of CPAs blind for three weeks, minimum, just to stand in its presence. He has moved on to programming a data visualization presentation to track the sum total of their work in one comprehensible interactive graphic, for themselves, initially, but ultimately for Nakamoto. If he welches on the million, it won't be because he can't see what they've done.

White-Blonde's attention is two-fold. In less than five hours, he has already completed the formidable task of booking drone photographers and aerial photographers for tomorrow morning. Specific locations pending. Yes, a considerable quantity of the power in this campaign will be organic, viral reach, as Americans flying around the country post their photos and video reactions. But to do this right, White-Blond will need high quality imagery of every site to slip Buzzfeed, video for the news networks, his Reddit Army, his Twitter Navy, his Facebook Grandmas, and his Snapchat Taki Brigade. He wants as much sunrise imagery as he can muster. Hope. Rebirth. A New Day. Nakamoto. Meanwhile, he's reaching out to every wonk, every reporter, every intern, every content monkey in his network and telling them to stand by for an exclusive. He's burning a few bridges with that fib, but a million bucks can buy a lot of drinks, and in DC, whiskey and weed can patch a whole lot of bridge. Plus, he'd owe them. People in his circles love being owed.

The work is going fast. Unbelievably fast. Can six people in a room spend $100 million in 18 hours. The answer appears to be yes. The world seems ever happy to accommodate money.

Sunday, November 1
7:59 p.m. E.T.

Are these Rold Gold?" the President mutters to the White House steward. "They don't taste as buttery as they should."

The steward inclines his head, "I will fetch some melted butter, Mister President."

"No, that's okay, I just–" The Presidential Tongue pauses to rescue a wayward crumb from the Presidential Upper Lip. "Well actually, that's interesting. Yes. Do that."

It is Primetime in the White House and the President is in the room they call The Mediary, seated in a gold, crushed-velvet upholstered throne he commissioned three years ago from Scotland's finest Chairbler to the Crown, a seventh generation shop that he often turns to when he requires not just quality but discretion in his furniture's construction. His family's crest has been etched by hand into an ornamental disc at the top of the chair's back. Soft, gold fabric lines the seat, back and arms of the monumental chair. It has a red velvet-lined seat cushion crafted to match the contours of the presidential posterior perfectly. Contrary to its appearance of unyielding, straight lines, it is the most comfortable chair in the White House. It may be the most comfortable chair in America.

The President is feeling bloated from his chicken binge of 90 minutes prior, and occasionally a secret-herbs-and-spices belch ripples up his esophagus, across his tonsils, and warbles into his vast dominion. He doesn't notice, though, as he is deeply engrossed in his element. His throne faces a royal-purple wall, across which are arrayed nine televisions in a Brady Bunch grid, each television a 75" monster. In the center square (informally "the Alice") is his favorite News Network. It always starts in that central position and earns the privilege of loudest volume, but he can shuffle the order of the networks across the grid through a system of pointing and screaming he has fine-tuned with Nelson, a White House telecom aide, once-fragile, now battle hardened, who sits in the back of the room before a switchboard of his own customization.

Apart from Nelson, no one can keep up with the President during Primetime. In his early days in office he made a regular habit of inviting one aide or another to join him for the 8 p.m. shows. None of them accepted the invitation twice.

For one thing, the President insists on hearing the audio for all nine screens simultaneously, if at varying volume levels. That cacophony is punctuated by his bellowed instructions to Nelson to adjust this or that volume, shuffle one program to this screen, that program to that screen. The sheer clamor of it is enough to drive nearly any person out of the room, out of the building, out of their own minds, but something about the President's unique visual cortex allows him to absorb nine separate programs simultaneously.

The initial array of Prime Time networks starting from the top corner, left-to-right, is as follows:

News, News, Business News

News, News, Another Business News

Nick at Nite, Business News, Russian News

Tonight, the President's focus begins on his favorite network, but knitting his eyebrows, he keeps flicking his eyes to the left, repeatedly, to his least-favorite network.

"Nakamoto in the A Block?" he mutters. "Nelson!" he shouts the name of his least favorite network and jerks his left thumb up in the air three times, and Nelson pots the audio up for the progressive network's voice to climb above the others.

Normally, it's that Weenie's Hour but it's election week and the network's pulling a stunt where they have their Prime Time host up and live around the clock for three straight days. Periodically, when they gloat about the stunt, the camera will cut to a physician in a white lab coat who waves and chuckles, gives the thumbs up. He's there in his thick-framed glasses and his tightly trimmed white beard, live on set, alternating shifts with a foxy little family practitioner from Foxborough in a similar white lab coat but dissimilar pink stilettos, to monitor the Prime Time host's vitals and reassure folks at home that their pundit is not taking any undue risks with her health.

"You're a national fucking treasure!" shouts the President. Some show. Why the hell is she starting with Nakamoto when the election is two days away? Hillary Jr. must be pulling her hair out. The home crowd is ignoring their own candidate. Who the hell's going to vote for a guy they've never even seen before? Not to mention, you know, the whole Japanese thing? Are we even really sure this fella was born here? His guys have been chasing that down hard and found bupkis, so far. But that's never really mattered before.

An animated bar chart fills the screen, and he can hear the left-leaning host introducing poll results just released that morning by a private firm contracted by PBS, NBC News and Jezebel. The scroll reads: Breaking News: Three-Way Dead Heat shows new polling.

Nakamoto hadn't blipped the radar a month ago, and sure his story has some legs, but these numbers don't resemble anything the President has seen before. Yeah, one of his stat guys tried to show him some bullshit this afternoon, but it was so weird that he dismissed it as the usual bullshit.

The President squints at the numbers. How many people did they even poll?

The host tells him: an unprecedented new automated polling system commissioned by the pollsters pushed a one-time text to a million cell phones at once with a single question: "America wants to know: Reply 1 for the President, 2 for the Democratic ticket, and 3 for Nakamoto." They didn't give Bernie as an option.

A million were asked. 200,000 responded. An unusually high response for a spammy text appeal.

The poll shows 35% for Hillary II, 33% for Nakamoto, 32% for the President.

The President bellows and jerks his thumb down five times, and Nelson slides down the progressive audio as the Host is saying, "To help us make sense of these numbers, I'm joined by..."

"Sean!" screams the President. "Sean! And crank it!" Nelson obliges him.

The President settles down a bit when he sees himself on the center screen. Gray jacket. Red tie. Good hand movements. He relaxes in his throne a bit and evaluates his performance. He looks good. Looks tall. Tan. That new spray's got less red in it than the old stuff. Looks pretty good. He wishes Melly had joined him. She'd have looked good up there, on the edge of the stage there, instead of that woman in the Army fatigues. Nice girl, but not so pretty. The Army could have done better for him today. Someone's going to have to look into that. Maybe if she tried a little bit. But that uniform. Hard to look good in the uniform. Shapeless. Maybe he should have some of his people look into that. Women like to look good, and our troops deserve the best we can give them. Why should they have to dress like men? It's the 21st century for god's sake. Let the woman soldier be a woman, soldier. He pulls a small gold case from his inside pocket to reveal a small notepad and writes: woman soldier uniforms? 21st century?! Cleavage? He tucks it back in his pocket.

He's got Paducah in the palm of his hand. Look at that crowd. That's more people than even live in Paducah. No way. He feels good, seeing himself up there again. It had gone well, been a good morning. Here it comes:

"On Tuesday," he says on-screen, he mouths the words as he watches himself. "I want you. To drop a house. A big old house, folks! One of mine, not some rinky dinky, you know, not some hippy's, you know, tiny house. Drop a house. Drop a big old house! On that. Wicked. Witch!"

The crowd loses their mind. There's a cut forward a few seconds. They should have kept the crowd response in. Why did they cut the crowd response? The crowd response was crucial. They went wild for like twenty minutes! He was going to talk to Rupes about that. Gotta show the feeling that crowd gave. They were going crazy. See here, this is where they start chanting.

"Drop that House! Drop that House! Drop that House!"

The President makes a half-hearted attempt to calm the crowd, waving his hands down, as in, let's settle down people. Then someone shouts, "Kill the bitch!"

"Okay," says the President to the crowd. He laughs lightly. "Now that's... we don't want to kill anyone. Settle down. I mean, a bucket of water, maybe right?" He laughs again.

The crowd starts chanting, "Kill the bitch! Kill the bitch! Kill the bitch!"

President, still laughing on the screen. "Now let's. Okay.

No killing. Let's... ha, ha. Well, maybe a little killing." The crowd laughs. "I'm joking. I mean, would it be the worst thing that ever happened to me?" President gives his comic shrug. The crowd roars. "But, no. Seriously. Don't uh... don't kill her. I guess."

Sitting on the couch, the President feels a mild chill run down his right leg. Why had they gone with that clip? He'd spoken in Paducah for 90 minutes. What's with that clip? What the fuck was with that fucking clip?

Cut to Seanny Boy, back in the studio, shaking his head slowly. "To shed some light on what happened in Kentucky today, we're joined now by our legal correspondent Maeve Jacoby. Maeve, can a sitting President be prosecuted for inciting violence against a rival Presidential candidate?"

The President drops half a Rold Gold in the melted butter ramekin. The hell was this?

"Well, Sean, to be honest, we're in unprecedented legal gray area here. While the President is immune from prosecution in some cases, there are other crimes for which he might be found culpable."

"So who gets to decide, ultimately?"

"Well, Sean, the Attorney General can appoint a special prosecutor to investigate this morning's comments and any aftermath that results. President or no, there are rules about calling for violent acts in a crowd."

"What are the odds that something like this can be initiated before the election in two days?"

"Well, Sean, absolutely nil, I would say, at this time, ahhhhh, from this vantage point if you take a ten mile view of the situation. It remains to be seen if voters will take matters into their own hands and punish the President themselves in two days."

"Do you think that's likely?"

"Well, Sean, the American people are a patient people, of proud, loyal pioneer stock. But when it comes to violence against women, America has always stood tall and said, 'Ah. Ah. Ah. No you don't, punk.' We value American women, Sean. Mothers. Daughters. Grandmothers. Aunts. All of them. Sisters. These are all women. America was built on the backs of our women. And the President's words today did not reflect those American values."

"But what do you say to the President's supporters, who are likely to argue that the President was, simply joking? About killing his opponent?"

"Well, Sean, there are jokes and there are jokes. And this one wasn't funny. Just because someone is laughing, it doesn't mean they're joking."

"Makes sense. But you're not saying people should vote against the President just because of one comment, are you?"

"Well, Sean, it's fair to say at this point that we're talking about more than just one comment aren't we? You know what they say. Fool me once, shame on you. Fool me 27 times, shame on me? Four years ago, we were gracious in accepting the President's apology for talking about 'grabbing women by the pussy'–I'm sorry. Can I say 'pussy'?"

"You may say 'pussy.'"

"Thanks, Sean. When the tapes came out and indicated the president was talking about how his celebrity status permitted him to squeeze unnamed women's genitals, America said, 'Okay. That's just guys being guys, grabbing the occasional kootch like men do.' Can I say 'kootch'?"

"By all means."

"Well, Sean. Then the long snaking line of women from his past showed up, and we said, 'Okay. This guy's a player. A real player. Does he dabble at the edge of acceptable sexual behavior? You bet. But lines are tricky things. Some of them are dotted. Some are dashed. And did we know that when we voted for him four years ago? Yes we did. Of course."

"But? I get a sense there's a 'but' on its way."

"Well, Sean there is. But when it comes to murdering women, there's a fairly strong majority, a decent number, in this country that believes, well, that's a bridge too far."

"So is America going to say no to murdering women, Moira? Is that what this election is finally boiling down to?"

"Well, Sean, I hate to say it's going to be a single-issue race, because nothing ever is. We live in a world awash in nuance and complexity. But if America does listen to the President's words and walks away convinced he didn't mean them, I will be surprised."

"Thanks, Moira."

"Sean, thank you."

"Coming up next, The Wall! Making us safer? Or just raising the price of guacamole and avocado toast? We'll take a look. After this message about pillows."

"Off!" shouts the President, swinging his arms in the air. "Off! Off! Off!"

Nelson hits the kill switch on the bottom of his production board, and the screens all flick off with an audible snap. Nelson dissolves into a curtain behind him and out a concealed doorway.

The President charges into his office screaming his aides' names. They enter after him, single file.

"What the fuck was that?" says the President.

"I don't know," says one. "I don't know what the fuck that was. Does anybody know what the fuck?"

They all shake their heads, a few quietly mutter variations on "the fuck?".

The Press Secretary, the administration's twelfth, ninth in the last nine months alone, and too new to know better, says, "You need to call Him."

"Excuse me?" says the President.

"You need to call the Aussie."

"You're fired," says the President. "Get the fuck out."

The Press Secretary leaves the room. Head lowered.

"The rest of you, out on the lawn," says the President. "Talk to anyone with a camera. It was a joke. America knows the difference between a threat and a joke. Fake news. The media's trying to pull one last rabbit from their hat. From their... No! From their ass. Everyone say that. The media's trying to pull one last rabbit from their ass. Exact words. Rabbit out their ass. Got it? That phrase exactly. Do it! Get out!"

They scurry, leaving the President sitting in his cushioned Aeron chair behind the Resolute desk. His heart is racing. Part panic. Part exhilaration. His back is against the wall. Before, he was just possibly losing. Now, he is being attacked. By his own network no less.

He pulls his phone from his jacket pocket and calls Rupes.

Sunday, November 1
8:23 p.m. E.T.

"I almost didn't get out of the parking lot because I couldn't stop staring at the sky. I nearly drove into a lamppost.

I've seen programs about the stars, but it was nothing that could have prepared me for the vastness of it all. I've known the world in two dimensions my entire life. And just to see it all in person. I could barely steer, I was crying so hard. But I made it out, headed northwest. That seemed the best, logistically and symbolically. North to freedom. West to freedom. I drove until the Tesla's battery conked.

Didn't quite know what to do at first, so I climbed onto the roof of the car and lay on my back. Off to the side of highway 361 near a sign that read Pimple Creek. An inauspicious respite if ever there was one. But there you have it. My first respite.

They didn't know I was free yet. They wouldn't know for a few more hours. I would therefore never be more free than I was in that moment, it occurred to me, for my liberty was a secret. And once that secret became known, my freedom would be ever imperiled. Father would see to that. Father is the most powerful man on earth.

Lying on my back on top of the car I beheld the vastness of the Universe. I knew glory. I should have been running, I should have kept moving. But if I were captured, I would not forgive myself for depriving my heart of this sky. This feeling. If only for a whisper of a moment.

I stared into eternity for twenty minutes. More than I could hope for. More than I deserved. And now it was time to trudge onwards seeking the impossible. Safety. Whatever that was.

I lugged the plastic bag I'd brought with me. The bag endured a lot, tied around my ankle, trailing behind me as I climbed up my tunnel. It held a change of clothes, four Kind bars, and a towel. Always bring a towel, a great man wrote, and the maxim proved its worth on the banks of Pimple Creek. I stripped down and waded into the fetid water. It smelled like an unflushed toilet, but it was cleaner than I was. A quick splash and I sprinted out of the water, as I heard things, animals, moving in the oily darkness. On the banks, I toweled off and changed, hurled my dirty clothes into the creek.

In the back of the car, I found many useful things. A toolkit in a vinyl satchel. A flashlight. A packet of flares. I dumped the toolkit out, and transferred my Kind bars, towel, the flashlight and flares into the bag, and closed the trunk.

Two options presented. Follow the creek or the road. Neither was safe, but for different reasons. I didn't yet know where I was going. I hadn't figured that out. I just had a feeling for what direction I ought to move. They'd be looking for me, but maybe they wouldn't be able to use the police. Maybe they'd have to be secret. Maybe just those guards. If I've got this at all right, they're the only ones who know I exist. I chose the roads. I started jogging. What a change! What a joy to progress as one runs, to feel new earth with every step, not at all like the futility of a treadmill. I ran until I arrived at a gas station. Then I asked for directions. Directions to your office.

I know it's difficult to believe. But that's why it is so important that I not be a secret any longer. The secret of my existence is my greatest peril. Once the world knows, I'll be free. They won't be able to put me back in that hole. They'll probably deny the whole story. They'll want as much distance from me as possible. I need to get to the point where I can merely be fake news. It's the only way they'll leave me alone. Until then, they'll do anything to get me back."

"Do you really expect me to believe all that?"

"I hadn't thought about it. I guess."

"I'll be honest. I don't. I think it's the most ridiculous thing I've ever heard. And your hair? It's a bad joke. A Mexican with that haircut."

"He made Rosita do it. Even though he wanted nothing to do with me, he still needed me to be as correct as he could make me. I don't know why."

"I think there are hidden cameras around here somewhere. There have to be. Is it in the bag? Is it in the wig?"

"No. What? This is just my hair. It's all true."

"Can you prove it?"

"Go ahead. Give it a tug."

"No. I've seen that gag before. I mean your story. Can you prove it?"

"I don't know."

"You better figure it out."

"I could take a DNA test."

"I'm guessing we won't get the President to contribute his sample."

"No. He wouldn't. But did you read about that cold case they solved in California? By matching the crime scene DNA to relatives of the primary suspects? It was on TV."

"Yes."

"So I bet there are some Presidential cousins that have their DNA floating around out there in one of those databases."

"Too expensive."

"What price, a Pulitzer?"
"You don't talk like you're 19."
"I've had a lot of time to think. I read a lot. I'm introspective."
"Sure."
"I don't even know why I'm here. I need to get to a TV station. Everyone on TV says that print is dead, but I couldn't tell if they were joking."
"Yeah?"
"You clearly don't have the balls to do this."
"Nope."
"And you're not easily manipulated. Which is annoying."
"I just think you're full of shit, is all."
"Well, remember this moment. You can even take a picture with your phone if you want. In fact, I want you to. I want you to remember the single greatest moment of failure in your career. In your entire life."
"Say cheese."
"Fuck off."
"After you."
"Which way is your bathroom?"
"Outside in the parking lot."
"I'll find it myself."
"Sprucing up for TV?"
"You'll see."
"Sounds good. See ya.

Sunday, November 1
8:28 p.m. E.T.

The three siblings are sprawled across sleeping bags, and two of them are still awake watching the conclusion of Running Scared. Empty pizza boxes are scattered across the white carpeting. Rico's right hand is shiny with Ruffles grease; he used to be a total chip addict. So bad his father hired a hypnotist from Long Island who tried to implant the idea that spiders lurk in every bag of potato chips. Didn't stick. Rico has fallen asleep on his sleeping bag, just like he always used to, his hand wrapped around a warm can of New Coke, and a smear of Keebler's waxen fudge striped across his right cheek. His sister's first thought is to remove the can to a safe space so he doesn't spill soda on the carpet. And then thinks, fuck it. When did she start caring about that kind of stuff? It's only carpet.

Tonight is about escaping all the trash that is adulthood. Recapturing something real and pure. Let him sleep. Rico snores lightly, nearly a kitten's purr.

The credits roll over a freeze frame of Gregory Hines and Billy Crystal and the one chick with their arms over each other shoulders, laughing, cigars lit. Victory.

Junejune's shaking his head. "Unbelievable film. Unfuckingbelievable film. I fucking love that film."

"I know," she says, "right?"

"You know, like, I get hassled a lot, but my favorite actor, my favorite actor! Is Gregory Hines. Never made a bad movie."

"White Nights."

"White Nights! And... he did Sesame Street."

"Yup, and..."

"God. He could dance couldn't he?"

"Oh he was an unbelievable dancer."

"Unreal dancer. And my favorite actor. I mean, what does that say about me? Really. If you think about it. Who else even says that?"

She stands and ejects the tape from the machine and puts it back into its case.

A look of concern flashes across Junejune's face. "Aren't you going to..."

"What?"

"Don't you want to rewind that first?"

"Why?"

"Well Dad always says..." He stops. Looks at his hands. "God."

They meet eyes briefly and then both instinctively look at the white carpet.

"I do it all the time, too," she says.

"Yeah," says Junejune. "It just happens. Doesn't it? I'll be, like, watching football, and they'll show some owner in the box with his kids, and I'll even think it. I'll think like, 'Dad always says, those NFL owners must drop their kids on their heads on purpose. Because I can't think how they'd all get so stupid and ugly on accident.'"

"Yeah," says his sister. "The other day, I was in the car and we drove past this homeless shelter on the East side, and it was like a reflex, I thought, 'Someone should knock it down. Luxury suites. Underground parking. Kill two birds with one stone. Where everyone else sees a problem, there's an opportunity.' But I thought it... I thought it in his voice. It was super weird."

"I know what you mean."

"Yeah."

Junejune slides his arm into a deflated bag of Ruffles and his hand emerges empty. "I've got more," she says. He knows he should stop her, but tonight, it seems like he should stop caring for a few hours. She arrives from the kitchen, pulling the bag open from the center and drops it next to him. "Police Academy 6?" she says, and waves the box in front of him.

"Oh God. Yes."

"City under siege" she says, as she pushes the tape into the machine.

"Michael Winslow is at least my second favorite actor," he says through a mouthful of chips. "I fucking love Michael Winslow."

"I'm still a huge Mahoney girl," says his sister. "I don't know what it is. Some crushes just burrow in deep."

"Even I had a little crush on him back then."

"What?"

"Nothing."

The golden Warner Brothers crest appears on the screen, floating before a blue sky dappled with puffy, perfect, white clouds.

"How does he sleep like that?" she says, pointing to Rico.

"I'd kill to be able to sleep like that."

"I don't really sleep anymore."

"Me neither."

"I'm serious."

"Me too."

"What? Like how many hours?"

"Maybe three. I don't know. No. I do know. It's exactly three. But not continuous. Really. Just sort of in and out for three hours."

"Same. Same. Every night the same."

"I'm always tired."
"I have these dreams."
"You too?"
"Yeah."
"Actually. The same dream. On a loop."
"Same."
"What happens in yours?"
"Other people's dreams are boring. You don't wanna hear that."
"No. I do."
"No."
"Seriously."
"Well. The abridged version. But it's weird. Cause first I hear things. Before I can see anything. I hear strings, like cellos. I hear these long low tones, like someone's playing twenty cellos in my head. It surrounds me from within."
"Same."
"Really?"
"Yeah. This is weird."
"So then... there's Dad. And he's standing on top of the Pyramid of the Moon. But instead of all stone, it's all, like–"
"Gold."
"Yeah. It's all gold. And it's the most amazing thing. Smooth gold steps climbing halfway up the sky. And no one else is there. Just Dad standing on the top block at the center of the whole thing. And I'm at the bottom. At the base. And he looks down at me, and he's giving me that one smile that I only ever saw him smile after he hit the dog with a rolled up newspaper. And he's gesturing for me to join him up there. And he's got these–"
"White gloves?"

"Yeah. How'd you know?"
"Same."
"Really?"
"Same. Exactly."
"Yeah. He's got these long feminine, like, 1980s country singer cowgirl gloves on. Long white spangly things with white fringe dangling from the wrist to his elbow and ornamental white scrolling of a silkier white fabric up the whole length of the glove. Like something Dolly Parton would have worn to a wedding."
"And he's naked?"
"Yeah. Otherwise he's nude. But he has a bodybuilder's physique, so it's not him, so it's kind of okay. Cause I don't think I could handle it if I thought it was actually, if..."
"Same."
"So then I start to climb the golden pyramid. And he's gesturing. Reeling me in. And the more I climb, the larger the blocks seem to grow. So I'm getting further and further from him, no matter how quickly I scramble. And I'm climbing and climbing. It seems to go on for hours."

They both watch the TV screen. It's one of those opening credits sequences that takes forever in some older movies. Neither of them is really watching it.

"Do you ever make it?" he asks her. "To the top?"
"No. I barely get close. Then I wake up."

He nods slowly. Leans back against a pillow and starts to watch the movie.

She looks at him with a wary look. "Same?" she says.
"No," he says.
"No?"
He shakes his head. "I made it once," he says. "I got to the

top."

"What happened?" she asks.

He inhales slowly through his nose. A long deep breath. She can see his chest gradually rising beneath his shirt. Then he puffs it back out in a noisy blast. "I don't want to talk about it," he says.

"Okay."

"I fucking love this movie so much," he says. He stuffs a handful of Ruffle crumbs in his mouth and crunches so loud she can barely hear the dialogue from the movie. She lies back on her own sleeping bag and nestles her golden hair back against one of the oversized pillows she's laid out for the three of them.

Nothing ever really changes, she thinks. Or maybe, nothing real. Ever changes. And everything, everything, everything, every thing that happens to you when you're a kid is real.

Sunday, November 1
8:28 p.m. E.T. / 7:28 p.m. C.T. / 6:28 p.m. M.T. / 5:28 p.m. P.T.

Nakamoto Spot #1283

Soft instrumental music rises. A family sits around a dining room table, buckling beneath the weight of a multicultural feast. Seated around the table: father, mother, white daughter, black adopted son, gender-free child, Native American cousin, Asian American neighbor.

Father: What a feast, honey!

Son: Yeah. Wow, Mom!

Mother: Oh yins.

Father: (to camera) Good evening, America. Are you tired of political ads like this one?

Neighbor of Asian Descent: People of every race, every income bracket, all the many splendid genders, united behind one political candidate? Sitting together for a non-traditional meal of foods appealing to every major demographic?

Mother: Maybe talking about the topics of the day. Like abortion?

Son: Or immigration?

Other child: Or which bathroom I should be permitted to poop in at the Dairy Queen Brazier?

Cousin: Or explosive pipelines through various people's backyards?

Daughter: Or health care?

Asian neighbor: Or tax rates on the wealthiest Americans?

Father: Well I'm here to tell you today, on November 3rd, cast your vote for–

The daughter produces a gleaming three foot katana sword from beneath the table. Its wicked blade catches the studio light as she swings it over her head in a graceful revolution. She leaps onto the table and sprints choppily over the feast, knees pumping like oil derricks, and charges towards her father. He still bears a jolly, if slightly puzzled, look on his face as the silver blade sings in her hand and splits the air. His eyes squint slightly; then his head tips backward off of his neck, and a vivid crimson spray of blood jets from the empty neckhole. The gathered family steps back from the table, each now warned and armed with a different weapon representing the five elemental skills representative of the Wu Hsing combat code. In short order, the daughter spins, slashes and hacks her way through the assembled dinner guests, who put up a valiant, if uninspired, defense, until they are heaped in their chairs or draining out into the expanding pool of blood on the floor around the dining room table. The daughter gives her sword a short, twitchy swing that stops abruptly, cleansing the blade of its freshly won blood with a snapping noise. A close-up of the daughter, then she rips a prosthetic nose and a pair of false, incongruous eyebrows from her face, which have been bothering, really, everybody watching, and the face beneath the makeup we all now recognize belongs to Golden Globe winning actress Uma Thurman, with the silver blade held before her face, and in sharp san-serif black text that reads: KILL BILL 3 and underneath it the words: "Coming November 4th. But only if Nakamoto has won the presidency."

Uma Thurman: And he means it. On Tuesday, vote Nakamoto. And I'll see you in theaters on Wednesday.

Sunday, November 1
7:29 p.m. C.T. / 8:29 p.m. E.T.

Gary's nightly chore list has ballooned over the last two weeks. In addition to the cooking, the cleaning, the shopping, and the usual around-the-house chores he takes care of, he has to empty Jean's bucket, enhance the soundproofing, call around to Jean's friends and make sure they don't get suspicious. A surprise two-week cruise is what he tells everyone. His treat for all she's ever done for him. But when he put their absentee ballots in the mail last week, that moment made it all worthwhile. He wasn't just giving her vote to the President, he was keeping it from Hillary 2.0. That's a two-vote swing if you think about it. Chaining your wife up in the basement isn't easy as it sounds, but the cause is righteous and she'll be fine and free in three days.

It's for her own good, after all. She doesn't have to believe that for it to be true. Gary knows.

In the evenings she's finally letting him sit on the couch with her. Not touching her, still got the empty middle cushion between them, but she seems almost relieved to see him now. Whereas at first she had been spitting furious, throwing everything she got her hands on, including her bucket, which was an unpleasant piece of business, believe you me. He could hardly recognize her in that first week. Like that time he caught the opossum in the Have-A-Heart. Caged rage.

In exchange for sitting peaceably with him for thirty minutes, Gary rewards her with a change of channel for half an hour (after Hannity), anything she wants. At first, she'd choose another cable news network just to piss him off, but at this point she is desperate for anything other than election news. Tonight, she's going to watch a show where Bobby Flay has to out-cook an AI-powered smart kitchen with a team of robotic sous chefs at its disposal. Plus the adult male actors from Full House have been reunited as the show's judges: Saget, Coulier, and Stamos.

Tonight, though, she's enjoying Hannity more than he is. That's for sure.

"Well, well, well," says Jean. "What was that?"

"I don't know," says Gary.

"Looks like Hannity just stabbed your man in the back." She giggles. "I did not see that coming."

Gary doesn't know what to say. She isn't wrong, and he doesn't understand it. Her giggling grows near hysteria. Very irritating.

But then, when the Nakamoto Kill Bill 3 spot airs, that's the first time Gary has to stop himself from hitting Jean.

"Oh oh, Gary!" she says, laughing. "Uh oh! Did you see that?" She slaps her leg and cackles.

"The act of a desperate man. How many people want to see that movie anyways?"

"A lot of people. A lot. And it's a tight race. So close. If all this cable news force feeding has taught me one thing, it's Nakamoto doesn't need to swing too many idiot votes away from your President to make a dent. And that is a beloved movie franchise. Something both idiots and the elite can agree on."

"Smells like desperation."

"Smells pretty shrewd to me. Looks like something you don't just do overnight. Looks like something that's going to get a lot of attention. Bring in a whole lot of eyeballs that are sick of this whole thing."

"People aren't that stupid."

She just laughs at him. Right in his face. Then she's bent over laughing, her breasts on her knees, laughing with a delighted, cruel edge. That's when he is tempted to hit her. First time in their marriage. Even through all this. He drugged the G & T he'd made her and carried her down, gentle as a lamb. Set her up the best he can and he's never raised a hand. And she said some pretty unforgiveable things to him in that first week. She cut him deep, as only someone who knows you as well as a wife can. But he never got angry. A little sad, maybe. He always knew it was the circumstances speaking, not her, and eventually she would settle down. And she pretty much has. But now, something about this laughter combined with... what?

With the fact that she might just be right?

He stands and walks towards the stairs.

"Wait!" she says. "Wait. Please change the channel. I'm sorry. Please. Just–"

He slams the bottom basement door behind him and climbs the stairs to his office. Slams the top basement door behind him for good measure. Sitting at his desktop, he opens Facebook. His newsfeed is already a mess, all this stuff about boycotting the News. Seems like a pretty quick overreaction, if you ask him. One five-minute glitch. But they didn't have to run that ad, did they? He clicks on a few links people are posting. There's a lot of speculation. People are wondering if there's a hostage situation or something. Are Hannity's kids safe? One guy's saying he knows for a fact that they hadn't been to school on Friday. Another guy's saying Hannity doesn't even have any kids. That that's just a rumor they put out there to draw any threats out into the open. Then his buddy in Sarasota's saying he'll never watch Sean again, and everyone is trying to talk him down, and then there's a few saying, me neither. People are wound tight, that's for sure.

He clicks the logo on the left that takes him to his private group – League of Traditional Husbands. There's a lot of upset people in there, too. He feels less alone, but not much happier, to read about all the SWs (Secured Wives) that are apparently gloating tonight. One guy writes: "Nearly jawed my wife tonight to shut her up. Help me Lord." There are a few comments that offer suggestions for "glee suppression" but the whole thing's supposed to be committed to non-violent means of securing the vote, so comments are getting taken down as quickly as they go up. Gary clicks refresh, reads the new comments. Clicks refresh.

Reads some more.

Refresh.

Refresh.

Refresh.

Refresh.

His anger is their anger. But the main thing is: everyone's confused. What the hell's going on down there with Hannity?

Sunday, November 1
8:35 p.m. E.T.

After three rings without an answer, the President says aloud to himself, "If he doesn't pick up, I'm going to fucking nuke Australia." The fourth ring. A fifth ring. Then a click.

"G'Evening Mister President," says a plummy Australian voice with a load of clotted phlegm crackling the "-ent" at the end of the word. The sound of a cough followed by the clearing of a throat and a solid, singular spitting noise.

The President hears a woman's voice say, "Not on the carpet!"

"Hold your tongue, harpy" says the Australian voice casually. "Sorry, not you, Mister President." He chuckles. "How's your evening?"

"Piss poor," says the President. "And you know it!"

"Me?" says the Australian. "What have I done?"

"You know exactly."

"Sorry?"

"I just watched Hannity lob softball hand grenades to Moira, and she smacked them all in my face. And I want to know why."

"Crikey, you'd have to ask her, now," says the Australian. "I wasn't even watching. I've got The Ozarks on over here. Have you seen it?"

"I've been preoccupied."

"Oh you should really watch it, mate. Absolutely brilliant."

"What the fuck is happening on your network?"

"Oh, they've got editorial independence over there. You know. I'm just the bean counter."

"Yeah, right," says the President.

"My hands are tied, mate," says the voice. "That's just Moira speaking her mind. Whatever she said. You know how it is. You should give Sean a call and give him a good piece of your mind, though. Might do you some good."

"I will," says the President. "But why bark at a dog when you can talk to the man holding the leash?"

"Oh now. That's just not the right metaphor, Mister President. I'm a figurehead at this late point in my career. Haven't you heard? Practically retired. Bed-ridden, the rumors are. Like I said, they value their editorial independence over there. I have an obligation to respect it."

"It's never stopped you before," says the President.

"With all due respect, I take umbrage at that, Mister President. Are you saying I've meddled in the politics of my network's coverage?"

"Christ. What's with this act? Knock it off."

The Australian voice laughs once, it's as much a bark as it is a laugh, and then another spitting sound, followed rapidly by distressed sounds from someone in the background. "Now look, Mister President," says the voice. "I'd help you if I thought I might profit from it. I really would. But the fact is, your act's gone a bit stale. The new circus has dancing elephants, and you're still trotting out a donkey that will take a piss on command and a seal that can bark the alphabet, but not very well. You know. 'Was that meant to be a "w"?' That sort of thing."

"That's not true."

"Ah but it is, though. It is. But you're looking at it all wrong, mate. I'm not talking about you growing stale. Just you in that office. Time to take a bow and move along to the next episode. Look at what you've done. Look at all you've accomplished! You've had an incredible run! Absolute legend. But it's not even close to over. You're on the cusp of something even more remarkable. Think about what you can do out of office. Just ponder it. I'm not talking about your own show. I'm talking about your own channel, mate. Your own network. Hire anyone you want. We'll reboot O'Reilly. Let's get Alex Jones. You name him, you've got him. My people can get you up and running. You think you're rich now? You'll have to hire a barge to take your money down old Caymans way."

"You're talking like I've already lost."

"Mate," says the Australian. "I don't know what your people have been telling you—"

"You are my people."

"Right, right. No. I mean your people over there. If they haven't told you, someone's got to. You've lost, Mister President. This chapter is concluded."

"They said the same thing four years ago."

"They did. I didn't."

"You don't get to decide."

The Australian laughs. "Mister President, it has been an absolute delight watching you work these last four years. So entertaining. You've been good for business, make no mistake. I am grateful for it all. You've made me a considerable nut, and we'll make a pile more together if I'm not much mistaken. I look forward to working with you again in the near future on many exciting endeavors."

"I'm not done—"

"Wednesday, Mister President. Maybe lunch. I'll have my secretary set something up. Nighty night."

"But—"

The Australian has already hung up.

The President lowers the phone from his ear.

He sets it down on his desk. And then he smells something. Just a whiff at first, and then it's gone. And then it's back again. Stronger. Distinct. It happens to everyone, eventually, the President knows. He thought he had another two years before it arrived. But here it is. There's no mistaking it now. It's everywhere in the Oval Office. Somehow. He doesn't know where it's coming from. The windows are all closed and sealed. Under the doors? Through the ducts? The heavy scent of eucalyptus envelopes the room. The President feels his sinuses opening and mucus thinning in the back of his throat. His eyes water. There's a term for this, in the industry. It's called getting koala fucked. And no one knows how he does it.

The President opens Twitter on his phone and scrolls down through his timeline with practiced flicks of his right finger.

The news is not good.

Sunday, November 1
8:56 p.m. E.T.

Hannity stands, pops his earpiece, unclips the lav mic from his lapel, the black box from his belt, and leaves a heap of wires and equipment in the warm butt-furrowed valleys of his desk chair's seat. He prides himself on the fact that he's had the same chair for eleven years. His assistant strides forward with an opened bottle of warm Mike's Hard Lemonade and a lit cigarette held out towards him. His post-show tradition. Nothing flashy. The same for the past 11 years. A working man's lemon-flavored malt beverage and one Kool cigarette a day. That's how Hannity rolls.

"So," he says to his assistant, a short blond woman in a dark gray skirt and a crisp white blouse. "He call yet?"

"No," she says.

"Tweeting?"

"Nothing yet."

"Probably trying to work it out."

"He probably already called the boss."

"You think?"

"Probably."

"And you know what to say. If the President calls. When he calls."

"I tell him you'll call him back."

"No. You tell him I'll call him back, eventually."

"Eventually." She scribbles on her ever-present notepad. "Got it." She studies him, expecting more.

"I'm an entertainer," says Hannity. "He's an entertainer. He'll understand."

"Eventually," says the assistant.

"Precisely," says Hannity. "I have an obligation to my sponsors. This is a business, after all. If anyone should get that, he should." The assistant nods silently, but continues to watch Hannity expectantly. "What?" says Hannity.

"So..." she says, "what was that? What's going on?"

He smiles at her, and she endures a fleeting vision of him reaching out to pat her on the head. He doesn't, of course, as the insurance company-mandated lawyer is standing in the shadows with one hand on his opera glasses and the other on the remote shock transmitter, finger trembling against the trigger.

"Going on?" parrots Hannity. "It's just reportage. Asking tough questions."

"Right," says the assistant. She nods. He nods. She tips her head to the side. "Will we be continuing to ask questions along that line?"

"We will see, won't we?" he says. He takes a long drag on the Kool and holds the smoke for a moment, runs his tongue along the base of his upper lip. He exhales a gray cloud over her head and studies the cigarette in his hand. "Is this a Kool Green?"

"No, Kool Blue."

"Hm," he says, biting his bottom lip thoughtfully. "If you say so." He finishes the hard lemonade and hands her the empty bottle. The assistant winces as Hannity sticks out his tongue and extinguishes his cigarette against it, like he always does. Flicks the butt casually onto the tiled floor. "Gotta make some calls," he says and walks back to his office.

Sunday, November 1
7:04 p.m. M.T. / 9:04 p.m. E.T.

Rocky Stanford's father had purchased plots of land east of Denver in the early 1980s hoping to cash in on the new airport once it was put in place. Seemed like a good gamble at the time. And in some ways it had been a good idea, but he'd missed the mark to an almost comical degree. Restaurants, hotels, gas stations, they all popped up, right between seemingly every plot of land the elder Stanford had purchased. And what was he left with? Arid, unfarmable land in a location where no one wanted to live, and therefore nobody wanted to build on. A disaster.

Rocky's dad cashed out what he could, which wasn't much, and took off for Florida with Rocky's mom, got an apartment in Orlando, sat themselves down on the couch, pulled the pin on their appetite, and inflated in place. Hadn't turned off the TV set in 25 years and counting.

Rocky had been a freshman at Boulder at the time. Dad had shown up at the dorm on a Thursday night, unannounced. Just knocked on the door, hadn't taken his hat off. He handed Rocky an envelope containing two pieces of paper: a check to cover the last three years of tuition and a deed to the last useless piece of land adjacent to an airport that wouldn't even exist for 11 more years. The deed had been signed over to Rocky.

"Good luck, son," said his dad as they shook hands. "I screwed up. Don't you do the same."

"I don't understand," Rocky had said, puzzled.

"Your mom's in the car. Gotta go."

"Where?"

"Florida, son. I'm out of the game. Visit anytime."

"But why?"

"Because Colorado can go to hell, is why."

"Oh," Rocky had said. And that was it.

26 years later, the bet Rocky's father had placed was finally paying a dividend. Not that Rocky really needed it.

After college, Rocky had followed in the old man's footsteps and become a real estate developer. Better at it than his old man had been. He and his wife have three little blond, soccer-playing kids and three golden retrievers: Elway, Terrell, and Shanny. They live in a big, new brick thing in a private subdivision, and his money makes money.

Tonight is just another penny from heaven. He gets a call asking about that last useless dust patch his dad handed him on his way out the door, he'd only held onto it out of sentimentality and as a cautionary tale. And now a voice on the phone asking can he knock some trees down over there in a particular pattern?

"Nope," says Rocky. "But only because a tree hasn't grown on that land in all recorded history."

"Oh," says the voice on the phone. Rocky hears clicking in the background.

"But I tell you what I can do," says Rocky, "if you're looking for some sort of large pattern to fill the bulk of my enormously valuable 277-acre plot of land." (He crosses his fingers and his toes.)

"Go on," says the voice.

"Well, how long does it need to last?"

"Two days."

"Election?"

"Can't speak to that."

"Well that's fine. Not my business. Yet. But if you only need two days, here's what you do. Where you calling from?"

"Not at liberty to–"

"Right. Well, I get the sense, based on your forestry query, that you're not from round here, so you don't even know we got four inches of snow yesterday. If you're looking for a pristine canvas, you've got it on my land. I've got four buddies with plows who can get out there tonight. I've got a team that can survey out whatever it is you want, mark it up, and we'll get that thing set up by..." he pauses and pretends to consult a watch, "11 p.m.. Local time."

The voice pauses on the other end. "That's a good idea," it says.

"Tell you an even better one. Got a buddy with a pump truck. He'll go through afterwards and spray the banks down so the snow doesn't drift over it. Plus I'll have my buddies plow it clean once a day to keep it nice and crisp."

Again, the voice is momentarily quiet. Rocky has the sense that a hand is being held over a microphone and a conversation is happening somewhere else. While he waits, Rocky tries to figure what he ought to charge for this service, at this hour, with this much manpower. What's it going to cost to get everyone out the door on a Sunday night? Tonight? Everyone's going to need a lot of incentive. Then how much to tack on for his own trouble? How desperate was the voice?

The voice returns to the phone and says, "Sounds like a plan. How much?"

"$780,000."

"Done."

"Good." Shit. Hurray! But shit. Should have started higher.

"We'll email you the design."

"Sounds good."

"11 p.m.?"

"Or your money back," he says. "But not actually. I'll take a grace period of a half hour or so."

"That's cool," says the voice. "Just has to be tonight."

"I know it's not my business, ma'am," says Rocky. "But how old are you?"

Limey, on the other end, stifles a yawn. "20," she says.

"I guess I'm gonna need a deposit of some sort."

"I've got your routing number," says Limey.

"Okay. So let's say 10%."

"No," she says. "It's all there. Already."

"All of it?"

"Yeah," she says. "I have to go. We appreciate your help."

"But who are you? Who do you work for?"

"It's all in the email," she says, and hangs up.

Sunday, November 1
3:12 p.m. H.T. / 9:12 p.m. E.T.

CIA Data Scientist, Dr. Sierra Cork has a song stuck in her head that could do with some exorcising. This happens to her with regularity, but it is the worst on Sundays when it's Sanchez's turn to DJ. She's tempted to cancel out the music, pop in her AirPods and make it all stop, but that goes against the spirit of the whole thing and it was Dr. Cork's own idea in the first place, so she ought to just hold her nose, plug her ears, and get on with it. Team building through music. It's usually pretty good, and Sanchez is no exception. It's just that Sanchez picks songs that stick where you don't expect, always songs that no one else has ever heard of, and these songs? They stay stuck. There is no proven antidote for a Sanchez track, nothing that can consistently handle the job. You just have to wait them out. Sometimes it will rattle around in your echoic memory for days, and then you'll see a dog food commercial, and –Poof!– the song evaporates and you can sleep again. Sanctuary head space until the next Sunday.

Cork's team is small but capable. They are eight strong analysts, chosen for their skill, their knowledge, their programming abilities, their loyalty, and their willingness to relocate to Hawaii (not the given you might think it is). The loyalty background check is probably the most important part of the equation (see Snowden, Edward, a.k.a. The Waipahu White Hat, allegations against) as the Pacific Data Traffic Center has access to pretty much all–no, who are we kidding–entirely all, of the world's internet traffic. Nothing is beyond their reach. But you'd be forgiven for underestimating them by observing the unofficial dress code of T-shirts, jorts, and Tivas and the location that houses them.

The team's workspace is sprawled out across the second floor of an otherwise empty three-story office building; from the street it's the sort of dead-windowed, brown, 1970s brick structure that makes anyone who walks past it immediately and involuntarily think of something else. That is by design and no happy coincidence. The CIA's Chief Architect in 1973, five feet and a full inch of genius, Carl Craft, wrote his still-classified dissertation on what he coined the "human response to structure." The title itself was a perfect mirror for the art of innocuousness described in its pages. Essentially, he wrote the book, the actual book, on how to get people to want to not think about your building. The building currently occupied by the Pacific Data Traffic Center was Craft's favorite design before he was killed by a neighbor's escaped pit bull. There are still some who whisper the pooch was a plant by an obsessed rival in the FBI architectural department.

As dull as the exterior was engineered to be, Cork allows her team to decorate the office interior however they see fit. They're a special gathering of minds, indoor kids all around, so she wants to cater to whatever healthy or harmless compulsions they have. Make the routine part of their routine, if you know what she means. Same principle the tech companies have been using for years to keep kids in their early 20s at work for endless hours. It can be a bit much, the Jean Luc Picard piñatas, the Mr. Robot posters, the blacklight lamps, the Sheldon mobiles, the stamps, coins, baseball cards, the authenticated autographed photo collections of Starship Troopers cast members, etc. She is constantly stepping on Legos. But that's the price of a great team. This great team, anyways.

Cork, with a Finnish house beat looping in her head, is headed for the roof to have a blue raspberry electronic cigarette when Lance Moller stops her with an awkward outstretched hand that is meant to indicate "Stop" but nearly lands on Cork's breast. Cork doesn't flinch, but Moller recoils in horror.

"Sorry," he says.

"What's up, Lance?"

"Sorry!"

"It's fine. What do you want?"

"So, you know how we had a hard time getting into some of our Russian hidey-holes this morning?"

"Yeah?"

"And how, like, Endrick was sending nasty emails to all of us, telling us to get his office back online so they could see what's going on over there?"

"Yeah."

"He was saying, like, we can't see shit!"

"Yeah, and?"

"Yeah, so it's a bigger thing than just our hidey-holes."

"What's a bigger thing?"

"Well, it looks like the entire nation of Russia, and Ukraine, and possibly Belarus, and probably Armenia, Moldova, Estonia, Latvia, Lithuania, Georgia, Azerbaijan, and Tajikistan, and... there's one other...?"

"It's okay. Finish your sentence."

"It's.... no..."

"What about them?"

Lance Moller tilts his head back as far as it will go on his neck and rolls it in tiny circles. Then he pops back to a normal posture with a smile and says, "Kazakhstan! Ah! My wife." He says the last word with a curious accent.

"What?"

"My wife."

"Excuse me?"

"Myyyyy wife."

"Oh. The... right. So?"

"So all of those countries are offline."

Cork's breathing hits a hitch. Moller is serious.

"How is that possible?" she says. "And explain this to me in a way that will allow me to explain this to idiots. Because it sounds like I'm going to have to do that."

"We don't really know how it's happened."

"Would a power grid outage explain it?"

"At least some of it, but most of their servers have back-up generators. We know that, because Johnson was working on that worm to knock them out."

"But he didn't do that yet, did he?"

"No way. He doesn't stand a chance of actually doing it. It's more a thought exercise as much as anything. So this doesn't seem like that. The whole thing. The whole thing? I don't think it's possible, but even if it is, it's been too long. They'd be back up by now."

"So what are the possibilities. Could they have shut it down intentionally?"

"They could have. It would take enormous coordination, not just in Russia, but with all those other countries, too. And it's not like Russia and Ukraine have been going on a lot of picnics lately. But even if they were, I can't imagine why they would do this to themselves. It hurts them more than anyone else, I would think. They're completely cut off. Unless they're doing something so secret that this is their way of going full radio silent as a country, as a bloc. But I don't even know what that would be. Like our satellites are watching all the time; they're not going to sneak into Poland again or anything without us noticing. We know where their nukes are, and we'll know if they start shooting."

"So they could have shut it down. But you can't fathom why. Got it. What else could knock that whole area offline?"

"A series of nuclear strikes would cut the mustard."

"Any in the news today?"

"Not yet."

"I'd have gotten a call, I think. What else?"

"An electromagnetic pulse. Maybe?" he says scrunching his face up in a doubtful fashion. "But you would need quite a few. And it's not like you could stop it at the border with any degree of control, so if you did that in the manner necessary to cut them off the way we're seeing, you'd probably fry most of Europe's circuitry as well. Which is not what we're seeing. So, no. Sorry. Had to talk that one out. I don't think that would do it."

"That's fine. What else?"

"I... I don't know."

"Okay," says Cork. She crosses her arms. "Can we talk this out on the roof? I have an addiction to feed." She wiggles her vape pen. It looks like Darth Vader's kazoo.

"Sure," says Lance. He follows her up a flight of stairs, then the narrow steel staircase that leads to the roof.

It's beastly hot up there, a fact that Cork well knows as she visits it at least five times a day to incrementally poison herself and burn homage to the goddess of solitude. Lance looks unprepared for the heat, though, and in less than a minute dark sweat marks bleed around the edges of the Steve Urkel logo on his t-shirt, lending an ominous air to the question printed beneath Urkel's shirt-tucked shrug in bubbly letters: "Did I Do That?" Cork takes a long, unsatisfying suck on her plastic vape's nib and as she exhales, wishes it was a real cigarette. She's easing off, but the transition's like moving from bourbon to Crystal Light. "Alright," she says to Lance, who is noticeably trying to pinch his arms against his side to limit her view of his dampening pits. "Let's say it was you."

"What?"

"I mean, let's say I tasked you with shutting down everything that's shut down. Russia, Ukraine, Belarus, Armenia, Moldova, Estonia, Latvia, Lithuania, Georgia, Azerbaijan, and Tajikistan and Kazakhstan. My wife," she recites from memory. "Could you do it?"

"From here? No."

"So not remotely."

"No."

"If I gave you unlimited funds, could you hire enough people to do it with you?"

He ponders the question. When Lance ponders he has a tendency to blink rapidly and non-rhythmically. It reminds Cork of her first computer and the electronic grunting noises it made as a program loaded.

"Unlimited funds?" asks Lance.

"Oh," says Cork, realizing her error. To describe the members of her team as literal-minded doesn't begin to capture their approach to encountering the real world. Her input has to be precise. "Okay. No. Let's say a billion dollars."

"Because..."

"Yes, I know. You could hire the world's population to log on and yaddah yaddah..."

Lance nods and recalibrates the question in his Central Processing Unit, blinks feverishly.

After nearly a minute, he says, "I could do it, I'm pretty sure. But I couldn't keep it down this long. Not the whole thing."

"Even with a billion dollars?"

"Not remotely. No."

"Oh. So let's try this. If I gave you a billion dollars, and a team of your choosing, gave you access to jets and vehicles, whatever tools, and set you loose to do this, in any fashion imaginable, could you do it?"

"Yes," says Lance. "Yes I could."

"Okay. Tell me how."

Lance clears his throat. His t-shirt is fully soaked in his sweat. "Can I tell you back inside? I'm dying up here."

"Sure," says Cork. The thing about a regular cigarette is that it's got this built-in timer. However long it takes to burn from the tip to the filter, that's a cigarette. A unit of time in a way that an e-cigarette just can't be. She slips the kazoo in her pocket and follows Lance down into the air-conditioned workspace.

Standing across from Cork in her office, Lance pats his forehead with a mound of paper towels he snared from the coffee station and appears more at ease. "Okay, so. If you gave me a billion dollars to do this, here's what I'd do. First, we'd work to map out the infrastructure of these countries' networks. We have most of it in hand, so it would be a matter of doing a terrestrial survey of cables and cross-checking it with signals we're not sure about, hunt down any strays we might have missed, and make sure we find them all. Because if we leave one open..."

"Like leaving one window open on your fish tank."

Lance pauses. Looks at her with puzzlement. "Why would you–"

"What's next?"

"After we map it, you give me however many teams of badasses I ask for. Fucking... spooky ninjas, strongmen, snipers, SEALs, to name a few, to watch my engineers' backs, which I'll need bunches of, because we're talking a lot of ground to cover, not to mention the coastal cables. But in some ways it would be a harder job almost anywhere else. Since the Russians have such tight controls over their traffic, there aren't as many entry points as there are in a lot of other smaller countries. It's all really centralized."

"Right."

"But you can't just snip a cable and run away. You have to really go to town on the cable at odd intervals, remove small sections, damage others but leave them in place so it's harder to work out what's damaged and where. I could make a frustrating mess in a short amount of time with good teams and all the right equipment."

"Would it be good enough to keep things shut down for, hypothetically, three days?"

"Not on its own. Probably not, if I wanted three full days of down time."

"What else could you do?"

"Well, I'd booby trap the shit out of the cable is what I'd do."

"Right."

"And–"

"And?"

"And I'd leave snipers behind to take out as many of the

technicians as I could when they showed up. I'd sync it up to a set time so they couldn't warn one another ideally. If you really wanted to slow them down for days, you couldn't do better than that. Take out the people who know what they're doing. Who know how to fix shit."

Cork pauses and looks at the ceiling for a few seconds. She shakes her head, mutters, "But that would be an act of war."

Lance blinks at her. "What do you think unplugging their internet is?"

Monday, November 2 / Sunday, November 1
4:19 a.m. Moscow Standard Time / 9:19 p.m. E.T.

Bogdasha Golidova brushes the snow from his arms as he walks from his truck to the signal box just off the edge of the road. It's been a long time since he was the first man on-site, but these are not normal circumstances. Golidova is the lead technician for the Pskov Oblast Federal Network Services team and it is unusual that he would be rousted from his sheets and the warmth of his wife Ula at 2 a.m. by a phone call from the Federal Oversight Manager. In fact this is a first. The manager never called him at home before. Every other network emergency could be handled by the modest overnight staff or by him the next day if the problem proved too tricky for Yuri and Taras.

But the manager had sounded more scared than frantic, so here he is.

The drive to this isolated signal box in Brunishevo, just a stone's throw from Latvia, took just over an hour from his home in Pskov. Golidova's already doing the math, and if he just has to flip the master power on and off, which accounts for 90% of the solution on trips out to this particular signal station, he can be back on the road, back home in bed for a full two hours of additional sleep before he has to wake up again for breakfast and coffee.

The signal box is not actually a box so much as a tiny metal hut the size of an old phone booth surrounded by a tall chain link fence bearing a number of signs that promise electric shock and sudden death to those who trespass around the facility. Golidova unlocks the fence, walks in, and hunts for the key to the switching station's padlock. It's dark and he left his flashlight in the truck, but after thirty second of scratching around, he gets the key in the lock, opens the station and hits the lights.

Golidova looks around the small room, studies the various indicator lights. Everything's powered. Everything looks good. He taps the keyboard on the old control station (he's asked for upgrades, but never hears anything back) and checks everything out on the monitor. Everything appears to be functioning. Except, big problem, the external international switch is showing absolutely no traffic. Which is weird. Golidova looks around the room as if he expects to find a large garden hose full of fiberoptic cable hanging loose from the ceiling. It is that kind of dead signal. But everything inside the station looks as it should.

Golidova pulls his hat down tight over his ears and walks back over to his truck, grabs a flashlight from the back and his ODTR. He sighs. It is doubtful he will be going back to bed this morning. He's not even sure what to look for at this hour, before the sun comes up at least, and still on his own, but with the Manager being the Manager, there is no way he can just take off. He is going to have to stay here and call all the other techs to join him. If he must suffer, all shall join him.

An inch of snow fell yesterday, so Golidova can watch his footprints multiply as he treks back to the station. He plugs in the ODTR, a boxy tablet that allows you to track how far an optical signal is traveling before it runs into a gap or a break. Then he jacks the device into the primary international cable. He is really hoping the break is on his side of the border, because if it isn't then he has no control over its repair. The Latvians will dick around with it for as long as they like and there won't be anything he can do about it other than tell the Manager, which is considerably worse than just waiting for the Latvians to stop dicking around and finally fix it.

The switch is 800 meters from the Latvian border. The ODTR says the break is 400 meters from the switch. Good.

No Latvian dickery tonight. Or, this morning. Shit. He's tired.

He gets out his phone and starts to call the dispatcher on her cell, and then pauses with his finger hovering over a green icon. No signal. Double shit. He could use the radio in the truck but there's no one in the office to answer. He's out here for another three hours before anyone else shows up in the office to hear the radio squawk. He can drive back towards Pskov until he gets a signal. That's one option. But maybe first, he should just go out there and take a look. If it's just 400 meters. The odds are good some farmer's backhoe dipped too deep or somebody dug a hole for a post and realized what they'd done when they looked down in the hole and saw this severed, government-owned cable, and just bolted. Golidova puts his phone back in his pocket, tugs his hat down over his ears, and walks back into the cold, out through the fence, locks it behind him, and this time rather than walking back to his truck, he follows the fence around the corner, around the back of the building, and tracks in a straight line, due south, following the path of the cable he helped bury many years earlier.

The sky is crystalline, cloudless, and the glow of moonlight reflects up from the thin strata of snow covering the flat fields around him. The point he's looking for, 400 meters distant, is on the far side of a grove of towering Scots pines, bursting from the white earth like a wall of dark giants. As he enters the grove, the path of the cable is marginally distinguishable, as any tree that might have impinged upon the cable's straight line had been hacked down and its trunk dynamited years ago. The light dissolves as he enters the trees, their branches thick and seemingly gapless. If a snowflake has made it all the way to the ground beneath these trees, it is alone and hiding in a layer of pine needles decades thick. Although the cable's path is still apparent, new branches have grown across the path, into the newly available light, and no one has bothered clearing them because the line is three feet beneath the soil, unbothered by tree limbs. Golidova keeps his flashlight pointed straight ahead, knocks branches aside and ducks as he plows his way forward through the grove.

Five minutes later he can see the glow of snow up ahead through the branches, and the brilliant edge of the nearly full moon emerges from the periphery.

Golidova trudges forward, out into the open plain, and the contrast feels so much like dawn that he turns his flashlight off and enjoys winter's early glow. The snow is stunning, really. Nobody's sick of it yet. Golidova's already ticking off the days until he and his friends can pull their snowmobiles from pallet racks, tear across frozen Lake Pihkva, and get buzzed in their shacks while they feast on whitefish.

He feels he has to be close to 400 yards by now and there's nothing to indicate that anyone's been out here for a while, let alone a rogue backhoe. But then he spots what looks like footprints in the snow up ahead. No tire tracks. He tilts his flashlight up and sees the tracks came from further south and went back that way as well. But there's an area, now Golidova can see it, where the footprints stopped and stayed awhile. It looks like three people. The snow is packed tight or kicked away entirely from an oblong area about the size of a kitchen table.

And in the center of that compressed snow is a black rectangular hole. As if someone has taken a hollow two-by-four and used it to carve a hole straight down. Straight into the network cable, it appears.

No accident, thinks Golidova. Not a post-digger. Not a farmer. Not kids. Deliberate. This is sabotage. He runs his flashlight further down the tracks and follows them, adding his own footprints alongside their trail. After 50 yards, he reaches another tamped down area where the three people must have spent some time, and looking down, Golidova groans. Another rectangular hole in the earth, undoubtedly on the cable as well. Not content at one break. His stomach clenches and he runs the flashlight's beam further down the line towards the border with Latvia. Golidova jogs another 35 yards and finds another tamped down area and another hole in its center. He doesn't know what tool they used to make such a hole. He's never seen anything quite like it. And he can't tell how many times they've carved up the line before it hits the border. And they probably put a few on the Latvian side for good measure, where Russian techs couldn't get at them. Which mean there would be Latvian dickery after all. God damn the Latvians and their relentless dickery!

Golidova shakes his head and turns to make his way back up the line. He needs to get to his truck, drive to a cell signal, and call the manager back, then probably... probably the police? And then his men, get all of them out of bed. If this is as bad as it appears, they're probably going to have to re-lay a big chunk of the cable, rather than just repair it at every break. It will be faster. But it will be at least a week. If you account for the Latvian foot-dragging dickery on the other side.

Ten steps heading back towards the station he feels something bite his ass. Like a bee sting in the seat of his pants, out of the cold dark air some fucking Latvian snow bee has... Golidova turns his head and looks down and sees a quilled dart jutting from the back of his pants. He puts his hand on it. What is this? But before he can pull it out, his body floods with a throbbing weakness, he slumps to his knees, slides forward onto his elbows, two narrow furrows in the snow, and then rolls on his side. He feels snow in his eyelashes as he blinks.

And then the remaining glow of white fields evaporates to darkness.

Sunday, November 1
9:29 p.m. E.T.

The centrist news network reached peak fever dream yesterday and its weekend anchors have begun to resemble a pack of zombies in crisply pressed shirts and ties. Sleeves rolled up by wardrobe too tidily, meant to look like a working man at the end of a day, but instead comes off as phony standing next to a touchscreen the size of a two-story bungalow, especially when you can see the stage hand steadying the rolling ladder the anchors and special correspondents occasionally have to climb to tap the upper half of the screen to activate the animated bar charts. The stage hands wear black pants, black turtlenecks and backwards black berets with the red logo across the foreheads. It's all descending into a strange carnival.

The Shining Star has developed a twitchy lip and a thick, marled southern accent that he can neither explain nor ditch, so executives have made an actual executive decision to lodge him in the Presidential Suite at the Peach Tree Ritz-Carlton with rotating visits by a psychologist, toxicologist, nutritionist, hypnotist, speech therapist, neurologist, dialect coach, and botox technician. The lip's in danger of developing a droop and his accent occasionally twists inexplicably into a Lowland Scottish thing, and things are looking overall bleak, but the executives are crossing the fingers that they can get him off injured reserve by Tuesday morning.

Until then, the young buck they snaked away from a CW affiliate in Des Moines to sub in has proven to be dynamite. A revelation. He's having a Wolf Blitzer Gulf War (Episode I) moment. Brokaw, if Brokaw was yoked and could bench thirty reps at 225. Former Hawkeye linebacker. Kid's got a jaw you can rest your beer on without fear of spilling. Dark brown hair, thick and lustrous as America's pre-European-contact forests. A voice, deep and silvery, that inspires not just trust and authority, but belief. That holy fucking grail. Sentences in the hallways of the corporation concerning his performance are punctuated with headshakes or high-fives, more often than not. No one's saying it aloud, but the unspoken thought is that even if The Star's lip mellows and drawl abates and the unfortunate #elayuhctorate stops trending... they should... they can't even finish the thought. They'd sooner dye the poor man's signature ivory coiffe black and pierce his septum than finish the thought. Yet...

This kid, Spark Jones, he's the real deal. An actual godsend in the minds of some. Smart, handsome in a way that everyone can appreciate and men don't resent.

Spark's on now and by 9:30 the Nakamoto ad is doing to the network exactly what it was designed to do, that thing that news does so beautifully. It is making it all about itself. The News is fully swallowing its own tail with ouroborotic delight. The commercial, aired an hour earlier on this very network, is now news itself. In addition to its original broadcast, the news network has now essentially replayed the spot three times for free, if only in clips interspersed with extensive analysis.

Spark, standing (towering?) in front of a brand-new holographic wall bearing a still-frame from the commercial (the one where the actress holds the grandmother's head aloft) says, "An unprecedented presidential sales pitch? Or just the same old political horse trading in new clothes? Or, as some are saying on Twitter tonight: is this a bribe? Or a threat? To help us shed light on this situation, I am joined by Paul

Dumphee, Assistant Professor of Political Science at Earlham College and author of the book Free Beer for the Kiddies: Bribing the Populace since 1776. Professor, how does Presidential candidate Satoshi Nakamoto's ad rank in America's history of political promises?"

"Well, Spark, and may I say, a real pleasure to meet you." Spark nods. "In the grand scope of things, this offer-slash-threat regarding the Tarantino film is actually just another chapter in the long, colorful history of politicians currying favor with voters through freebies. Giveaways. Although on a grand scale."

Spark nods, "Now we aren't sure about ticket prices at this time, so it isn't clear if he's giving the film away or just saying it will arrive in theaters, or not, based off of the election results. Do ticket prices help clarify whether this is a bribe or a ploy?"

"That's right, Spark," says Dumphee. "Very astute observation and just, just marvelously well-phrased." Spark nods, but not in a boastful fashion. "The fact is, if he was offering something material of financial value in exchange for a vote, that would run afoul of election laws. You can't stand on a soap box and tell everyone that you'll give them a five dollar bill for voting for you. That would be electoral fraud. Vote buying. But because he's only offering the opportunity to purchase tickets to something, that's a whole other ball of wax. Now, without a doubt, the other candidates are meeting with their staff to weigh the merits of filing complaints and lawsuits to undermine this tactic. However, it's likely they'll just have to let it go and live with it."

"And why is that, professor?"

"Such a good question, Spark. They'll swallow this pill because if they don't, they'll look like the guy or gal who hates Kill Bill and wants to keep a lid on this film. They'll look every bit the spoil sport, and the sort of people whose votes might be swayed by this movie gimmick are also the sort of people who will come after you if you try to shut it down. I don't know if you've ever been to a... a uh... Comics Convention? But it draws a colorful and devoted crowd. Very zealous. Did you know I saw a 50-year-old woman dressed up as calico cat in a cape once?"

Spark nods sagely and asks, "Historically, what are some comparisons we might be able to draw to this particular sales pitch?"

"Well, Spark, nearly every campaign is doing a version of this exact same thing. The wording is different, but the subtext is identical. When a politician says they're cutting taxes, they're saying: 'I. Will. Give. You. Money.' When a politician says they're making health care affordable, they are saying 'I will give you money.' Even when they say they're going to kick immigrants out of the country, what they're mostly saying is, 'I will give you their job.' And therefore, guess what?"

"I will give you money?" says Spark.

"Brilliant! Yes, exactly. So in some ways you can't name a campaign in American history that hasn't done pretty much the same thing. But what's different here? Two things. One, he's not saying the government will give America a new Tarantino film. He's going to do it himself from his own pocket. Two, Nakamoto's offering each American citizen something their money can't just buy on its own. Because he already owns it. He had the foresight to gain control of this franchise. He owns that movie, if I understand the situation correctly. He owns an experience, a piece of art, whatever you want to call it. And he can release it or not, according to his whim. So even if I'm a billionaire, I can't get my hands on it unless he lets me. He has something I want and I won't have the opportunity to buy it. Unless he wins."

"In your evaluation, then, professor, is this a gimmick or a tactic that may make a legitimate difference in the election?"

"Oh I think this is the savviest tactic I've ever seen."

"Ever?"

"Oh yes. Oh my, yes. I don't know if you've noticed, but we just spent the last five minutes talking about one candidate and one candidate alone. And it wasn't negative. It was all speculative and new and interesting, two days before the election, Nakamoto just dropped a positively charged viral bomb on the entire thing. Just when everyone thought they'd be sick to their stomach if they heard another word about the election. He'll have the youth market in the palm of his hand here. Plus, I imagine you're not done talking about this tonight, am I right?"

Spark rewards him with a charming chuckle. "Probably not," he admits.

"No. Probably not. And you'll keep talking about it tomorrow, too, if I'm not mistaken. That ad just bought him the front page of every news site, of Reddit until tomorrow morning, Twitter for four hours or so, SnapChat for thirty minutes. Forget buying ads. He just bought 50% of all American social media at a crucial moment. You've heard of recency bias? This is exactly the sort of last-second move that swings things a candidate's way. Gimmick or no."

"Food for thought, Professor Dumphee. Thank you for joining us this evening."

"Oh an absolute pleasure, Spark. Thank you for having me. And if you're ever in Richmond, Indiana..."

"Coming up next! The Nakamoto Spot. Who vetted it? Does it cross a line? Should we have even aired it? Should we air it again? We'll hear your thoughts via Twitter, Tik Tok, Bumblz, Periscope, and Instagram and check in with our own ombudsman to see if we're in hot water. We'll be back."

The lights blasting Spark Jones dim a bit and the director makes a roundhouse motion with her finger. Spark widens his eyes and snaps three large blinks to adjust to reality. He nods at Shelley, the director. "Okay?" he says.

"Amazing," she says.

The producer in his earpiece says, "Back in two minutes thirty. Do some stretches. Get a drink. It's a marathon not a sprint."

Spark nods. He paces over to the low-slung desk that is more a prop than anything in this age of the standing anchor and pulls his silenced phone from the thin shelf where he had stowed it. He unlocks it and glances at his texts, mostly kudos from all over, friends, family, classmates, former teammates. He opens up Signal, on which he only has three contacts labeled: SN, YN, and HN. He taps a quick note to SN himself. "Still all good."

SN responds within seconds: "Watching. Keep going."

He taps back: "KK" and hears the producer in his ear, "One minute."

"Airing any ads I ought to know about?" he says to the open air.

"Depends," says the producer in his ear.

"On what?"

"No. Just Depends. Plus-size and Night Defense."

"Probably leave that alone then."
"Copy that."

Sunday, November 1
9:43 p.m. E.T.

The President is back on his sofa in the Oval with his head propped against the armrest, the back of his hand resting against his forehead. He has hurled his favorite pillow across the room. It rests on the floor where it landed after ricocheting off a portrait of Franklin Pierce (second-best-looking president). Nothing is broken, but if one were to pick up the pillow they'd find moist bite marks on the smooth unlogoed side. The smell of eucalyptus has thinned, yet lingers.

The President opens up messaging on his phone and texts the kitchen steward: "chikwhopr" and sighs loudly. The ChikCrunchWhopper is his own proud innovation, one he has pitched to two successive BK and C-F-A CEOs without response or success. Not so much as a postcard. Didn't seem too much to ask. They didn't even have to put his name on it. They could work something out if they wanted to license The Name, but really, he just wanted to be able to buy the thing off the shelf, so to speak.

ChikCrunchWhopper Recipe

1. Procure a fully loaded Whopper hamburger, everything, absolutely everything on it and place it in a medium wooden salad bowl.
2. Open that burger up and take the pickles off. You want a little taste of pickle but only sickos would intentionally place that weird slippery, seedy disc in their mouth. Place pickle coins in Zip-Lock bag. Discard or burn.

3. Procure a Chik-Fil-A sandwich. Withdraw the singular lump of chik-n from within the bun. Again, discard pickles in Zip-Lock bag. Burn bag. Place chik-n lump on open face Whopper.
4. Open one 5.5 ounce bag of Utz Sour Cream 'n Onion chips and empty the entire thing on the open-faced sandwich, spillage is unavoidable and to be embraced.
5. Replace top Whopper bun.
6. Serve while still warmish.

The steward always carries the sandwich in on a tray that also bears a moistened wash cloth in a fancy china bowl and a compactly folded bath sheet the steward sets on the coffee table for post-consumption mop-up.

It's the sort of sandwich that requires a lot of attention while it's being consumed. Both hands on the superburger, elbows planted on table, shoulders hunched to allow face to hover over the wide salad bowl placed beneath chin to catch drips of grease, sauce, oily crumbs, salivary foam, and the like. Once you start eating it you can't set it down until you're done or the whole thing crumbles into an unmanageable pile that cannot be lifted twice. You must hold on for dear life until it's all over. Then you towel off.

The distinctive knock of the kitchen steward sounds, and the Presidential salivary glands begin to pulse.

November II

Monday, One Day

Monday, November 2
6:50 a.m. E.T.

"When I got here last night the doors were locked."

"We lock them overnight. Yeah. We get a lot of crazies coming around. You know. Especially this time of year."

"Well I'm not one of them."

"Okay."

"I'm not."

"That's fine. Okay. How can I help you?"

"You can help me tell my story. You can save my life. And my liberty. My happiness... that's probably beyond anyone's reach."

"Okay. Sounds dramatic. I've got five minutes. But then I really have to go to a story meeting to prep for the 9 o'clock cast."

"I am your story."

"Okay. That may be, but whatever it is, you have to get on with it. I really don't have time today."

"I am the President's son."

"Oh. Okay."

"I know how that must sound. And for me to show up today, asleep next to the concrete bumper at the end of your parking spot when you pulled in. I know that none of this does anything for my credibility."

"Well–"

"That's fine. I understand. I already went to the newspaper across town and I have already seen the look you're giving me."

"It's not that I don't believe you. But I'm not sure I'm–"

"My mother was a maid, is a maid... I don't know for sure

if she's even still alive. At a golf resort in Palm Beach."

"I can guess the one."

"Yes. She was an illegal immigrant from Mexico, employed by that resort. Or so I've gleaned. I don't know anything more about her because I've never met her. I was raised in an underground bunker, imprisoned in luxury, but imprisoned nonetheless, my entire life. Armed guard outside the door, 24-7, and nothing to keep me company but the television and nobody but Rosita. She is... she was... my pseudo-mother, my maid, my caregiver. My captor. And then there were two doctors, one each day. And once a year, on my birthday, one other visitor..."

"Not your father?"

"Yes. My father."

"Every year?"

"Every year. As far back as I can remember."

"Well, that's at least something, so far as verifying your story goes. When is your birthday?"

"September 12."

"And what year were you born?"

"2001."

"Ah. Right. So. You're 19?"

"Yes."

"And you've never been out in the world? Not once?"

"Never. Not until today."

"How did you escape?"

"I tunneled. Into a wine cellar."

"You tunneled."

"Does this mean you believe me?"

"No. Not yet. No. This means I'm willing to believe you. God knows I want to believe you. But I need to know an awful lot more. I need to know everything."

"You don't have a meeting, do you?"

"No. I thought you were another loon. You might still be. You know, the hair doesn't really scream... integrity? I'll be honest, your whole look feels like a bad gag."

"It's all I've ever had."

"I'm going to call in a colleague, okay? And the rest of our conversation is going to be recorded. As we follow through, as we do our research, call around, verify what we can, we may decide to have you do the whole thing over again with our station manager. And then again with better cameras in our studio. And again with our lawyers. The scrutiny is going to be thorough. Relentless."

"All I have wanted to do for years is to tell my story. I'll tell it a thousand times if you ask me to."

"Okay. That's what I needed to hear. Because the P– your father, is a litigious man."

"I know."

"He could destroy me. And you."

"I am destroyed."

"Well just me, then. If we don't get everything, if we don't have this nailed down tight, it simply won't air. They won't let me. I won't allow it myself. I don't like your odds as it is."

"I understand."

"Alright then. Let me call in Mary. What's your name again?"

"I never said."

"So what's your name?"

"Well you know my last name."

"Right. I suppose."

"Well it's the same as my first name. And my middle

name."

"You mean you're–"

"You can just call me Triple T."

"Oh my god."

"Or Tonio. Rosita calls me Tonio.

Monday, November 2
3:53 a.m. P.T. / 6:53 a.m. E.T.

Monday mornings are the hardest to get if you want to see Los Angeles's most respected dental specialist. The specialist, known to those who can afford her work as Doc Sharon, is a notorious early riser. She detests traffic, and if you want an appointment, you have to arrive half an hour before your appointment. That's why Shirley Hutcherson arrives so early for her 4:20 a.m. appointment with the specialist.

Shirley sits in a wobbly wooden chair in the waiting room reading a Time magazine from December, 2016. Patients aren't permitted to use their phones in the waiting room, dentist's strict policy and Shirley's seen people kicked out for violating it. The old Time is what she's left with. Leafing through the rag, she relives what for her was a time of horror and disbelief. Articles about re-counts. About the history of the electoral college. Headlines predicting trade wars. An article about why white Obama voters in rural Pennsylvania voted the way they did in 2016. Shirley's grown somewhat numb to the whole thing.

Nothing like the dentist to wake her up, though.

"Ms. Hutcherson," a hygienist in spotless white scrubs says from the doorway.

Shirley follows the woman back through a winding hallway, buffeted by the sounds of drills and polishing tools, suction, hoses, clanks, and whirring. Here and there, she swears she hears people crying and moaning and someone saying, "Oh no no no no, please. Oh please, no no no no." She shivers.

"Have a seat," says the hygienist, gesturing to an avocado

green dentist chair, upholstered in thick, shiny plastic that looks impervious to damage. The sort of chair that can easily be hosed down. The tools for her cleaning are laid out on a spotless aluminum tray next to the chair, and a television set mounted on the wall opposite the chair is playing muted conservative news with the closed captioning enabled, so one can read every word being said. Over the distant sounds of buzzing, and humming, and grinding, as Shirley slides into the seat, she hears music from a round speaker embedded in the ceiling overhead. It sounds like some sort of collegiate a cappella group covering Rage Against the Machine songs of the late 1990s.

"Hm," says Shirley.

"What's that?" says the hygienist.

"Who picks the music?"

"Doc Sharon herself. Do you like it?"

"No. Not really."

The hygienist nods and studies a clipboard full of paperwork. "Mm hm. Just a cleaning, it looks like?"

"Yes."

"Okay," says the hygienist. "I'm going to put these spacers in your mouth, okay? It will help relieve the strain in your jaw while I'm working on your teeth. It looks like you're straining already. Like you clench your jaw?"

"Ung," says Shirley in reply, as a small plastic wedge has already been crammed in the left side of her mouth. The right one follows shortly.

"I'm afraid it will leave you at a disadvantage, conversationally," says the hygienist with a smile so wide it bridges her ears. "But then, you didn't come here to talk. Did you?"

"Ung," says Shirley.

"That's right," says the hygienist. She scoops up a small dental mirror in one hand and a silver tarter scraper in the other, the sharpened tip at the end of the hook catches the light and shoots a sparkling beam into Shirley's eye. She winces. "Whoops!" says the hygienist. Then she twitches the scraper and the flash of light blinds Shirley again. The hygienist doesn't acknowledge it, but begins to tap thoughtfully on Shirley's gums with the end of the hook. "These gums look a little inflamed, I can tell already. How often do you floss?"

"Ung ung ay," says Shirley.

"Hm," says the hygienist. "You're sure about that? I'll show you some technique when we're through, make sure you're doing everything in an effective fashion. Oh. Can you see the TV from this angle? Want me to pivot you?"

"O."

"Here. Let's make sure." The hygienist rotates Shirley's chair so unless she wants to stare directly at the hygienist or close her eyes, she has no choice but to watch the news as the cleaning continues. Shirley is watching footage from the President's speech from yesterday morning. "That was some speech yesterday," says the hygienist. "Some speech. He says things that need saying. You know?" The hook scrapes ferociously against Shirley's teeth as the hygienist speaks, occasionally catching on something, some impossibly hard substance, and the hook tugs violently. Shirley feels like a tooth is slipping, like it's going to succumb to the yanking and pop right out. The hygienist keeps after it, and Shirley can feel a crumble of something chalky land on the back of her tongue.

"The thing I like about him, I think, is that he's real and he's looking out for us first, you know? He could be chilling in his mansion at home right now. Or at any hotel in the world, cause he practically owns them all. But he wants to help. Even with the media. And all those jealous ladies saying whatever they said. Even with Mueller harassing his family and telling everyone he's like a Nazi or whatever he says, you know what? Even after impeachment? It's too important to quit now. There's too much left to do."

"Ung."

"I know, right? And like, look at everything he's done. The wall's nearly done? He's turned our enemies into our friends? Did you see him hugging that little North Korean fella? Cutest little thing. I don't even mind the haircut, you know, because at the end of the day who is he? He's just another human being, just like you or me, and when the President scooped him up and twirled him in the circle like that, you know? That just tells you all you need to know about the man. It's just like he said. If you treat someone like your enemy long enough, eventually they'll become one. All we had to do was stop acting like they were some sort of Bond villain nation state thing, you know?"

"Ung gah."

The sharp tip of the hook now traces a path along the base of Shirley's top teeth, outlining the gums and occasionally jabbing into them. Shirley can taste blood in her mouth, but the rinse and suction keeps not coming. She tries to swallow accumulated spit, but the spacers in her mouth make it an awkward choking swallow.

The hygienist pays no mind and continues in the absentminded tone of someone speaking while focusing intently on something they're doing with their hands. "I guess tomorrow's going to be pretty exciting. We're going to have a reelection watch party over at my sister-in-law's house. She's got all sorts of stuff planned. She bought these ICE jackets online and this, uh, pin the tail on El Chapo game where you do a shot of tequila and they spin you around... you know, and you stick a donkey tail right on his old be-hind. Whole family's going to be there, young and old. We're bringing the kids, all the kids. My niece just turned 18 and she's pretty fired up to vote. The grandparents already voted early; they took pictures and put them up on Facebook and everything. Got 400 likes, and it started this whole thing at their retirement home, they live in Florida, so all these people kept doing the same thing, showing them filling out their ballots and handing it in, and you'd have probably seen it on the news if they'd voted for her, you know, but the media sits on stuff like this. I mean I know the polls show Florida is close, but it looks like everyone, I mean absolutely everyone? in Sarasota voted for the President this year. Cause really, who answers a poll, you know? Like who answers their phone anymore if it isn't a number they know? These polls are all total trash, so I'm not even worried in the slightest. It's just four years ago all over again. And my niece and her friends, they've got the kids on board too, started handing out these wigs at the dance clubs and that started this whole kind of kitsch-uprising, because if you take a look at what he really stands for, really, like, what he's done for this country, you have to admit that things are pretty good all around for us. I mean, really. I think we're pretty free. You know?"

"Ung gah."

The hygienist is still scratching away with the sharpened hook. She seems to have found something worth delving into between Shirley's front teeth, and her eyes squint with focus as she continues to speak and scrape.

"You know the first thing I hope they get passed after the

re-election? Is term limits. Just get rid of them."

"Ung!"

"We don't really need them anymore, now that we've got the right man for the job, right? I mean, if it ain't broke, don't break it. Let's see how far we can go with this thing, you know? That's something my uncle in Ohio is pushing for on Facebook, I just saw, and people really seem to be getting on board. So I don't know. We'll see. My uncle's a state legislator there, and he says he's pretty sure they've got what they need in the state governments to get this thing going and really, you know, change the constitution. Not that the constitution is flawed, don't get me wrong. But let's let a man finish the job he started you know. Let the work work. And with all the media and the obstructionism, I mean, eight years isn't enough these days. In this new world."

The hygienist finally pulls out the rinse wand and sprays down Shirley's teeth. She floods the back corners of her mouth and Shirley starts to gag. She puts the vacuum wand in Shirley's mouth and says, "Close." Shirley pinches her lips around the nozzle as best she can and a great relieving slurp empties her mouth of most of the water, which she can tell has a lot of blood swimming in it.

"Okay," says the hygienist. "I'll go get the doctor for the final check-up. I'm leaving the spacers in. Don't try to take them out." She wags a playful warning finger and shakes her head once, then leaves the room. Shirley takes the opportunity to wipe the tears off her cheeks with the back of her hand. She's breathing hard and her pulse throbs in her ears. Doc Sharon appears in the doorway, mirrored sunglasses, black hair pulled back tight, wrapped from the waist up in a black leather smock, black leather lace-up gloves that run all the way to her elbows, fishnet tights bulging around the knotted muscles of her legs. A pair of white Nike cross trainers that look as though they've been tied too tightly. She carries a cordless dental drill in her hands and revs it once.

"Weren't you just here yesterday?" growls Doc Sharon.

"Aag," says Shirley, nodding.

Doc Sharon turns up the volume to the television set and the news starts thumping from speakers mounted on the four corners of the ceiling.

"Is that better?" shouts Doc Sharon.

"Angh," says Shirley.

"What are you going to do? What will you do tomorrow if this all comes sliding to a stop?" she says. She revs the drill again. Shirley whimpers. "Won't you get bored? What are you going to do?" Doc Sharon smiles. "Are you still going to need me?" she asks.

"Aahaa," says Shirley.

"That's what I thought. Maybe more than ever. Now. Let's take a look at what's going on in here." She pumps her index finger to rev the drill again and leans low over Shirley's open mouth, over Shirley's quivering ecstatic lips, Shirley's eyes glistening, reflecting the chilled white light of the buzzing halogen bulb.

Monday, November 2
6:58 a.m. E.T.

The sun has been up on the east coast for exactly 30 minutes and Cell 20-L of the Manzanita Hyatt is busy tracking, pushing, and coaxing their way into America's morning conversations. They have been lucky with the weather, good sunrises in nearly every location. The official Nakamoto campaign Twitter account had sent out fresh tendrils at 6 a.m. with a note: "Be sure to look out your windows this morning, America. Together, we can do anything!"

The campaign is still coasting off of the previous night's Kill Bill pitch, which the network morning shows were taking their cracks at, but the morning tweet has sparked a smattering of interest and the usual online speculation, as the account doesn't Tweet frequently. The team at the Manzanita knows the pictures and videos, as they come, will be the main factor in pushing things forward. If they can grab the headlines on the east coast, then as the sun rises across the country it should feed the fire as newscasters in the central time zone and then mountain and Pacific time will fan out to see if there's a landscape Easter egg in their own neighborhood. Not to mention Alaska Standard Time and eventually Hawaii Standard Time, neither of which have been neglected.

Honolulu has been one of the toughest to work through, actually, but Limey eventually fixed something up with a golf course owner involving two fairways and a prodigious amount of red clay soil which even now is being spread strategically, battery-powered work lights illuminating the progress of a hundred workers. It is not cheap and it will only be up today.

Anchorage had been one of the easiest, thanks to a forested, city-owned park next to the airport, a mayor staring down budget cuts that were suddenly and simply far less daunting thanks to the Nakamoto jackpot, and a surplus of local residents capable of and interested in felling trees at any given moment.

Each of the young people in the suite is tasked with monitoring three TV stations at a time. As their spots hit, they update it in the Outcomes tab of the monster spreadsheet (the spreadsheet has now won the nickname Thad, for some reason), provide the length of coverage, and score it on a positivity of coverage scale from -5 to 5. "If you feel like we've struck jackpot, highlight relevant cells in gold in Thad," says Atticus, "wave your hand and I'll come take a look. In addition to doing everything we've already accomplished, now we need to prove what we've done. We need tangible results. The video people are going to splice the best bits together later this morning for an ad we'll run tonight. We're looking for anything ecstatic."

The prize for most effective location so far, no surprise, is New York. At first glance, it seemed impossible to secure a space remotely malleable enough to do what needed doing, but Cell 20-L and their mother trucker pills have proven their worth.

New York City, with its multiple airports and insane, even by Bitcoin multi-billionaire standards, real estate prices offered an incredible challenge. It was the White-Blonde man who suggested they use Central Park, to much initial protestation, before he pointed out the number of well-populated buildings surrounding it, and explained the idea of corralling 2,000 people together, at $100 apiece, in supplied white t-shirts with "Nakamoto" tastefully embroidered on the right sleeve. Cell 15-B, previously stationed at the LaGuardia Ramada have been re-assigned, sent down by Acela that morning to get everyone in place with megaphones and a simple but ingenious system of popsicle sticks and twine. They have it all up and running and taken down in under an hour. They annoyed a number of Tai Chi groups on The Great Lawn this morning, but only briefly, and with promises of brevity and donations to their various organizations, many even joined the promotion. The drone footage that 15-B's AV guy captured is truly stunning, and is widely distributed to every network and newswire. The NYC piece is on every station and the frontispiece to every national news story as well.

Miami, also, is performing well in every way, thanks to the discovery of a company that specializes in ethically sourced fish food containing a glittery compound. Spread in sufficient quantities by a fleet of pre-programmed feed-spraying remote boats working by dawnlight to finish at sunrise, and then for a brief, glorious hour, the Nakamoto symbol appears glittering on the surface of the Atlantic Ocean, just off the coast of Coconut Grove, and the effect is enhanced by the glimmering schools of fish that arrive to consume the feast. It is short-lived, but spectacular and beautifully documented from Miami high rises, news helicopters, and local photographers, of which there is an abundance.

The Nakamoto social teams are tracking the best of the posts and giving them their own boosts. The news anchors, especially the locals, go full-blown bonkers for the imagery, although a number use the unfortunate term "publicity stunt." But in general the team at the Manzanita Hyatt has achieved the impossible. They have purchased America's attention for a full six hours on the day before the most expensive, fiercely contested election in history in an era where six hours is the equivalent of sixteen days in 1984 time (the math is solid).

The conference room in the Manzanita Hyatt is misty with exhaustion and human vapor at 12:35 p.m. when Atticus answers a call from Yoshi. He doesn't bother moving to the bathroom to take it.

"Heyo," says Atticus.

"Good work," says Yoshi.

"Thank you, sir. This team is unbelievable."

"Tell them the bonuses drop in an hour."

"You serious?"

"Of course. And send them to bed. Tell them we won't need them until 6 a.m. tomorrow morning."

Joy, fatigue, and the thought of sleep are suddenly too much, and Atticus sobs once into the phone.

"What?" says Yoshi.

Atticus inhales sharply. "Nothing. Sounds good. Anything else until tomorrow?"

"No. Sleep tight." Yoshi hangs up.

Atticus deposits his phone in his vest pocket and looks around the conference room. Five sets of expectant eyes look at up him. "Good work," he says. He smiles. "Time for bed."

A cheer erupts from the small group but then devolves rapidly into tears and hugs, and then tumbles into the sort of uncontrolled, lurching heaving sobs that no one in the room can remember experiencing since they were small, small children. Life's earliest disappointments locked deep in six memories flood the room in those sobs like sinister madeleines. The childhood ghosts of dropped ice creams, parental slaps to the cheek, being lost in the grocery store, deceased grandparents, dog bites, Simba's daddy, waking up in the crib and realizing for the first time what it means to be alone in the Universe, the sensations return at once, abstract feelings outlined in fragments of concrete baby-thought. Tears, tears, tears like they've never known and will never see again.

And then they leave the room for the comfort of a sleep closer to death and nonexistence than anything resembling life.

Monday, November 2
7:22 a.m. E.T.

He's decided. He's not leaving the residence today. Maybe not tomorrow either. He doesn't care what his aides say anymore. No more events. He's tired of pandering. Meeting people. He's so sick of thanking people. Of asking people for things. Votes. Money. Endorsements. "Support." The President is propped up on his chaise lounge in the living room watching his morning show and scrolling through his feed.

It's over, he thinks. It's all over. He's been outdone by this Nakamoto guy. It's over.

"Melly!" he shouts towards the master bath. His wife appears in the doorframe, stroking her hair with a gold handled brush.

"Yes, darlink?" she says.

"Can you do that in here?" he says. It calms him to watch her brush. It always has.

She frowns a little, not an unhappy frown, just her unfocused default, and sits next to his feet on the chaise, angles her shoulders so he can still see the screen on the wall beyond her. "Is darlink sad?" she says.

"Yes," says the President. "Darlink is a little down this mornink."

"Maybe darlink Tweets, yes?"

The President sighs. "I don't know," he says.

"Tweet, darlink."

"I'm beginning to think it's just not reaching people the right way. Look, just... look what this guy's doing out there. I mean, I mean... whole landscapes he's got..."

His wife looks at the TV for a while. "Hm," she says, unimpressed. "You own lawnmower too, darlink. Big whoops."

"That's not bad." The President opens a new Tweet and writes "Neat. I have a lawnmower, too. And PEOPLE KNOW WHO I AM." Sends it.

He doesn't feel much better. Maybe a little. But he does enjoy watching his wife brush her hair.

A yellow-haired person on the TV is standing in front of a green screen displaying a series of images from this Nakamoto aerial footage bullshit that he can't seem to escape, no matter what channel he turns to. They pause to superimpose the President's latest tweet across the lower-left-hand corner of the screen. The blonde reads it aloud and gives it an unconvincing laugh and says, "Good one, Mister President. Thanks for watching this morning." But then they go on and show even more of the images. The one next to the Atlanta airport is shaped like a peach, with Nakamoto written in cursive, diagonal across the fruit. Outside Charlotte they did a controlled burn in the shape of a full rack of ribs and bold boxy text that reads "Carolinans for Nakamoto."

Then the Miami thing? Unbelievable.

The whole thing is genius.

The President turns back to his phone. He tweets, "Hearing experts think Nakamoto ocean glitter causes fish cancer? May spread to humans? SCARY IF TRUE! EXPERTS!?!"

Then he sighs again. He opens his thread with the kitchen steward and types, "Oreo Blizzard. Gumy bears on bttm."

"Where are you going today?" he asks his wife.

"Mmm. Children's hospital. Then event at Veteran's hospital. Then animal hospital. I think."

"Why don't we just stay in?" he says.

"Here?" she says.

"Aren't you tired of all this parading around? All this touching strangers?"

"No, darlink. I like it. It's nice to do." She looks at him with concern. "Is your blood sugar low, darlink?"

"I think it may be," he concedes.

"You have Blizzard yet?"

"No," he admits. "I just ordered it."

She tuts. "Really," she says. "They should just brink it to you."

"Well I don't know what kind I want until I'm a little awake so–"

She tuts again. "You should decide night before. Like underpants and necktie."

He shakes his head. "It doesn't work like that," he says. "I don't know."

"Blizzard! Blizzard! Blizzard!" she says, and slaps him playfully on the calf. "Then we talk." She leaves the room, still brushing her hair.

Watching her leave almost makes him weep. She's so beautiful. She's the most beautiful. He wants her to sit by his feet all day, brushing her hair, making him feel good, cheering him on. He wants to ask her to stay again, but then she'll see what he's planning and she'll make him get up and go out onto the lawn for half an hour "Do some puttink, go do your puttink" and he's just not got it in him.

No. Today, he'll just stay where he is. He needs a break, and he's a grown man, and by god he's going to take one. I mean, everyone's already made up their mind at this point and even Rupe–

A polite tap at the door, precedes the arrival of the white

gloved steward bearing a custom, silver, jumbo-sized DQ cup on a beautiful golden tray.

He lays it on the end table next to the President's chaise, bows, and leaves.

The President jabs his spoon into the Blizzard and shovels three quick scoops into his mouth. He presses his tongue up against the melting lumps of soft serve speckled with chocolate cookie and squeezes the ice cream against his palate with his tongue. He feels his scalp tighten and his brain press forward against the back of his eyes. The soft, awakening pain.

He swallows.

Perhaps he'll go into the office for a few hours. Just a few.

Monday, November 2
7:28 a.m. E.T.

"You tell him."

"You tell him."

"I told him about the North Korean thing last time."

"I had to tell him about the Chinese take-over of Hong Kong."

"What are you guys even complaining about? I had to tell him when the Saudis leaked the Mecca Resort plans to the Times."

"That was ages ago. It's your turn."

"You must be shitting me. It will never be my turn again. That was the worst thing I've ever endured. And in case you've forgotten I was held prisoner for three months in a Bosnian outhouse. My thing was ten times anything you've ever had to tell him."

The members of the National Security Council are seated in an antechamber off the Oval Office, vaping vigorously. None of them can say when the vaping thing took off in the Council, none of them actually talk about it, but it is certainly a thing now, to the extent that the President has begun to complain about the smell of tangerines the Treasury Secretary seems to carry wherever he goes. But the President also recently complimented the National Intelligence Director on his cologne (which was, in fact, residual cinnamon e-liquid).

The members of the council now sulk in silence, puffing away, waiting for someone else to voluntarily inform the President that we currently have no communication with Russia. Or the former Soviet states. Our satellites seem to freeze up as they pass overhead even. Static. We have no pictures. We can't get into their systems. Our spies have fallen silent. Unreachable. Our embassy has gone incommunicado, as have the U.S. consulates in Yekaterinburg and Vladivostok. Not good. Their embassy here is answering the phone but not any questions. They keep saying, "The ambassador has no comment at this juncture." May the good lord smite the runny nosed consultant who taught them that phrase. The International Fucking Space Station has gone eerily quiet.

"They could be doing anything," mutters the grizzled Chair of the Joint Chiefs, exhaling a plume of mint-chocolate mist. "Absolutely anything. They could be reformulating the U.S.S.R.. They could be setting up an invasion force to point at Alaska. Jessie Hopscotching Cripes. They could be, they could be, they could be shuttling Iranian Revolutionary Guard up on into Scandinavia to kick off a big old Western European cock grab. Judas Cropdusting Lice. Could be anything."

"Settle down, Todd," says the Assistant to the President for National Security Affairs.

"You settle down, you old fucking marshmallow-smoking-ass piece of shit."

"I don't need settling. And it's cotton candy, I'll have you know."

"I stand both corrected and fucking tickled pink to know it. 'Have you know.' I'll have you know the contents of my ass. 'Have you know.' That phrase tells me everything I need to know about you. That's probably etched on your coat of arms, I beg your pardon, escutcheon. I tell you what. If that phrase isn't on your gravestone someday, I'm buying the plot next door and I'll put a little monument of a scraggly old jackass with a little text bubble saying "I'll have you know..." and an arrow pointing right at your dusty-ass skeleton."

"All right, all right. Give it a rest," says the Secretary of Defense. "I'll tell him."

"Oh sure you will."

"Yeah right."

"No, I will," says the SOD. "I'll do it."

"You never break bad news."

"Yeah. You always have an underling do it. Or trick J-Kushy into doing it."

"Well, the buck stops here on this one. I'll do it."

A puzzled silence follows.

"Why?" says a suspicious Vice President.

"Yeah," says the Treasury Secretary. "Why?"

"It's the right thing to do," says the Secretary of Defense. "I'll take my lumps this time, gentlemen."

"Bullshit," says the Assistant to the President for National Security Affairs.

"The hell," says the grizzled Joint Chief.

"What's your angle?" says the Secretary of State.

"No angle," says the Secretary of Defense. "It's my turn to face the music. That's all. My staff should have seen this coming, whatever it is. And I have to own that."

"Bull. Shit." The Assistant to the President for National Security Affairs shakes his head. "You're already planning for his successor, aren't you?"

"Oh! I get it!" says the Secretary of State.

The grizzled Joint Chief guffaws. "You smell someone burning lame duck à l'orange in the oven, you sniveling son of a bitch. And you're hiding it in your napkin and sneaking out to the Pizza Hut buffet afterwards like a damn coward."

The Secretary of Defense shakes his head stoically. "No,"

he says. "I'm just doing the right thing."

The room cracks up, everyone but the Secretary of Defense.

"Oh my God," says the Treasury Secretary.

"That's rich."

The grizzled Joint Chief fans himself with his hand. "Son, you haven't done the right thing for a selfless reason since you been potty trained. You been shitting in your hand and calling it Hershey's ever since."

The Secretary of Defense offers him a quizzical look. "I don't even understand what that means."

"Never mind," says the Vice President. "I'll tell him."

"But–" says the Secretary of Defense. Grumbles tipple across the table from every side.

"No," says the Vice President, pointing his hands towards the group, his fingers pinching against his thumb in a closed-sock-puppet-mouth gesture. "I outrank all of you–" Again, a mild grumble of disagreement runs through the room. "I outrank all of you! And I have a meeting with him before the NSC meeting, as a matter of fact. So I'll tell him."

The room takes a collective drag from their respective e-cigarettes. It is crypt quiet. The Vice President stands, smooths his suit jacket with the palms of his hands, and strides out of the room towards the Oval. When the door clicks behind him, a cloud burst of flavored exhalations mingles in roaring laughter.

"Oh that poor dumbass," says the grizzled Joint Chief, wiping tears from his eyes.

"Woooooooooooooooooo!" says the Secretary of Defense. "Woo."

"You'd think a man would have to learn something in four years," says the Secretary of State. "Even just by accident."

"And you would be wrong," says the Assistant to the President for National Security Affairs. "You would be wrong."

Monday, November 2
7:34 a.m. E.T.

Yoshi Nakamoto is halfway through his five miles on the Holiday Inn Express fitness center's treadmill. He's cranked up to a vigorous walk and the little built-in television screen on the treadmill allows him to bounce back and forth between channels and monitor progress. Progress is excellent.

He's also got his Bluetooth headphones connected to his phone and is dialing around the various Political Cells for status updates and new assignments as Satoshi rolls them towards him on Signal. All cells have at least two people focused on pushing the "rising landscapes", as some are describing them to news and social outlets. But the day is only beginning and the biggest fish are yet to fry.

The real pitch arrives today. The stunts have done their job. The attention is real. The stories are in place. The opponents have been choked out of the narrative. But now you're left with an interested group of people, the serious voters, who are asking themselves: "But really. We mean it. Who are you? And what will you do?"

Satoshi Nakamoto will be unveiled today. The real Satoshi, a flesh and blood human. It's essential if there's any chance of capturing 270 electoral votes. This has to go beyond a novelty act. Nakamoto doesn't have the institutional advantages of a Democrat or a Republican. There is no party line to vote for Nakamoto. It takes a little effort. You have to step out of line. And the early voters and absentee ballots are guaranteed to be a loss, as the month-long surge only peaked this week.

Today must be about reality. Or a version of it, thinks Yoshi, as he pumps his fists in concert with his treadmill stride.

He taps the side of his headphones and says "Call Cell Four".

It rings once in his ears and he hears a woman say, "Cell Four. Lisa."

"Yoshi here. Status update."

"Project Ground Game is blowing up. We don't even need to push this thing. It's rolling downhill and gaining speed on its own."

"Good. In 300 minutes there will be a new push. A bigger one."

"Bigger than this?"

"Bigger. More important. Essential."

"Any hints?"

"Nope. But any media people you're in touch with, give them the heads-up that something even bigger is on its way."

"They'll want more than that."

"That's the idea," says Yoshi. Hangs up. Taps his earpiece, "Call Cell Five."

"Cell Five. Martin."

"Yoshi here, Martin. Good start?"

"Great start. Everything's spinning."

"Endorsement videos?"

"All set. Finally. Just uploaded to the Media folder. They're queued up in the YouTube folder, set to Private."

"Highlight reel?"

"Same. All set."

"We got clearance on the U2 track?"

"Yup. And the Beyoncé and the Johnny Cash and Lil Nas X. Not cheap."

"Sure."

"My people are wrecked over here."

"Almost done," says Yoshi.

"Nick of time."

"Start teasing your media contacts."

"Funny. Two weeks ago, I couldn't get a call returned. Now I can barely set my phone down for thirty seconds without someone blowing it up."

"The price of success."

"Can I ask you–?"

"Nope. Gotta go." Yoshi hangs up. Taps his earpiece, "Call Cell Six."

Monday, November 2
7:45 a.m. E.T.

The President has the last bite of cookies 'n cream blizzard and the final gummy bear in his mouth when Secret Service knocks twice. They can burst in if they need to, but there's a formal knock established for needs deemed non-life-threatening. The President buzzes them in on his phone, and the door opens. Instead of the Lead Agent, though, it is a man wearing a black turtleneck, black jacket, black beret, and black pants. No insignia.

The President's eyes widen at the sight of Johann Microsystems, CEO, Founder, and Eponym of Stern Microsystems. As part of their contract, Johann is not permitted to contact the President via phone or written communication. No intermediaries, either. The contract was updated four years ago to stipulate that if information needs to be communicated, it should be directly, face-to-face from CEO to the President in the Executive Residence only, and only in the event of one of three circumstances.

None of which are good circumstances.

The President wipes his chin with an oversized linen napkin stitched with the DQ logo. He stands up.

"Are there recording devices in the room, Mister President?"

"Yes," he replies. He fumbles with his phone for a moment before decisively tapping the screen. "Go ahead."

"You're sure?"

"Go."

"We had a containment breach. The subsidiary is at large."

"You said that was impossible."

"I was incorrect, sir."

"You said it was fucking impossible."

"Yes I did."

"And you were fucking wrong!"

"I was, sir."

"Oh my god. When did it happen? Do we know where he is?"

"Midnight, Sunday morning. And not exactly, no. We're zeroing in on a region. Tapping some law enforcement contacts. We still believe the situation can be contained."

"It better be. It goddamned better be. I'll sue you for everything you have. I'll own your company just to burn it to the ground. I will end you, if this isn't resolved immediately."

"No you won't," says Johann.

"What?"

"You're not suing me. And you shouldn't try to threaten me. It's idiotic and counterproductive. We will continue to do our best to track down the subsidiary in good faith."

"Who the hell do you think you are?"

"I'm the man who holds your greatest secrets. I'm your accomplice in a crime, ongoing for 19 years. What? You're going to sue me for failing to take care of something or someone and never have to explain in court what that something or someone is?"

"Christ."

"I'm the man who saves you from yourself. I'm far from alone in that, but no less crucial to you as a result."

The President drops into a chair. "I know. I know. I'm... sorry. That was a knee jerk reaction."

Johann nods, conciliatory. "I understand, sir. And I apologize for not telling you sooner. I had hoped to have this sorted by now."

"But?"

Johann shakes his head. "We'll find him, but I don't know how quickly. We need a break. Soon."

"Right."

"I'm not just here to tell you about the breach, though. I need your permission."

"For what?"

"When we do find him."

"What?"

"Exactly. What?"

"What do you recommend."

"The same thing I recommended 19 years ago, sir. My opinion is not only unchanged but stronger."

"You want—"

"Alternate arrangements, sir."

"You want me to have my own—"

"I don't want anything, sir. I am making a recommendation. If this were me, if I were in your shoes, this is what I'd do."

"Why can't we just put him back in the... you know."

"Because the subsidiary isn't who he used to be. Before, he was placid, subdued, easy to maintain in a humane fashion. Now? We know he's been planning this, doing this for years."

"Years?"

"Tunneled, sir. Tunneled. Right through the wall and into the wine cellar."

"My God." The president draws circles on the arms of his chair with both hands. "Through the wall?"

"Through the wall, sir."

"He always seemed happy."

"We're now dealing with an uncooperative subject. Which means we can continue very few of our past procedures. We'll need to add restraints. 24-7 surveillance inside the facility. A less charming cleaning and dining staff. Something more like a prison, to be frank. If I were you, looking at this situation, with the added expense, the decrease in the quality of life, abject misery really, for the subsidiary... I'd just as soon pursue alternate arrangements. It would be mercy."

"Mercy," says the President softly.

"Yes. He'll never even feel it. It will be over quickly. Like hitting a light switch. Now on. Now off." Johann flicks an imaginary switch with his finger.

"Mercy," says the President.

"The kindest thing you can do," says Johann.

The President looks up at him. "And then our contract is concluded?" he says.

Johann nods. "That will effect its termination."

The President looks down at his sticky, silver Blizzard cup. "Okay," says the President. "Do it. If you can find him in the next 36 hours, make your alternate arrangements."

"But if we don't find him in that timeframe?"

"Then leave him be."

"He'll still be a risk to you."

"He'll have earned that right, then," says the President. "Tunneled, you say?"

"Yes, sir."

"How far?"

"60 feet. Into the wine cellar."

"60 feet. Hard soil?"

"Limestone, sir. Mostly."

The President whistles. "Chip off the old block," he says. "36 hours?"

"Yes."

"Either way our business is concluded, Mister President."

"That's correct. No need to see you again, regardless of the outcome. This is it."

"Well, if you and the Misses are ever in–"

"Get the fuck out, Johann."

"Yes, sir."

Johann gets the fuck out.

Monday, November 2
6:58 a.m. C.T. / 7:58 a.m. E.T.

Even through the soundproofing panels he installed in the basement ceiling, Gary can hear Jean clattering around in the basement. He can hear the chains dragging. She's pacing again. He wonders if that's normal. There was a discussion thread about Secured Wives that still gives him the willies. This guy in Houston has his wife manacled because he could just not keep her in one place. Hands cuffed, ankles cuffed, and cuffs linked with chains, the sort of thing you do to prisoners being transported from one prison to another. A pretty severe rig by the sounds of it. But necessary. The man down in Houston says she tried to take his eye out when she woke up after dessert and found herself on the basement floor. Took a mighty swipe with her free hand, and yanked so hard against the cuff around her other hand that she dislocated her wrist. So he got out the emergency tranq gun, standard ops, and put her down. Watched a YouTube video on how to pop the shoulder back in place, but it took him three goes, with her waking up each time screaming bloody murder. But eventually he got it set, and in his words, "she aint yankin round no more."

Sad it's come to this. One day left of all this business, and then life can get back to normal.

Gary sits on the edge of the bed and stretches. He walks to the kitchen and starts the coffee. Fills a pot of water, drops four eggs in it, sets it on the stove and lights the burner. Flips on the small TV mounted beneath the kitchen cabinets. He watches while the Mr. Coffee burbles in the background. And it just doesn't make any sense. His news folks fawning over these lawn sculptures or whatever... well, the one on the water is something. But what's the deal? What about the issues?

What is happening to his channel?

Gary smells corruption. Maybe terrorists have taken over the building. How would anybody know? They could just get the building locked down and put out whatever stories they wanted, because they'd own the network. And it's not like the mainstream's going to cover that story. They'd be delighted. Well, okay, it's probably not that. But maybe they've got something on the honchos at the network. Blackmail. Or bought up all their stock; hold the company hostage. Or get their kids held hostage. If Gary wanted to shut them up, that's how'd he do it. He thinks of Jean. The couch down there is corduroy and she's got this ripply pattern all over her at this point: arms, face, legs, everywhere. Won't be permanent. Will it?

The water on the stove is boiling. He snaps the lid on the pot and drags it onto a cool burner.

Wednesday will be a new day. He's got it all planned out. He's even got a script in mind.

First, French toast. Her favorite. He hasn't made it for her this whole time, just so he could use it on what the e-book calls "The road to recovery."

Second, a heart to heart. "Well, Jean. I want to talk to you about why I've done what I've done." In his script, that's where she starts screaming and swearing at him, and he waits her out. Even if it's an hour before she simmers down, he waits. And when she's worn herself out, he just keeps going. He doesn't acknowledge a word of what she's screamed.

"Jean, you married me knowing I was a good man, a principled man. I love you and I care about you, and sometimes I have to do things for you that you might disagree with, but they're for your own good, and I know you know this. Like the time you wanted a red Ford and I wouldn't let you because everyone knows cops pull over red cars at three times the rate of a dark gray car. At first you were upset, but eventually you came around to my way of thinking and you grew to love that gray Chevrolet. And every car in the garage since has been gray, and it wasn't cause I said so. And then there was the time you wanted to go see Springsteen play, and although I admire the man's music, I'm sorry, I just can't put money in the pocket of a man who hates this country. But then we went to that Lee Greenwood show, instead, and you had a ball. You said, I quote, 'I had the time of my life.' That's verbatim. And I didn't say a word when you asked him to sign the back pocket of your jeans and he did it, and he took his G-D time doing it too, and I didn't say a word.

"You think about it. This is really just the same thing. Yes, I went against your wishes. Yes, what I did here may be considered by some to be a criminal offense. But I did it for the right reasons. And I did it..." Here, Gary can see himself choking up a little bit. He doesn't think he will, but it might help seal the deal if he does cry a little bit, because she's only seem him cry once before and it did seem to affect her in a way that might prove helpful. "I did it, because I love you. You're my darling." And then he'll take the key from his pocket, unlock her cuffs, and fall to his knees. And then she'll kneel, facing him. She'll slap him. Once. Hard. Then she'll embrace him. And they'll hug it out.

The coffee brewing burbles to a halt and Gary pulls the carafe from the machine and starts to pour the first mug but stops mid-pour because he thinks he hears something.

Is that the front door opening?

Gary walks into the living room. Out the big picture window, standing in front of a black German sedan, Gary sees one of the largest women he's ever seen. Her arms are crossed, forearms bulging through the black sleeves of her shirt. The back door of the sedan is open, and Jean is climbing into the car. After she takes her seat, Jean leans out with a scowl and flips the bird. Flips that bird so hard. Right at Gary. The enormous woman ensures that she's tucked her legs in before she closes the door for her. The woman doesn't glance back at the house. Just gets in the driver's seat. Pulls away.

Pale. Confused. Terrified. Gary slumps into a floral-patterned love seat.

Monday, November 2
8:08 a.m. E.T.

Vonkers wakes up soaked in her own sweat. The sleeping bags are cozy as you fall asleep, but they retain every bit of heat and slow-cook you in your own salt water and oils overnight. She's forgotten that aspect of sleeping over. Her mouth still tastes like stale chocolate cookies. She hadn't brushed her teeth last night, first time in years she's fallen asleep with a sugary mouth. Her brothers are still conked out, the three siblings laid out on the thick carpeting like a trio of enormous silk worms.

She slides out of her sleeping bag as quietly as she can and pads to the restroom to take a pee. She decides not to flush, a tribute to their father's rules growing up concerning whether to allow it to mellow or send it down, washes her hands and goes to the kitchen. In the freezer, she finds the three breakfast burritos she'd had Melda pick up at the 7-11 and heats them in the microwave. While they cool, she pops a plastic capsule in the Nespresso machine and boosts herself up to sit on the counter while she waits for the beverage to gargle into her "Blondes Do It In the Mall" mug (another childhood keepsake).

At the moment her cup fills, Rico walks into the kitchen, rubbing his face with both hands. He's still wearing his blue onesie, his hair is sleep-spiked on the right side, and his right cheek has a vivid four-inch zipper impression linking his lips to his right ear.

"Morning!" she sings. "Burrrrito?" She rolls the "r".

"Unnnng," he says. "Give me my phone back. And some

fucking coffee."

"Cartoons," she says. "Cartoons for one hour. Then phones. But yes. Here comes coffee." She inserts a new capsule and presses a button. Slides a yellow mug beneath the spout; the side of the mug reads "NKOTB".

"You found my New Kids mug?"

"I couldn't find the original. But this is it, right?"

"Yeah. Oh my gosh. Oh my fucking gosh."

"You're welcome."

"Can I... can I have hot chocolate instead of coffee?"

She smiles. "It's a hot chocolate pod."

It looks like, for a moment, as if he might hug her. His shoulders bunch a bit and her eyes widen in alarm. His head twitches to the left once and his shoulders relax. "Cool," he says. "But I do need my fucking phone."

"Sorry," she says pointing to a small purple safe. "Time release. 9:30 you'll get it back."

"What the fuck?"

"I set it to unlock at 9:30."

"You've got to be fucking kidding me. I need it now."

She shrugs. The microwave beeps and she pulls out the plate with the three breakfast burritos. The Nespresso glugs and spews hot chocolate into Rico's mug. He grabs it and takes a slow sip. His scowl softens. "Which cartoons?" he says.

Junejune appears in the doorway to the kitchen, drool stains on the shoulder of his green onesie. His hair is unruffled by sleep, but his eyes have the dusty, sunken aspect of nascent consciousness. "Where's my phone?" he says. "Give me that coffee." He points at Rico's mug.

"It's hot chocolate," says Rico.

"Oh," says Junejune. "Can I have hot chocolate?"

"Yours is brewing," says Vonkers, tilting her head to the Nespresso machine.

It burbles, as if on cue, and a ropy stream of steaming brown liquid spews into a red mug that bears a white outline of Boy George's face on the side.

"My Culture Club mug!" shouts Junejune. "Holy shucks. Fuck. Where'd you find it?" She shrugs and giggles. His delight dies. "But where's my phone? Seriously."

Rico points at the safe on the counter. "She set it to open at 9:30," he says.

"You must be shitting me," says Junejune.

"Nothing we can do about it now," says Vonkers, walking back to the living room. "Grab your burrito. I've got Garfield and Friends."

"This isn't funny," says Junejune.

She doesn't say a word from the next room. Her brothers poke at the safe for a few futile minutes. "Google its manual," says Rico.

"With fucking what?" says Junejune.

Rico looks at the refrigerator. He slaps it half-heartedly. "Fucking dumb fridge. I hate this apartment."

They abandon hope, snatch burritos and join Vonkers in the living room, where she is shoving a tape into the VCR.

"Should we watch the news first?" says Junejune.

"Do you want to watch the news?" says Vonkers. "Or do you just feel like you're supposed to?"

The brothers look down at the carpet. After a prolonged silence, Rico says, "I want to watch Garfield."

"K," says Junejune. "Garfield. And friends."

"Here we go," says Vonkers.

"I fucking love Odie," says Junejune.

"I like Nermal," says Rico.

"Nobody likes Nermal," says Vonkers.

"Nermal is the worst," says Junejune.

"I like him," says Rico, and sips his hot chocolate. "I like him the best."

Monday, November 2
7:14 a.m. C.T. / 8:14 a.m. E.T.

After she finishes a long bath, Olive Smith turns on the TV on the back porch and settles into her rocker with her oatmeal. Kokomo gets the Indianapolis stations. Mostly she just wants to know the weather, but sometimes they do something nice about an organ donor or about someone who got killed by a drunk driver, but then the family of the dead person forgives the drunk driver, and then they do a scholarship and that's real nice. Sometimes someone saves a puppers or a kitten from a tree or a well or a storm drain or a ceiling or something, and that's nice too. She could do without knowing about all the murders, but then, it's good to know what to be careful of, too. And the phone scams. She nearly bought that grifter on the phone, who said he was from Microsoft, gift cards at the CVS last year. Standing at the checkout and then remembered, hey. What about that WISH Investigates special report? And then she asks the checkout boy if he's ever heard of such a thing as a Windows Shark Attack, and he looks at the pile of VISA gift cards and he say, "Oh ma'am. No no no..." So there's another reason to watch the news.

Tony walks out on the porch in just underpants and undershirt, holding a coffee mug and still smelling like last night's beer. "What's the poop?" he says.

"That little Nakamoto fella' built all these signs and sculptures you can see from the air when you're flying over."

"Who?"

"This Nakamoto. Sashimi Nakamoto."

"Who's that?"

"He's running for President. He invented the... uh. You know. Bitscoin."

"What's that?"

"It's like a money or something."

"What do you mean it's like a money?"

"It's like a computer money or something. I don't know. I just know he's a billionaire with a 'b'. And he wants to be president."

"Of what?"

"America."

"What?"

"Yes."

"Why'd he make a sculpture?"

"He's got these big signs, you know, like you can read them from an airplane, they're so big."

"Why?"

"Advertising."

"For what?"

"'cause he's running for President."

"When?"

"Tomorrow."

"Tomorrow?"

"Tony, are you messing around?"

"What?"

"You didn't know there's an election tomorrow?"

"I guess not."

"Well you better go vote."

"Why?"

"Because it's important."

"Who you voting for?"

"I don't know. Maybe this little guy. I like these signs. He

did one by the Indy airport. It's a big racecar and the exhaust out the back spells his name. It's real nice."
"That's all right."
"Yeah."
"He's a little guy?"
"I think so. I haven't seen him. People don't know what he looks like."
"Is he Japanese?"
"Nobody knows."
"What?"
"It's a mystery."
"But he's gotta be Japanese, right?"
"Maybe. Maybe not. You know how Tina at the Suds f'r Now has those symbol tattoos on her arm?"
"Yeah."
"Could be like that."
"Huh."
"But there's gonna be some announcement later today."
"He's gonna step out?"
"That's what people think. That's what they're saying."
"What if it's Bill Cosby?"
"What are you talking about?"
"What if it turns out it's Bill Cosby? Secretly."
"It's not going to be Bill Cosby."
"But if it is?"
"Well then I won't vote for him. But it isn't Bill Cosby. This guy's a, a, a, uh, you know, computer guy. Genius."
"I don't know what Bill Cosby knows about computers."
"Well, he's your age, so probably not much."
"Hey."
"Hey yourself."

"What if it's Bobby Knight?"

"Well then I guess I could count on seeing you at the voting booth tomorrow."

"You know you would."

"But it's not Bobby Knight."

"You don't know that."

"Yeah. I do."

"Think about it. When's the last time you saw him?"

"This morning over the mantle in the family room."

"You know what I mean."

"I really don't, Tony."

"I mean he hasn't been doing hardly any color commentary the last year or so. And he's not coaching. So makes you think. What's a man like that get up to? Because he surely isn't sitting on his hands. Man like Bobby Knight, not that there's two such men, but man like Bobby Knight, doesn't just disappear without a reason."

"So you think he's Mister Nakamoto?"

"Just saying it's possible."

"About as possible that I am."

"Are you?"

"I don't know. Maybe."

"So that's—" Tony points at the screen.

"That's outside Chicago. See. They did a big Michael Jordan head in the cornfield there, and then there's a big word bubble and it says 'I heart Nakamoto.'"

"Well that's something."

"I like it. 'Snice."

"Lotta work."

"Well I don't think he does them all himself."

"Still. Lotta work."

"Nicest political ad I ever saw. And I've seen about a million this year."

"How many of those they do?"

"Over 100, the news thinks. Sun's not up on everywhere, so they're waiting to see."

"Mm hm."

"Where you going?"

"Getting the lawn mower out."

"You mowed yesterday."

"It's looking shaggy."

"I said you just mowed yesterday, Tony!"

"It's shaggy!" he shouts from somewhere inside the house.

Monday, November 2
12:22 p.m. W.E.T. / 8:22 a.m. E.T.

After circling the unfamiliar green peaks of the island chain once, the pilot of a Sukhoi Superjet descends towards the Faroe Islands' international airport with his heart pumping double-time. The cockpit is a riot of swearing and sweat. The wind swipes at the large Russian passenger jet's wings with capricious power and direction and the passenger cabin trembles and swings with stomach-roiling speed. The seats are stuffed with programmers, hackers, and technical personnel, terrified pale faces tinged blue and green, hands clenching armrests, eyes peeled wide or clamped closed. As the runway clarifies in the windshield, the plane settles into a tremulous direct line. A sudden dip, and the wheels touch earth with a buckling thump that sends the passengers' heads whipping towards the seat in front of them. But they are finally down, safely. The pilot and co-pilot are a mess, cackling with hysterical relief over the sounds of complaining brakes until they slow to a crawl and turn towards the terminal.

Viktor Paralinka is the first off the plane at the Vágar airport, down the wheeled staircase, and out into the wet chill of the fresh Faroese air. The Russian ambassador to the Faroes stands on the tarmac with a shiny smile and his hand extended. Paralinka scowls at it.

"You shouldn't be here," says Paralinka.

"Welcome!" says the ambassador. "Sorry?"

Stormont is next down the staircase, an enormous and powerfully built man with a complexion untouched by the turbulent landing and a permanent scowl that throws darts of fear into men who otherwise think of themselves as important or unshakeable. His gait emotes doom. The ambassador's smile departs at Stormont's approach. "The bus will just be a moment," says the ambassador.

"This is unacceptable," says Paralinka. "Everything about this is unacceptable. What are you doing?"

The ambassador has his phone out, texting his assistant to hide the Russian-Faroese Accordion Appreciation Society Welcome Ensemble as quickly as possible. "I am checking with my assistant to ensure the facility is ready for your men," says the ambassador.

"Put your phone away," says Paralinka. "And don't mention any of this to anyone who isn't less than a foot from your mouth. And even then, make sure that person is me."

"Never fear," says the ambassador. "Torshavn is ready for you."

"All the supplies?"

"Yes, sir. Everything as you requested."

The plane is unloaded on the tarmac before the bus arrives. Russian technical specialists huddle in small clusters, each carrying one Kevlar duffel and one backpack of equipment. They've been informed that clothes, toiletries, all personal necessities will be provided at the unrevealed destination and to leave all identifying documents and materials at home. This last instruction leaves the techs particularly nervous about the conclusion of this expedition.

The bus finally pulls up, a large blue coach with no markings on the sides. The techs load up, followed by a stewing Paralinka. Stormont is last aboard, but before he climbs the steps, he rests a hand on the ambassador's right shoulder. "If news of our arrival is made known to anyone, you will be recalled to Moscow to attend your mother's funeral," he tells the ambassador.

"My mother is dead?" Stormont looks at him. "Oh," says the ambassador and shakes his head as if to clear the cobwebs. "I see. Of course."

He nods and the bus pulls away, leaving the ambassador standing next to the diesel golf cart he'd driven to meet the plane. A member of the ground crew pulls the staircase away from the plane, and the hatch closes above. The plane starts back towards the single runway, and within five minutes it's airborne, tottering in the swirling gales of Faroe on its return trip to Moscow.

The blue bus, meanwhile, has been waved through a diplomatic hole in the fence on the west side of the airport and is already hugging the curves that wind through the island contours. The view from the bus is a dramatic moonscape carpeted in thick green grass and moss from edge to edge. Infinite, gray water surrounds it. Smatterings of homes, black with bright red paint around the frame, turf roofs or sloped steel. Dots of white and beige on either side of the road clarify into sheep or rocks as the bus flies towards them. The techs look out the window, astonished at the landscape flying by, and restrain gasps as the bus passes a raised gate and blinking lights and signs of every shape and descends into a tunnel that runs beneath the water on its way towards the capital city of Tòrshavn. A tunnel that seems to have no conclusion. The light disappears behind them and doesn't reappear ahead for kilometer after kilometer. At last the bus emerges from darkness into a world surrounded by a wall of black rock on one side and forbidding water on the other. No one says a word through the entire bus ride.

After 45 minutes, they arrive at a three-story, unpainted concrete building. The bus turns into a parking lot, and pulls around to the back of the building, obscured from the road. The techs disembark and file into the building's lobby. Stormont is last off the bus. He stands on the top step and gestures for the driver to turn off the engine. The driver, an older man with a bit of blonde still peeking through his white hair looks at Stormont, puzzled. "Come," says Stormont, and gestures for the driver to follow.

"No, sir," says the driver. "I have to head back to the depot."

"No," says Stormont. "You come. Just for a minute. We'll pay. Come."

The driver picks up his radio, but Stormont gestures with a menacing index finger. "No," he says. "Come, immediately."

The driver sets the radio back on its cradle and follows Stormont down the bus steps, looks around nervously, and follows him into the concrete building.

Although unfinished on the outside, the interior is clean and ready to go. The techs are already picking up folding tables from a pile in the center of the space and setting them up next to outlets and ports around the edges of the large ground floor space and next to pillars equipped with electricity and networking. No partition walls divide the large open space, so Paralinka is able to watch with arms folded as duffels are emptied onto the tables and equipment is stacked, arranged, connected with quiet deftness. A pallet of monitors is wheeled to the center of the room, and the techs get busy unpacking and arranging workstations.

The bus driver watches the silent Russians set up camp for

a minute before Stormont gestures for the older man to follow up the staircase. The driver ascends two flights of stairs side by side with the large man. The third floor of the building is unlit. A window at each end of a long hallway illuminates the edges with a sickly glow, but the center is one long, dark shadow. Stormont escorts the driver down the center of the hallway, stops and opens a gray, metal door and motions the driver to go in. Stormont flicks a light switch as the driver enters, and the driver sees the room has been transformed into a tiny prison apartment. It has a cot, a toilet, a sink, and a small television. A large box of Meals Ready-to-Eat is on the floor at the base of the cot.

"What's this?" says the driver.

Stormont tosses a rubber-banded stack of Euro notes on the cot and holds out his hand. "Phone," he says.

"No," says the driver.

"Three days here," says Stormont. "And then, go home with that." He gestures towards the money.

The driver walks to the cot and flips through the stack of money. He raises his eyebrows. Looks at Stormont. "Three days?"

"Three days. That's all."

"And if I said no?"

"It's not that type of invitation," says Stormont.

The bus driver hands him his phone. Stormont powers it down, slides it in his pocket and leaves the room.

The driver watches the steel door close behind Stormont and hears a deadbolt snap into place. He turns on the television and sits on the cot, pulls a cigarette from the pack in his jacket pocket, and pats his pants pocket, looking for his lighter. He has a brief vision of the lighter, resting on his lunch pail. It is still on the bus, next to his elevated driver's seat. "Oh no," he gasps. "Three days!" He stands and pounds on the door. But no one answers.

Stormont is already back on the ground floor. The work there is moving efficiently. The monitors are nearly all unboxed, and the nests of wires on the tables is growing rapidly. A tech with a thin mustache approaches Paralinka. "Excuse me," he says. "Do you know where the chairs are?"

Paralinka scans the room and points to the room the monitors had been dragged from. "Not there?"

"I hope not," says the tech.

Paralinka walks to the room and stops at the doorframe. Fifty inflated yoga balls, all red, return his stare. He sighs. Then he starts kicking them out of the storage room and into the general work area. The techs halt their assembly and watch the balls bound into the room, deflect those that skip towards the expensive equipment. Once all 50 are in the work area, Paralinka stands at the threshold of the storage area and shout, "Okay! Enough gawking. Operation Double Eagle is back up. Take a ball and get to work." Paralinka walks to Stormont. "Yoga balls. Would it be stepping on your toes if I kill that ambassador myself?" he says.

"These are good for your core," says Stormont. "You should try it."

"What's that noise?" says Paralinka. A high pitched whine fills his ears from every direction.

Stormont squints. He can't place it. Then Stormont notices one of the techs wobbling on his yoga ball. They're deflating," he says. "All of them." The tech spills off of his ball in slapstick fashion and lying on his back, rolls over to study the offending ball. It continues to shrink. The tech's head wobbles and falls back against the concrete floor. The same sequence repeats itself around the room. The programmers and hackers are collapsing like dominos as Paralinka and Stormont watch. Even the balls no one is sitting on are deflating around the room.

Without notice, Paralinka drops to one knee, braces his hands on the floor. He looks up at Stormont, astonished. "Gas," he says. "...balls."

Stormont nearly changes facial expression. Conditioned for action at all times, he vaults into a sprint towards the entrance they'd arrived in but only makes it four steps before he slides onto his belly and skids to a stop with his arms sprawled above his head and his left leg pinned awkwardly beneath his body.

For the next three minutes, the only sound in the room is a soft hiss. 52 bodies litter the room like an upended box of dolls. All motionless.

The door to the parking lot swings open and three men enter wearing black unitards and lime green gas masks and carrying semi-automatic rifles with silenced muzzles. They pull the door shut behind them and fan through the room. None of the Russians so much as twitches. While two of the new arrivals stand in the center of the room panning their weapons back and forth, the third runs a survey of the closets and smaller rooms off the periphery of the main room. No one there. He makes a circular motion to the other two men around his wrist and then jogs up the stairs. The other two men open a nylon bag of zip ties and begin binding the wrists and ankles of the unconscious Russians. They start with the largest man, Stormont, and work their way through the room. When they're done, they prop open the door to the building and take their masks off.

The third man appears at the base of the stairs. His weapon is casually slung by its strap around one shoulder and he guides the bus driver through the labyrinth of unconscious, bound men and out towards his bus.

The man in the black unitard hits the latch that causes the bus door to swing open. "Now," he says to the bus driver. "Not a word for two days. Yes? Not even your wife."

"Yes," says the driver. "Absolutely nobody."

"You stay quiet, another 10,000 euros in your pocket. Yes?"

The bus driver smiles and lifts his cap. He has €5,000 in his pocket already. This is a good day. "You have my address?" he says.

"Yes I do," says the man in the unitard. "And I will visit you whether you speak or not. Understand?"

The bus driver continues to smile and nods. "These bastards were kidnapping me for three days anyways. Excuse me. I need a smoke."

The man in the unitard nods. The bus driver clambers up the bus stairs and lights a cigarette, closes the door to the bus and gives the man in black a little wave, but the man has already turned his back and is re-entering the concrete building.

Monday, November 2
8:36 a.m. E.T.

"Is she awake yet?"

"Yup."

"Any better?"

"Marginally."

"How marginally?"

"Less than a percent better."

"Thin margin."

"Yup."

"Is the smile... settled down at all?"

"Nope. Still full blown."

"What's the neurologist say?"

"Says he's not sure. But. Thinks this will be over by 10 p.m."

"Tonight?"

"Tomorrow. But."

"No promises."

"Exactly."

"We're sunk."

"I don't know. She's done some dynamite radio interviews."

"We've canceled every public event for the last 24 hours and the next 24 hours. The media's all over this. They want to know if she's even alive."

"So we're getting coverage."

"Yeahhhhhh."

"Attention is something she was lacking."

"Uh-huh. Look. This whole line of response to the quarantine needs something different. We've got to tell them something more than 'The candidate is turning to the good people of radio and podcasts to tell her story.'"

"She's the Voice of the People."

"Yeah. People aren't buying that. There's a lot of nasty speculation that makes more sense than the story we're slinging."

"Like what?"

"Like she got into a playful food fight with staffers, but things got ugly and she caught a nasty slash from a fish stick and now it's infected."

"What?"

"And I heard another that she passed out on an escalator and her nose got caught in the machinery and was torn off and had to be reattached."

"Seriously."

"That's what The Splinter is 'insinuating'."

"I hate the internet! So much."

"We have to deal with this differently."

"What do you suggest?"

"She needs to come out of this heroic. It needs to be big. We need a rumor so unlikely, so preposterous, that you both can't believe it and kind of have to believe it at the same time. Because who would bother inventing something this bizarre about themselves? We need to out-crazy all this crazy."

"Create something wacky to hide something mundane and relatively harmless. But embarrassing."

"Because it is embarrassing. That she's bad at smiling."

"And wanted to get better at it."

"So the media hear hoof beats. We'll scream zebras."

"Zombie zebras."
"Exactly."
"What are you thinking? Tangibly."
"Assassination attempt."
"What?"
"Yeah."
"We can't."
"Yes we can."
"We can't manufacture an assassination attempt."
"We won't. We'll manufacture rumors of an assassination attempt."
"No."
"Why can't we?"
"Because the Secret Service won't let us."
"They can't stop us."
"They'll deny it."
"Secret service policy is to never acknowledge thwarted assassination attempts. They downplay foiled plots to limit copycats. And to avoid revealing security methods. All that. They only acknowledge the loons that make it into the White House daisies because there are witnesses all over the place."
"Really?"
"So long as the attempt is thwarted they don't acknowledge its existence. They won't. Unless real damage is inflicted."
"But if we don't produce her after the news is leaked..."
"That's where we have to get creative. There has to be a reason, a really good reason, why she can't surface until Tuesday night."
"It can't look like she's scared."
"Or hiding."
"Right. So why else would she stay under wraps?"

"She lost both legs in an explosion? Being fitted for prosthetics."
"Too much. Too much to explain away."
"One leg?"
"No."
"Two toes."
"Yeah. That's no good. She can be singed but not damaged."
"Poisoned?"
"She kind of was poisoned."
"We can say she nearly died. She had to learn how to walk again over the past 48 hours. She nearly died but now she's fine."
"They'll hear 'She's brain damaged.'"
"The people are accustomed to that."
"Who poisoned her?"
"The Russians?"
"The Chinese?"
"Angry hedge fund managers?"
"I like that."
"Previously unknown gang, Defenders of the 1%."
"But..."
"What?"
"It still makes her look weak. Like when Bush puked on the Japanese Prime Minister's crotch. Americans don't like a sickly president."
"Or a puker."
"No."
"Hm."
"More heroic."
"Maybe she took a bullet intended for a family member."

"That's not bad. In the shoulder. Flesh wound. Bruce Willis-style."

"But she keeps it under wraps. Doesn't want that to be the headline. She doesn't want a fuss."

"But there would have to be official reports. Something like that. Because it would be successful. Not lethal, but still wounded."

"Damn."

"It doesn't have to hold up for very long, though. We leak everything, but publicly deny everything. It only has to appear true for 48 hours."

"But it can't be her."

"Maybe her husband caught one. She's by his bedside. Won't leave until he regains consciousness."

"That's not bad. Selfless. A devoted wife. Appeal to the traditionalists. And spin it the other way: a servant leader."

"And then she can still emerge unscathed. Nothing to explain."

"Because it was only a rumor to begin with. And we publicly denied it all along."

"And he'll be by her side at the acceptance rally. Will he wear a sling?"

"Oh he should definitely wear a sling."

"But will he?"

"Have you met the guy? He'll wear a cactus in his undies if she tells him to."

"We'll have to burn every journalist we know."

"It's a Hail Mary. We don't have anything left."

"And that smile."

They shudder in unison.

"All right then. Brass Tacks. Let's go."

Monday, November 2
8:00 a.m. C.T. / 9:00 a.m. E.T.

The woman known as Moshi Nakamoto sits across from Jean Crest in the Best Western suite she'd reserved for the occasion over a month ago.

"You're ready for this?" she asks Jean.

"Oh sure," she says. "Yes."

"How much prison time do you want for him?"

"I get to choose?"

"Pretty much."

"Two weeks should do. Tit for tat."

"That's it?"

"Enough time for me to move out. Let him stew."

"Okay. Two weeks."

"And you'll pay for the divorce."

"All set. Paperwork's ready. Undated. In the satchel with the money. We appreciate everything you've done. What you've suffered."

"Small price to pay."

"Most would disagree."

Jean looks at the dark leather valise on the floor. "Two million?"

Moshi nods. "As agreed."

Jean nods. "You snared my ballot?"

"Plans changed on that count," says Moshi. "Complication. He dropped it in a blue box, rather than out the front door of your house. But the D.A. says they can pull it this afternoon at the County Office before it gets counted. Special powers. Little tiny loophole for voters under duress."

"Okay," Jean says. "Let's go."

"Press will be at the police station."

"Grace is driving me in?"

"Yeah. I can't be seen there. Grace is in the lobby."

"Okay."

Moshi hands her a blue blanket. "Wrap this over your shoulders." Jean does so and starts to primp in the mirror. "Don't fuss," says Moshi. "It's better rumpled."

Jean nods and takes a long, deep breath, holds it, and exhales out her nose. "Do I look victimish enough?" she says. Her face is pale and sad. The corduroy stripes across her cheeks are striking. Deep and pink. She's still pretty, in a mussed way.

"The perfect victim," says Moshi.

"Thank you."

"You know the lines."

"I've been practicing for two weeks."

"One last time," says Moshi. "Mrs. Crest! Mrs. Crest! Why'd he do it?"

"My husband, Gary, is a fanatical supporter of the President. He drugged me. Chained me in the basement. Stole my vote. Mailed it in."

"Did he act alone?"

"He told me... he said he was part of a Facebook Group. Something. League of Traditional Husbands. Some sort of cult for the President. There may be thousands of women like me. Chained in basements. Right now. Someone needs to do something. They need help. I got lucky. A friend found me when they did."

"Mrs. Crest! Do you blame the President for this?"

"I do. Of course I do! The way he talks! The screaming!

The blaming! He's a rabble-rouser, not a president. My husband never would have done something like this. Never. If not for this President. His lies. The way he tramples people. Like he owns the world. Like a dictator! Of course! Something like this was bound to happen. And it did. It happened to me."
"So are you going to vote tomorrow?"
"Oh you can bet your cookies I will. Bet. Your. Cookies. It's my right as an American. As a Midwestern Wife. My obligation. They tried to steal it from me. The D.A. says they can pull the absentee vote my husband cast for me. Illegally."
"So who will you vote for?"
"Not that it's any of your business. But I've had time to think. A lot of time. (Then I wait for a laugh.) Tomorrow, I vote for Nakamoto. An end to this system. This hatred. The two party system is broken. It's time we were good to each other. To unite. It's Nakamoto for me. Nakamoto on Tuesday. Nakamoto every day. For America." Her voice cracks on the "-ca". Moshi nods. She smiles.
"You have been practicing."
"I was hoping there might be a bonus."
Moshi cocks her head, admiring the scale of her greed. People are as predictable as animals. Jean's perfect for the job. How Yoshi found her and the dozen others, Moshi has no idea. But this one's perfect; Yoshi is right. Moshi nods. "If Nakamoto wins, then. If Nakamoto wins, expect a bump." She nods again.
Jean stands. "Let's go," she says. "I'm hungry."

Monday, November 2
9:30 a.m. E.T.

The three siblings have climbed back into their sleeping bags and the Garfield and Friends VHS tape has nearly reached its end when they hear a shrill beep and the electronic lock of the small, purple time-programmed safe in the kitchen unlock itself.

Rico is sound asleep. Vonkers rolls on her side and looks at Junejune. "9:30," she says. "Want your phone? I can get it."

"Not really," he says. "But I guess I should. I'll get them." He pulls his legs out of the sleeping bag and gets up on his knees. The pajamas are so comfortable. It's going to bum him out to return to his tux. He stands up.

"The NES is hooked up," says Vonkers.

He freezes. "It still works?"

"Yup."

"What games?"

"All the games."

"Punch Out?"

"Yes."

"Mario?"

"Of course. All of them." She points to a narrow closet door to the right of the television set. "Go look."

Junejune walks over and opens the closet. From carpeted floor to ceiling, the narrow closet is stuffed with racks of gray Nintendo game cartridges. He is agog. The collection is alphabetized. Junejune pulls out one cartridge after another, studying each colorful label in disbelief. "Oh!" he keeps saying as he finds a game title he is looking for. "Oh!"

Vonkers laughs watching him.

"It is everything," says Junejune.

"Yes," she says.

Junejune pulls out one cartridge and stares at it confused. "There is no Super Mario Brothers 4 for the NES."

"Not in America," she says.

"What?"

"Japanese bootleg. Underground game developers."

"What? Is it any good?"

"Beats me."

"Where did you even get this? All of these?"

"I have a friend who knows about this stuff."

"Not Kushie-J?"

She smirks. "Definitely not. He's too busy freaking out over mushroom caps."

"Fuck."

"Do you know, around the house, he calls daddy "Daddy" too?

"He does?"

"Yeah. Creeps me out."

"Fuck. That guy. No offense. He's got his nose so far up dad's ass he can smell his shampoo."

"No joke. It's been... tough. After tomorrow... depending on how things go..."

"Yeah?"

"Well it depends, of course."

"Right."

"If daddy loses. Then, I'll probably go on a vacation. Finally. By myself. I need sleep. Do some reevaluating, you know? You know, Gwyneth wrote last week, 'If you really want to find yourself? First you need to take some time to look.'

That really hit me. And the sleep. I just can't..."

"Yeah. Last night was the first night I didn't..."

"Wake up screaming?"

"Yeah."

"Same."

"In quite a while."

Junejune looks down at the cartridge in his hands. The label artwork is clumsy. Mario's hat is all wrong and his face has Asian features. He is holding hands with a cross-eyed ostrich with a smutty smile, wearing a pink dress and a tiara. The ostrich is winking at the Italian plumber.

"I need to play this," says Junejune. "Immediately."

"Yeah? I can get you your phone."

"No. No thanks." He turns to his sister. "Can you lock it up again?"

"Of course. Sure." She slides out of her sleeping bag. "How long? An hour?"

He looks at her, and she can see the sadness in him, so plainly, the desolation that strikes him at the thought of leaving this moment. This place.

"How long can you set it for?" he asks.

"As long as we want?"

"Set it for 36 hours."

"Won't... won't someone worry?"

"No." He sighs. "No, I don't think so."

"The polls will be closed."

"Everywhere but California."

"Oh right."

"So make it 38 hours."

"Really?" she says, giggling. "No way."

"I saw how full the freezer and fridge are. You're ready for anything."

    She shrugs. "Can we really just do this?"

    "What? Are we going to get in trouble?" He laughs.

    "It feels like it," she says.

    "We're adults."

    "Are we?"

    "Yes. So we can act like children if we want to."

    "What will he say?"

    "He'll say we're acting crazy."

    "Hmph."

    "He'll scream and shout. So what's new?"

    "Let him shout."

    "Yeah."

    "Should I wake Rico?"

    "Let him sleep."

    "He'll be pissed if he can't get his phone for 38 hours."

    "It'll be fucking funny."

    "Yes," she agrees. "It will." She goes to the kitchen to reactive the timed safe, and Junejune pulls three gray cartridges from the closet. He crouches before the Nintendo and pushes the bootleg Super Mario down into the slot. He unwinds the cords wrapped around two game controllers and plugs them into the console.

    When Vonkers gets back to the living room he hands her one of the controllers. "It's two player," he says.

    "Thanks," she says.

    "But I'm player 1," he says. "All-time player 1. I call it."

    "That's fine." She sits down. They both focus on the screen and the endless morning continues as unexpectedly as it began.

Monday, November 2
7:23 a.m. P.T. / 10:23 a.m. E.T.

The staffers at the Anyone But Him office in Seattle are melted in their chairs. Exhausted, depressed, massaging their temples and rumpling hair. Others clean their glasses absentmindedly as they gaze into the past. Remembering happier times. Moments of hope. They are all in their early-to-mid-twenties but wear the collective mien of a grizzled cadre of elderly accountants on the cusp of dying at their desks in the employ of a company that has never shown them any affection, but still they stayed to the end.

They are not jaded. They are just so tired. So very tired. Forlorn. They have spent six months trying to slay a dragon who turned out to be a hydra. Everything they tried appeared to work. Seemed to work so well. And then inevitably dissolved.

A man of forty appears in their midst, blue button-down shirt, open at the neck, sleeves rolled halfway up the forearm, thinning sandy hair.

"Hey guys," he says. "Hey. Heads up." He claps his hands twice and laughs for no reason they can discern.

They stare at him through unfocused eyes. They hate him. They don't have a reason to hate him. When they try to understand the revulsion he induces in them, they can only think of reasons to like him, this well-intentioned, cheerful, goodhearted, selfless, blameless, marvelous, likeable, sincere son of a bitch.

They hate him so much. They would hate anyone who tried to talk to them this morning, and he is talking. So they hate him.

His smile is real. He never stops smiling, the smiling bastard. "Hey," he says, smiling, while they hate him. "It's the homestretch. We're tired. You're tired. I'm tired." He doesn't look tired. He looks like he has never known tired. He has only ever read about tired. He saw a Netflix documentary called Tired one time and thinks he knows tired now. He dated a girl once who was half-tired, and now he thinks he's full-tired himself. He spent a semester abroad in Tireland and won't stop speaking with a Tired accent. But he isn't tired. You can tell, because he keeps talking. "But we're nearly there. We've nearly done it!"

God, they hate him.

"Excuse me," says Priyasha, oh, there goes Priyasha, she always knows what to say. Thank God for Priyasha. "Mister Lanket."

"Please, Priyasha. Call me Alex. How many times do I have to—"

"No, sorry, Alex—"

"Mister Lanket was my history teacher, who married my mother after a parent-teacher mee—"

"No, yes. Sorry, Alex. Please. Don't. Alex. It's just, if we seem a little down, it's just because we're not really convinced that we've really done anything. Is all."

"Well that's no way to feel! Just look around!"

"Yes, sir, Alex. Sir. The root of the problem. All the looking around. We've lost. We're going to lose. I know that goes against your Principles of Forward Focus, but... it's time to face facts."

Alex smiles at Priyasha and shoots her with an invisible benevolence laser. "Let's dialogue," says Alex.

Priyasha's head rocks back on her neck, just a little, like a gnat has flown past the tip of her nose. "Okay," Priyasha whispers. "Okay," she says, louder. "We arrived here together to prevent the re-election of the President. Anyone but him. We're all over the place in here, politically." Priyasha gestures around the room, "Terry's a Democrat, Mina's a libertarian, Jess is an anarchafeminist, Tristan's politically agnostic... we don't agree on much of anything. Except that he must be stopped. But now the polls are kinda showing that nobody's going to hit the number for the electoral college."

"That's right!" says Alex. "We are part of the movement. We destroyed the President's electoral majority. You did that. All of you. All of us."

"Right, right," says Priyasha. "But now, it's divided four ways, so now the House is going to pick the President."

"That's right!"

"Yeah, that's not good, though."

"No. It's excellent."

"No it isn't."

"It's at least very good. Wouldn't you say?"

"No. No it isn't."

"But it is."

"You're wrong, Alex." Priyasha throws both arms up in the air.

Alex continues to nod sagely. "Hey," he says softly. "I'm here, Priyasha. Communicate with me. We're storytellers. Tell me a story."

"Okay," says Priyasha. "A story. A tale. I got one. There once was an idiot from Portland, Maine. He had tooooo much money when he was born–"

Alex stops nodding and bites his lip. "Now–"

"So he decided: I'm going to fix the world with my money! He took a pile of filthy lucre from his wholly unearned trust fund, whose source, I might mention was—"

"You know, some stories—" Alex holds up a hand.

"...a lead mining operation that leaves in its wake, even today, three uncleanable waste sites so polluted that the only halfway viable Superfund solution on the table involves airlifting via zeppelin fleet a portion of Hancock County, Maine and dropping it on Quebec. But I digress. That young idiot shuffled a chunk of cash into his own tax-exempt, non-profit Political Action Committee and recruited from the ranks of America's young idealists a cadre of talented, earnest people willing to pour their very souls into his pet effort in exchange for housing and cold brew coffee and protein bars. People so young and earnest, that they never stop to think about what it means to only fight against something, but never for anything, all the while concealing his congenital brainlessness behind a curtain of dynamic hand motions, personality mirroring, buzzwords, and cocaine fueled—"

"—and they all lived happily ever after great story!" Alex shouts and punctuates his own ending with frantic hand claps. "That was super. Just extraordinary storytelling. Super job. I have heard you. But what we're hoping to excavate—"

"Not done!" says Priyasha.

"Done," says Alex, his tone loses its fun-love and his voice drops an octave. He throws a Muay Thai jab into the air for emphasis. "Done. Sit down, please, Priyasha."

"I won't," says Priyasha.

"Listen," says Alex, calm again. Happy again. "This vote in the House. I promise you. It will be fine."

"No. It won't be fine, because it isn't a regular vote. Each state gets one vote. California will have the same-sized say as Wyoming. Or North Dakota. Alaska has one congressman. New York has 26. But for this vote, they'll stand as equals. 1 to 1."

Alex nods. "I know," he says. "Of course. Yes yes. I know I know I know." He scans the room. "Cool cool cool." He smiles.

Priyasha is agog. "Then why are you still smiling?"

"Because you're forgetting one thing."

"What?"

"The House only gets to vote on the top three winners in the electoral college."

"But..." Priyasha wobbles on her heels.

"And if we keep going, if we keep working, if Nakamoto keeps gobbling his base..."

"You think he'll finish fourth?" asks Priyasha.

"I do," says Alex.

"Oh," says Priyasha.

"Oh," says Terry, the Democrat.

"Oh," says Mina, the libertarian.

"Oh," says Jess, the anarchafeminist.

Tristan, the political agnostic, whistles softly.

"Oh," the room says softly. It builds to a rhythmic "Oh. Oh. Oh. Oh."

"Oh!" the chant grows louder. They stamp their feet and chant: "Oh! Oh! Oh! Oh! Oh! Oh! Oh! Oh!" Alex jumps onto a desk and swings his arms like an orchestra conductor, and the "Oh"s ring from whiteboard wall to whiteboard wall and the plate glass windows shiver in their frames, and outside the window the first sunbeam to slip past Seattle's cloud army in two weeks slices through the gloom and sprays the room in golden showers of sunlight, washing their cheering faces with a resplendent glow. They abandon their laptops and cellphones to form a swaying circle that consumes them in a hopeful, unchoreographed dance of optimism that takes possession of their weary hearts and stagnant limbs and transforms them into ecstatic, acrobatic puppets of dance, cavorting and roiling with movements that are not of their own will, and yet none will ever forget.

Because Dani, the intern from the University of the Pacific, is standing off to the side recording the entire thing on xer cellphone.

Monday, November 2
10:34 a.m. E.T.

The Vice President never makes eye contact with Karen, the President's secretary. Karen has noticed but, ever the tactful professional, she's never made mention of it. Still, it is odd. She's never fully sure he's speaking to her. She's held her job for thirty years, as much an institution in The Office as the walls around her, but she's never met a man who treated her this way.

"Is he in?" says the Vice President.

She pauses. "Who, Mister Vice President?" she asks.

"The President."

"Yes," she says. The Vice President reaches for the doorknob to the Oval. "But–" she says, and stops, deliberately enticing.

The Vice President stops with his hand on the knob, turns and looks two feet over her head. "What?" he says.

Karen purses her lips and plays with the top button of her blouse, fidgeting between thumbs and index fingers playfully. She slips it from its buttonhole. "Oops," she says. Her fingers fiddle with the next button down, a translucent ivory disc. It, too, slips from its hole, and the upper rim of her cleavage pops into the room as the blouse grows slack beneath its collar. "Oh my," she says. "Mister Vice President."

"What are you doing?" says the Vice President.

"Why? Say, can't you see?" says Karen. "Mister Vice President?"

"I don't see anything," he says, staring pointedly, another foot further above her head, seeming to study the seam where

228

wall meets ceiling.

"Well that's too bad," she says.

"Why?"

"Well I was thinking, maybe you and me, you and I, we could go to lunch some time, Mister Vice President."

"I'm afraid I–"

She is playing with the third button now. The office is very much hers alone. A foyer to the Oval she shares with no one.

"I love lunch," she coos. "We could eat here. Private. We can get delivery from," she pauses, the button half-in, half-out of the shirt's hole. "Anywhere," she whispers huskily.

The Vice President's gulp is audible.

"I've always admired your hair," she says. "It's so smooth. Like combed whipped cream."

"Thank you," he says. The Vice President's face is growing blotchy, red patches bloom on his neck and cheeks like spilled ketchup on a white floor. "I must go," he says.

"Think about it," she breathes.

The door closes behind the Vice President, and she buttons back up. She smiles. What an ass.

Inside the Oval, the Vice President finds the President lying face down on a couch. The presidential shoes and socks are off the presidential feet, settled side-by-side beneath the couch, and a familiar Thai national is grinding her thumbs into the bottom of the presidential soles. The President groans like a monk who's forgotten Latin.

"Mr. President," says the Vice President.

The President ignores him. The Thai woman ignores him with her eyes, but stabs a black-gloved index finger to her lips.

"Mr. President, I would never intrude normally–"

The woman shushes him.

The President rocks his head five degrees and side-eyes the Vice President. He doesn't say anything, just glares at him.

The Vice President, accustomed to this posture, continues, "Something's up in Russia."

"What?" mumbles the President. Three-quarters of his lips are pinned against the massage table's face-rest.

"We don't know."

"Well find out, and then bug me."

"Well, so, the thing is, we do know... well, we know that we don't know anything. At all."

"Are you drunk again?"

"No. Not this time, Mister President." One time, three years previous, the Vice President had a misunderstanding at a golf club involving his first (documented) encounter with a fuzzy navel, which he had assumed must be a virgin beverage, and the President is disinclined to allow anyone to forget the incident, sometimes referring to him as "Drunky O'Hoosier" or "Larry Beered".

The President grunts.

"I'm not," says the Vice President. "The thing is, we're not getting any intel from Russia. Nothing at all. Public lines. Secure lines. Nothing. State website is down. Satellites are down overhead. Sir, the fax is down. We can't reach our own embassies. The phones are dead. The microburst backup gets nothing but silence. We can't reach our spies. Sir, Mister President, the International Space Station is down. The border lines are down. The radar's coming back weird. We have lost all contact, all pictures, all everything of Russia."

The President moans and sits up. He waves the Thai woman away from his feet. "Mrs. Soang. I apologize. Could you please come back in an hour?"

"No," she says.

"Tomorrow then? Please?"

She stands and glares at the Vice President. "I'm busy tomorrow," she says to the President, while holding her gaze on the Vice President.

"Can you find an hour?" pleads the President.

"No!" she shouts, as she throws bottles of lotions and oils into the handwoven basket she carries to clients' homes. "Tomorrow I am busy! Tomorrow! I rub Mister Nakamoto!" She hoists the basket over her shoulder and charges out of the room. She pauses at the door and shouts something in Thai before disappearing.

The President glowers at the Vice President. "I'll call Vlad," he says, after assuring himself that the Vice President is sufficiently uncomfortable.

The President heaves himself off the table, allowing the towel previously covering his posterior to slide to the ground. The Vice President averts his eyes, averts them feverishly, and in the process notices on the massage table there is a vinyl applique of the Presidential Seal where the President's, uh, oh my, private parts had formerly rested. The Commander in Chief, naked as a budgie, picks up the receiver from the red phone on his desk. He waits.

The Vice President has turned his back and is pretending to study the brush strokes of a landscape by Andrew Andrews, feigning engrossment so fully as to raise an index finger and outline the shape of one of the trees in the air before him.

"Nothing," says the President.

"Nothing?"

"No," says the President. He sets the receiver down. "Will you grow up?" says the President.

"I'd never noticed the shadows—"

"Will you turn around? I'm not talking to the back of your snowy head."

"Excuse me?" The Vice President turns around and stares at the President's forehead.

"Haven't you ever been in a locker room?"

"Mr. President, are you saying even the red phone is dead?"

"We're just a couple of guys here."

"Yes, Mr. President."

"It's fine. You can take your pants off too, if you like. Just a couple of guys."

"I don't... I don't wish to remove my pants at the moment, Mister President."

"Right. Yeah. You want to talk about Russia. Yeah, the phone's down. Blah blah blah. Probably the weather." The President bends down and takes his time picking up his towel, yawns and turns it into a bouncing toe touch stretch to provide the Veep a nice full moon. Full and still waxing. The Vice President turns back towards the painting.

The President secures the towel around his pale white belly and shouts "Olly Olly Oxen Free!"

"The NSA doesn't believe it's the weather, sir," the Vice President says, still addressing the painting.

"What does the NSA know? Bunch of dorks."

"Of course, sir. They've made their mistakes. But—"

"Fine, fine. What do you want me to do? Send a drone over Moscow and see what happens? Sounds like fun."

"No, sir. I just felt you ought to know."

"You understand what tomorrow is, right?"

"Of course, Mister President."

"Very busy. Extraordinarily busy."

"Of course."

"Don't you have things to do?"

"Yes, Mister President."

"Get out."

"As you please."

The door closes behind him.

The President is left standing before his desk. "As you please," he mutters. "Who the fuck talks like that?" He uncinches the towel, allowing it to plop to the ground again. He enjoys being nude in the Oval. Sometimes, he lies on the carpet for an hour or so, just thinking. He doesn't even want to do that, today. What he wants is a super nap. The President pulls his official White House robe from the coat rack by the door and cinches it tight.

The day before. Is that too late to change running mates? Everyone will say it's too late. No one's ever done it before. It's crazy.

His pupils dilate.

No one's.

Ever.

Done it before.

It's crazy.

He reaches for his cell phone.

Monday, November 2
9:49 a.m. C.T. / 10:49 a.m. E.T.

Marguerite walks up the steps to a small concrete porch and rings the doorbell. Her maroon puffy coat is zipped up to her chin, but she has decided not to wear a scarf or hat so people can see her entire face. The red, white, and blue clipboard is tucked in her left armpit, her right arm hangs loose, ready to shake hands if the opportunity arises. A handshake is a powerful thing. If you can get to that point, no matter how the conversation goes, you are walking away a winner.

She has been to 22 houses so far this morning, starting with her next door neighbors and working her way down the street and around to the next block. She is ignoring the list they gave her yesterday at headquarters and is trying every, single door. What are they going to do? Fire a volunteer?

After eight seconds, the door opens and a small child appears, or the top half of him anyways, above the white metal of the storm door, still closed between them. He is a very small boy with sulky features, by Marguerite's assessment, and a half-eaten Twix in his hand and a stripe of chocolate trailing from the corner of his mouth to his chin.

"Good morning!" says Marguerite, through the storm door's glass. "Is your Mommy or Daddy home?"

The boy shakes his head and puts a gooey hand against the glass.

"Grandma?" says Marguerite. "Or grandpa?"

The boy shakes his head. He presses his nose against the glass and looks up at her. His focus is on the button on her down jacket. He points at it.

"Do you like my button?" she says. "Would you like one?" She reaches into her pocket and pulls out an identical pin.

"No," the boy says. He presses his lips against the glass, goggles his eyes, and makes a carpish sucking motion against the glass.

"Brayden?" a deep voice bellows from inside the house. "Brayden, what the hell are you doing?"

The door behind the boy swings open wider and a man appears, towering behind the boy. They have the same nose. The same ears. The same eyes. This enormous man was once this small boy, Marguerite has no doubt about it.

"Helloooo!" says Marguerite, waving her right hand at the man. The small boy tries to keep his lips on the glass, even as he tips his head back and rolls his eyes up to look at his progenitor. The man places his hand on the boy's head, palms it like a softball, and gently pries the tiny head away from the glass. The boy's lips make a soft popping noise as they detach from the storm door. The man guides the boy by the head around the edge of the door and out of sight with a motion that both father and son have clearly practiced.

"Hi," says the man. "We don't want any. Sorry."

"Oh, I'm not selling anything."

"Yes, you are," he says pointing to the pin on her jacket. "Sorry. Not interested."

"I'm a registered nurse," she says, holding up her hand. "I'm not some politician. I'd just like to talk about..."

"You're a nurse?"

"Yes I am."

The large man pushes up the sleeve of his thick, black sweatshirt and points his elbow towards Marguerite. The skin on his elbow is rashy and has three white pustules in the center of the rash. Nasty red stripes, fingernail width, trail up the man's forearm. "What's this?" says the man.

"Oh," Marguerite doesn't recoil from the elbow, held at her eye level through the glass door. "I'm not really qualified to diagnose that, I'm more of a..."

"But what is it?"

She studies the elbow, in spite of herself.

"You've been scratching it," she says.

"Yup."

"You shouldn't scratch it."

"Okay."

"How long has it been like that?"

"Two days."

"Did you do anything? Did you cut it on something or spill something on it?"

"Nope."

"Have you recently switched soaps or lotions?"

"I don't use lotion."

"You switch soaps?"

"No."

"Laundry detergent?"

"Nuh uh."

"Did you clean it up with soap and water?"

"Took a shower."

"Well clean it separate, too."

"Okay. Then what?"

"Pour some alcohol on it."

"What kind?"

"Rubbing alcohol. Or hydrogen peroxide."

"Oh. Okay."

"But it could be an allergic reaction."

"I'm not allergic to anything."

"Sometimes you can get allergic to things. Develop new allergies."

"No," he says. Shakes his head. "Nuh uh. No."

"Okay," says Marguerite. She raises her eyebrows. "You may want to put some antibiotic ointment on it. That might help."

"Yeah?" says the man. "You got some?"

"Yes," she says. "But I'm not really..." She has a small backpack full of campaign materials and her purse. She unslings it and roots around in the bag, before producing a small white tube of generic antibiotic cream. "May I come in?" she says, looking up at the enormous man. "Just for a moment."

He returns her look thoughtfully. "No," he says after a moment. He pops the storm door open enough to stick his hand through, palm up. Marguerite places the ointment and a political pin side-by-side in his large paw.

He frowns at the pin.

Marguerite smiles at him. "Be sure to get out and vote," she says.

"Nah," says the man. "But thanks for the stuff." He closes the door.

Marguerite sighs, descends the steps, and makes her way towards the next house.

Monday, November 2
10:52 a.m. E.T.

The Vice President storms into Karen's foyer again, and this time he's not making eye contact because his head is buried in his cell phone. His brow furrows as he charges past her. He has a desperate look in his eyes. The Vice President yanks the handle of the Oval Office door and finds it locked.

"Buzz me in," he says to her.

"I'm very sorry, sir," says Karen. "I'm afraid it isn't possible."

"Yes it is. Let me in."

"No, sir. I'm not permitted."

"What the hell is this? Do you know what the hell this is supposed to mean?" He holds his phone's screen towards her.

"I couldn't say for sure," says Karen, without looking at the screen. She knows what it says, and she knows precisely what it means.

Five minutes previous, the President had tweeted: "After much consderation, prting ways with Crew Cut Quaker Oat Man. #Yourefired Off the ticket. Replacement announced soon. Stay tuned for exciting news!"

"Am I 'Crew Cut Quaker Oat Guy?'"

"Yes, sir. I believe so."

"He calls me that?"

"Sometimes. Yes."

"Where's your protocol? It's 'Yes, Mister Vice President.'"

She smiles. "I'm not sure it is. Anymore."

"Don't you contradict me. He can't fire me. He literally

cannot, constitutionally. Or kick me off the ticket! The election's tomorrow for Pete's sake! It's not even possible. I'm on all the paperwork. I'm on the ballot!"

"It kind of looks like he did it anyways."

"But he can't!"

"But he did."

"It's. Illegal! It isn't possible!"

"We've certainly heard that before."

"Sweet, merciful Jehoshophat," the Vice President says. He throws a dismissive gesture at her and returns to the Oval Office doors. He grabs the door handles and throws his weight back against them. They don't so much as rattle beneath his effort.

Karen smiles as she slides her hand under her desk and taps the panic button twice.

Two secret service agents tear into the room like a pair of bulldogs, hands on holsters, prepared to kill or die. They pull up short at the sight of the Vice President tugging at the doors to the Oval. They turn to Karen with questioning expressions. She points one index finger towards her ear and makes a circular motion. She points the other index finger at the Vice President. She mouths, "He just got fired," to the men.

One of the men positions himself between Karen and the Vice President. The other takes a step back and places one hand over his ear and speaks softly into the collar of his jacket. He watches intently, clearly listening to instructions while the Vice President alternates between pounding on the door and jerking the door handles.

After a minute of uncertainty, both agents approach the Vice President, hands at their sides.

"Sir," says the taller of the men.

The Vice President turns and stares at the two agents. His doughy face is maroon with exertion. "Unlock this door," he says. "Immediately."

"We need you to come with us, sir."

"That's Mister Vice President to you!"

They look at each other, then back to him.

"We need you to come with us."

"Where?"

"We've been instructed to escort you from the premises."

"What do you mean from the premises?"

"From the grounds, sir. Immediately."

"What are you talking about? I'm the Vice President. Juniper flipping Creesus! You can't just..." He turns and starts pounding on the doors to the Oval Office again. The two agents lock eyes momentarily, and Karen can hear the older of the two sigh in a professional, just barely audible manner.

"Sir?" says the older man. "It's better if we just follow you out."

The Vice President wheels on him. "Better than what?"

"Better than the alternative," he says. His tone is dry and clinical.

"What do you mean, the alternative?"

"We escort you out," says the agent.

"You wouldn't dare. You would not dare."

"As I said, sir. It's better if we just follow you out. No one will even notice us, alongside your usual detail. We'll provide you a five yard cushion if you leave immediately."

The fight dribbles out of the Vice President. Anger gives way to resignation. Resignation rapidly transitions to calculation. Karen watches it happen, watches his facial expression ricochet from emotion to intellect. It happens swiftly but she catches it and marvels at his expedience.

"Very well," he says. He twists his neck once, as if to crack it, but no sound results. He straightens his tie. He pulls his phone and turns on his camera, switches to its front-facing lens and checks his hair. It hasn't budged. He sets his jaw. Squints his eyes, too much at first, then relaxes them. Locks the facial expression in. Pockets the phone. Turns to the older agent. "I want ten yards," he says.

"We'll give you seven," replies the agent. "If you go straight to the South exit. We have a car waiting for you."

"Eight," says the Vice President.

"Seven, sir. And if you deviate in any way from a direct route, I will tackle you." It is clear that the agent has no intention of haggling further.

"Seven, then."

The Vice President marches out of the foyer, followed by the two agents at a distance of precisely seven yards.

When he has left the area, Karen unlocks the Oval Office doors and pokes her head into the room. "The Quaker has left the building," she says quietly.

The President is leaning back in his chair, grinning. It has been a while since she saw that particular smile. "Thank you, Karen," he says.

"My pleasure," she says, and closes the door again. "Twit."

Monday, November 2
11:30 a.m. E.T.

Paralinka's mind awakens before his body. He cannot open his eyes, but he can feel the mattress beneath him. What happened?

What happened?

He remembers arriving on a plane. The bus ride. The green landscape. Everything so green. The sky so gray. The water so blue. There are only three colors here. Then the setup. People flopping over. The pilates balls... deflating. The look on Stormont's face. Oh. The look on that face.

He's dead, Paralinka must be dead. If he's not dead, already, he will be soon.

His eyes flick open, finally. He sees a clean white ceiling. An exposed fluorescent lightbulb blazes down on him. He can't turn his head. His arms won't listen. His legs won't move either. Such a strange feeling. This paralysis. He rolls his eyes, trying to get a glimpse of anything. All he can see is the ceiling and the tip of his own nose. The room is silent.

He focuses on wiggling a toe. Just the big toe on his right foot. After a minute, at last, he convinces it to twitch.

Thank god, he thinks. It had not taken him long to believe it might be permanent, but if he can get a toe to move, his furthest extremity, he's confident the rest will follow as that gas, whatever it was, gradually wears off.

It takes an hour. An hour before he can pull himself up to a seated position. His head still spins as he surveys his prison.

He sits on a thin mattress, on a tiny metal bed frame. The room he is in is clean and white. It feels new. In addition to his bed, there is a metal toilet against one wall. A small white plastic table and a red plastic chair. On the table: a stack of books. Novels. In Russian. A tin plate containing a few small apples and a thick pastry speckled with raisins. A plastic cup of white yogurt. A bamboo spoon. A tin cup filled with water. A packet containing two aspirin. A sheet of paper.

The walls are cinderblock, painted a glossy white. The door to his cell is white, thick metal, and windowless, with a thin slot at knee height, secured shut from the outside, clearly intended for the passing of meals and other material.

The ceiling is at least twelve feet high. In one corner, a black glass dome stares at him.

Paralinka studies his clothes. He has been clothed in a thin, white cotton long-sleeved shirt and white cotton pants without pockets. The clothes he was wearing before are nowhere to be seen.

He lowers his legs over the edge of the small bed, rests his hands against the plastic table and tries to stand. Too wobbly, too weak. He can't lift his butt from the mattress more than a few inches before he drops back down. Every inch of him feels exhausted. He has never felt so worn.

How long has he been out?

With no clock, no watch, no phone, no window, he has no sense of how much time has passed. It could be five minutes. It might have been five days.

He abandons his attempts to stand and flops forward so his arms rest on the table. His fingers fumble with the paper for a minute before he is able to grip it. He lies back on the bed and reads what he discovers is a typewritten letter.

"Welcome Viktor Paralinka!

Please pardon the involuntary nature of your stay. We hope to provide you with as safe, comfortable, and brief an experience as possible, given the circumstances. If you desire, you will be returned home in three days.

The rules of your captivity are simple and few, and though we are sorry to impose them, please know that if you are cooperative your stay will be as pleasant as we can make it.

If you violate the rules, we will be forced to flood your guest suite with the same gas that brought you here. We regret the necessity of this initial anesthetization and hope to avoid repeating the experience. We tried it on ourselves, first, and we understand first-hand how unpleasant the after-effects feel.

The Rules
1. *Please do not attempt to escape or communicate with your fellow guests.*
2. *Please do not attempt to disable the camera on the ceiling.*
3. *Please do not make excessive noise.*
4. *Please do not attempt to harm yourself.*
5. *Please do not attempt to make a fire of any sort.*
6. *Please behave yourself in a civilized manner.*

Thank you for observing these guidelines. We hope you enjoy the peace and reflection that solitude can offer, however coerced it may be.

Yours Sincerely,
The Management

P.S. We recommend taking the aspirin as soon as you feel able.

It helps immeasurably."

Paralinka reads the note twice. He crumples it up, and tries to throw it defiantly towards the camera on the ceiling. The attempt is pathetic. The motion of his weakened arm is less that of a grown man and more like a baby throwing a piece of buttered bread from his high chair. The effect is similar, and the wadded paper plops, embarrassingly, two feet from the release point.

He lies back and closes his eyes.

His thoughts are of Mother Russia. And how she will execute him.

Monday, November 2
12 p.m. E.T.

The video is released everywhere at once. YouTube. Bought the Front Page of Netflix and Hulu. All the social networks. Votenakamoto.com. 4K live feed to every network, all prepped and primed to interrupt programming for the unveiling. Soap operas are interrupted. Game shows. Everything. The day before an election, no one has demanded the country's attention so thoroughly as Satoshi Nakamoto's machine has accomplished in this buildup. The organization has mastered spectacle as no one else before them.

Satoshi's video was filmed the day before in a specially outfitted studio room.

The backdrop is meant to be distinguished. Impressive, but relatable. Satoshi even filled a bookshelf, carefully selected each title. Made sure the spines read the same direction and everything.

The video has no title card. It fades up from black to a shot of Satoshi standing in front of a desk. The caption at the bottom of the screen reads "Satoshi Nakamoto: Presidential Candidate".

She smiles genially into the camera.

"Hello," she says. Satoshi speaks from memory, but in a manner that is clear and candid. As if she is speaking to each viewer individually. As a friend.

"I'm Satoshi Nakamoto. It's a pleasure to finally meet you. To really meet you. I know I've played up the mystery, but I needed to get your attention before I made my pitch to you. In person."

She makes a sweeping gesture along the side of her body. "I know. Perhaps, not who you were expecting. Hi Mom!" She laughs. It's a winning laugh. Then she grows serious again. "I'm a private person. At my day job (I teach math) I'm Sarah Harvest. I only legally changed my name to Satoshi Nakamoto on the sly a few years ago. So that I could ensure your vote for me really is a vote for me. I live a normal life within, until recently, relatively modest means. I have never been rich. I've only had this weird... possibility of wealth, because I never touched the BitCoin genesis block. If you don't know, that just means, I never spent the very first pieces of BitCoin. They're worth a lot of money now. I knew that if I cashed them in, it wouldn't be long before everyone would discover me.

I am not a politician. I never wanted to be one, and I don't think I'm one now. But I do want to be your president. It took me a long time to figure out how I could do that without first becoming a politician. I'm awkward at parties. I'm no good at small talk with strangers. I'm not politically connected. How could I still succeed? By now, you've seen some of what it took. I had a lot of help, and I want to say thank you to the wonderful workers who brought us to this point.

But, see? I ramble. I'll cut to the chase.

Who am I? What will I do if you vote for me?"

She laughs. It's charming. It's a deeply charming laugh.

"I will release that movie. It's true. I'll probably release it anyways, to be totally honest. It's just too good.

I also promise to use the power of the Office of the President to make your life better. Your life. I will end armed conflict between our country and the world. On inauguration day, I can and will. Will we still monitor the world for threats and intervene when necessary? 100%. Of course. Will our allies in the world, the friends of democracy, be able to rely on us? Absolutely.

How can I promise this? If you're like me, you're tired of politicians making promises that they never keep.

So here's an example of what I will do for you. Even as you watch this, I'm doing it. And I'm not even President yet. I invested some of my own money in a private operation to stop Russia from interfering in tomorrow's election. That's something no government has managed in the past five years. And I did it without spending a single government dime.

Right now, Russia is unplugged. Offline. It has no connection to the outside world. No internet. No phone lines beyond its borders. No satellite connections. I have hit the Mute button on Russia.

In an act of desperation, the Russians sent a crack team of hackers to the Faroe Islands, a tiny isolated territory in the Atlantic, in a last ditch attempt to infiltrate and corrupt our election. That nest of spies has been subdued. And they will face justice.

After the election.

When you think of me, when you choose to vote for me, I hope you'll remember deeds such as this, not as stunts, but as proof that I know how to solve problems. Really solve them. I know how to get things done. And that's something we haven't had in Washington D.C. in a very long time.

Even more important, I pledge this to you: I will take money out of politics. You may be thinking, money's the only way you got here. And that's right. That's both the problem and the solution. This conversation we're having? We're only having it because I spent over ten billion dollars.

There are too many billionaires who can buy their way into

office. And too many billion dollar companies control the world you live in.

As a result, only a billion dollars can land someone in the White House. That's what it costs. Or more, in my case. With your help. And that means by the time anyone gets there, they owe favors to a lot of people. Hundreds of corporations. And in some cases, to a number of foreign governments.

So how will I stop this corruption?

As we've seen over the past four years, an Executive Order is a powerful tool. One person can get quite a lot done. But I'll do even more. I will issue five executive orders targeted directly at removing money from politics in America.

I won't bore you with the specifics. But essentially, lobbyists won't be able to leave behind a single paper clip in a D.C. politician's office by the time I'm finished. And all those political ads cluttering up your favorite TV shows, your online videos, your Facebook wall? Those are gone. Especially my ads. You won't miss them. I won't miss them.

People will say I can't do it. That it's a free speech issue. And they are wrong. I can. And I will. If you vote for me tomorrow, I'll do it.

You're thinking, will big money really allow one person to do this? To fix this? Won't congress try to stop you? Aren't they addicted to those lobbyist bucks? Or, even if they don't take money from lobbyists, aren't they frightened of SuperPACs running ads in their districts, asking the congressperson why they hate America?

Or why they want to raise taxes?

The answer is: yes, they'll try.

But that's why I'm launching BitPAC, a non-profit devoted to supporting politicians committed to removing money from politics. I am transferring $5 billion of my personal funds into that political actional committee..."

Nakamoto pauses mid-sentence and produces a large, glowing red button in her right hand. She presses the button and it makes a satisfying "ding!" noise.

"Now," she says. "We'll be fighting money with money. Don't worry. I see the irony. I hate to say it's the only way. But it is. If you're a congressperson or a senator or a state legislator or a governor and you're looking for a way out of this greed-fueled carnival, please visit 1bitpac.com to learn more. 1Bit-PAC will offer you direct financial support and indirect political support to counteract and silence the money of the elite. If you're a politician who isn't willing to change the system? If you're looking to keep the status quo? Well. Get ready to play. I just bet $5 billion that you're going down.

Finally, you may be wondering, what will I do without a Vice Presidential candidate? The answer, of course, is that I will follow the Constitution. The senate will select my Vice President from the top two finishers in the general election. I really don't mind who they choose, so long as they pick a candidate committed to removing money from politics. If they do that, we'll get along fine. If they don't, then I'll put them in a political kennel.

I know that's just a start. Our first real introduction. But I believe we're going to get to know each other very well in the next four years. Think of this as my last campaign commercial. Thank you for taking the time to listen to me. Tomorrow, when you cast your vote, please vote for me: Satoshi Nakamoto."

Monday, November 2
12:43 p.m. E.T.

The President lets his head fall back against the Commander in Chief throw pillow. His face is sculpted into a portrait of despondence. He just fired the Vice President the day before the election and only wrestled 45 minutes of news coverage away from this... woman? She's unbelievable. Maybe an 8 for the face? 7 for the bod? Kinda multiracial, kind of exotic beauty. Was she, like, Indian? Like an actual Pocahontas? Or mixed? One of those ones you can't tell. Maybe 45 years old? Maybe 30? Well, has to be at least 35? Again, some chicks, you can't tell. And talk about media catnip. And the strategy? The unveiling the day before? Theatrical doesn't begin to capture it. The President knows from showmanship, and this is the best he's ever seen.

The President knows wealth, too, and this lady is nothing but liquid. There are plenty of billionaires (he knows most of them) and some will even brag about how poor they are, how they have less than a million in the bank. They own stuff worth a billion at the moment. An estimated billion. But their money isn't actually money, there for the spending. This chick? She made her money making money. Making the idea of money. Unbelievable.

Few things depress the President more than feeling poorer than someone else. Right now, he feels as though he might as well be broke. Again.

Plus, the whole change of Vice President thing hasn't played quite how he expected. He was thinking the speculation would have turned to the replacement, right off the bat.

All the excitement, the questions: who's next? Who will be next? That's how it always worked before. He ran through the news cycle in his imagination even as he'd reached for his phone to fire that vanilla wax doll. He could hear poor little Chuckie Todd having to bite: "Who's the next veep? We've gathered a panel to speculate, blah blah blah."

A feeding frenzy! Who will it be?

Pompeo?

Bill Belichick?

Tom Brady?

Bill O'Reilly?

Sarah Palin?

Rudy G?

Kanye? Wouldn't that kill them, though? Adding a black man to the ballot and daring them, just daring them, to say something mean about him. A Kardashian in the White House? There isn't a spoon big enough to satisfy the way the media would gobble that up. Good luck exercising restraint. Good luck stopping that train.

That was how he thought it would go. Then the bastards flipped it so fast. So damn fast. "What's going on in the White House?"

"Has the President finally lost his mind?

"Breaking the law. The President has lost control and tried to do something it isn't Constitutionally possible to do."

He flips through the channels so quickly his remote blister comes back again. It is all bad coverage. No speculation on a replacement. Just speculation as to whether what he just did was even possible. Not in a good way.

Geeze. He's not a guy to second guess himself. Goes against everything he's ever achieved and how he achieved it. But maybe...

His head plops back again.

Then Nakamoto shows up and mops the floor with him. Slicker than seal snot, this lady. They were already obsessed with her, and that was before they'd even seen her. Or knew she wasn't a guy.

If he hadn't told Karen he wanted Full-Stop Executive Time he knows the room would be full of staffers. The White House lawyers, those guys. What a box full of pains in the ass they are. Karen's probably out there with a crossbow, keeping them from knocking at the door. She's a good egg, Karen.

The President tries to count his blessings, like Gwyneth told him he should do every time he's feeling down (on TV, he doesn't actually know Gwyneth). He hasn't really taken the advice, but now seems as good a time as any.

One. He likes this pillow. This is a perfect pillow.

Two. The kids. He does like the kids. They all pretty much grew up right. Good looking. Smart. Tall. All very tall. Except, of course... his thoughts turn to that chip off the block, floating around. Out there. Somewhere in the wilds of Florida. On the lam. Well, even that's a blessing, really. A little wild, Mexican oat.

Where are the kids? He sits up. Taps at his phone. He's been so caught up in things. Wasn't he supposed to meet them for something today? Or just the rally tomorrow? Were they coming for lunch? Last text was yesterday.

Lunch. He's hungry. He's famished. He's never been so hungry. What does he want? What doesn't he want? He wants everything at once. All of it. The kitchen will be ready for him. Karen will let Chef through. That's the only exception, she knows, for Full-Stop Executive Time. Chef is always welcome.

The President opens his message thread with the kitchen and types: "honey buttr tost" Hits enter. "bigmac, extra ss" (special sauce). Hits enter. "chikn nuggs" Hits enter. "caramel sauce." Hits enter. "curly fries." Hits enter. "chocolate cherry shake" Hits enter. The TV drones on in the background. "fried apples." Hits enter.

He drops his phone to the floor beside him and settles his head back against the pillow again. Oh right. The kids. Where are the kids? The kids will know what to do. He drops his arm over the edge of the sofa and fumbles blindly for his phone. After ten seconds, the fumbling slows to a cartoonish prodding of the carpet. His eyes close. His arm stills. The snoring begins.

After a lull, the side door opens and Chef rolls his silenced dining cart into the Oval Office, only glancing at the President's slumbering form as he wheels his way to the Resolute desk. Chef unloads the gold domed platters and plates onto the desk carefully, noiselessly, and wheels out of the office as quietly and efficiently as he arrived without waking the President.

Monday, November 2
1:51 p.m. E.T.

The lawyers have heard his story, taking notes the entire time. The station manager, too. Then the corporate parent company's lawyers. Then the lawyers hired by those lawyers. Everyone's freaked out for having even heard this story. Like they're afraid of being accused of slander for so much as encountered this guy. Each meeting has been recorded. He has given blood samples. Hair samples. Urine samples for toxicology. He has been through two polygraph tests. A mental health evaluation. Things have moved quickly at the television station.

It has been a long seven hours for Tonio. Probed, prodded, insulted by questions and insinuations, but he's stood tall against the deluge of doubt and answered every challenge as good naturedly and honestly as he can. Even so, there is so much he doesn't know about himself, he worries that he can't give them enough of the substance they need to reassure themselves that he is who he claims to be.

His arrival at the station has been the well-source of hundreds of guarded and vaguely worded phone calls. No government channels have been approached for confirmation, as there is a real fear on the part of those in the television station that if this guy's for real, as crazy as the whole thing appears, he will be disappeared the moment his presence is revealed. He'll be locked away or worse, and the most incredible story of their lives will be flushed away.

Also, they don't want to be sued into oblivion by the President.

The place is filled with panic. Excitement. Dread. Skepticism. And at the center of it all is a young man of nineteen, now seated alone in a small conference room, devouring his third breakfast burrito and drinking orange juice from an enormous plastic WORN TV coffee mug.

He has already seen more people today than he has met the entire course of his life combined. It is something of a relief to be alone for the moment. But also frightening. Surely the next person through the door will be an armed guard to take him back home. Or a pair of them. Or three men in white jump suits carrying a restraint jacket and plastic zip ties.

But when the door opens again, it's someone else, altogether.

A short man in a handsome gray suit, carrying a much-abused brown leather satchel under one arm, opens the door, closes it behind him, and flips a dead bolt switch to lock the door. Smiling, he takes a seat across the table from the boy.

"Hello," says the short man. He has a mild southern accent. "My name's Horace Swinney and it is a great pleasure to meet you." He reaches his hand across the table and they shake hands. "A privilege," says the smiling man. Swinney's face has a smoothness to it that seems unnatural. Like someone has patched his wrinkles with putty. He could be a very old thirty or a very young seventy.

"Charmed," says the boy.

"You've raised quite a stink up in here," says Swinney. "Quite a stink indeed."

"I'm sorry. I guess it was unavoidable," the boy says and nods. "I didn't know where else to go. You might say that television has been my sole, lifelong companion."

"Well I, for one, am glad you found us when you did."

"You are?"

"It's my station after all. My station that you wandered into, right off the street. Like some underground angel come crawling out of the underworld."

"You own the station?"

"In a manner of speaking," he says. "But I prefer to call myself its caretaker, more than an owner. As such, I have many responsibilities. To my family. To the people who work here. To the fine folks at home watching in their living rooms, or on the go, via our W-O-R-N App. So I need you to deal plainly with me. You must not embellish a word you say to me. I hope you don't find me rude, making so direct a request. But so much depends upon the truth."

"No, sir. You are a principled man. I understand the stakes."

"You're well spoken. More erudite than your father. Or your brothers."

"Thank you, sir. I hope you won't mistake it for flattery or mimicry if I return that compliment."

"Not at all. I've made a fine living off of speaking well. Now. As you may have surmised, time is of the essence."

"Perhaps even more to me than to you, sir."

"So allow me to inquire: What is it you want? Personally? What would you say is your motivation in all this?"

"I'm just a kid," says the kid. "Just trying to get free. To stay alive. And I know no one in this world. No one I want to know, in any event."

The small man nods in reply. "Are you looking for revenge? Revenge against the President."

"Perhaps someday, sir, perhaps one day my fear will transform to rage. And then to retribution. But at present, all I do,

I do to save my life."

"You fear for your life?"

"Yes. I think I do. But even more, for my freedom. And therein my life."

"Do you love your father?"

"I find I do."

"Do you hate your father?"

"I fear him more. More than I hate him."

"I see. And do you recognize that in stepping from the shadows you will be his destruction."

"I can see that one part of him will fall away. Yes. But he will survive with more in his pocket than most."

"But politically."

"Yes, that part of his life. That may be done."

"He may be sent to prison."

"He's avoided it this long. I doubt that will happen now."

"But if he were put on trial? If your word was needed to send him away, would you give that word?"

"Yes."

"Don't tell me what you think I want to hear. I mean it. Are you willing to go on the stand, and face the world, and say that the President of the United States of America, your father, held you captive in an underground bunker for 19 years?"

"Yes."

"Yes, what?"

"Yes. My father, the President, held me prisoner against my will. My entire life. Separated me from my mother before I could ever meet her. I don't know if she's alive or dead. Yes. Visited me on my birthday like I was some sort of zoo animal. Kept me locked away beneath the ground. I never saw the sun. I never saw the moon. Would have continued to do so until... my dying day or his, I suppose. Yes. Yes he did."

"Who is your mother?"

"I don't know exactly," says Tonio. He recounts the story, as he has so many times in the past six hours. At this point, the story has some polish to it; he's practiced.

"And how did you finally escape this prison?"

The boy recounts the years-long escape process. The planning, the digging, the training, the deception, and his first moments of freedom and escape from the resort property. Swinney lets him speak, uninterrupted, and during pauses encourages him to continue with quiet nods as he listens. "And then I came here," says Tonio. "And your morning show producer listened to me and gave me a chance to tell me story. And here we are."

The small man lets the silence settle for a moment. Then he unzips his leather bag. "These," Horace Swinney produces a sheaf of envelopes from his battered satchel, "are the results of your DNA test. Obviously, we don't have the President's precise DNA as a measuring stick, and we don't know who your mother is. But, happily, a number of the President's close relatives had their DNA sequenced through genetic genealogy companies and then posted those results to GEDMatch, an open source website that people use to track down relatives. Because we have those relatives, including, even, one of the first daughter's DNA, we essentially have the President's genome. As a result, according to our research staff and three independent geneticists (none of whom were made aware of the identities of the subjects involved), there is a 99.9% chance that the President, as you claim, is your father."

The boy nods. "So you believe me."

"I believe this," says Swinney. "So, in turn, I'm inclined to believe the rest of your story. Your pedigree is a fact. That is true. And if that part's true, then the rest of your story may have credence, as wild as it seems. But we here at W-O-R-N take our news seriously. The truth is everything to us. So I called a friend of mine who lives near the resort in Palm Beach this morning. Asked her to do a little undercover work, to wander the grounds of the resort where you claim to have been held for 19 years."

"What did she find?"

"Obviously, we needed to employ tact, but I can tell you with certainty that the parking lot of that resort is teeming with black trucks, licensed to a shell company which we have discovered is owned by Stern Microsystems, a private security company. The grounds are being scoured, even now, by squads of men in black turtlenecks carrying high powered firearms. In particular, there seems to be a high concentration of those men coming in and out of a tiny, nondescript shed."

"I see."

"We also found the car you borrowed from the resort. Just as you described it. Abandoned. Battery dead, but otherwise no worse for wear, not too far down the road from here by Pimple Creek." Horace pulls a stack of photographs from his satchel and lays them out before the boy. "Also, we found the bag of clothes you threw in the creek. An alligator had mangled it up a bit, but we got what was left. And footprints that match the soles of your sneakers. Along the bank of the creek. Here."

"You did it all so quickly."

"Time is of the essence, as they say," says Horace. "And everything, every single word you've told us is the truth."

"Thank you," says the boy. He is near tears. "Thank you for taking the time... for believing me."

"I admit," says Horace, shaking his slowly, "at first, I thought you came here on the crazy train. We get a lot of that. But no, my boy. You've been a victim of your father, the President of the United States, your entire life. Every word of your story that we can prove, we have."

"Thank you."

"And we're determined to keep digging. For you. For our viewers. And for America. This is Horace Swinney for W-O-R-N News. Tallahassee's trusted news leader."

"I beg your pardon?" says the boy.

"All set?"

"What?"

"Yup. Went even better than I thought. Okay," says Horace Swinney. He looks above the boy's head. "Yup. Get it to New York." He keeps staring. "Already? Okay, then. Super." Swinney lowers his gaze to meet the confused eyes of the boy. "Alright then, son," he says, removing a small flesh-colored earpiece from his left ear. "Why don't we repair to my office?"

"Will I be going on air?" says the boy.

The papers and photographs are already back in Horace Swinney's bag. The small man tucks it under his arm, rises, and unlocks the door to the conference room. He turns back to the boy, who is still in his chair, and with a slight bow from the waist says, "You just did."

The small man opens the door, and gestures for Tonio to follow him. When they emerge into the hallway a crowd of people gathered around the door bursts into applause and cheering. Tony sees the morning producer he had first met this morning among those applauding. There are tall men wearing suits and perfect hair, women in colorful blazers, and people in less formal apparel, jeans, t-shirts, and headsets. The crowd parts cheerfully as Horace wades through, shaking hands as he walks. He turns back to the astonished boy and gestures for him to follow. Tony does so. People hold their hands up as he passes, and when he mimics the gesture, they slap his hands. His first high fives. A blond girl in yoga pants and a chunky knit sweater throws her arms around his neck and gives him a long, blistering kiss. His first kiss.

Startled. Happy. Confused. Overwhelmed. He follows Horace Swinney through the gathered crowd, down the hallway, and through an open door that bears a placard reading simply, "Mr. Swinney".

The door closes behind him.

Monday, November 2
1:59 p.m. E.T.

Satoshi Nakamoto idly flips through her phone and smiles to herself. Everything is going better than planned.

The response to her video is explosive. She's got commentariat from both sides of the aisle shilling hard for her new third way. As they should, considering what she pays most of them. And even beyond them, the organic reaction is exactly as she'd hoped. She's grabbed the mantle of "Change" which is enough for most people. She is the newness.

Then this Presidential prisoner son? She only wishes she could have invented something that awful. She'd have paid $100 million and here's the President just giving it away. Satoshi's got to help that kid keep going today; keep that story rolling for more than an hour. She shoots a Signal message to Yoshi to have the Florida office devote themselves to digging up everything they can and the midwestern offices focus on blasting the President for child cruelty. And, of course, for using eminent domain to build The Wall. Let's not forget. People in the country despise eminent domain.

Yoshi's already on it. He's irreplaceable.

An alarm sounds on her phone. She nearly forgot! How could she forget?

She wants to pause and memorialize this moment. Satoshi reclines in her high-backed chair and allows her mind to travel far, far away.

If all has gone well, somewhere, someone is receiving an unpleasant surprise.

Monday, November 2
2:15 p.m. E.T.

The President's acting Deputy Press Secretary, Jessica Mossani, six hours into the job and three coffee mugs of caffeine-infused vodka into her day, taps "Mute" on the chunky remote control and looks around the war room.

"Shucks," she says, massaging the back of her neck. "Shucks, shucks, fucking shucks."

Five staff members are frozen in agonized poses around the room. Maria, the intern from GW is the only person in the room seemingly capable of movement, and she demonstrates that ability by removing her ID lanyard from around her neck and setting it on the large conference table, walking out of the room, sliding the pocket doors closed behind her, insinuating herself into a passing White House tour group, and eventually exiting through the gift shop, out the front doors, never to return.

The five staff members she leaves behind do not mark her departure. They share a watery-eyed condition, still gazing towards the television without truly seeing it.

"I guess," says Bob, Deputy Press Officer, a man of serious suits and whimsical socks and whorling combover, who makes a point of always being the first to volunteer a suggestion in the cherished belief that doing so offers value and demonstrates a resonant brand of decisiveness to his superiors and colleagues, as the sort of man who "gets the ball rolling" even if that ball is rarely the ball still in use at the end of the metaphorical ball game, he always "gets the conversation started," and in this instance, acting purely out of habit he repeats the phrase again, "I guess..." before attempting to regroup, but again merely to muster a meager: "I guess..." and then one final time whispers "I guess," and then rejoins the silence that proves to be the natural response to the interview they have just watched courtesy a small CBS-affiliate in Tallahassee, Florida.

The 7-footer on staff, Watkins, Deputy Assistant Writer and formerly a center on the basketball team at John Madison in distant, younger days, leans back as far as his chair will allow. Bob decides to watch this, rather than think about Tallahassee broadcast news, as the immense, thin man leans further and further back. Bob silently roots for the chair to tip all the way backwards and send Watkins reverse-somersaulting into the coffee banquet.

It doesn't happen for him. Watkins finds an equilibrium and hovers, sideways, like a palm tree in a hurricane, fronds slapping the ground but never fully giving way to the gales.

Greggins, Associate Deputy to the Deputy Assistant Writer, just entering his second year in the office has his elbows planted on the table and his hands buried in his thick tangles of black hair. He startles with a whistling gasp, and realizes that he had stopped breathing for some unknown measure of time. He looks around the table with alarm, as if unsure how he arrived here.

His eyes stop and stare at a young woman with striking auburn hair, Mathilde, Deputy Director of Social Outreach, who is biting her lower lip and goggling into the abyss with empty eyes. Bites her lip so determinedly that the delicate vermillion gives way to the pressure and her two front teeth, her central incisors, puncture her lip's soft, pink tissue. She doesn't seem to notice. Doesn't flinch as two thick stripes of blood descend from her lower lip, trace the dip of her cleft and flow down and over her chin, dripping thin threads of crimson on to the conference table's gray molded plastic where it pools in a compass-perfect circular disc that expands as the blood flows uninterrupted from her mouth.

This proves disturbing enough to end the nightmare reverie in the room.

"Mathilde!" shouts Press Secretary Mossani. "Stop it! Gee. Suss." The rest of the room recoils at the gruesome sight of the young woman's bloody catatonia, which continues, uninterrupted by their outbursts, the shouts, the slapping shut and scooping up of laptops, and the backpedalings from the table as the blooming circle of blood creeps wider and wider across the table. Mathilde continues to goggle, silently, motionless. The Press Secretary stands up from her rolling chair. "Let's... give her some space. We can regroup in my office," she says. The three men follow their boss out the door, leaving the unfortunate, young woman in her chair.

"Should we..." says Bob. "Do something?"

Watkins nods his concern.

Greggins says, "I think we should."

Mossani continues walking and says, "She'll be fine," over her shoulder. "Just give her a minute to gather herself. I did the same thing during the Contra affair. She just needs some air."

Watkins nods his agreement.

Greggins says, "Good idea."

"Let's do this," says Bob.

Mossani walks behind her desk and drops into her chair as the men fill three of the four chairs arrayed in front of the desk.

"Should we consult with the President," asks Bob, "before we commit to messaging?"

"Sure, Bob. You want to go ask him if he's really kept his secret, half-Mexican bastard living in a golf resort dungeon for twenty years, Bob?" asks Mossani. "God dammit, Bob."

Bob shifts his butt cheeks side to side in his seat in reply.

"No. We prep until we're called upon. Walk in prepared. Everyone," says the Press Secretary, "compose three plausible, one sentence statements of denial. Right now. Five minutes. Go."

Watkins and Greggins tap at laptops. Bob flips open a fresh page in his reporter's notebook and scratches away with a sharp #2. The Press Secretary pecks at her phone.

At five minutes, she looks up. "Watkins, go. Give me your favorite."

Watkins reads in his natural slow-motion voice, "I have no idea who this young man is, but I can imagine why such an accusation might be cast the day before the most important election in American History."

"Not strong enough. Greggins: go."

"We don't know where the liberals dug this guy up, pun intended, but they can put him right back. This is utter nonsense."

"Maybe. I'm not sure I like puns for the moment. Bob. Go time."

"This is the desperate act of a fake news media intent on assassinating this President on the eve of his landslide re-election. This is Lee Harvey Osvald holding a shotgun microphone. And this White House does not. Will never. Bargain. With. Terrorists."

"That's barely lucid," says the Press Secretary.

"I know," admits Bob sheepishly. "You liked it?"

"I love it. Give that page to Greggins to type up and distribute."

Bob rips the page out of his notebook and hands it to the younger man. Greggins takes it with disdain. The Press Secretary knocks back a hearty slug of caffeinated vodka and dismisses the men. She picks up her phone and says, "Ellie. Hey. Get a roll of paper towels and check in on Mathilde in the conference room? 'Kay thanks."

Monday, November 2
10:36 p.m. Moscow Standard Time / 2:36 p.m. E.T.

The Russian President has been sitting on the toilet in the handsomely furnished bathroom that adjoins his office. He has been perched atop this toilet for 37 minutes, and he doesn't know what to do.

He is mid-bowel movement, and, to be brief but clear: it is stuck. Half-in. Half-out.

The gnarled tube of stool, which he has had sufficient time to name (Putivic, since you asked), refuses to commit to a complete departure from his body. Said night-soil is equally adamant that it will not return from whence it came. The concrete-dense tube juts a full six inches beyond the event horizon of his anus, but, and he can just somehow tell that this is the case, it extends, coiled, at least another full ten inches inside his body.

Viewers at home, and may your mind's eye forgive this, may wonder, why doesn't he employ one of their methods for abandoning this pesky hanger-on? This unwanted guest.

Well, the President might reply, he's tried everything he knows.

He's tried to "tilt the turnip cart," as his mother taught him, for instance, leaning all the way over, the entire 45 degrees, until one blanched thigh is wholly rocked off the toilet seat and all of his weight is left to press down on the remaining, seated thigh. To no avail. He has tilted the other way, as well, going so far as to extend his arms high over his head as he rocked and held the pose, trying to goad his bowels into action. But nothing.

He has attempted the slow-breathing Buddha. Both hands resting, palms-up, on his bare, chalky thighs, his posture straighter than a Soviet apartment bloc, he relaxes in systematic fashion and listens to his breathing. He closes his eyes. The pace of his inhalations slows to a crawl. His exhalations wouldn't rustle a canary feather. Centimeter by centimeter, he flexes and relaxes every muscle he can discern, one by one by one by one by one. He is attuned to his pulse and his thoughts focus on an image of an unwinding spool of white thread connected on its receding end to a kite. The kite rises and rises and the thread feeds steadily off the spinning spool. He follows the progress of the string and as the spool turns and turns, the coil of white thread grows thinner and thinner around the spool's wooden core until the kite exhausts the thread and rises, unimpeded, trailing the full length of string behind it. The Prez watches the kite rise higher and higher, into the invisible distance that swallows it. He looks down at the empty spool in his imagination. He opens his eyes. Still, he cannot conclude the matter below.

Pinch it off, the reader may be shouting into the page. Just pinch it off!

It is not possible. It simply is not. Don't you think the Russian President would have already tried this after 37 minutes? Of course he did. Of course he would have been happy to raise the soft, white flag of defeat long before this point. But Putivic is a beast of previously unencountered qualities and strength. Yes, Putivic smells of the old familiar funk. Yes, Putivic has a traditional color, a healthy hue, even, by popular standards. But His density is unfathomable. Pinching it off is not feasible. He is unpinchable. He refuses to be broken, not just via the usual methods but even after the most unorthodox lower body contortions. Wriggling, shaking, hopping, gyrating: nothing moves The Beast. The Russian President moves beyond even these measures, and squat-waddles off the toilet with his pants around his ankles, Putivic's head and torso protruding from between his legs the entire time. The President arrives at the sink and secures the electric toothbrush he keeps on the bathroom counter for a mid-day brushing.

Sacrificing both his dignity and his favorite toothbrush to the cause, he returns to his perch on the toilet and swipes and pokes at the offending Putivic periscoping towards the toilet water. But Putivic feels nothing and surrenders nary an inch. He parries every stab and every swipe. He will not be moved, neither in nor out, nor diminished in the slightest by the clumsy hacking of an electric toothbrush. The toothbrush, however, is terribly diminished by the experience. It is determinedly worse for wear, smeared with unmentionable ooze grazed from the President's flank. The Russian President, disgusted and frustrated, tries to throw the toothbrush into the sink across the room, but in his rage overthrows the target. The toothbrush hits the mirror, shattering a spiderweb crack that distorts the President's scowling reflection. What's worse, the impact causes the toothbrush to power on, and now furiously sprays bits of Putivic residue in all directions as the device bounces around on the counter, and then onto the floor until it finishes the full 90-second brushing cycle.

Those 90 seconds are a nightmare eternity for the Russian President. The gorgeous cream tiles, the gold bathroom fixtures, the mirrors, the doorknob, his useless fucking cell phone, the Russian President himself: everything, everything, everything is flecked in brown. Spattered with his brown. Everything.

The veins on his shining temple bulge with frustration. He reaches for the mottled roll of toilet paper beside the toilet and winds a generous measure of double ply around his right hand, winds and winds it around his hand forming a thick, crude, white oven mitt. Satisfied that the hand is shielded, he shifts his weight to his left leg and reaches beneath his right buttock and grabs ahold of Putivic's protruding bottom half.

Then he pulls.

He grits his teeth and pulls as hard as he can. But the thing won't give. He can get no purchase on the slimy thing. Worse, when he does manage even the slightest friction and pulls down, it hurts terribly. Like he's yanking on his own intestines. He stops to catch his breath. The toilet paper mitt starts to absorb the surface excrement. Whatever immovable material it is that forms the core of Putivic refuses to bend or be moved. After a frantic minute, the toilet paper glove is a mess. It takes the other hand to remove it from the Russian President's right hand and drop the mass into the crystalline water of the toilet bowl.

He cannot call anyone in to help him. It is mortifying. Humiliating. No one can know.

He sighs and crosses his arms across his legs, folds himself over them and dips his head below his knees.

He must... He'll just wait. He has waited longer for less. He will wait for this to pass.

Monday, November 2
4 p.m. E.T.

Tonio sits in a plush leather chair opposite CBS's Vice President for 2020 Election Coverage on a corporate jet. She hands him a long narrow menu and says, "We aren't permitted to pay you, as an interview subject. Network ethics policy to keep everyone honest. But we can feed you." She gestures to the top line of the menu. "I recommend the lobster tail."

After the original interview aired, things proceeded quickly, and the boy has been summoned to New York City to be interviewed by a distinguished newsman on a national news magazine. The network has rewritten its evening programming, shoving aside an hourlong *Charles in Charge* Reunion special to take advantage of the fact that they essentially own this jaw-rattling story. Through dumb luck and the proximity of their Tallahassee affiliate to the highway, they own it like nobody else and intend to make some hay.

This young man hasn't a dollar in his pocket or a friend in the world. He doesn't own a phone and he doesn't know anyone to call. No one has access to him but them. And as the old adage goes, a man without a friend or family, is also a man without a booking agent. And in this case, a man without legal representation, a change of clothes, or a mailing address. No one can get their claws in him. By default, from their perspective, CBS has assumed custody of the President's son, and they're in no rush to share that bounty.

The Vice President for Election Coverage is leaning towards Tonio as he studies the menu carefully. He can smell her. She smells like citrus and vanilla. He's never held a menu before, but he is doing an excellent mimic of people on television studying a menu. "We can also," the VP is continuing, "assist with lodging in the city. We have an executive guest suite on the top floor of our headquarters you can use for the duration of the week. We also have a capable wardrobe department that will meet us at HQ to take measurements and get you set up with some clothing."

"But you can't pay me."

"Not exactly."

"But maybe you could offer me a per diem? Is that how you say it? A per diem isn't payment. Right?"

"I suppose that might be right."

"I noticed you have a second bag." He points to a black nylon backpack on the floor across the aisle from them. "But you aren't even spending the night in Florida. Just flying down and back right?"

"That?" she says. "That's not my bag."

"Oh yeah?"

"Maybe that's your bag."

"Oh?"

"Because it isn't my bag. It isn't the pilot's bag. So I guess..." she scratches her head with an exaggerated motion. "I guess it's your bag."

"Okay," he says. He walks over to the bag and unzips it. It is stuffed with banded bricks of 20 dollar bills. "Oh right," he says. "I forgot. This is my bag."

She smiles at him as he returns to his seat. "I'm so glad you found it," she says. "You really are your father's son, you know. CBS is proud to be the network you've chosen to share your story. We want to be the ones to help you tell your story your way."

"Right." Tonio leans back in his seat abruptly and stares out the window. His expression is alarmed. "Excuse me," he says, straining to keep his composure. The plane has taxied to the end of the runway and its engines are roaring. Although the jet is beautifully sound-balanced, the noise is still the loudest thing Tonio has ever heard, and this is the third vehicle he has ever been in, the first being the commandeered Tesla and the second, the sedan that took him to the airfield outside Tallahassee.

"Of course," says the VP leaning back in deference to his panicked eyes. She picks up her phone from the table beside her seat and idly flicks at the screen.

Tonio glances at her, but returns his focus to the most urgent matter at hand, the forward motion of a vehicle intent on leaving the ground. He has spent his whole life beneath it, and in a moment he will leave its surface. He will fly. The concrete of the runway rolls beneath his view, faster, faster, and faster, and the white lines that intermittently stripe the surface grow closer and closer together as the plane gathers momentum, faster and faster and faster. His breath is tight in his chest as he's pressed back in his seat by the plane's speed and his own anxiety.

And then.

The pressure relaxes against his chest. The plane seems to unclench, freed of earth's friction. So sudden. So easy. The runway disappears beneath the plane. The landscape stretches out beneath him. They are aloft.

Tonio leans forward and presses his head against the window's cold plastic. He watches the world miniaturize. Everything that had moments before seemed impossibly imposing rapidly becomes a toy in the distance. The highways become gray stripes, speckled with little toy cars. Is that a lake? How can that possibly be a lake? It sparkles beneath the plane. He sees a toy boat chugging across the puddle, trailing a widening V of wake.

Tonio glances up at the VP; she is lost in the little black rectangle in her hands. While they are flying. They are actually flying! Flying! Tonio wants to shake her shoulders. He wants to shout. "Don't you get it? We're flying! Flying! I saw a bird this morning for the first time. I nearly screamed! I really did! I've never... They're like aliens! They are magical flying nymphs! And now we are flying! Flying! Human beings. Through the air!"

She continues to stare at her phone. Looking mildly annoyed.

Tonio turns back to the window. He shakes his head in disbelief. The landscape below spreading wider and wider as they rise. Then there's a twinkle. A small burst of light, far below. Then something trails light through the sky, trailing a white stripe behind it.

"What is that?" he asks the VP, pointing down toward the burgeoning white stripe.

"Hm?" she says, not breaking eye contact with her iPhone.

"That?" he repeats. "The little glowing thing? The... white line. There?"

"Ah?" she looks up for a moment. She smiles at him. "I'm not from Florida," she says. "I don't really know the–"

"No, the white line, there. That seems to be curving towards us?"

She turns to the window and squints. "I don't see it," she says.

"There," he points.

"Where?"

"It's—"

A flash, a burst of daylight and the cracking noise of the jet's hull splitting in half interrupts him. The VP disappears. The blue of the sky is overwhelming. The seatbelt tightens against his chest and the wind blasts him back against the seat.

He is no longer flying.

He is falling.

He is in the back half of the jet, now severed from the front, from the wings, from everything. The air whips his fantastic blonde hair, and as the back half of the jet tilts forward, he is confronted with the earth again. There is a moment, a moment of time so immeasurably brief that no fraction of a second is small enough to describe it, when the remnant of the plane he occupies is neither rising nor falling nor moving forwards, frozen for that moment in its final apex. The wind pauses between breaths, and all is still. Everything below. Glistening lakes. Green fields, the mottled green of trees from above. Ribbons of roads winding through it all, white specks of cars drifting forward.

Then the landscape gathers clarity.

Grows.

It is wonderous. All of it.

It grows closer. Larger. The outlines of trees gain definition. Clearer, larger, closer. Faster. Faster. Faster.

He passes out in his seat. A sad smile on his face.

Monday, November 2
4:09 p.m. E.T.

Surface to Air Specialist Clarke lowers his shoulder-mounted rocket launcher and watches the white trail of smoke chase the Learjet as it passes overhead.

It does what God made it to do. An orange blaze of light flashes. Maybe a mile past Clarke's station in the cypress trees around Silver Lake. He watches the white jet split in two and its halves begin their unscheduled descent. The front half takes its time, still propelled up and forward by its flaming engines. The back half slowly tilts towards the earth below and falls.

Clarke lowers the launching unit into its case and snaps it shut. He doesn't even wait to watch the plane crash. Doesn't need to. What he needs to do is get in his Stern Microsystems-issued black SUV and get out of this swamp before the Podunk Florida mall cops show up.

Monday, November 2
4:30 p.m. E.T.

Spark Jones is finishing his fifth set of prison push-ups (handstand position with legs leaning against the wall for stability, and not a single grunt as he cranks out the reps) in his makeshift office at his network's New York studios, they'd flown him north that morning for the homestretch, when an assistant producer pokes her head through the door. "Excuse me," she says, and pulls up short, blushing at the sight of the young anchor upside down and testing the tensile strength of his white tank top.

He hops to his feet and beams the winning smile that flew him all the way from Iowa to today. "No problem. Sorry. What's up?"

"It's. They're. They want you on camera in five. If you can manage it." He isn't supposed to go on until 6.

"Absolutely," he says, already pulling on his shirt and smoothing his collar stays. "What's going on?"

"Oh. Pretty much everything," she says, admiring his neck as he buttons the final button of his shirt and begins tying his gray, knit necktie. "Your hair's good. We'll get you to makeup."

"I don't really need to," he says.

"Don't they make you?"

"Apparently I produce this oil that just sort of does the equivalent," he says. "Genetic thing. I don't know. Let's go straight to set."

"Diane said she'll brief you there."

"Sounds good."

On set, it's mid-commercial break and the crew is milling,

making small adjustments. Interns are jog-running from place to place, and Spark watches two of the best producers in the building on their phones, walking figure eights around each other, gesticulating as they pace. The network president is off to the side of the chaos, standing by himself with his arms crossed, watching the tangled action spin around him with a look that speaks of satisfaction.

Diane, executive producer, approaches Spark at a jog, headset bobbing as she goes, a handful of paper extended towards his chest. She hands them to him.

"Good evening," says Spark. "What's on tonight's menu?"

Diane speaks faster than most people think, and now she's speaking faster than she thinks. "Forget everything we said in this morning's story meeting. Have you been keeping up?"

"No. I was asleep. What's new?"

"Well first, this morning, the President starts tweeting that he's fired the Veep, so that's news. Of the, you know, insane-slash-impossible variety the day before the election."

"Right."

"Interrupt that bizarre drama to find the first confirmed video message from Nakamoto himself. Herself, I mean."

"Sure."

"Well then, CBS in Florida literally digs up a beautiful biracial son of the President this afternoon. He spills his guts all over America. DNA tests checks out. No one can find a hole in his story. It all makes weird amounts of sense. The timing. The resort staff. Every ounce of it. The next thing you know, the plane the kid's riding to CBS New York gets heat-seeking-missile-blasted out of the sky and he is toast."

"Yikes."

"I know? And now we have this whole Basement Housewives story that you pitched at the story meeting, and–how did you find out about that before the first wife was even freed, anyways?– and we don't have the proof we need yet, but that's exploding all over the place and nobody knows how fucking high that dumpster fire's going to blaze. We're going to be writing copy as you speak. You could be throwing to Rockford, Florida, Washington, I don't even know where the fuck this starts or how it ends. You're just gonna have to stick to the script as we hand it to you and stay smooth in choppy fucking water, right? Buckle up, big boy, we've got 22 seconds left before break ends."

"Right," says Spark. He glides onto the set, nods to the anchor he's replacing, an ashen-faced veteran of the network who tries to return the nod, but can barely lift his chin, and limps out of the spotlight. Exhausted. Broken by the day's reporting. Poor bastard sweat right through the back of his suit.

The trumpets blast through his earpiece and the stage lights blaze. Centercam's light goes red and the prompter is rolling. Spark Jones feels a flame behind his eyes, like a moment of prophecy is at hand, and locking eyes with the camera's lens he swears he can feel America looking back at him. All those eyes on his.

"Good evening," he tells them. He ignores the script rolling across the screen and riffs: "On the eve of America's election, the race for the highest office in the land belongs to anybody and as a result: nobody. But in the midst of pollsters and hucksters, false prophets, soothsayers and sham shamans, we are the Voice you Trust, and we're here to help you sort through a nation in crisis. Welcome. To the Evening News." The music rises in his earpiece and he watches the title credits roll on a

TV in the background.

Diane, in the control booth, is losing her shit. Slapping an assistant producer in the back of the head with the palm of her hand and seething. "Read the fucking prompter. What is he doing?" she hisses. "What are you doing, you absolute fucking yokel."

Therese, running the board, turns her head but not her eyes and says, "Shut the fuck up, Diane." She hits a button and the tight focus brings Spark even closer to the audience. "He's doing the god damned news. Old school. Free style."

"He's out of control. Go to commercial," says Diane.

"No," says Therese. "Loosen the reins. Give him his head. Let's see where this goes."

"Dammit," says Diane. "Dammit dammit dammit. I don't even have a choice. Spark," she says into the control room mic, "read from the prompter or I'll tear those corn muffins you call ears off your head."

Spark's face, on the monitor, doesn't register that he heard the threat, but as the music fades behind him, he segues back in by saying, "The eyes and ears of America have seen and heard some doozies over the past four years. But what we heard today, took the cake..."

Diane slumps back in a rolling chair and scowls at the screen. Of all the days for this walking slice of country ham to go rogue, he does it today.

Monday, November 2
5:30 p.m. E.T

The President's wife finds him asleep on a chaise lounge, a string of caramel sauce lashes his upper lip to three fingers of his right hand. A tray of upended bowls and dirty plates on the end table. His white shirt is flecked with scraps of breading, which the First Lady identifies from experience as the remains of Arby's curly fries. The chaise makes the President look even larger than he is. He's a tall man and his first Presidential term has left him swollen. Splayed across the furniture he reminds his wife of a baby grown too large for his crib. A hermit crab uncomfortably ready for a new shell. So cute.

She could watch him like this all day. But she didn't come here to admire her beloved, but to stir him to action and update him on the latest media lies. No one else will do it. They're all refusing or hiding. Or in the case of one particular trio, morosely drunk in a room with the lights off, giving everyone the creeps.

"Darlink," she sings softly. "Darrrlink. Time to wake up!"

The President's tongue peeks from between his lips and finds the line of caramel. He laps it into his mouth. His eyes flutter open. "Hungh?" he says.

"Time to wake. There is new fakeynews."

The President pulls himself forward on the chaise, his arms dangle parallel to his sides like a seated panda for a moment before rising into a full yawn-stretch. "Yes?" he says. "What is it, sweetheart? It can't be that bad if they sent you to tell me."

She is silent. A chill climbs the back of the President's

neck.

"No one else would tell me?" he says.

"Is nonsense," she says. "There's a little Mexican boy on TV, he says you are his daddy. And you kept him locked in a... a uh... what's the word... a tiny room in the ground, with the bars... what is the word?"

"Nonsense," says the President. Beads of sweat ooze through the pores of his forehead. "They'll say anything. They're desperate!"

"Yes. Is crazy. He looks just like you! Only Mexican. Same hair! Is like a clown."

"That's an act of desperation. Obviously. I know the type. He'll be yesterday's news in 72 seconds."

"Oh, is already gone, darlink! Like I said to Karen and Beel and bald one and the other bald one. 'Out of sight. Out of mind.'" And they say, 'No. Is so much worse!' And I say–"

"What do you mean? Gone? He just did the interview and disappeared?"

"No. Is even better. He is note coming back. Kaboom!" She splays her fingers out dramatically and waggles them.

"What do you mean? Kaboom."

"After he gives the interview, he goes on a plane to New York. You know. Because he was in Florida. And the plane takes off and goes: Kaboom!"

"Oh my god."

"All gone." She dusts her hands against each other. "Problem solved."

"Oh my god."

"Is okay. It serves him right."

The President slumps back against the chaise lounge.

"Darlink. Ohhh. Is okay. Do some tweety. You'll feel better.

Tweety! Tweety!"

    The President is not listening. The President is sad.

Monday, November 2
6:14 p.m. E.T.

Moshi is back in New York for three more errands before boarding a jet to Italy. The first task is the simplest. She walks six steps up to the landing of an older brick building in Queens, surveys the buzzers, and uses her elbow to press the bottom, white button labeled: "Vasiliev" for three seconds. Moshi hears a buzz from the doorframe, pulls her hand into her sleeve and uses the edge of her shirt to open the door, enters the dirty front hallway, and descends to the basement apartment.

The door to a shabby apartment is already open. A strung-out woman in a red terrycloth robe that has seen better days stands by the door with her arms folded, gray vape pen shaped like Eeyore dangling from her lip. She coughs a plume of surprisingly pink smoke into Moshi's face Moshi walks past her into the apartment.

"Sorry," the woman says, in a bleary Russian accent. Moshi continues past her, ignoring a smell that suffuses the place, that if she had to guess its origin, was the result of someone eating nothing but rose petals for three days before enduring an hour-long bout of shattering diarrhea.

Moshi breathes only through her mouth as she approaches a card table piled with unopened junk mail and magazines, opens the duffel slung over her shoulder, and dumps a pile of money on the table. Thick rolls of rubber-banded $100 bills.

The woman approaches the table and picks up one of the rolls, and, for no clear reason, sniffs it.

"Two million," says Moshi.

"I like this bag," she says, pointing to the duffel.

"Me too," says Moshi.

"I want it."

"Sorry."

"My cousin risked his life for you. He may be killed for this."

"Two million," says Moshi. "The bag is not part of the deal."

Moshi turns and leaves, careful not to touch anything, jogs out of the building and down the block, tosses the duffel in a construction dumpster, and catches a bus heading downtown. Everything on schedule.

Two transfers, one train later, she's in lower Manhattan and slides into the flow of people flooding the sidewalks. She appreciates the anonymity provided by the ever-moving, ever-present crowds of New York.

The drop-off is on the 15th floor of a new hotel that looms over its older, brick neighbors. The top floor is a cocktail lounge whose primary selling point is its view. Windows on all sides peer out over the glittering skyline. Drinks start at $30.

Moshi leans in to the bartender and orders a flute of champagne. She points to a smiling man reclining in the corner of the lounge who waves to her. "His tab," says Moshi, to the bartender.

Moshi sits across from the man, who seems incapable of wiping the smile off his face. Perhaps because he's about to be significantly wealthier than he was when he woke up this morning. "All right," says the young man in a soft Southern accent, "champagne. I like your style, sister."

"You've got your wallet up?"

The young man nods and holds his phone towards Moshi.

"You type," says Moshi. "I'll dictate."

The man shrugs.

Moshi recites from memory an 18 character alpha-numeric code and the young man types into his phone. Taps enter. His eyes widen briefly. He's staring at a number on his screen that he has difficulty believing now belongs to him.

Moshi drains her glass of champagne in one swallow and tucks the empty champagne flute into a jacket pocket.

The young man pulls his eyes away from his phone to watch the strange smuggle. Moshi stands and buttons her jacket.

The young man points and says, "You really like that glass."

Moshi says, "Some people feel a need to leave their fingerprints on everything they do in life. And some do not."

She leaves without a handshake, gesture, or a word of farewell. Just walks away. Outside the hotel, Moshi removes the champagne flute from her pocket, reaches into a trash can and cracks the glass against the inside of the can like an egg, sending its shattered shards into the trash bag within.

Moshi descends the stairs of the Bleecker Street subway and boards an uptown train, finds herself at the base of a shiny new building on 30th street. She's early by a minute. Moshi doesn't wear a watch, but years of specialized Coast Guard M.P. training has her internal rhythms synchronized to the Atomic Clock in Boulder. She's usually good to within 12 seconds when she tests herself.

Moshi leans against a gargantuan polished marble orb in front of the building and doesn't have long to wait. The chiseled young news anchor walks past, appearing for all the world like a man stretching his legs and taking the air.

"Excuse me," says Moshi.

"Yes?"

"May I get your autograph, please?"

"Of course. Who should I make it out to?"

"Cash," says Moshi.

Spark Jones smiles and takes a fat Sharpie and small notepad from Moshi's hands and signs his name. He hands the notepad back.

"Keep the pen," says Moshi.

"Sure, thanks."

Moshi strolls away towards the nearest hotel to catch a taxi for the airport.

Spark Jones hustles back into the building. He knows he has five minutes until he's back on-air. As he rides the elevator up, he twists the doctored Sharpie and unscrews it at a secret seam to examine its two hollow halves. In one, he sees the rectangular socket of a flash drive. Rolled up and secreted in the other is a scroll of paper the size of a fortune cookie fortune with handwriting on one side. He tucks the paper carefully into his wallet, and reassembles the Sharpie.

On the 24th floor he pauses at Diane, the producer's, desk on his way back to the soundstage.

"For fuck's sake," she says. "Where have you been? You're on again in less than five and you haven't even been briefed in on–" He hands her the flash drive. "What's this?" she says.

"It's the pee-pee tape," he says.

It takes her a second. Then she shakes her head. "Fuck you, it's the pee-pee tape."

"It is."

She narrows her gaze at him. "I don't know what passes for funny in Iowa, but this ain't it."

"I'm not joking."

"You're on in four. This is not the move."

"I'm deadly serious. We have thirty minutes to be the first to air it. If we don't, they're giving it to NBC."

"Bullshit."

"It's the pee-pee. The actual pee-pee tape."

The producer's pupils flare and shake for a millisecond. The technical director, watching this exchange from the monitor bank rolls her chair to peer over Diane's shoulder at the flash drive. Diane grinds her teeth. "Right. Where did you get it?" she says.

"A connection to a highly placed Russian intelligence official. That's as far as I can go."

"Sure. Yeah. Of course. Even if this were real, which it isn't, it won't be enough for legal."

"It's as far as I'm allowed to go. It will have to be enough."

"Get out there and get ready. You're on in three."

"That has a shelf life of 28 minutes remaining."

"I heard you. Get out there."

Spark leaves the room, his manner as unruffled as ever.

Diane leaves the production booth and walks to her office, plugs the flash drive in, and taps at her mouse a few times. Five video files.

She double-clicks one and it begins playing.

Her head slowly tilts towards the screen and her eyebrows rise at corresponding speed. She can hear her pulse. Her hands tremble. The back of her neck tightens.

She pauses the video and opens the second file. It's the same event but from a different camera angle. The quality is studio superb. There's nothing glitchy about it. The footage is crisp. The voices are clear. The faces are unmistakable.

Her voice starts low and rises to a scream: "Fuuuuuuuuuuuuuuuuuuuuuuuuuuuuuuuck!"

Diane copies the five video files onto the secure shared server and then onto her laptop's local hard drive. Terrified to lose what has just fallen out of the corn-fed, fucking, blue sky.

She shoots a poorly worded email, mostly exclamation points, to three of her bosses, directing them to the video file on the server. Then picks up her phone to call them. She ejects the flash drive, and while the phone rings she slides the precious footage into her inside jacket pocket.

She sprints down the hallway, phone held to her ear, yelping all the way back to the studio.

Monday, November 2
7:45 p.m. E.T.

The back room at Marx Sharks is elbow-to-elbow dudes. Black t-shirts or blue denim button-ups with the sleeves rolled back is the uniform of the pack. They're all wearing "Hello, My Name is..." stickers, mostly on unorthodox parts of their body–foreheads, shirt sleeves, navels, one over each nipple, upside down, angular– and one of their Reddit usernames scrawled in blue Sharpie in the sticker's white space.

u/disaffectedopossum is a tall dude of the blue denim variety, one of those tall guys who you can tell never played basketball, and has spent his whole life telling people he hates basketball when they ask if he plays basketball, which is all the goddamn time, which is why he fucking hates basketball. He has black hair and a pair of chunky Warbies that keep sliding down his nose. He's drinking mead from a tall vessel akin to an hourglass and talking to u/fakeusername1984, a short man with a shaved head and a crisp, waxed mustache, in hushed and urgent tones. The shorter man is in a black t-shirt and swigs occasionally from a brown bottle of Michelob Light, punctuating each sip of beer with a look at the bottle as if someone has mistakenly filled it with hot buttercream.

The tall man leans in to be heard over the din of the full room, and, somewhere in that tonal gap between hollering and conversing where most bar conversations occur, says "Of course I know he's the man, but I'm like having doubts about the utility of voting for him."

"Polls like that are designed to have that effect. It's a self-fulfilling prophecy. You won't vote for him because you say he can't win. But he can't win because everyone thinks that way and won't vote for him."

"Just because it sucks, doesn't make it false."

"It's fucking defeatist."

"It's just realistic. I can't live through a second term of this shit."

"If she wins, it's just as bad. Four years of circle-jerking stalemate. The electorate disenfranchised, and then in another four years, the elite throw out another game show host puppet with name recognition. But this time, 2/3 of a brain, so way worse. So much worse."

"The Veep."

"I said 2/3. The Veep can't work a toaster."

"Maybe a smart toaster. Siri, toast my toast."

"Exactly."

"How did that guy get this far?"

"Because he looks like a butch George Washington."

"Washington's got those cheeks."

"Veep looks like a general knocked up a Gideon Bible and the resulting baby was homeschooled on a parsnip farm by Tom Landry's angriest uncle."

"That's Veepers."

"I'm done compromising. If I voted for the Dem on Tuesday, and she still lost, I'd have to off myself. I couldn't look in the mirror. I'd drain a bottle of Gorilla Glue."

"Bernie's my boy. Don't get me wrong. But she isn't that bad. And she can beat him."

"If you're not going to vote for Bernie, at least make it Nakamoto."

"Why the hell would I do that?"

"Because at least Nakamoto's outside the two-party system. In particular, the party that continuously fucks Bernie and anyone else with ideals at every opportunity. Plus, it's fucking interesting. And, I'm not even shitting you, I think she's got a better shot than Hillary Junior or Bernie."

"Shut up."

"I'm serious."

"People do love billionaires."

"Yes they do, for some reason. They're fascinated by all that cash. And Nakamoto is Bruce Wayne and Batman all wrapped up in one. Like a Bruce Wayne who doesn't put on the front in a famous mansion, and pretend to take down two playmates per night, and host soirees that are the constant target of cartoonish terrorist hits. Which by the way, Master Wayne, take a note and if you find yourself near a chandelier with a glass of champagne in your hand, probably time to skate. For the common good. Right?"

"Right?"

"Nakamoto's getting that good press, too. Sucking up the jet fuel, you notice?"

"Yeah. It's been a day."

"There's a lot of people want to see the two-party system fall apart."

"Present."

"Nakamoto's more viable than Perot was."

"Isn't he just going to steal votes away from the Dems, though?"

"Some. But there's plenty of people from both parties who don't see themselves in their candidate. And then there's plenty of people who just want things to be... interesting."

"That's how we got here in the first place."

"Reckon so."

"So... I don't get it. Why aren't you voting for Nakamoto?"

"Like I said. It's a personal principle for me. No judgement on you. Plus, there's this part of me, I don't know." He takes a drink, winces, and glares at his bottle. "Part of me that wants Bernie to pick up the paper on Wednesday morning, sit there at the kitchen table, open up the Times. His wife's got the beef bacon going low and slow. The eggs are on standby so the food can be all done and hot at the same time. She fills his coffee cup. Big chunky Vermont ceramic mug. Same as every day. He went to bed the night before at 8:30. And he's sitting there with the sun streaming through the gauzy blue curtains on the window over the sink, and that early morning, golden light landing on the paper, right on his name, and he can see that he got at least 5%. You know?"

"And then he dies? Or what?"

"What? No."

"It sounded like maybe he was about to die, in your telling."

"No. Just. He gets this gentle revelation. Like a thank you. 5% isn't nothing. 5% of America in the face of everything is, you know. A legacy."

"But if he told you to vote Nakamoto?"

The short man pauses and finishes peeling the label off his Michelob Light. "Well I guess I'd vote for Nakamoto then."

Monday, November 2
7:49 p.m. E.T.

A conference table with six chairs, four of which are filled. Two more have Skyped in.

"We can't run it."

"We have to run it."

"He has to give us a name. We don't have to share the name, but he has to give us the name. We need more."

"He says he can't."

"We run this without more information, we destroy the entire network. The entire network. The parent company. It's our jobs, it's everyone's jobs. We have a responsibility. If this thing's a deepfake... It isn't ethical. Our credibility will be worthless. And that's without the lawsuits, which would bury us... it's... reckless beyond belief."

"If we sit on this, the night before, our credibility is worthless. We are purposeless. There's as much danger in waiting as there is in proceeding."

"It's an opportunity, Bill. It's a golden gift from the gods."

"We've at least got to blur out the nipples."

"It's too good to be true, Stacy. The timing. The way it arrived? We're being taken for a ride."

"It's bigger than this moment. I mean it. If we run this, and it proves to be fake, that will be the genuine death of real news. And it will be our fault. We really will be fake news. Active participants. This will confirm every ounce of paranoia this country already harbors. And if the President loses because we run it, and then it turns out to be a fraud, then the next guy in office... we're talking about the delegitimization of the entire government. An actual civil war. This needs more than 22 minutes of vetting. We need to—"

"Our deepfake guy at Berkeley says its legit. There's none of the—"

"I don't care what one guy at Berkeley says. I'm telling you, this thing needs more—"

"We have seven minutes left and—"

"I have concerns about the nipples."

"We cannot air this—"

"We'll add a disclaimer that—"

"Be quiet."

"If we—"

"Quiet."

"Sorry."

"We're running it. We're running it now."

"But—"

"Quiet."

"Sorry."

"It doesn't matter. It doesn't matter if it's fake or if it's real. It just doesn't. Haven't you been paying attention? That's the lesson. That is the lesson. Right and wrong are now independent of the Truth. The truth is, most of the people who want to believe it will believe it. And those who don't want to believe it, won't believe it. If it's real, it's newsworthy. If it's fake, it's newsworthy that someone went to so much trouble to fake it. So, we're going to run it. Unedited. Nipples and all. All five files. No commentary. Just a caption along the bottom. 'Exclusive: Pee-Pee Tape Unearthed.' Loop it twice. No commercial breaks. Go."

"Yes, sir."

297

"Go. Do it now."

Monday, November 2
6:00 p.m. M.S.T. / 8:00 p.m. E.T.

Jerry Sheehan idly flips through the channels after the local weather forecast has wrapped up, as is his custom. And, as is custom, the weather is nice. His wife, Rosie, knits, halfway through a rainbow scarf to mail back to their daughter in Fargo. A framed photograph of the "Welcome to Sun City West" sign hangs above the TV set. Their recliners are perfectly aligned, aimed at the television at matching 35-degree angles, with their leg rests levered up and occupied.

Rosie's eyes are intent on a tricky bit, so she doesn't much notice that Jerry has stopped changing the channel. There's voices speaking in Russian and English and a generic sort of techno beat in the background.

"God. Damn," says Jerry, softly, to himself, unaware he is speaking aloud.

Rosie looks up. "Jerry!" she shouts.

"It's the news!" he shouts.

"Well I don't like this news! Change the channel! Oh my word! What is she... change the channel, Jerry!"

"But it's the news!"

"Change the channel! Jerry!"

He changes the channel.

"Guess I'll just watch Jeopardy," he grumbles.

Monday, November 2
2:01 H.T. / 8:01 p.m. E.T.

Mrs. Jacobsen's Current World Affairs class, mostly 12th graders, stares at the screen aghast. Nobody says a word. Mrs. Jacobsen herself has left her desk to use the restroom and top up her coffee in the break room, telling her class to take notes. Outside the door of her classroom, she feels as though she can hear what sounds like hoedown clapping and the President's voice shouting something like, "Just like mama used to whistle!" Puzzled, she opens the door to find 18 students, 20 empty notebooks splayed open, and, on the floor, two puddles of vomit creeping towards each other.

She surveys the mess and the stunned atmosphere; she identifies two empty desks next to the puke. The lone 9th grader in the class, tiny Crystal Iosua, extends an arm and an accusing finger towards the smartboard. Mrs. Jacobsen turns to the subject of the students' collective gaze with the slow, head-turn of horror, reads the caption at the bottom of the screen and dives for the button on the side of the smartboard. Hits the power button just as... just as...

"Okay," says Mrs. Jacobsen. "Okay! Well..."

The class blinks at her.

"So! The... um..."

The class blinks again. Has their blinking synced up? Are they blinking in unison?

"Now!" she says. "Let's...."

They are blinking in unison.

Blink.

Blink.

Blink.

"Okay!" she says. "So then... go ahead and, uh..."

They blink again.

Not a word.

"Open your books to..."

There isn't a book in the room. They read websites and magazines.

The class blinks.

"As I was saying..."

They blink again.

"Let's just... go ahead and... yeah."

A knock at her classroom door, and she sees department chair Ms. Lambert's round face through the glass rectangle in the door. The department chair mouths the words "Pee. Pee. Tape!" to Mrs. Jacobsen. Mrs. Jacobsen nods slowly. The department chair flails her arms in the air like a distressed marionette and disappears from view.

Mrs. Jacobsen's eyes return to the blinking chorus, and without another word, she takes her seat. Her blink joins their rhythm.

Nobody says a word. The bell rings.

Nobody moves.

Monday, November 2
7:02 C.T. / 8:02 p.m. E.T.

The TVs above the bar are muted in favor of a seemingly endless loop of Bob Seger's "Old Time Rock and Roll" pounding out of the jukebox. It's played six times in a row. Someone thinks they're a comedian.

The Blues don't play until 9 o'clock, so the news is on. The foursome of regulars who know each other only in the context of their usual positioning at the bar are struck momentarily dumb as the anchor has disappeared and been replaced by the steady flow of footage. The closed captioning is on, but even though people on the screen are speaking, there are no captions apart from that single headline.

"This ain't real, is it?"

"Can't be."

"What'd he say?"

"I can't read lips, man."

"Looked like, 'I am the Dia-per man.'"

"What's he doing? Is he dancing?"

"Whoa."

"Wait. This isn't the, uh... this isn't actually the..."

"Oh my god."

"This can't be real."

"Sure looks real."

"Can't be."

The footage continues unabated and uninterrupted.

The bartender joins them, leans back against the bar and cranes her neck to see the screen.

"Wow. Wow, wow, wow."

Periodically, they recoil in concert, and say, "Ohhhh."

"Is this real?"

"Can't be."

"Looks real."

"I mean, it's the news." The footage starts again, this time from a new angle.

"It's real."

"It is real."

"Oh!"

"That is real. You can't fake that."

"You could, but... not that. No."

"Nope."

They lower their eyes and re-center their attention on their beer.

It has lost appeal.

"Gonna switch to wine," says one, signaling the bartender. "Wine. Red. Please."

"Same."

"Same."

"Same."

The bartender takes their half-empty beers and empties them into the sink while the regulars avert their eyes. As the bartender retrieves four wine glasses from the rack overhead, the hammering piano notes that mark the start of "Old Time Rock and Roll" ring out for the ninth time. One of the men swivels on his stool and says, "I'm-a-kill somebody."

Monday, November 2
8:03 p.m. E.T

The festive tumult in Times Square is at a standstill. The tourists, the actors in costume, the cops, everyone, frozen in their tracks, fixated in distress at the enormous, nine-story, 4K screen, so bright it could illuminate the square without any help from the 100 other screens blazing from on high.

Tourists clamp hands over children's eyes. Never in human history, never, have 15,000 people made so little noise.

A few people, born to the moment, have their cellphones out, videotaping the transfixed crowd, heads rocked back, jaws slack, turkeys in a rainstorm.

Silence. Stillness.

Then a man bellows, "Oh like we didn't know!"

It snaps the trance.

Some giggle. Some grimace, and gulp, and rattle their heads as if to dislodge the images. 14,978 people, give or take, lower their eyes and keep them lowered, as they move again, gradually, with heavy motion, cancelling plans with every step, intent on abandoning the streets to search out quiet spaces where other people are not.

Monday, November 2
8:05 p.m. E.T

"Now clap like you're a seal!" her husband's voice says. The First Lady turns off the television and rolls her eyes. Please, she thinks. As if he would do such a thing.

Is there nothing they won't stoop to? She slides her feet into her slippers and shuffles towards the bedroom.

"Darrrlink!" she calls. "Fakeynews alerts! Darrrlink!"

Monday, November 2
9:22 p.m. E.T

Yoshi Nakamoto is off the clock. Tucked beneath his drum-tight Holiday Inn Express high thread-count sheets, he is pointedly not going to turn on the television this evening.

His phones are off.

Today's laptop is blissfully incinerated (there's always such release in that).

Work-life balance is so important, he thinks, thinks it with such vigor he nearly says it aloud to himself. He spins the wheel of his old iPod to a classical music playlist. Taps the button and is surrounded by music that was composed hundreds of years ago.

There is peace in Bach. A peace so pure and perfect, as if the old man had opened some vein in the collective unconscious and set some truth loose for anyone willing to listen.

Yoshi thumbs through his novel until he finds the most recently dog-eared page.

The only light in the room shines down from the bed-side lamp.

Perhaps, he thinks, someday, when all is revealed, people will wonder: how did he sleep at night?

Like this, he thinks, and makes a sweeping gesture with his hand. Like this.

Beautifully.

Tuesday, November 3 / Monday, November 2
6:11 a.m. Moscow Standard Time / 10:11 p.m. E.T

The Russian President has swung between silent prayers and torrential threats. Prayers to the Lord above to unclench the fist below and release this Kraken. Prayers to any and all deities who might, in passing, free him of the steely monster coiled in his insides. Prayers, even, pleading prayers to little Putivic himself. "Please let go," the President mewls between his legs. "Please."

And then the threats, very specific threats, to anyone who dares to knock or tap on the bathroom door. Threats to life, liberty, family, loved ones, body parts, children. Terrifying threats. Detailed threats. Followed by calmer words, "I'm fine! I'm fine. I just need a minute."

Eight hours. Eight hours and twelve minutes. He is aware of how long this battle with Putivic has sustained.

The government is paralyzed beyond that thick door. Communications remain severed from the outside world, and those who sally forth to reconnect the Russian state keep disappearing.

Those men nominally in charge of the state are unable to act, fearing the wrath of their absent President, should they overstep or step in the wrong direction.

The Russian President is exhausted. Beaten. Distraught.

This is his lowest moment. He knows it. He has known life's struggles, and this is the deepest depth. He hasn't cried twice since he was a child, and now he has wept three separate sessions in one day.

And the smell. Just when he feels he is fully immune to the

stench, some wandering waft will wend its way up his nose and prick his senses anew.

Can he sleep? He wonders. Can he safely sleep in this state? Perhaps that is precisely what he must do. Perhaps only sleep will relax whatever it is within him that must be relaxed to allow resilient little Putivic to relent.

The Russian President folds his arms across his knees and rests the side of his face across his wrists. Soon, the exhausted man is asleep.

He dreams of falling trees crashing in silent forests. He dreams of a man called Robechev, a man he knows not, a man born of his imagination, splitting trees and yodeling into the clear blue sky as he swings his axe. Over. And over. And over. And over. Bold chops of the axe send clouds of splinters to blister the air. Trees become wood. Wood is rolled into a boiling river. Drifts swiftly away into the distance. So satisfying to watch the wood drift away. Flooosh.

The axe falls. Chop! Chop! Chop!

The President's eyes flit open. The knocking at the door again.

"Leave me alone!" he shouts. "Leave me alone or I will freeze your limbs off and drop what remains of you down a well!"

The knocking stops. Or had it ever started?

Had the knocking been real?

Has he begun to confuse his dreams with his very real dilemma? Would this be life now? Is this what remains to him?

He checks. Though, of course, he knows already. It's still there.

For the fourth time today, he weeps.

November III

Tuesday Chooseday.

Tuesday, November 3
9 a.m. Central European Standard Time / 3 a.m. E.T.

The novelty of The Pope's "man among the people" act has by now worn so thin in the neighborhoods around the papal apartments that the staff of his favorite cafe no longer even wink at the old man in his touristy "The Vatican" sweatshirt and "Italy Rox" baseball cap. His Holiness politely places his order at the counter and takes his usual seat in a corner by himself to settle in with the International Herald.

The cafe's atmosphere shifts, though, as a tall woman rests her hand on the chair across the small table from The Pope and says in Spanish, "May I?"

"Claro," says The Pope and lowers his newspaper an inch. He studies her over the top of the paper, as this lovely woman, dressed in a simple black t-shirt and black twill pants lowers herself into the chair. "Good morning," The Pope switches to English.

"Good morning," says Moshi Nakamoto. "Am I so obviously American?"

"You are familiar to me," says The Pope. "Your face."

"Another life, perhaps," says Moshi.

The Pope chuckles. "Perhaps metaphorically."

"Perhaps," says Moshi.

The Pope looks at Moshi, thoughtful. He folds his newspaper and rests it on the small table. Shakes his head. "I know you. But I cannot place you," says His Holiness. "I am sorry."

"We have never met."

"You are just here for coffee?"

"I need a favor," says Moshi.

The Pope smiles. "How may I help?"

"We may help each other." Moshi produces a narrow envelope from her back pocket and lays it on top of the folded newspaper.

"What is this?" asks The Pope.

"Photographs."

"Of course," says The Pope. "Do you have a pen? A... marker?"

"I don't want your autograph," says Moshi.

"Oh," says The Pope. He picks up the envelope, studies it, and opens its flap. Pulls out a slim stack of black and white photographs. Flips through them. His face never drops the benevolent smile, but his hands betray him with a gentle tremor. He straightens the stack lightly against the table and returns them to the envelope. Then he slides them into the folded newspaper. When he looks back up at Moshi, the smile remains but his eyes have steel in them that wasn't there before. "What is it you want?" says The Pope.

"A political endorsement."

"I've been paying you people for forty years." He spits the words.

"Not us."

"No?"

"You don't have to worry about those people any longer."

"No?"

"No." Moshi holds her hands up in conciliatory fashion. "You'll never hear from them again. Those people. They have nothing. They are nothing."

"No?"

"No."

"I have you to worry about now, eh?"

"Not that, either. One favor, and you're done."

"Of course. A phrase I have heard. Many times."

"The negatives are destroyed. Two sets of prints exist. That one," Moshi pointed at the newspaper. "And one other. The other is yours after you give your endorsement. Your troubles end there."

"Of course," says The Pope.

"I am sincere." Moshi sits back in her chair.

The Pope sighs. Thumbs the thin pages of the newspaper. "It is not so easy," he says. "People think this office... that I can do or say what I please. There are layers of people, a machine, between me and the world. The press office. They will never release such a message. Nothing political."

"They won't need to," says Moshi.

A waiter interrupts their conversation, arriving with a tray bearing two coffees and two croissants. Sets them down and leaves.

"You have excellent taste," says The Pope.

"I asked for whatever you're having," says Moshi. They take a bite of their pastries. Crumbs rain down on plates.

"Why should I trust you?"

"You can simply fear me for now," says Moshi. "If you'd prefer." The Pope raises his eyebrows in agreement. "But," continues Moshi, "you can turn to page 13 of that newspaper. It may put you at ease."

Intrigued, The Pope rests his croissant on his plate and opens the newspaper, scans the page, finds the right article. His head disappears into the newspaper. Moshi finishes her croissant in three bites. She is on a schedule. She is always on a schedule. The Pope emerges from the newspaper with a new expression on his face. Astonishment. More beatific. A tinge of hope about him.

"They won't bother you further," says Moshi.

The Pope nods to Moshi. "I am in your debt," he says.

"Not for long," says Moshi.

"These photos," The Pope pats the envelope. "I was very young. It was meant to be funny. In Argentina this was funny."

"They are funny."

"Just a thing a young man does."

"Of course."

"Yes! But people don't understand."

"No."

"The Pope. He moons the camera?"

"The Pope's ass."

"Oh my God. The Pope has two butt cheeks. Oh no!" The Pope waggles his fingers in the air in mock horror.

"Forget about it," says Moshi.

"Exactly. Forget about it," says The Pope.

"Forget about it. I'm here to help you truly forget about it."

"How do we proceed?" asks The Pope.

"You come and go as you please, I gather?" says Moshi.

"I do."

"You can take me into your apartment?"

"Yes."

"Good. We go there. You put on your vestments. Your tallest hat. We record two one-minute messages. I have a short script. One in Spanish, one in English."

"Then?"

"Then we're done. You swear, on a stack of Bibles, I assume you have one handy, not to retract the message. I leave. You're done with..." Moshi gestures towards the secreted envelope, which The Pope has unconsciously rolled back into the newspaper. "All of that. For good."

The Pope studies Moshi. "I don't know why," he says. "I feel I can trust you."

"You can," says Moshi.

"I could use someone like you," says The Pope.

"You are," says Moshi.

"Beyond this matter."

Moshi pats her pockets and smiles. "I don't carry a business card."

"No," says The Pope. "I wouldn't guess so."

"Okay?" says Moshi.

"May I finish my coffee first?"

"It would be a sin to waste it," says Moshi. The Pope smiles. Takes a sip. The waiter arrives again and brings Moshi a second small cup of espresso. Moshi drains the cup, comically small in her expansive hand, and sets it next to her first cup.

"You like coffee, no?" says The Pope.

"Si," says Moshi.

The Pope nods approvingly. Drains his cup. "Let us roll," he says.

Tuesday, November 3
6:00 a.m. E.T.

Being first in line is a tradition on Election Day for Shirley Lanofil. From her first election in 1958 until today, Shirley's been first in line every time. The same polling station in Charleston for 62 years. Always wears something red and something blue. And now, she jokes, that her hair is white she wears the full flag. She doesn't have a party. She has a country. That's what she tells people impolite enough to ask.

She's rarely had much competition for the first slot. Voting isn't the sort of thing that people camp out overnight for.

Until today, apparently.

She is crushed when her niece drops her off in front of Burke High School, a full hour before the polls open, and she sees at least fifty people, a few of whom are taking down a row of tents lining the path that leads to the front steps of the high school.

She walks gingerly towards the line with a look of disbelief. The line is nothing but young people, she realizes as she gets closer. This is even less likely than a line in the first place. Half of them are black. Half of them are white. Maybe a few straddle the line, one way or the other, racially speaking, but as a whole, the impression she gets is of a group of friends? A club? A biracial voting club? What is this?

Shirley reaches the end of the line and taps a towering young woman on the elbow. "Excuse me?"

"Good morning!" The woman lowers a smile at Shirley. This young woman is lovely. She could be an actress.

"Are y'all in line to vote?" says Shirley.

"We are. Yes. Are you here early, too?"

"I am. Yes. I always am."

"That's good!"

"Did you sleep here?"

"We did! It was so much fun."

"Didn't you get cold? I'd get so cold, sleeping out here on the sidewalk."

"It wasn't so bad. We've got good sleeping bags. Coats. And we have these little battery space heaters." The woman pulls what looks like a pink, plastic lantern from a large hiking backpack.

Shirley studies it. "That's real nice," she says. She pokes it with an index finger, purses her lips, and nods. "Y'all got it all laid out real nice."

"Mmhm," says the glamorous young woman. "We've been planning for weeks, so we kind of turned it into a party, you know. To help get a few of our friends who might've dragged their feet to come out and vote."

"So you know everyone here?"

"I do now. It was a good party."

"Oh yeah?"

"It was an evening. I can tell you."

"Didn't the police come shoo you away?"

"No. My friend Marigold," the woman points down the line to a woman wearing a chunky knitted beret featuring a plastic, orange flower on its brim, "she works in the Mayor's office. She helped us get a permit."

"Y'all got a permit to throw a party on the high school lawn?"

"To camp out."

"Hmph," says Shirley. She leans around the woman and

studies the line again. It isn't even a good line. Jagged to the point of amorphous. Too much mingling to be a good line.

"Would you like some coffee?" The tall woman flourishes an aluminum thermos.

"I don't want to put y'all out," says Shirley.

"Not at all."

A sleeve of paper cups appears from the camping backpack. Shirley pulls one from the top of the stack the young woman tilts towards her, then holds the cup as the girl pours out steaming brown coffee.

"Thank you kindly," says Shirley.

"For a civic minded friend, a pleasure," says the young woman. "I'm Margaret."

"Nice to meet you. Shirley." They don't shake hands but nod to one another.

"Have you lived in the neighborhood very long?"

"My whole life. I was born in the house I live in."

"Wow! That is. Insane."

Shirley raises her eyebrows. "And you?"

"Moved here in June. We rent a condo on Rutledge. My friends and I?"

"That's nice." Shirley sips the coffee. "Thank you for the coffee."

The girl smiles, then responds to a dinging noise. She pulls a phone from her puffy vest's pockets and studies it. She turns and says something to the man in front of her, a short man with a shaggy beard, clad in a brown, corduroy jacket. He's a sloppy little fella. He is not taking care of himself, this tiny man. Surely this cannot be Margaret's boyfriend. Shirley takes a step to the side and eyeballs the line again. She tries not to stare, but just look at them! They're all so young and happy.

317

So smooth. These girls are so smooth. So pretty. And the boys just look derelict. Tousled. Bearded. But then the smooth faces and shining eyes. They betray their youth. Their money. Even rumpled, these unwashed boys are beautiful.

Part of Shirley wants to shuffle to the front and ask that young woman in the rainbow overalls and the stars and stripes stovepipe hat if she can cut in front. She could tell her, "I've been here first, every election since 1958. Would you mind if I stepped in ahead of you?"

She decides against it. She knows she can't, because she knows exactly what she would have said herself, in 1958, if some little, old lady had tapped her on her shoulder and said, "Excuse me. May I cut in line front of you? I've voted first here in every election since 1920."

Shirley would have demurred and said, "Yes. Of course, ma'am." She'd have allowed the little old lady to cut in front. And then she wouldn't have been first in line. And then she wouldn't have made a point of being first in line every election. It wouldn't have meant as much. Not as special. Maybe she wouldn't even vote every time an election came along. So no.

No. Shirley steps back in line and sips the coffee carefully.

Best all around if she stays where she is. She counts the line in front of her. Today, she will be voter number 53.

53's a good enough number.

Tuesday, November 3
7:00 a.m. E.T.

The President is still lying on his back in bed, gold lamé top sheet pulled tight over his face. The First Lady has been up for two hours getting ready. She's been patient, but over the last twenty minutes she has begun to bang around a little bit. Her heels clomp on the bathroom tiles like hooves on cobbles. She brushes her teeth as loudly as she can. At last, she stabs at the control panel next to the bed, and the blinds open. Daylight crashes into the room and through the thin, shiny fabric, bright enough that even through closed eyes, the President can see a reddish glow.

"Darrrrlink," she whispers.

He ignores her.

"Darrrrlink," she whispers again and taps the mattress three times.

He growls from beneath the sheet.

"Time to wakey," she sings. "Shakey, bakey, here comes a–"

"Nooooo," he groans.

"Earth quakey!" she shouts and pounds her fists on the bed next to his head. She giggles and swipes the pillow from under his head and pounds him on the face with it. He catches it and clenches it over his face, as if to smother himself.

"Oh my God," he mutters into the pillow.

"What? Darrrrlink! Time to get uuuuup! Time to win!"

"Nooooo," he moans into the pillow.

"Forget Tuesday. It's Youse-Day!" She takes a step back from the bed and waits. He doesn't move. Keeps the pillow in

place. "You want me play my music?"
"No."
"Time to get up."
"No."
"I'm going to put it on."
"No!"
"Then get up."
"No."
"Here it coooomes." She taps at her phone a few times. Slovenian folk polka pumps from the speakers embedded in the ceiling over the bed. She spins and dances to her favorite accordionist.

The President endures the jolly oompah thumping for as long as he can, but, as always, he submits. Throwing the pillow and sheets off his face, he gasps, "Okay." He waves his arms in the air, surrendering. She pretends not to see or hear him and continues dancing. She knows she hasn't really won until his feet hit the carpet.

"Okaaaay!" he shouts. She ignores him. He tears at the sheets and swings his feet over the edge of the bed. He hurls a pillow at her, aiming for her calves, conscientiously avoiding her dress. She taps her phone, and a blessed silence ensues. The President storms past her into the bathroom and tries to slam the door behind him, but the door is one of those designed to whisper shut at the last second, so he can never get the desired –BLAM!– he wants in moments such as these. He plants his palms on the bathroom counter and looks in the mirror. The pouches under his eyes seem deeper today. Rimmed in purple.

He reaches to the back of his neck and unpins his black satin sleeping bonnet. Tosses it to the side of the vanity. He rolls his head from side to side and watches his hair bounce with the motion. "There you are," he says softly to his hair. "There you go, baby."

He uses the toilet and washes his hands, drying them carefully. Then moisturizes thoroughly. His reflection scowls at him. He exits the bathroom and finds his wife sitting at the edge of the bed waiting for him. She glances at a chunky gold bracelet as if it is a watch. Which it is not. "Let's go, sweetyheart!" she says. "You want Blizzard on plane? I'll tell them breakfast on plane."

They are scheduled to fly to the Southern White House to cast their votes this morning in the Sunshine State. The victory party is scheduled to be there tonight as well. Then the plan is to stay on for a week or so, entertain friends, some dignitaries, maybe get a few rounds in. It's all...

"I'm not going," says the President. He sits down beside his wife and grabs her hand. Tight. She is taken aback by how tightly he holds her hand. She is fully dressed. Hair perfect. Accessorized. Made up. He remains barefoot in his favorite red, silk pajamas. "I can't," he says.

"Don't be sorry, darlink, it's—"

"It's over," he says.

"What do you mean? It's—"

"No. No. It's over."

"That's what everyone says four years ago. And then you go Boom! Big win! Win win win!"

"It's all over. Not just this." He gestures around the room. "I mean us. You. Me. Everything. We're done."

"Darlink!" She stands. "What are you saying?"

"Rudy's filing the paperwork this morning."

"What?!"

"You deserve better. Much better. It's time for you to move on."

"I–"

"Take the boy with you when you go." He shoos her away. "Go. Take the plane. Go to Florida. It's too cold here."

"No, I–"

"Get the fuck out." He stands up and looms over her. She is suddenly aware of his size in a way she never has been before. His shadow smothers her, and she takes a step back.

"Darlink." She can barely whisper. "But I luff you."

"Now."

She takes another step backwards. Neither says another word.

She leaves the room.

He lowers himself back into bed. Pulls the sheet back up to his chin.

He stares at the ceiling, his jaw set. His eyes are dry but an observer, an intrusive and judgmental observer, could be forgiven for assuming that this might not be the case for very long.

I am alone, he thinks. Finally. Alone. This is all I've wanted. Solitude. And everything I've feared.

Where are my children?

Tuesday, November 3
7:22 a.m. E.T.

Vonkers answers the knock at the door where she finds the doorman in his dark blue uniform holding a brown paper bag aloft. He presents it to her with both hands. "Ma'am," he says.

She takes it without a word, closes the door, and carries it into the kitchen where she empties its contents onto the counter. A box stuffed with doughnuts of every description: crullers, bear claws, jelly-filled, chocolate covered chocolate, birthday cake, maple glazed, blueberry cake. A carrier with three coffees. Three hot chocolates. A narrow brown paper box. She opens the lid to reveal a pile of crispy, thick, pepper bacon.

At this rate, her brothers might never leave.

The time-controlled safe has been reset for another 24 hours. It's been a relief to be free of their phones. They've talked about it a number of times since this strange vigil began. More than they've talked in years, really, to anyone, let alone each other. Life without a phone in your pocket or purse, it's like a monastic retreat. It couldn't last forever, this respite, but it could last another 24 hours, surely.

Would their families be worried? Maybe. Maybe a little. But everyone knew the days leading to the election would be madness. They were scheduled to be apart. Their lives would not be their own; it was understood.

But here they are, together, during this brief window.

Junejune appears as if from the sky. "Bacon," he says, and plucks a piece from the paper box, snaps a piece off in his teeth. Disappears again.

Rico appears from the other direction and assembles a

stack of his favorite donuts. "Maple. Chocolate. Cruller. Tower. Bacon chaser."

He disappears.

She pulls down her favorite yellow plate from a shelf and arranges her own collection and joins them on the couch. Each of them sits, Indian style, food in the diamond formed by their calves and thighs.

"Dark Crystal?"
"Little Monsters?"
"Herbie?"
"Fuck Herbie."
"Fuck Little Monsters!"
"Guys."
"Sorry."
"Sorry."
"We are the World."
"Oh."
"You have that?"
She holds it up.
"Oo."
"Oh."

She stands, opens the box, and slides the cassette in the VCR.

Tuesday, November 3
7:34 a.m. E.T.

The lines at the 7th Presbyterian Church of Oxford, Ohio are longer than anyone can remember. All the way to Milligan's front door, which is handy enough, as you can dip in for a cup of coffee and a biscuit sandwich before you commit to the line. The counter kids are jolly sprites, too young for the line. The owner's at the end of the line in the church, scrutinizing people's driver's licenses before they can get a ballot.

Gregory Jemson is three people away from the door when a fight breaks out behind him. The fifth fist fight of the morning? People need to speak with their votes and shut their mouths beyond that.

It's those red hats. They're a provocation, he thinks.

As are the blue hats. Whoever came up with "Grake Mamerica Gate Atain" deserves a pat on the back. At first, dismissed as absurdist proto-protest-wear, they started popping up in Williamsburg and Portland and all that, then bled into the suburbs and thence to the Midwest, where all beautiful things go to make money.

Either/Or is the spirit of the day in the college town. The brick streets of Uptown are a mélange of student groups and old folks groups, segregated by red, white, blue, and black. The Nakamotans in black shirts, black headbands. "Nakamoto" in white across their chests. "Why Not?" across the headbands in white.

Bernie Bros in festive baldcaps and whimsical wisps of white cotton, four feet long, that dance in the wind above their

325

heads, high-fiving every few steps in their rolled-up white shirt-sleeves.

Red Hat Crew in white t-shirts and jeans walk up and down the length of the street, trying to make eye contact with people walking past. Shouting, "I want to dialogue!" periodically and giving everyone the creeps.

Blueys. Loads of blueys, blue t-shirts up-top, yoga pants below for the women and tapering khakis for the gents, singing chants and cheers about the nominee. Handing out little blue poms and Dixie cups of coconut chai latte.

Classes are canceled for the day and the bars are open. Very open, and very full, especially considering the early hour on a Tuesday. The Society of Concerned Tavern Owners held a pow-wow with the mayor and the police chief and have come to a secret agreement that they won't be carding today. Not anyone. But you do have to show your "I Voted" sticker to be served. Doing their bit.

Some poor sucker dressed as an ice cream cone stands in front of the IDF handing out samples of red, white, and blue ice cream with chocolate chips on top. Something for everyone. And no one wants to hear that. Cups of the stuff litter the roofs of any building unfortunate enough to be shorter than three stories, which is most of them. It becomes the thing to do, chucking the small cups of unification ice cream. Eventually, the ice cream man has to take shelter from an overeager black-clad fraternity that half-hatches a plan to throw him on the roof of a low-slung vegan taqueria. Too drunk to half-accomplish the feat, but still, the teenager in the ice cream man suit has no interest in discovering the extent of their will or the flaws in their plan. Retires to the break room to ball up and have a nice cry.

The fights come and go. There's no blood. It's all shoving and posturing and someone keeps shouting a guttural mantra of, "Come at me, bro," and it rings in the air like a round of "Row, Row, Row your boat."

Upon entering the church's social hall, Gregory is relieved at the silence he finds within. It's as if out in the world, the shouting, the chanting, the jeering, the hooliganry and the festivity, all of that is a carnival. And this is a place of worship. A serious room where adults gather to determine the fate of the free world. And he is one of them.

He extends his hands, one laid on top of the other and receives his ballot from a serious-mouthed woman who looks for all the world like Barbara Bush in a yellow blouse. All of the poll workers are in logoless yellow tops. Clearly prearranged to avoid the appearance of bias.

Gregory takes his ballot to the privacy of a table, shielded from his neighbors by a white plastic panel on three sides of the desk. He uncaps one of the thin, black, felt-tipped marker pens at the desk and begins the slow, careful work of democracy.

For each office, he scans the options listed and goes to the bottom line where there is a blank straight line next to the final bubble. He carefully pens the name "Fartstick McGillicunty" into each write-in line for every possible office and fills in the bubble next to his chosen candidate.

Satisfied, he walks his ballot to the exit and feeds it into the machine, supervised by a short man wearing a garish black t-shirt featuring a bald eagle in leather playing an electric guitar. "You wanna sticker?" says the man, proffering a round "I Voted," sticker with a tiny American flag next to the words.

"I certainly do, good sir," says Gregory.

He slaps the sticker on his forehead and strolls back into the chaos of the election day crowds, a confident sway in his stride to let the world know he has voted, and that all the nonsense outside could mean nothing more to him now, for his work here is done for the day. He is a participant.

Tuesday, November 3
8:00 a.m. E.T.

Gary wakes up with a gasp, stiff and sore from neck to ankles like he's never been sore before. The flannel blanket he'd curled up beneath the night before is bunched in his arms. He is facing the wall, but he can feel someone watching him. He rolls over to discover a slender man crouched at eye level, next to the bottom bunk, squinting at him. Gary starts backwards and tries to sit up, hits his head against the bottom of the top bunk and pushes himself up on one arm. The man doesn't move, but his squint does widen by a millimeter.

"Morning," says the man, and nods.

"Hello," says Gary.

"You know you snore, man?"

"Sorry. Yeah." Gary rubs his head and tries to read the man's neck tattoo without appearing to stare, but it's difficult because the letters are ornamental gothic letters that will require more focus than Gary feels it's safe to give them at the moment.

"It's cool. You might want to see someone about it, though."

"Yeah." This man is concerned for his health.

"They moved me in here to look after you, man," says the thin man. "Last night." He finally stops crouching and leans back against the concrete wall, still half-squinting at Gary.

"Who did?"

"The guards."

"Why?"

"Dunno. I think they thought you might top yourself."

"And you're supposed to stop me?"

"I don't know. I guess I was supposed to shout or something if you started making a noose."

"Would you have?"

"You want me to?"

"I'm not going to."

"It's twenty bucks."

"I'm not going to try to kill myself."

"You say that now."

"What?"

"Everybody says that, man. Even the ones that go ahead and do it. Especially those guys."

"Oh."

The man raises his eyebrows and makes a face to indicate that he knows of such things.

"I'm Gary," says Gary.

"Okay," says the man.

"What..." Gary sits up carefully, has to slouch to avoid cracking his head again, and swings his legs over the edge of the mattress. "What are you in for?"

"You're not actually supposed to ask people that, man. That's just in movies."

"Oh. Sorry."

"Prison etiquette, man. You ask a guy like that, first day you're likely to catch a shiv."

"Oh. Sorry. Okay. Thanks."

"I'm just kidding, man."

"Oh. Ah. Ha ha. Yeah."

"Just kidding."

"Yeah, so–"

"Shit. That's all we talk about. That's the ice breaker.

That's the main course and dessert. Shit."

"So what'd you do?"

"I killed my aunt with a rolled-up newspaper." The man picks his nose.

"Oh," says Gary. "That's..." He stops. How to phrase it? Best not to round out the phrase. Maybe just shut up. Gary nods. "Yeah?"

"No," says the man. He giggles at Gary. "Shit, man. This is just jail, man. Not prison. No. I did a little B & E. Allegedly. I don't know what they have yet. How would you even kill someone with a newspaper, man?"

"I don't know your aunt," says Gary. "Maybe she's frail."

"No. All my aunts could kick my scrawny ass," says the man. "Half of them have. But I'm being rude, man. Monopolizing the conversation. What are you in for?"

"I–"

"I'm joking, man. Everyone knows what you did."

"They do?"

"Yeah man. You're fucking famous in here. And abroad. Your ass is on every TV channel."

"Oh."

"You're like a folk hero, man. Not everyone's cool with your politics, of course."

"Right."

"But most of them are all for taking control of your woman. So that's cool, man."

"Oh."

"Of course not with me, man. I frown on it. I'm an enlightened modern man. Think of myself as an ally. But with most of these guys, you're alright."

"That's good."

"Of course, you'll want to watch out for the ones who are not alright with you. There's always a few, man. Always a few that want to make a name by taking out a jailhouse celeb."

"Oh."

"And you do fit that bill."

"Oh."

"But I wouldn't worry about it, man. The guards'll keep you safe. You got a few fans on staff here, for sure, man. You're probably untouchable, since you're famous and all. Nobody wants to be a guard on-duty when a famous person gets snow-capped."

"What's snow-capped?"

"You don't wanna know man."

"Oh."

"You really don't wanna know."

"Okay."

"But if you see a guy with, like, filed teeth, man, like fangs, and a question mark tattoo on his nose, like... don't make eye contact with him and try not to, you know, like touch him, and like don't be alone with him, and like if you do, man, just try to knock yourself unconscious against the wall or the floor, 'cause like... no, man. Seriously."

"Okay. Thanks."

An enormous guard appears at the cell door. "Johnson!" he shouts. "Hands through here."

The scrawny man walks to the back of the cell and studies the wall while Gary submits his wrists and hands through the designated gap in the bars and receives the cuffs. The guard unlocks the door and slides it open for Gary to pass through.

"Good luck out there, man," the man shouts over his shoulder.

"Thanks," says Gary.

"Shut up, you!" says the guard, pointing a baton towards the man. He slides the door closed and gestures Gary to walk ahead of him. The guard mutters to Gary, "Don't know why they've got you with that guy. Freaking weirdo."

"Yeah?" says Gary. They walk down a narrow concrete corridor past mostly empty cells.

"Oh yeah," says the guard, through his teeth. "We've had our strange ones in here, but that guy's off the charts."

"Why?"

"You didn't notice the teeth?"

"I was mostly staring at his neck."

"He filed his teeth, his bottom middle teeth, he filed them down to these sharp little fangs." Gary looks back over his shoulder at the guard who rambles on. "It weirds me out every time. And he talks about himself in the third person like he's a supervillain. Probably in the wrong facility if you ask me. But they keep shuttling him back in here saying there's nothing wrong with him. But really they're just as freaked out by the guy as we are."

"Is he violent?"

"Allegedly," says the guard. Gary turns and sees the guard's half-smile. "Allegedly very violent."

"Where are we going?"

"Your lawyer wants to meet you."

"I don't have a lawyer yet."

"Apparently you do."

"But I didn't–"

"You made bail. And you have a lawyer. Kind of a famous one, too. I've seen him on TV. Smart money says you'll be out of here in an hour."

"What?" Bail had been set at three million dollars. Gary has no chance to make bail.

"Turns out guys like you have a lot of friends."

"But I don't."

"There's a GoFundMe that says otherwise. Here we are."

"GoFundMe?"

"I threw 20 in the pot." The guard gives him a conspiratorial wink. "Enough's enough, you know?" He opens a heavy metal door and guides Gary into a room outfitted with a small table and two chairs. A man in an expensive three-piece suit stands as Gary enters the room. Gary recognizes him from television as well. Holy cow.

"Sorry about these," says the guard as he unfastens Gary's handcuffs. "Rules are rules, and my boss is not sympathetic to our ideals. But I get you."

"Thanks," says Gary.

"It's a privilege. I'll see you in 20," he says to the lawyer.

"Make it 30," says the lawyer.

"You're the boss," says the guard and swings the door shut behind him.

The lawyer extends a hand and shakes Gary's. "Let's get you out of here, Mr. Johnson."

Tuesday, November 3
7:30 a.m. C.T. / 8:30 a.m. E.T.

It is the strangest sensation, thinks the Democratic candidate, catching her reflection in her laptop's screen, the most bizarre experience to feel so morose but appear so euphoric. She tilts the screen forward to lose her reflection. How odd to lose control of one's facial expression. She never fully grasped, not until now, how much she uses her face to communicate. How awful to wear this mask and to never be fully understood. In fact, to contradict yourself with every miserable word. Words are not enough.

She finishes an email and hits "Send."

The TV blathers on in the background. Local Green Bay news. Weeks earlier, staff decided it would be good visuals to finish the campaign in the Midwest, so here they are. Freezing their November nuts off. She'd worn her scarf into the hotel, through the lobby, with her sunglasses on. Near fiasco. Wisconsinites think it's the snobbiest thing in the world to wear sunglasses indoors. They'd hustled her into a staff elevator and made it to the Holiday Inn Express Presidential Suite unscathed.

Three staff members filter in and out of the room and their faces betray them. Things are not going well. Of course they aren't going well. They're going dreadfully. They're in the homestretch, and she's become a ghost while Nakamoto is dropping publicity bombs, and that's perhaps an insensitive way to phrase it in light of... yesterday's... good God, but she's only thinking here, so, in light of that, just let it go, but while she's blowing up, nope, wrong phrase, while she's pulling into the lead, the Dem's nowhere to be seen. Invisible. She's doing comedy podcasts, for God's sake, phoning in to Maron? Conan? Even the semi-serious ones are head-scratchers. Brokaw? Who even knows he has a podcast or why? She hears he does it out of a Jamba Juice in Connecticut. Just pounds juice and records phone calls and forwards them to his niece who majors in digital humanities at Oberlin to edit.

And the aides all try to paint a rosy portrait, but she knows what it smells like. There's a dead body around here somewhere. And you know what they say. If you're sitting in a room with a corpse, but you can't tell who the corpse is... it's probably you. She was a staffer once, herself, of course. She's been around enough cadavers to see the flies in everyone's eyes.

And of course, someday, this all comes out. Any day. Gringate. The first staffer to blab is the only one who gets paid, and tomorrow morning, they'll all be unemployed for the most part, so what will keep them all in line? She's surprised, in fact, no, she's touched, actually, that it hasn't made the news yet. She can barely believe it.

Her phone rings. Her husband. She dismisses the call. Feels bad immediately. Doesn't deserve that. Calls him back while he's still leaving her a voicemail. He switches over and answers her call. Like he always does. She's never had to leave him a voicemail. It's one of the reasons she loves him.

"Hey, babe," he says.

"Hi," she says.

"Hanging in there? Get you anything? I'm with the staff down here at the uh... you know, shoot. What's it called? This little cupcakery downtown, pressing the flesh."

"Having fun? How's the sling? Did the rash go away?"

"Oh yeah! No, it's great! It's relaxing. It's like a little vacation for my right arm. Love it, babe."

"I don't know why they made you put it on the right arm. I really don't." (Although she does, because it had been her idea to make it look more realistic if his dominant arm was incapacitated.)

"It's fine! It really makes you think, you know? How dependent you get on one specific hand? It really makes me grateful, or it's going to make me really grateful, when they take the cast off. But I'm grateful already! What am I saying? I love my right arm! I love you!" She can tell he's talking to his arm. "And I love you!"

"That's great, honey."

"You hanging in there, babe? I can usually tell, but with the... thing, I can't tell. Doing okay?"

"Yeah. Full-speed ahead here."

"I've always said it. I've always said you only ever had one speed. And it is: 'Now.'"

"Thanks, sweetheart."

"You're sure you don't want me to bring you something? These young gentlemen make some very interesting swirly-looking muffin things and the lamination on their croissants is just, I mean, you couldn't–"

"Thank you, sweetheart. I'm fine."

"No problemo! We'll be back your way in an hour! Okay, babe! Richard is making that face."

"Right."

"He says I shouldn't say 'Problemo.' Isn't he a crack-up? You're a crack-up, Richard!"

"Okay."

"He's still making that face. The one that says I'm talking

too loud near open microphones."

"Okay, bye then!"

"Okay, babe! See you in sixty sweet–"

She hangs up.

She loves the jolly idiot. When this is over, she's going to buy him something nice. He's going to need a hobby that is not her career. What should he do? They'll do something with the shed in the back. Nothing creepy. Nothing figurine-y. No dolls. Pottery? Woodworking? She can't picture him using a lathe. Maybe not woodworking. Little model ships? Planes? Blacksmithing? They could put a forge back there. He could– no. That's not it.

He could go the Bush route; do some painting. Water colors? Maybe water colors. She thinks Bush does oil paintings, so this would be same but still different. He could take lessons.

And she'll write her book. Her "tell-some" tale of rise and fall.

She sighs at the thought of it. The writing.

She consults the spreadsheet. "Michelle!" she shouts. Michelle's head appears around a door frame.

"Ma'am?"

"Is it Aukerman or Ackerman?"

"Aukerman, ma'am?"

She sighs. Adjusts her headset. Dials the number.

Tuesday, November 3
8:50 a.m. E.T.

Sister Adeloga's third period Moral Theology class is gathered around Therese Martinique's cell phone in Our Lady of the Perpetual Sigh High School (mascot: the Fighting Sighs, long story). Sister is in the hallway, as all teachers are required to stand sentry during passing periods, while the students in her classroom watch the video. It isn't often that their interest in social media overlaps with their religious instruction. When she re-enters the classroom, the students scramble out of their scrum and back to their desks.

"What's the fuss, Gus?" asks Sister Adeloga.

Silence greets her.

"What's going on?" she asks again.

Again, they stare at her. She returns the empty stare. A standoff. Their blue sweater vests aligned in rows like seated soldiers. The silence lasts for thirty seconds.

"Amnesty, sister?" says Peter Pham, finally.

She sighs. "Is it serious?" says the nun.

"Depends," says Peter. He scratches his head, gauging the offense. "No. I guess not," he says. "Yes and no. But no. Not really serious."

"Amnesty," says Sister.

"So–"

"No!" says Therese.

"She won't take it," says Peter.

"What's going on?" says Sister Adeloga.

"We were looking at–" Peter says and pauses. "A cell phone, sister."

"Yes?"

"And there was a video."

"Okay."

"Of The Pope."

"Yes?"

"And he was endorsing a Presidential candidate."

Sister Adeloga frowns at the young man. "I doubt that very much," she says. "Whose cell phone?"

"Dammit, Peter" says Therese.

"Amnesty!" Peter beseeches her.

"Yes, yes," says the nun. "I just want to see it. Who's got it? No. Never mind. I don't want to know." She sighs. "I'll just look it up."

The nun opens her laptop and types a few words into a search engine. The students watch as she views the video with subtitles on. Her eyebrows knit in confusion. She closes the lid and looks over her pupils' heads.

"Does this mean you have to vote for Nakamoto?" says Imelda VanDeezen, a girl with long braids nearly to her backside.

"I'm voting after school," says another boy. "Does this make it a sin to vote for Bernie?"

Sister Adeloga taps her finger thoughtfully on her desk for a moment. The students watch expectantly as she mulls the matter. She stands. Walks to the back of the classroom. She does this sometimes. Looks out the window. At present, a squirrel is dragging the remains of a fast food submarine sandwich along a thick tree branch outside the window towards its leafy nest. A meatball slips from the bread and tumbles to the ground. Sister watches the squirrel struggle until the paper wrapper disappears into the nest. She turns away from the window and returns to her chair behind the desk. She rests her elbows on the cold metal of the desktop, and lays her chin on her intertwined fingers.

"Yes," she says. "If you are to continue as a member of His Church, you must vote for Mr. Nakamoto. As must I."

The class is stunned.

"And will you?" asks Peter.

"Yes," she replies. "It is a Papal Bull. And I have made vows. I shall obey him."

"But–" says the cross-eyed girl who Sister can't remember the name of on a good day, although she's somehow sure it rhymes with "crisp".

"Plus, why not?" says the nun, interrupting the girl. "Anything else would be an improvement." The class raises an eyebrow. "Now," she continues. "Open to page 224. 'The Informed Conscience.'"

Tuesday, November 3
7:15 a.m. M.T. / 9:15 a.m. E.T.

The line leading to the front doors of the Mountain View Dispensary hasn't been this long since the grand opening six years ago. In fact, it's two parallel lines. The owner of the shop offered up the dispensary's private event space to the city election commission, and after a series of contentious hearings, the commission had finally accepted the offer. Their only condition is the placement of a clearly labeled velvet rope to guide people into the voting area, and then an exit from the polling station out the back, rather than a return trip through the foyer. If you wanted to make this one-stop shopping, you'd at least have to make a trip back around to the front of the building from the alley.

Despite that mild obstacle, the dispensary is still doing a brisk business, mostly customers who have just cast their ballot and looped back around to the front entrance.

People are walking out of the voting booths flushed. Red faced with exertion. Like they just voted so. Fucking. Hard.

Voters of all ages. Pounding through the exit like they just righteously kicked someone's ass in a bar fight. They hit the alley. Turn the corners. Walk into the dispensary. Asking for something that will make them feel like they've been shot to the moon.

The Wambassadors try to talk them down, encourage them to pursue the mellow of the moment, find peace amid turbulence, etc. but ultimately, the customer is always right.

If the customer doesn't want to participate in consciousness as polls close and results roll in, that's the customer's right and nobody else's business.

Well. It's kind of the Mountain View Dispensary's business. But only literally.

And as agreed by the membership of Colorado's Society for Patriotic Dealing, nobody scores today until they've voted. The bar for proof is low enough. An "I Voted" sticker. Easy enough to borrow off a friend or whatever. Still. It's another nod to civic responsibility. Marijuana must snare what opportunities it can to prove itself a good neighbor.

Tuesday, November 3
8:30 a.m. C.T. / 9:30 a.m. E.T.

Marta double-checks the four sandwiches on the counter, each laid before the correct lunchbox. The chips are the correct chips. Then celery for Daniella. Carrots for Isabelle. Radish coins for Adolphus. Persimmons for Emily. Coconut Greek yogurt for each. A small pouch of gummi vitamins for each. Adolphus buys the school milk. Isabelle gets a tiny aluminum can of pineapple juice. The other two get a can of LaCroix.

Good.

She packs the contents into their lunchboxes and stands them up, handles on top, and arranges them by the age of their corresponding owners. Oldest (Emily) to youngest (Isabelle). Just as she always does.

Marta's own son will find lumpia in his lunch bag in a few hours. A special day. His school day already began an hour ago, so he doesn't have long to wait. Sometimes Marta likes to picture what her boy is doing at any given moment. She sees more of the quads than her own boy. She feels guilty about that, so perhaps picturing him, thinking about him, helps level the score slightly. Whatever, she likes doing it.

Right now, she sees him sharpening his pencil at his desk in a very tidy and focused manner, just as he always does. The curl of brown wood shaving falls in one piece onto a square of notebook paper he has rested on his desk as a receptacle. When he's finished, he folds the square in on itself, keeping the wood shavings in the center as he goes until he has a little paper packet the size of a single Monopoly die. He puts the little paper square in his red, plaid shirt pocket and pats it three times. Beautiful little man.

Mrs. Fitzpatrick appears in the kitchen and skeptically surveys the line of lunches like a wedding planner eyeing the cake one last time. Just daring that frosting on top to wilt. Not that she knows which lunch pail belongs to which of the quads.

Marta has a fantastic passive face. She can do stoic better than most people can breathe. She ignores Mrs. Fitzpatrick's evaluative mood and turns her attention to cleaning the breakfast dishes. She knows Mrs. Fitzpatrick is not a cruel person. Maybe lonely. Definitely understimulated. Massively insecure.

Marta has learned, and of course it takes practice, that other people's moods nearly never have anything to do with her or anything she's done. Easy enough to say, but believing it took years.

"Marta," says Mrs. Fitzpatrick.

"Yes mom." Mom is her ma'am.

"Have you had the chance to vote yet?"

"No mom."

"But you will. Right?"

The quads have swim practice after their string quartet rehearsal, the cutest thing, and Marta drives them to and from each activity. She should be done by 7.

"I think so, mom."

"You absolutely must, you know. It's the most important thing you can do. Our country's at a turning point."

"Yes mom."

"Do you know who you'll vote for?"

Marta's dishwashing catches a hitch for a moment, then continues at a slower pace. "Yes mom."

"Can we talk about this? Can we talk about something real, for once?" says Mrs. Fitzpatrick.

Marta turns off the running water and dries her hand on a towel. She doesn't turn towards her employer but continues to stare at the blue and white Valencian tiled backsplash. She sighs. She has never sighed in front of Mrs. Fitzpatrick. "Yes mom," she says. "I have to drive the children to school in ten minutes. Maybe when I get back?"

"Why not now?"

"I think maybe, you mean more than ten minutes?"

"Oh. No. I think we can chat now. Just for a minute."

"Yes mom."

"Okay, so...?"

Marta just stares at her in reply. That infuriating, patient way of hers. Mrs. Fitzpatrick hates that shit. It makes her feel so unreasonable. It makes her feel crazy.

"So? Who will you vote for?" says Mrs. Fitzpatrick.

"Mom?"

"For President."

"Mom? Who will you vote for?"

"I asked you first. And you know who I'm voting for. You've seen the signs on our front yard. I'm not shy about it. For Pete's sake, Marta, you've worked for us for six years, I think you know which way Danny and I will be voting. Don't you?"

"Yes mom."

"So?"

"Mom, I work for you for six years, yes?"

"Yes."

"So maybe politics is not a good idea, mom?"

"Marta. It's a simple question."

"Yes mom."

"So?"

"But it isn't simple. I am afraid that maybe–"

"You can't seriously be voting for him, Marta. Not after everything he's done to your people. Said about your people."

"Mom, it's not so simple–"

"How can you say that? How can you possibly say that? After all the horrible... all the horrible things he's said. Rapists! Marta, rapists! All of your people?! That's hate speech. It's a war crime! That's what it is. It's a verbal atrocity. And his policies–"

"Mom–"

"You cannot possibly, possibly be thinking of voting for him. I know your people have very strong feelings about abortion, and I get it, I so get it, but think about everything you've been through! How hard you've worked! And all the awful things he's said about you in return? And how many of your sister workers are employed in his hotels and restaurants and who knows what else?"

"Mom–"

"I mean, build that wall? Where would you be, Marta? Where would you be if that wall were finished? What would your family be doing? Right now? With the cartels?"

"Mom, I'm Filipina!"

Marta's facial expression has finally changed, and it isn't happy. The hand towel lies on the ground between them. They stare at each other. Have they ever made eye contact of this duration? Marta wears a scowl and Mrs. Fitzpatrick (Helena, if you're wondering at this point) wears a face both astonished and appalled.

"I am so. Sorry."

Marta's face has returned to its native neutral state. "It's fine. It's okay mom."

"No. Oh my god. I am. So. Sorry."

"Mom, no."

"I was about to... Oh my god."

"No, Mom. Please." Marta has already returned to the dishes.

"Marta, please."

"It's fine, Mom."

"But I never, I never even asked. I just. Assumed."

"Is okay."

"But you made us tacos. Every Friday for the past five years, you've made us tacos, and they were so good! And I asked you to! And you never said a word."

"I like tacos."

"And yours are very good."

"Thank you mom."

"Oh my god." Mrs. Fitzpatrick laughs. "Oh my god." She sits on a stool at the kitchen island. "And dia del muerte?"

"Wikipedia!" says Marta. She chuckles as she continues to finish the dishes. "Is good."

"Oh my god. And tamales."

"Is okay. I learn a lot!"

"Marta. I love you, Marta." Mrs. Fitzpatrick is buckled over on the stool. Cackling now. "Oh my gawwwwd."

"Is okay!"

"Marta! It's not okay!"

"We are all people, mom. Is no problem."

"But." Mrs. Fitzpatrick straightens up on the stool. "You aren't going to vote for him are you?"

Marta pauses mid-task. She turns to her employer. "Yes mom," she says. "I am."

"But why?"

Marta shrugs. "You know."

"Abortion," says Mrs. Fitzpatrick. "But you know he doesn't really care about any of that. He's probably paid for a bunch of abortions. You know he's a womanizer. Right, Marta?"

"Maybe," says Marta. "Yes, maybe. Okay. I don't like him. But it doesn't matter what he thinks. Look at what he does. Look at what he does."

"But," Mrs. Fitzpatrick is foundering. She looks at Marta. Really looks at her. "What do you care?"

"About the babies?"

"They're not babies. Not yet. They're just, little beans. What do you care? What about a woman's body? What about her life?"

"What about baby's life?"

"It's not a baby!"

"Is a baby. I think so."

"Well," says Mrs. Fitzpatrick. She picks up a towel and absentmindedly dries a cup from the drying rack. "What about the Pope?"

"Huh?"

"What about the Pope?"

"Yes?"

"The Pope. What he said?"

"What are you talking about?"

"This morning. The Pope's video?"

"Huh?"

"Here." Mrs. Fitzpatrick pulls her phone from the kitchen island and taps its screen a few times. She tilts it towards Marta, who watches, rapt. The video ends.

"Papa," murmurs Marta.

"I know," says Mrs. Fitzpatrick.

"But..." Marta looks anguished.

"He's made his peace with it," says Mrs. Fitzpatrick.

"But I never vote for her."

"The directive is clear. You have. To vote for Ms. Nakamoto. That's the freaking Pope, Marta."

"Yes."

"It is."

"I know."

The dishes are done.

Mrs. Fitzpatrick smiles. "Are we going to go vote together?"

"What?"

"Let's go vote together."

"I don't vote same place as you."

"That's okay. You'll come with me. I'll go with you. Girl's day out!" Mrs. Fitzpatrick flings her hands over her head playfully. "Woo!"

Marta smiles. She nods and juts her lower lip for a split second. "Okay," she says. "Let's go vote."

They high five. Their first high five.

"You know. I don't vote for her."

"That's okay! Just don't vote for him."

"Okay."

"Okay!"

"I don't like him really!"

"I always knew it, Marta. Marta, you're the best."

The quads appear in the kitchen, crisp, clean, and ironed. They scoop up their lunches with tiny hands and head for the door.

I am so blessed, thinks Mrs. Fitzpatrick, watching Marta smooth their hair and straighten their collars, zipping up neglected backpack zippers. The housekeeper opens the door, and the quadruplets file out towards the Range Rover. Marta pauses at the door and holds the door open for Mrs. Fitzpatrick.

"Shotgun!" shouts Mrs. Fitzpatrick and jogs out the door in her boots. "Shotgun!" She playfully nudges Emily towards the back door. Emily pouts and shuffles towards the back door. "Yay!" she says, buckling her seat belt.

"Yay," says Marta.

The quads, in the backseats make four-way eye contact and sigh.

Tuesday, November 3
7:35 a.m. P.T. / 10:35 a.m. E.T.

Seated before a bank of nine monitors, Ivory Jenkins leans forward and squints towards the bottom half of the screen devoted to global Crypto exchanges. BitCoin's been all over the map the last six months, starting when a quarter of the Nakamoto shares finally moved. The price plummeted initially. A scare that the whole block would go up for sale. If that had happened, who knows? The price could have dropped to a penny. Ivory is a Cryptobull. His job was nearly toast.

But the rest of the Nakamoto shares didn't budge. Things stabilized. Then the campaign announcement. Ever since, the thing has looked like an EKG during a heart attack. Up and down with zero predictability. Nobody's been able to build an algorithm remotely capable of keeping up with it. The news is constant. Giant dips, then gargantuan recoveries. Mammoth rallies.

Overall, the trend has been up. You have to take a really big step from the chart to see it, the line so jagged, it's like a magic-eye portrait, but yes, if you bought a year ago and sold today, at the right minute of a lucky hour, you'd make ten times what you paid.

Ivory's grown immune to the minute-by-minute volatility of the stuff.

Or so he thought. The price just spiked. Like 1000% in a minute. Someone, somewhere just made a God-bet. Like a sovereign nation-level bet. And not some small sovereign-nation. This was not Swaziland throwing their teacher's pension away, this was like, Switzerland switching over from their Franc. And then you'd expect a dip. People cashing out, hitting some auto-sell number, there's always a dip. But it just keeps spiking. And spiking. And spiking. But he can't rightly call it a spike because a spike has two sides, and this just keeps climbing. He hears someone in the room scream and hit the floor.

Ivory is sweating. His stake in BitCoin, his own modest stake alone, has just surpassed 50 million dollars. The firm's investment is... Dear Lord. He taps the "Event" button all the traders have at the base of their monitor stand. He's never tapped that button. The only people who have tapped that button in the office have been fired. That button is for World Wars and events that in thirty years will have names that start with the word "Great." Events that defy hyperbole.

The other traders flock to his desk. Jeremy, the Chief, elbows people aside and plants both hands on Ivory's shoulders. Leans over his head. Ivory's head is bowed forward by the weight of Jeremy's blacksmith-crossfit-pumped torso, so he can no longer see the top screens at his station. Jeremy makes a noise or possibly says "Calliope" or sneezes or something and then the pressure on Ivory's head and neck relaxes.

Jeremy has fainted. Jeremy with the bronze casting of (supposedly) John D. Rockefeller's testicles on his desk, Jeremy who makes seven figures a year for precisely these moments, Jeremy who once called then-Baltimore Ravens linebacker Ray Lewis "a shiny little beyatch" to his face at an American Heart Association fundraiser, that Jeremy would be on the floor, if it weren't for the crowd of mostly pudgy quants crowding around the desk, now barely supporting his significant bulk before it hits the ground.

Ivory turns to watch the titan fall. What now? What is he supposed to do? His job is to spot trends, not pull triggers. He turns back to the screen. If you hit the sell-switch at the right moment now, it's the difference between hundreds of millions and... billions. But who even knows? What is happening?

"Do I sell?" he shouts. "What do I do?" No one responds. The primary decision maker's eyes are rolling in his head. The partners are away. The only one who calls them directly is Jeremy. The system's always worked before because Jeremy's never lost consciousness. There is no failsafe.

"Fuck it," says Ivory. "I'm selling. 75% of our stake." Even if he's wrong, he's wrong and rich.

He sells. He hears an "ooo" noise around him, the quants quiver. Ivory can hear them recalculating their respective net worth as a percentage of the firm's massive holdings.

They were all rich before. Now they're all wealthy. Generational wealthy. PayPal founder wealthy. Unbidden, an idea flashes into one of their heads for a foldable car. Another wonders, for the first time, why Mars gets all the attention when Venus is sitting right there, begging to be colonized? But still they watch the price. Please plateau, thinks Ivory. Please plateau. Please plateau. Or drop. Go ahead and drop.

But as the gathered men watch, the number keeps rising. Rising and rising. Their spirits fall. They are all insanely wealthy. But just look at how much wealthier they could have been if this idiot hadn't just sold. Over thirty seconds, they watch their wealth diminish and fall away in the face of the wealth they could have had. Ivory can hear the sound of their arms crossing. Behind and beside him. They pace away to their own stations to mourn in solitude.

Ivory watches.

It just rises and rises and rises. On and on and on and on. It's a disaster.

Tuesday, November 3
10:39 a.m. E.T.

Satoshi Nakamoto's phone pings.

She ignores it.

It pings again. And again. And again.

One ping, she understands. She expected at least one alert, but...

It pings again.

She pulls the phone from her jacket pocket.

Huh.

It pings in her hand repeatedly. Gathering steam until it takes on a cadence like morse code. She silences it and just watches the screen, moderately surprised. The pings are set to fire every time the price doubles. Doubling is the only marker that interests her at this point. Or used to be.

She clears her throat.

She is now worth a trillion dollars.

Worth.

At a certain point, you know, what's the difference? What's the difference between 10 and 20 billion dollars?

What's the difference between 100 billion and 200 billion dollars?

But a trillion?

Something about that number is different.

Satoshi says the word aloud: "Trillionaire."

Tuesday, November 3
11:21 a.m. E.T.

The Secret Service detail outside the apartment building have begun to whisper among themselves, speculating as to what in the hell is going on up there. Since the initial sweep three days ago, before Codename Dolly announced her intention to have a little get-together, nobody's been allowed in. The vaunted Secret Service professionalism is beginning to fray.

All three details have been milling around since Sunday evening, their itineraries constantly being cleared of events and travel. The tenants of the building don't even look twice as they pass through the lobby at the somber mass of dark suits, dark glasses. The residents pass through the screenings, resigned as airport travelers, while their Trader Joe's and Whole Foods bags gets scanned and man-handled.

Three details means the Secret Service can divide up the active response and take turns. It would be quite a relief if the whole situation weren't so weird. Or if they knew when it would end.

Two-thirds of the details are enjoying their turn in an impromptu HQ established in the doorman's office, playing cards and drinking diet sodas, and keeping half an eye on the TV mounted on one wall. As secret service agents, they're used to waiting, but this isn't the time of year when they're used to it. This is usually a stimulating window in the calendar.

A lanky Virginian pauses at the precipice of flinging three trump cards on the table (left bauer, right bauer, ace, cha cha cha!) when all the men and women in the room freeze in place at the whisper through their earpieces.

Big Boss is coming, too?

The cards are hastily swept up and chucked in the trash. The details are shuffled to various floors. The rooftop, surrounding buildings, everything's already covered. But don't get spotted playing cards on-duty for God's sake, unless you want to spend the remainder of your career walking Laura Bush's cockapoo past Dallas McMansions. They don't even have sidewalks, you know? You take your life in your hands walking a cockapoo in suburban Dallas.

The fourth detail pulls up outside the building and Big Boss is trundled through the lobby and into the elevator. On up to the old apartment with the rest of them.

Does anyone have any idea? Curiosity of that sort is frowned upon, but who can help themselves?

The Model's down in Florida on her own with Babycakes. Kooshball's down there too.

Marlita's back in D.C.–still going to classes.

Everyone else is here?

Today?

The Kiddos haven't even left to vote.

The Press is on to the whole thing now, too, so the pain in the ass for all involved is amplified. And the Press seem to know even less than usual. Drones buzzing around the top of the building. Some poor idiot parachuted in. They don't even have the right floor.

No one knows a thing, and now he's here too?

What in the hell is happening in that apartment?

Tuesday, November 3
11:25 a.m. E.T.

Rico is asleep on an oversized beanbag chair holding a stumpy glass bottle of Original New York Seltzer brand root beer. Even asleep, the bottle is tilted, half-raised towards his mouth, frozen in time. He still somehow hasn't spilled a drop.

Vonkers is lying on her stomach, her elbows planted in the thick shag, her chin resting on her hands, left folded over right, while she watches Beverly Hills Cop 3. The best of the series. Her long, blonde hair looks a little stringy at this point, draped just to the edge of her field of vision. One small line of her hair is pulled forward, a braided bang bisecting her eyebrows, tucked into her mouth, coiled around her tongue.

Junejune has put on ten pounds in less than three full days. Hasn't looked in a mirror since he put on the pajamas and has no intention of doing so. Only leaves his sleeping bag to use the half-bath and even then closes his eyes to wash his hands. Seriously.

The timer on the phone safe still has three hours to go.

Junejune has forgotten the plot of BHC3, as he used to call it, so each plot twist is a surprise. He is falling in love all over again and Eddie Murphy is a genius. Such a genius. Junejune is 17 again. Having those dreams, those waking dreams that used to wash over him at school. Those dreams where he's holding hands with... Half-shy. Sun rising over campus. For a moment, he can see the morning sun flashing across the Pennsylvania treeline. Looking down on trees, such a thing, to look down on a treetop from the height of the library's top floor.

Maybe, he thinks. Maybe becoming an adult is just one

long attempt to understand what you knew as a child without even trying. Maybe all that irony and all that cynicism all that dirt, it's as if the world has buried you alive. You've got to dig out and rediscover yourself.

He fills his mouth with Cheetos.

That's it. That's what this is. This is a rediscovery.

And then the door opens.

Dad walks in. Alone. The door closes behind him. He stands there, looking at them. Rico's tiny kitten snores, the only sound. Vonkers looks over her shoulder at Dad. She could be 13 again. That little braid in her mouth. The look too-cool to ever be surprised. Defiant eyes.

Junejune tries to stay calm, but there's a fear, more elemental than his conscious self can control, climbing his spine. The sight of his father. That look on his face. That thing his jaw is doing.

Junejune is unmanned. If childhood is truly his destination, he just arrived.

Dad walks towards them, into the living room. His eyes on the screen. He watches. Eddie Murphy is on a Ferris wheel for some reason. Climbing from swinging car to swinging car. Still wearing that varsity letter jacket.

Without a word, Dad sinks into his old La-Z Boy recliner. Without fumbling, reflexively, Dad knocks down the lever with a practiced motion and the chair reclines. The built-in ottoman springs forward so fast that Dad's legs bounce in the air above the footrest before settling in.

Dad sighs.

Vonkers turns back towards the television. The muscles around Junejune's spine relax and he turns back to the TV, too. Rico continues his nearly subsensory snoring.

A family reunited.

So, thinks Dad. So, so, so. Here we all are. The family. No harm, no foul. Hopefully.

Tuesday, November 3
12:25 p.m. E.T.

Moshi catches the airport bus and transfers to a second bus that carries her back to her neighborhood. She doesn't even go to her studio first. Gets off the bus and right into line.

The single-file procession trickling into the building at Moshi's designated polling station is nearly three blocks long. It trails back out the double doors of the elementary school, down the main walkway to the sidewalk, then turns the corner. Then turns another corner!

And oh, shit, is it ever cold.

Moshi pulls the sides of her hat lower over her ears and gets in line.

The man in front of her wears a heavy flannel coat, the red and black tartan of much of New England's folksiest folks. He wears a blue baseball cap with a dark red letter "B" outlined in white, and a navy hoodie pulled tight over the hat. He turns, looks up at Moshi and nods. "Democracy at work. Am I right?" The man throws his hands in the air. "All this, for what?" he says.

Moshi does not respond. Just looks down at the man. Squints a little.

The man continues, undeterred by silence. "I mean what's the point? Stand here for hours? Out here in the cold. And does my vote mean a thing in this state? No. State's so blue it swallows you up. So if you, you know, vote with the Dems you're a drop in a full bucket and, you know, if you vote with the Republicans, you know, you're pissing in the ocean, you know. And if you vote for the libertarian, you know, you're like doing performance art. It's not even voting, you know. Just martyring yourself or something. Like ooooo you're so principled and everything and good for you, but like, hey man, hey. Hey. You know. Real world called, man. Can't go live on the moon yet, you know? Uncle Sam's still gonna take his cut. Even if you do go to the moon, you know. First thing they did when they got there, what'd they do? Put the flag down. Why? So they can tax it. But–" He juts his jaw forward and his lower lip rises over the rest of his mouth as if to say, "What are you gonna do?" Then he goes right ahead and says, "What are you gonna do? I only have the one vote. But it's mine and I'll be god damned if I let these hordes of maniacs take it away from me. You know? You've got to do something. I mean I know. I'm preaching to the choir here, 'cause I can tell, you know, you and me are on the same page, and there you are and here I am and here we are. But still. You know? Kinda feels like a waste of time. Don't get me wrong. They're not gonna keep me from doing my part, but you know. It does feel like a waste of time. It does."

The man looks up at Moshi. He appears to be waiting for a verbal response. Or is he listening. To someone else. "Are you on the phone?" says Moshi.

"What?" says the man.

"Are you on the phone? Or are you talking to me?"

"What?"

"Sometimes I can't tell."

"What do you mean?"

"If people are talking to themselves or to me or on the phone."

"Sorry. There's some lady here. I can't hear you over this lady." He turns and his voice drops to a stage whisper, "You should see this lady. She's the biggest lady I've ever seen." The man clamps his hands over his hooded ears. "It's election day. The loonies always come out of the woodwork on election day. It's no wonder the country's such a shit show. She's jabbering at me like a lunatic."

The man ducks his head, hands still clamped to the sides of his head, and mutters on.

Moshi considers cracking the guy in the throat with her elbow. Dismisses the idea. Not worth the trouble. She cranes her neck to try to see around the corner of the building. The line hasn't advanced an inch since she joined.

Tuesday, November 3
2:25 p.m. E.T.

Yoshi Nakamoto gets the texts he's been waiting for.

"Turn off the machine."

"Pick ten highest performers & formulate a victory cell in DC"

"Pay out everyone that needs paying"

"dont skimp"

"Ten million extra for yourself. job well done"

Thank the Lord.

Yoshi opens his wind-down document and scans it once, top to bottom. His memory is superhuman, but this project needs to finish as well as it began.

He starts his calls. Shuts down each cell, one by one. The news is greeted on the other end with relief. With jubilation. Tears in a few instances.

Bit by bit, he disassembles everything he's built. East to west.

It's so much easier to destroy than it was to build, Yoshi marvels. He even cranks up the pace on the treadmill and keeps the calls moving as he churns out the mileage.

At last, he finishes the call to the final cell.

"That's it?" says the young woman running the Hawaiian cell.

"That's it," says Yoshi.

"Oh! That's... Do you think there might be opportunities. In a Nakamoto administration? For someone like me. Maybe?"

"Maybe," says Yoshi. "I'll put your name down as interested."

"That's cool. So what's next?" says the woman. "Or. What's first?"

"Gotta keep moving," says Yoshi. "Be in touch."

"How?"

He hangs up. Slaps the red stop button on the treadmill. Drapes a hotel gym towel over his face and sits on a padded bench.

That's that. Whatever it is. That is that.

Either they've done it. Or they haven't. Whatever it is they've done. Or nearly done.

Yoshi catches his breath. Mops his bald head, sweeps the sweat from his eyebrows.

What has he done?

    What has he done?

        What has he done?

Tuesday, November 3
3:45 p.m. E.T.

The crew in the Manzanita Hyatt sits around the conference table for the final time. Rolling suitcases line the walls, and Atticus is reading from a fax that just finished printing. The same message is being read by leaders at each of the cells, except the final ten being preserved for celebration follow-through.

"Friends," reads Atticus. "We did it. We did it together. Thank you for your work. Without your time and energy and brilliance, none of this would have been possible. In the days, weeks, and months ahead, you will see first-hand how we have united our country in the name of Change.

Your contract with Nakamoto for President is now officially terminated and the agreed upon payments and any supplementary bonuses and incentive-based bumps have been transferred into the bank accounts and digital wallets you provided our organization.

Each of you now qualifies, in the eyes of the federal government and the world at large, as a wealthy individual. Congratulations and pay your taxes.

If you'll take a simple piece of advice from a person who knows from experience: wealth isn't everything. In fact, it isn't much of anything. Wealth is the illusion of safety in a dangerous world. Never mistake it for anything more than that. The sense that you are safe is the most perilous trap you will encounter. There is no net to catch you. Not really. You must live dangerously in this dangerous world.

That's it for advice.

The laptop you were issued upon hire is yours to keep. Please enjoy it in good health. The device has been wiped remotely, as some of you may have already noticed, and restored to factory settings. Your access to official email accounts, shared drives, and all other Nakamoto for President materials and resources has been disabled. I apologize for the abrupt nature of that housecleaning and hope you understand.

Friends, I thank you from the bottom of my heart. Whatever happens next, know that you made it all happen.
Namaste,
Satoshi Nakamoto
a.k.a.
your friend, Sarah."

Atticus lowers the letter to the table. "Sarah," he repeats.

"So..." says Limey. "That's it?"

"That's it," says Atticus. He tears the letter into strips and drops them in the wire trash basket.

"Does anyone want to go grab a drink? Or something?" says Limey.

Michelle shakes her head. Everyone else does the same. Atticus says, "No."

Everyone attends to their messenger bags, half studying their phones as they pack. Atticus pulls on enormous Finnish, silver, noise-canceling headphones and intermittently bobs his head as he slides his laptop into his bag. Without a word to each other, they depart the room, one-by-one, wheeling black bags behind them until only Limey remains, seated in her chair.

She removes the laptop from her bag and slides it to the center of the conference room. Lays the power cord on top of it. Sets her phone next to it. She'd purchased it shortly before taking the gig.

Limey doesn't trust any of it.

She stands and backs away from the table, slings her bag over her shoulder and snares the extended handle of her suitcase as she walks out the door alone.

Tuesday, November 3
4:24 p.m. E.T.

The Pussy Hats are out and they have been. Day? Drinking? Everyone has the day off so it. Is. On. So on? It has been on, if the full story is told, for six hours.

First: vote.

Lines had been: hellacious? But so what? Like, got in eventually. Selfie with the ballot. Tag that m-f-er. So many likes. Like, instant likes. Fucking, Ellen liked that shit. Fucking, Oprah liked that shit. Fucking, Bey, liked that shit? We are all viral today. On out into the chilled air with the roomies and besties to the local, organic micro-distillery slash café that is on the verge of becoming "basic", they can sense, but is not totally there yet, so it's good.

Hats of every color. And you know what? It's cool. It's all good. In the hood.

Scouts are dispatched from tables and a conciliatory vocabulary rises from an organic place. Hands are placed softly over hearts. People find themselves bowing to one another.

"You are my sister," a woman named Bristol in a pink hat tells a woman in a yellow hat.

The woman, Siobhan, extends a hand. "And you, you are my own."

The tears puddle between them. Puddle.

The young men trickle in. Wary at first. Greeted by guarded gazes.

Bernie Bros. Nakamotans in Black. Hu-man-Allies clad in pink and blue "I'm with Her" shirts.

Is there tension? Yes. Obviously. It's been a minute. But

the spirit of the day, the being-finished of it all, suffuses the room. The alcohol has a pacifying effect and the only-recently-legal edibles play their part in mellowing the space.

Peanut butter cups.

Red licorice whips.

Chocolate chip cookies.

Someone brought, like, bowlsful.

It's a children's birthday party that has chewed through its leash.

Shift manager takes the cue and dims the lights two hours earlier than usual. Fires the playlist she programmed yesterday: "Peppalection." Joyous jams with a minimum 160 beats per minute. Pumps the music two notches higher to accommodate the crowd, the vibe, crosses her arms and nods to the beat. Cool. Tips will be alright tonight.

The television sets are off.

The truce extends itself across every line.

Gender? Race? Sexuality? Go ahead and explain all that to the past if needs must. Tonight, wait it's tonight already?, how is it night already?, anyways, tonight is for everyone. For all Americans.

Is that what it is? Is that what they're feeling? Is this patriotism? Love for a country? Love for that common thread connecting them all? Isn't that normally saved for sporting events and disasters?

Who cares? Tonight?

Tonight.

One way or another.

This is over.

Tuesday, November 2
9:19 p.m. W.E.T. / 5:19 p.m. E.T.

Paralinka gradually regains consciousness with a tightness clamping his gut. Turns out to be a seatbelt. He plucks at it with his index finger, bewildered. Looks around. The situation clarifies. He is on a plane. A dazzling plane. First rate by any standard. He has the row to himself. He is so thirsty. Dizzy. Parched. He fumbles with his seatbelt for nearly a minute before he is able to release the latch. Grabs the headrest in front of him and pulls himself to his feet. The plane is even nicer from that vantage point. Every row is business class.

His staff fill the seats. Most are still well asleep. Unconscious. A plane full of Russia's most experienced hackers, technicians, and computer scientists.

No Stormont. Thank God. The deadly giant is nowhere to be seen.

A gentleman in a smart blue vest approaches at the sight of Paralinka's wobbling stance.

"Good morning, sir," says the man in vaguely accented Russian. "Would you care for some breakfast?"

"No," says Paralinka. "Or... yes. But first, I need a restroom."

"Of course, sir," says the man, proffering a hooked arm. "Please allow me to assist you. The anesthetic leaves people mildly disoriented."

Paralinka accepts the arm, and the man escorts him past row after row of Mother Russia's finest minds to a washroom that he is surprised to find both spacious and well-stocked. It contains a full-sized shower, toilet and bidet, a neatly stacked tower of freshly laundered, white hand towels (mildly lemon scented) next to the spotless ivory sink.

He might cry.

"Whatever else," thinks Paralinka, "at least I have lived to see this airplane restroom." The sentiment is absurd, he knows, but he feels it no less for that fact. As he empties his bladder he reflects that this relief can be no less than a gift of angels. After, he splashes cold water on his face and pats himself dry with a hand towel.

Emerging from the washroom, he finds the man who led him there holding an oblong copper tray bearing a glass of orange juice and two neatly-arranged aspirin on a tiny, red plate.

"Sir," says the man, with a modest bow of his head.

"Thank you," says Paralinka. He pops the pills in his mouth and gratefully knocks them back with the orange juice, the most delicious, the most refreshing orange juice he has ever known.

The man guides Paralinka back to his row without the slightest condescension, not a hint of being burdened by the task. He is so gracious, this man.

Paralinka settles back into his seat. He can hear the plane stir as the fleet of technicians begins to come around. More men, dressed in blue vests, appear from behind the curtains at the front of the plane, ready to assist with every stage of recovery, guiding people to restroom, arriving, unbidden, with just the right foods and drinks. Name it, and it appears.

Confusion reigns on the plane, but it is a satisfied sort of confusion.

Paralinka considers the conditions. They are being pampered. Are they being wooed? Or are they being lulled? Is this the lead-up to a sales pitch or an execution? He's far too cynical to think it could be anything else. He decides a sales pitch is imminent. Who would go to such lengths to subdue a doomed cadre?

No, he decides.

An offer is in the making.

But what offer? Who is this? Who can afford such a thing? This plane is custom-fitted to such a purpose. He gathers himself and staggers to his feet again, slides into the aisle.

A blue-vested man appears.

"Which way to the bar?" asks Paralinka.

"This way, Mister Paralinka," says the man, with a nearly imperceptible bow. Paralinka's legs are steady now, and he follows a pace behind the tidy man, down the length of the plane. At the sight of him, various technicians recoil in their seats, jarringly reawakened to the details of reality. He ignores them and follows on.

The blue-vested man pulls a thick, velvety curtain aside at the back of their cabin to reveal a darkened room. The man stands aside and bows his head again, inviting Paralinka to walk past him into the room. Inside, Paralinka is greeted by subdued copper light and a horseshoe bar, behind which stands a cleanshaven man with a professional smile.

"Good evening," says the man in a refined Russian accent. "A drink?"

"Please," says Paralinka. "Scotch. Neat."

"Will a Macallan suffice, sir?" says the man.

"What year?"

"1970," the man says with a genuinely apologetic downward glance.

Paralinka nearly chokes on his spit. Makes a noise like a

dying moped. Recovers. "That will be fine," he says.

The man nods his gratitude and pours a crystal tumbler three-quarters full. Presents it on an ebony coaster. Disappears to a corner of the horseshoe, pretends to dry glasses that are not wet.

Paralinka sips the valuable liquor. An analogy involving angel wings intrudes upon his thoughts.

A screen atop the bar begins to glow. Fades up from black. A woman, not unlovely, greets him, greets all of them, as the message plays across the seatback screens throughout the plane to the entire Russian crew.

The sales pitch. He knew it.

It's a good one.

She offers options:

Return home. To whatever. To God knows what. Shame. Demotion. Siberia. The unknown is the only guarantee. Possible execution.

Or: Fiji. Their families relocated. Extended families, too. Homes. Salaries. Opportunities to help the world. Wealth, comfort, and security. Arrangements are in place.

Everything is optional. It is a choice.

No one is being abducted.

Smart, thinks Paralinka. Very smart. The illusion of choice.

A gentleman in a blue vest will be by in a moment to take each person's order for dinner and will make note of each person's preferred destination.

Fiji or Moscow?

Paralinka has another sip of scotch and smiles.

A man in a blue vest (possibly the first man to assist him?) appears at his elbow.

"I beg your pardon, Mr. Paralinka."

"Yes."

"I've been instructed to invite you to the rear of the plane for a video call."

Paralinka nods and follows the blue vest around the edge of the bar and through an automatic sliding door, down a narrow hallway, and into a dark, walnut-paneled study at the back of the plane. A large television screen above the back wall of the room is illuminated, and the image of a woman in a gray turtleneck, black jacket awaits him patiently. She nods and gives a small wave from the screen.

"Viktor," she says. "It is an honor."

Paralinka bows. "I am honored to meet my host," he says. "Your hospitality has been exceptional."

"You are more than welcome," she says. "I apologize for the coercion you encountered on this journey."

"I am at a disadvantage."

"I am Satoshi Nakamoto," she says.

He flinches, but recovers with alacrity and bows again. "A pleasure, Ms. Nakamoto. An honor."

She waves it off. "We meet as equals, Viktor. Please. You are a genius with fewer resources at your disposal and less self-interest. That is all that separates us. And 3,000 miles."

"You flatter me."

"I speak the truth. It's what I do."

"Let us converse in clear language, then. What are your plans for me?"

"I wish to give you the same option as your countrymen. But I realize that you possess significantly more status... and let's say, initiative, than they do. I am familiar with your work. Your career. There are less than ten people walking the earth with your abilities. I know that anywhere I send you, you could be a danger to me. And I would rather be a colleague. If not a friend. Your men have all chosen Fiji. To a man. Not a solitary exception. I admit I sold the option well, but even I'm surprised that not a single person chose to return home."

"Moscow is cold in November."

"Yes, well. As to your options, I feel it would be unwise to pretend I could limit you to two. I would be happy to arrange to have you delivered anywhere you please."

"But?"

"But if I may make a suggestion..."

"It's your dime, yes? Is that what they say?"

"Yes. I would prefer you lead the team you've gathered on this plane. In Fiji."

"To do what?"

"To work with me. To rule," she says. "To lead the world down a new path. Nothing less than that."

"From a desk in Fiji?"

"Poolside, if you like. Or from the beach."

"Is it so simple?"

"Where do you think I am?"

Viktor considers the question. "It doesn't matter," he says.

"That is correct," says Satoshi.

"The pay?"

"Unlimited. Essentially. You will have whatever you want. Money as you've known it is going to soon be somewhat..." She makes an ambivalent gesture with her hand towards the camera and screws up her face. "...different."

Paralinka sits in an elegant wooden chair, a curved swooping thing that gathers him up as much as allows him to sit. In a sense, the other men on the plane have made a decision for him. To return home without them was a demotion in itself.

Starting from scratch. Even if he is allowed to live. To return to work. What awaits him? Nothing promising.

Plus, if this woman is about to wreak havoc on the world's currency, he'd rather get paid in whatever she's got.

Plus, Fiji.

He sips the gorgeous, golden scotch and raises his glass towards the camera built into the top of the television. "I accept your proposal," he says. "Without reservations."

Nakamoto smiles and nods. "Wonderful," she says. "Your plane will have you there in less than half an hour."

Paralinka laughs. "Were you so sure of my response?"

"Of course not," says Nakamoto. "But I was optimistic. Hopeful. You'll learn that about me. I am a hopeful person."

"You will learn that I am very much the opposite," says Paralinka, again raising his glass.

"I already know that," says Nakamoto. "And I hope to show you a different way."

Tuesday, November 3
7:20 p.m. E.T.

Breathless election coverage pauses for commercials (gotta pay those bills) and Spark Jones takes the opportunity away from powerful cameras to glance at his phone. His digital wallet is so, so satisfyingly thick. He could walk off the set right now. Just walk away from it all. Like a quarterback who throws one perfect pass. Walk off the field, arms raised, unwilling to jeopardize perfection.

But this? The cameras, the lights, that's a wealth all its own, and not the sort that money can buy. He knows this.

He's got cache now. Traction. Say-so. Sway. Heft.

Power.

He looks past the lights towards Diane in the control booth, staring at him over the board. He waves at her and deposits his phone in his pocket. She doesn't trust him. Despite the story he dropped in her lap. Maybe because of it. Nobody's this good, this fast. You don't hop off the tractor-pull, brush the straw from your shoulders, and walk in the door waving the pee-pee tape your first week on the job. You just don't. It simply isn't done.

Well, Diane, he thinks. It's like his mama always says: People and bread ain't that far afield. Some just rise faster than others.

He doffs an imaginary cap in Diane's direction. She does not acknowledge the playful gesture.

He'll have her fired before Inauguration Day.

Tuesday, November 3 / Wednesday, November 4
9:01 p.m. E.T. / 5:01 a.m. Moscow Standard Time

At last. A change. The Russian President cannot begin to explain it, but something changes. He hears it first. It is audible before it is physical. He experiences it with every sense. His bowels relax, his stomach unwinds, and the business that began nearly 30 hours earlier comes to a swift conclusion.

The tears, he thought he'd run dry but here they come again, streaming unbidden down his cheeks as his guts empty into the toilet, soft and wonderful. Pillowy.

He weeps, even as it terminates, coiled beneath him like a dreaming eel.

The Russian President unspools a length of triple ply Charmin and dries his eyes. But the stream of tears keeps flowing. He has never known such gratitude. He is overwhelmed, so tired, so happy. So deeply and truly relieved. He'd thought, he'd really believed, that this is where he would die.

He unspools another length and gets to the business of wiping. Remarkably, no blood.

He is alive. So glad to be alive.

He pulls his pants back up for the first time since Monday night, and whispering a quiet farewell he flushes little Putivic into the unknown. Farewell, Putivic, he thinks. Farewell, worthy adversary. May we never meet again.

He washes his hands. Returns to the roll of toilet paper and makes another Charmin mitt. Wipes down the floor, the mirror, the walls, as best he can. Mortifying labor. But he will have it clean. He will erase this moment. This never happened.

The work is long and he is so tired. Hands and knees and

nothing but toilet paper and drips from the sink. But finally, he is satisfied.

Apart from the stench, you might never know what had passed in this room.

Still.

As he bathes his hands once more, he plans. He will have this bathroom torn apart and replaced. The walls stripped. Lights ripped out. That mirror? That mirror will be ground to powder. There will be no witnesses.

No one will use this room again, least of all himself.

He studies his proud reflection in the cracked mirror one last time.

Exits the bathroom.

He limps to his desk. Studies his cell phone which rests next to his desk phone. The lock screen image has changed. Someone's changed it. Now, it's a plain pink background with black graffiti text slashing across the foreground at an angle.

It reads: "I can do that anytime I want. Mess around however you please. But leave America alone or never shit again."

He lowers himself gingerly into his desk chair and powers his phone down.

Fair enough, he thinks. Fair enough. There's plenty of life to be lived without enduring that twice.

He has been infiltrated at the deepest, unknowable, depth.

Understand when you are beaten.

It has been so long.

He buzzes his secretary. She sounds tired. He tells her to bring him a pizza. She says okay. The battle has left him famished. Hurt and hungry.

He shuffles to a long couch situated beneath an oil painting of his likeness wrestling a pair of albinotic circus bears in

Dvortsovaya Ploshchad. The Russian President slumps into the couch, swings his legs up, and throws his head back onto the cushioned arm, and falls into a dense and dreamless sleep from which he will not rouse until the following day.

Tuesday, November 3
10:16 p.m. E.T.

Harper Commaro is on her third night as a manager trainee, when a young man with a smooth, shaved head appears in the lobby of the Campus Ramada and asks for a room. With 40% occupancy, she's glad to see anyone. Things have not been going well.

"I just need a credit card and ID," she tells him.

He apologizes and explains that he was recently robbed and has neither ID nor credit card, but he can leave a cash deposit.

It's Harper's first time in such a situation. She flips through the pages of the Ramada Quality Guide in her memory, searching for the policy but she can't seem to find it.

The young man slides $500 across the counter. "Will this be enough?" he asks.

Commaro nods. "I believe so," she says. "How long will you be staying with us?"

"One night," he says. "That's all."

"That should cover it," says Harper. After filling out a few more fields on her computer screen, she activates a key card and slides it into a paper sleeve before sliding it across the counter to the young man.

"Is there a good place to eat nearby?" he asks her.

She makes a few suggestions and points him to the elevators. Harper watches as he slings a black, nylon backpack over his shoulder and scoops a large paper Publix grocery bag under his arm as he limps towards the elevator. At the elevator's doors, he pauses, and she watches as he studies the two elevator buttons. After deliberation, he hits the "Up" button and looks back over his shoulder to her. She smiles and gives him a thumbs-up.

He returns the smile.

Gives her the thumbs-up.

His first thumbs-up exchange with a cute girl.

Tuesday, November 3
10:45 p.m. E.T.

She can finally frown. Without even tugging with her fingers, which the doctors cautioned against, she can frown of her own volition. The corners of her mouth still curl up, mildly, by default, when she relaxes her face. Probably, the pills are finally doing what they were intended to do, albeit three days too late.

What a lovely smile! Now that there is nothing to smile about.

The results are in, and she's ahead of the President in the election. Ahead of Bernie.

Behind Nakamoto by 15 points. He's going to have the Electoral College majority. Looks like.

The people have spoken. And they are very weird people.

Her staff penned their first draft of a concession speech months ago. Of course, she doesn't know that. No one tells a candidate that sort of thing. But it's the sort of thing a good campaign manager gets done months in advance. There's an acceptance speech as well, a magnificent piece of prose that no one will get to hear this year. The campaign manager has squirreled it away for use by some other, future candidate. It's too good to just throw away.

The version of the concession the candidate reads on her tablet is the 23rd iteration of that original concession speech. Obviously, the name of the victor had to be changed. A new emphasis on both losing and winning the election. Losing, because she just lost. Winning, because as the speech says: "At least this bag of toxic gas will be dispersed into the atmosphere."

Seems harsh. Plus environmentally unsound. Really. Just not necessary. Just kinda mean.

The concession speech is meant to be a call for a united country, even one so thoroughly divided at present.

She deletes the self-satisfied pocket of venom from the speech.

"We are winning," she writes. "Winning because tomorrow is a new day. A new day with new leadership."

Maybe she'll land a cabinet post.

"Winning because our country has once again exercised her most cherished principle."

Or an ambassadorship. Something plummy. England. Ireland. Australia. Something where they speak English for God's sake. Wales? Does Wales have its own ambassador?

"Winning because democracy has yet again risen and prevailed in a world of creeping fascism."

Maybe not the British Isles, though. Maybe not this year. A bit messy. Maybe Belgium. Everyone in Belgium can speak English. Basically England with more stability.

"Winning because that's what America does. Again and again and again."

Ugh. Walk that back. She deletes the passage.

"Winning because our country is turning a new page. A historic new page. Where your political party is no longer your identity. Where we aren't just... one of two things. Republican or Democrat. Liberal or conservative. Where shades of gray can have their day. Where you can agree and disagree with the same person and walk away friends."

If not Belgium, maybe just a parting gift. Maybe a few mill for an endowed chair at Stanford or a think tank. A think tank of one.

"Winning because Ms. Nakamoto has opened the door for a third way. Our options used to be Yes. And No. And now? Now America has banded together. United. And said with one voice: Maybe."

What the fuck does that mean? Doesn't matter. Keep going.

"Winning because our nation has discovered the power of Maybe."

I mean, this sounds good for some reason, but it doesn't actually mean anything. But maybe that's been the point the whole time.

"And Maybe is as Maybe does. And Maybe is the United States of America! God Bless you. And God Bless America. Maybe!"

Yeah.

Sure.

Maybe.

Why not?

Tuesday, November 3
11:45 p.m. E.T.

Aaron Burr VI sits in his great-grandfather's chair in front of his great-great-great-grandfather's fireplace watching the flames dance atop a pile of logs. He sips brandy twice his age from a pipe snifter as old as America and listens to a radio playing the British Broadcasting Corporation's live coverage of the election results. He has always preferred to listen to the election results. Prefers it to television. Prefers it in a British accent. It is a curious thing to trust one's ears over one's eyes. But he does.

Ironic, then, that he never hears that hulking Amazon, Moshi Nakamoto, enter the room and slide the pocket doors closed behind him. Thanks to Moshi's specialized Coast Guard training, if she doesn't want you to hear her approach, you will not.

"Good evening," says Moshi.

"Oh!" says Burr, nearly upsetting his snifter in surprise. The tip of the glass pipe curling from the glass briefly darts into his nostril. He dislodges it in as dignified a fashion as he can muster. "Hello," he says. He studies Moshi, standing like a shadow before him in black jeans, a black jacket, black t-shirt.

"Is it arranged?" says Moshi.

"Of course," says Burr. "Although," he gestures towards the radio, "there is a chance my efforts may be moot. Your employer seems to have nearly wrapped it up on her own merits and efforts."

"Our employer," says Moshi.

"Er, yes," says Burr. "Of course." He prefers not to think of himself as working for someone else. But then. He is. After a fashion. He prefers to think of Ms. Nakamoto as a partner. Or an investor.

"Nonetheless, she wants reassurance," says Moshi.

"Yes. You have my word."

"Yes. She's had that for a while. She has your word that you'll break your word on her behalf. I'm not talking that sort of reassurance."

"Oh. Well that's... I don't know what more I can offer, really. We have a gentleman's, we have a... civilized agreement, albeit without the face-to-face handshake one would normally prefer. If she would accept you as a surrogate, you and I could shake hands. I don't imagine she wants a written contract as that would be... potentially problematic for both of us."

"No. Not that sort of reassurance either."

"I see. Well?"

"Give me your glass."

"My... this?" Burr points to his snifter, confused.

"Yes." Moshi extends her hand and takes the glass from the puzzled man.

She carries the snifter to a desk along one of the tall, wood-paneled walls and sets it down. Moshi produces a skinny, silver tube from inside her jacket and unscrews its cap. She pours a shimmering stream of powder into the brandy, and swirls the snifter to mix it as she walks it back to Burr.

He accepts the glass back and studies his brandy. It looks mostly the same, but small particles shimmer in the golden fluid now.

"Bottoms up," says Moshi.

Burr looks stricken. "What is it?"

"Brandy, if I'm not mistaken."

"What did you put in it?"

"Nothing of any danger to you, so long as you follow through when called upon."

"But what is it?"

"That's complicated."

"It's poison?"

"No. Of course not. You understand how valuable you are."

"It's poison. Isn't it? Slow-acting. And you'll give me the antidote after we've finished?"

"No. There's no such poison. That would be absurd. Just drink up, do your job, and never think twice about it."

"I can't just do that," says Burr. "I need to know what this is."

Moshi sighs. "I can only give you the short version. It's basically a combination of iron filings and supercharged nanobots that can be activated either remotely or on a timer. In this case, remotely."

"I don't understand."

"It swims around in your system for six weeks or so. If you hold up your end of the bargain, all of that will eventually pass out of you on its own."

"But if I don't?"

"If you don't, then Ms. Nakamoto hits a switch. An app on her phone, actually. And then you never, ever shit again. Not the way you're accustomed to, anyways."

Burr nearly drops his snifter. "Dear Lord."

"I'm led to understand it is unpleasant."

"Dear Lord."

"Drink up."

Burr eyes the snifter nervously. "This is very expensive

brandy."

"I happen to know you can afford another."

"Very strong. It is not meant to be slurped."

"Hold your nose."

"What if she triggers it by accident?"

"She doesn't make mistakes. She won't. Prost! Let's go!"

"I–"

"I'm on a schedule," says Moshi. "Knock it back. Now."

Burr sniffs his glass, as if it may be the last time. Puts it to his lips and tilts his head back, drains the brandy in a single swallow. He makes a wheezing noise and pounds his chest as he sets the glass down on the end table by his hand.

"Now, recite the pledge of allegiance," says Moshi.

"Excuse me?" says Burr.

"The Pledge."

Burr recites it.

Moshi nods. "Just making sure you swallowed. The stuff is photosensitive, by the way. We'll know if you puke it up." She turns and leaves the room, leaving a threat swimming in a pool of brandy in the old man's belly.

Tuesday, November 3
11:59 p.m. E.T.

Ignoring the secret service agent protesting her movements (a horde of suits showed up yesterday evening and proved immediately as annoying and cumbersome as she'd feared) Satoshi Nakamoto pushes aside the gauzy curtains and opens the large French doors of the Airbnb suite. She walks out onto the balcony and surveys the crowd gathered seven floors below and waves down to them. A roar of approval erupts from below. Word of her location has spread. Thousands of high-pitched "Woooooo!"s. She looks past the crowd towards the National Mall stretched out like a somber theme park. Satoshi glances down at her cell phone and after three seconds, she sweeps her left arm forward.

Music rises from hundreds of speakers, hidden throughout the area. Rousing trumpets and strings, the sort of music that accompanies slow motion footage of people riding horses. On cue, 10,000 bright lights dart through the sky from all directions, and swoop into formation and assume the shape of a spectacular, luminous American flag. They even drift back and forth, just slightly, to create the illusion of a flag curling and flapping in an imaginary breeze. The crowd cheers and whoops even louder at the sight of the glowing spectacle. Then the drones rearrange themselves into large letters, alternating in red, white, and blue stripes until they spell out in gigantic block letters, "Thank you, America!"

From Nakamoto's vantage point, the moon hovers just

above the upper-left corner of the tableau. The display continues in that manner, the drones serving as pixels in the world's largest television as dubious interpretations of various moments in United States' history are re-enacted against the blue-black night sky.

Jefferson signs the declaration of Independence as men in tights and wigs lean over his shoulder to watch.

Abraham Lincoln draws a sword from his scabbard and slices off the scowling head of a confederate general.

A clearly defined Reverend Martin Luther King Jr. and Rosa Parks fly with angel's wings, pumping their fists victoriously, over the oooo-ing crowd.

Nakamoto doesn't stand on the balcony for long. It's too cold.

"Idiots," she mutters, waving to the crowd one last time. Most of them don't see it, have their backs to her, their heads tilted up, absorbed by the largest drone display of its kind. Nakamoto backs into the penthouse and pulls the doors shut again.

The secret service agent, a bulldog with a necktie, latches the door behind her and mutters something into his shirt sleeve.

"I need some space," says Nakamoto. "I want you to leave." The man considers arguing; he doesn't move. "I won't go out on the balcony again. I promise," she insists.

He abandons an argument before it begins and steps into the hallway.

Nakamoto has a yellow legal pad laid out on a massive rolltop desk that the Airbnb's property manager had started to explain the historical significance of when she had told him to leave. Something to do with Chester A. Arthur and brown sugar? She hadn't paid attention.

Nakamoto sits. She is a list-maker. Always has been. Lists are effective. Paper lists are superior.

One list, in particular, has grown lengthy in her mind, but she has never committed it to paper. This seems the right time and the right place. Flames snap and shimmer in the fireplace beside the desk. An oil painting above the desk shows a musket battle between young men wearing tights, vests, and jackets, epaulets waving in the breeze. Bristling mutton chops. Men fall and horses rear, but there's not a drop of blood on the canvas.

She begins: "To Do: commencing January 20, 2021"

1. vet and fill cabinet. Necessary: loyalty, leverage, 25th-proof
2. withdraw diplomatic corps from all nations
3. nuclear strike: n.k.
4. full pardon, all federal offenses. empty all fed pens.
5. withdraw troops from all foreign postings. no exceptions.
6. withdraw all budget proposals. submit none.

She taps the sharpened tip of her pencil against her top lip, pensively. There are so many ways to break something, she thinks. So many small and incremental methods, so slight that hardly anyone notices what you're up to. Like sanding down a chair's legs a little every day. Like being slow-cooked to death.

People can get used to anything.

And they will.

That's the lesson.

If you really want to fix something, really fix it, you've got to break it properly. Completely. Spectacularly. Publicly.

You've got to follow through on each worst-case scenario. Remind people that there is still something worse than worse. That worst is possible.

You cannot simply run the Constitution through the shredder and reassemble the parts in a better order. The machine is built to protect itself. And its flaws.

No. Some things, you don't fix. Some things, you burn on the front lawn.

You start over.

She folds the paper five times. Lines up her throw. Spins the creased list into the crackling fireplace where it lands on a log, sparks, and flares into a sputtering flame.

Acknowledgements

This book was made possible through the generous hospitality of Martha Kesler and the Kesler Family Writing Retreat of Cape May, New Jersey. Their generosity deserves a book less crass than this. Ah well. Many thanks to friends and family for encouraging me to continue to write, if not grow and mature as an adult, and to my colleague James Cleary who offered a deeply helpful response when I asked him what he would do if he had billions of dollars to throw at the Presidential election. In addition, this book and all good things in life would be impossible without my Bird. Thank you is too meager a phrase. Please, instead, accept this ellipsis...

About the Author

Andrew McDonnell is one of the best-reading readers of the *New York Times*. He has written numerous radio plays, short stories and an earlier novel: *All Animals Versus All Humans*. He writes and teaches in Wisconsin.

Learn more and read more at www.November123.com or watch him rarely Tweet: @drewmcdonnell

Questions, complaints, book club requests, and lucrative film rights inquiries accepted via email at:
ikilledshamu@gmail.com

Made in the USA
Monee, IL
14 February 2020